THE GENE OF LIFE

THE GENE OF LIFE

Ted Takashima

Translated by

Giuseppe di Martino

MUSEYON

New York

Copyright © 2011 Tetsuo Ted Takashima
English translation copyright © 2021 Museyon Inc.

Library of Congress Cataloging-in-Publication Data

Names: Takashima, Tetsuo, author. | Di Martino, Giuseppe, translator.
Title: The gene of life / Ted Takashima ; translated by Giuseppe di Martino.
Other titles: Inochi no idenshi. English
Description: First edition. | New York : Museyon, 2021. | Identifiers: LCCN 2021008605 |
ISBN 9781940842516 (paperback) | ISBN 9781940842523 (ebook)
Subjects: GSAFD: Suspense fiction.
Classification: LCC PL862.A424144 I5613 2021 | DDC 895.63/6--dc23
LC record available at https://lccn.loc.gov/2021008605

First edition 2021

First published in the United States of America in 2021 by:
Museyon Inc.
333 East 45th Street
New York, NY 10017

Museyon is a registered trademark.
Visit us online at www.museyon.com

Printed in USA

This book is dedicated to those who have died from COVID-19, to those who are suffering because of the pandemic, and to those brave heroes and scientists who are fighting every day to vanquish the virus. May 2021 be the year the vaccine reaches every corner of the world.

CONTENTS

gene
a distinct sequence of DNA forming part of a chromosome, by which offspring inherit characteristics from a parent.

DNA
deoxyribonucleic acid, a self-replicating material present in nearly all living organisms as the main constituent of chromosomes. It is the carrier of genetic information.

chromosome
a threadlike structure of nucleic acids and protein found in the nucleus of most living cells, carrying genetic information in the form of genes.

telomere
a compound structure at the end of a chromosome.

telomerase
an enzyme that adds nucleotides to telomeres, especially in cancer cells.

—New Oxford American Dictionary, Third Edition

PROLOGUE

He held his breath.

Through the binoculars in his right hand, he watched the plaza fill with people. In his left, he gripped a detonator. Over twenty pounds of a new plastic explosive, Semtex Alpha, were ready to blow—enough to take down a building. The accomplice beside him wiped his sweaty palms on his pants, and raised a Galil sniper rifle.

A man in a khaki military uniform appeared on the plaza's stage. The crowd grew quiet.

The assassin's heart skipped a beat. Failure was not an option.

"Alles klar, fangen wir an," he said. "Okay, let's get started."

He pushed his left thumb down. There was a deafening roar.

In July 2008, the public square in the western German city of Dörrenwald was packed with thousands of young men and women.

"We will regain our former glory and create a new world under a new order! We will tear this corrupt world down! We will restore *der Führer!*" The voice boomed through the speakers and reverberated through the plaza. *"Heil Hitler!"*

Crowds of young fascists clicked their heels and performed the Nazi salute, the same salute that changed German culture more than seventy years ago—and was now illegal.

Thousands of onlookers surrounded the square, some began shouting.

"Organizers estimate around 4,200 people are in attendance," a reporter, a young woman in her mid-thirties, yelled into her mic. TV cameras weren't allowed, so it was an audio-only broadcast. "Members of the *Schwarzes Kreuz* Party have gathered here from all corners of the world!"

Seats on either side of the stage were occupied by elderly people, with the exception of one middle-aged couple. The man watched the crowd and smiled, reliving a distant past.

"Heil Hitler!" The words became a chorus, a chant.

A cool breeze blew through the trees around the plaza.

Suddenly there was a deafening roar, then whirls of smoke and dust. For a split second, all sound was muffled and the crowd was silent. A gaping hole appeared in the center of the stage. Shrieks. Cries, both tearful and angry, rose above the scene. Thousands of people began running in different directions.

A thick cloud of dust covered the stage. Mangled bodies and severed limbs jutted out from the debris.

TV cameras that had been snuck in were turned on, and the clicks of camera shutters began recording the scene.

"Explosion—explosives went off near the stage!" shouted the reporter, her voice cracking and her face filled with fear. A cameraman staggered after her. "Over ten top *Schwarzes Kreuz* executives are lying on the ground! And Chairman Friedrich Heiper is nowhere to be seen."

"Wait!" She halted, almost screaming her words now. "All that blood is from people's limbs! They're dismembered body parts!"

The cameraman turned his camera on the carnage.

"There are many—there are innumerable wounded. The ground is covered with bodies! The number of lives lost . . . it's considerably high. This rally—" Her words were cut short. She covered her head with her hands and collapsed. Blood gushed between her fingers.

Gunfire, then more explosions were heard in the surrounding forest.

"They're firing," shouted the cameraman. Suddenly the camera jerked violently, and the back of his head sprayed red.

More screams. More enraged shouting.

The square reeked of blood and gunpowder. Sirens of ambulances and police cars shrieked in the distance.

———

Limone sul Garda, Italy, July 2008.

"Could it be?" whispered a man despite himself.

He had read and re-read the research. He was sure he understood it. But, seeing it before his eyes, he just couldn't believe what he was seeing. At long last, could this be what he'd been searching for?

As he watched the screen, a red liquid was forcefully flowing against a beautiful blue background. It was intravascular blood, as shown via ultrasound diagnostic equipment.

"Only forty people in the world share this privilege," stated a physician in a white lab coat standing behind him.

The man's eyes were fixed on the screen. Suddenly, the display split in two. One half showed coursing blood, while the second section showed blood squeezing through veins that looked extremely narrow. "On the right are her veins. On the left are the veins of a person of the same age group."

The man turned to the smiling woman in her seventies lying on the bed. The blood vessels of a person of her age would normally contain accumulations of cholesterol, forcing her blood to pass through narrow gaps.

"I understood this from all the research papers, but it's beyond belief to see it with my own two eyes." He turned back to the display.

"Everyone says that when they see it for themselves," the physician said, his voice tinged with pride.

He placed two tubes on the desk. "These test tubes are both turbid with cholesterol." With a grand flourish like a magician, he added white powder from a glass vial to one of them. The liquid turned transparent. The difference between the tubes was perfectly clear.

"The powder is protein refined from the blood of the *portatori*, that is, carriers."

The man was speechless. He was moved more than surprised.

"A single letter of genetic code, out of the three billion base pairs, was all it took to create this wonder protein capable of disintegrating cholesterol. Just that one, single-letter mutation has granted its carriers a perk ordinary people don't have access to." The physician smiled, embarrassed. For a moment he forgot he was talking to a world-renowned genetic scientist. Two books on his laboratory shelves were written by him.

The geneticist shifted his gaze to the petite elderly woman again. She was a carrier of the apolipoprotein A-1 gene, which produced a cholesterol-killing protein that prevented arteriosclerosis. She and her fellow *portatori* lived in a picturesque village of less than a thousand on the edge of Lake Garda, at the foot of the Alps.

"They are blessed by God," said the physician with feeling.

"It's nothing more than God's whim," Max muttered, before he could stop himself.

● ● ●

I

—

BERLIN

Chapter 1

Maximillian Knight gingerly descended the flight of stone stairs in front of Technische Universität Berlin's grand lecture hall. He looked up at the great city's cloudless summer sky. He had lived in Germany for a year now, but this was the first time he had noticed such a clear blue sky. A cool breeze was blowing. Groups of students filled the lawn, which stretched all the way to the park. Max took a deep breath, and the crisp air expanded his lungs.

He had just finished giving his farewell lecture on the subject of "21st-Century Genetic Science and Humankind." He could still feel the enthusiasm of the audience of seven hundred, and he sensed the students seated on the steps were looking up at him.

He was in his mid-thirties, around five foot eight and 150 pounds, and hadn't changed much since his twenties. He had finely chiseled features, thick eyebrows, and long black hair that covered his ears and fell over his dark eyes. He didn't give off a friendly or cheery vibe, and he was aware of that. He had heard that his students called him "the gloomy professor."

He looked up at the church in front of him. The sun's rays reflected off its steeple and blinded him. He squinted against the harsh glare. A dull pain began to throb in his head. He balled his hands into fists and tried to shake off the heavy feeling.

In ten days he had to return to America. But before he left Germany, he needed to sort out his research materials and pass the baton, as well as say goodbye to people. He had a lot to do. As he turned to walk down the stairs, he stopped. A gently sloping lawn stretched from the base of the steps, and a gray Mercedes sedan with tinted windows was parked about a hundred feet away.

A slender man in sunglasses was leaning against the car. Max could tell he was looking at him, but he was used to having eyes on him, so he ignored him and took a step forward.

When he'd reached the bottom of the stairs, a voice from behind called, "Professor Knight!"

He turned around, only to find a thick book thrust in his face. The title read *Die Zukunft der Gene* (The Future of Genes). It was his third book, released in February of that year. Written as a primer of genetic science, it was his first book aimed at lay readers. His first two had been more technical, and had been translated into five languages as textbooks for students.

"Would you please sign my book?" asked the young woman.

Max didn't even look at her before retrieving his pen from his chest pocket and signing.

The man in sunglasses paced briskly toward him. Max was seized by a fear he'd never felt before. He pushed the book back at the woman and practically ran across the lawn. He heard someone call to him, but didn't look back. When he reached the road, a Volkswagen van came rushing toward him. It swerved in front of him and blocked his path.

"What the hell . . ."

"Don't speak. We are not going to hurt you," the man in sunglasses whispered. Max was dragged to the van.

Max looked back at the stairs. The woman clutching his book was watching, puzzled. Max was about to shout, but he was already halfway in the van. It started moving before the door was even closed.

It happened so fast he'd had no time to think. Clearly these guys were used to this sort of thing. Witnesses might have guessed the man was simply a friend of Max's, taking him for a ride. The van's tinted windows hid what happened inside. Max was sitting between two men. In the seat facing him sat a third, a broad-shouldered, silver-haired older man. The earthy smell of cigar smoke hung in the air—probably Cuban. Max tried to get a good look at him, but the man in sunglasses placed his hand over Max's mouth. The older man mumbled something and grasped his arm.

A foul-smelling cloth covered Max's nose. He tried to pull off his captor's hand, but he was overpowered from both sides. He could feel his strength waning and his consciousness fading.

Pure darkness.

It was vast, endless. His soul drifted within the soundless expanse. It yearned for light, for sound, for smells and flavors. It wandered in search of anything that could anchor the mind.

His whole body was constricted by a powerful force. He felt like he was dissolving into the darkness. He was being sucked into a deeper, blacker void.

Where am I? But he couldn't speak.

I know this place. I've seen this world countless times. It's the plane of death. It is death itself. For death is nothingness. Boundless, never-ending nothingness.

From a great distance, he heard the growling of a wild beast. The sound brought him back to consciousness. After a few minutes, he realized that what he heard was coming from an air conditioner.

He opened his eyes. Everything was blurry, but he was looking at a face. It was the silver-haired man from the van. When he tried to get up, multiple arms reached out to hold him down.

"Like we said, we are not going to hurt you." The man had a British accent.

Max stopped struggling. He focused on the shafts of light coming through the slats of the window blinds. He realized he was lying on a bed. The old man peered down at him. He had to be over six feet tall, and his wrinkled face was as deeply chiseled as a Michelangelo sculpture. He was expressionless, and Max could only imagine what color his eyes were behind his brown-tinged glasses. He seemed quite old, and he was dressed in a tailored double-breasted suit with a soft silk scarf around his neck. A handkerchief poked out of his chest pocket, and he wore blue cuff links. He had the look of a snobbish, rich British gentleman. He didn't exactly seem threatening.

Max remained motionless, only moving his eyes. He noticed an old-fashioned writing desk and chair against a gray wall. There were four other men in the room, two in their twenties and the others in their thirties or forties. They were all standing around the bed, staring at Max. He tried to speak, but couldn't. His words stuck in his throat.

"We used ether. This ought to wake you up a little," said the old man, breaking a capsule under Max's nose. The smelling salts made his head jerk up. Suddenly he was fully aware of his surroundings.

"Professor Max Knight," said the old man, reading a dossier. "Thirty-five years old. Researcher at the California Institute of Technology's genetics lab. A year ago he was invited to TU Berlin as a guest professor, where he has continued his research. That was until this weekend, after which he plans to leave Germany and travel around Africa before returning to America. Max Knight quickly rose to global prominence seven years ago for his gene analysis research. He discovered the RN1 and 2 restriction enzymes, developed software for gene reading and analysis . . . and particularly impressive, he unraveled the molecular biological mechanism of the mouse anti-aging gene and the klotho gene, greatly influencing subsequent research regarding the genes of life. His method was widely employed for functional gene analysis, and gene research advanced rapidly because of it. Furthermore, it was applied to embryonic stem cell research, and contributed a great deal to the development of new drugs and medical treatments. Since then, he has continued to present revolutionary ideas revolving around genetic science, and he is known in the field of life science especially as the scientist who altered man's notions of life itself. Though he is young, he is undoubtedly an icon."

The old man placed the file on the desk and took a deep breath. "You *are* Max Knight, correct?" he asked, staring.

"I don't know about . . . that last part." His voice was even hoarser than he'd expected. "Who are you people?"

"We have no intention of hurting you," replied the old man unhurriedly.

"You already have!"

"Please forgive us. We had no time to explain, you see. And even if we did, you would certainly have declined. Not to mention that many in our group are aggressive sorts." His tone was amicable, even sympathetic.

Max glanced at the alarm clock on the bedside table. It was past six. He'd been out for an hour.

"My name is Joseph Feldman, but please, call me Joe."

"Where . . . am I?"

"You're in the headquarters of Feldman Antique Dealers. More accurately, the guest bedroom. You're not in danger here. We buy and sell antiques, that's all."

"What you did to me is a crime you know!"

"We know there is no excuse, but this is how these gentlemen do things." Feldman looked to both sides. The other men stared at him, their expressions unchanging.

Max tried to get up, but a dull pain stabbed in his head.

"The pain ebbs quickly," Feldman said, signaling with his eyes at his men. "You know that better than I."

All but one of the men left the room. When Feldman turned his head, Max caught a glimpse through an opening in his scarf of a patch of reddish-brown scarred skin going from his right ear to the nape of his neck.

Max tried to get up again. This time, however, Feldman offered a hand.

"I never thought they'd use a rag on you. But though they're a little rough, they are a dependable lot."

"Dependable for what?" Max sat up, his headache receding. The pain had jolted his brain awake.

"Meet my assistant, Jake Horowitz," said Feldman, pointing with his eyes to the other man in the room. "He's American."

Jake smiled bashfully and cast his eyes down. He looked to be around forty. Bulky and plump, he only reached to Feldman's shoulders, but he commanded attention all the same. He was the only one among them who seemed to have any emotions, as he flashed his softhearted eyes Max's way.

"Would you like some coffee? Or maybe some tea? We have scotch and brandy, too."

"Coffee."

Jake nodded and left.

"Let's go to the office." Feldman pointed to the door beside the writing desk.

Max stood up. He was unsteady, and Feldman swiftly stepped in to hold him up. His muscular arm was strong for a man his age. They entered the adjacent room. A bookshelf took up two walls, and the remaining walls held rows of filing cabinets. Under the window was a large desk, in front of the desk was an expensive-looking table and sofa. It looked more like a tasteful library than an office.

Feldman's eyes invited Max to sit. Max took a seat on the sofa.

"Now then," Feldman began, "I have a favor to ask of you."

"This isn't how people ask for favors."

"I know. But we are being constantly surveilled."

Max looked at Feldman's face. He was well-mannered, and had a classy, sophisticated air. But when he fixed his gaze on him, he saw a glint of danger in his eyes.

Jake entered with a cup and coffeepot on a tray. He placed the cup on the table and poured. When Max brought the cup to his lips and took a sip, he started feeling more at ease.

"Please be discreet about what I'm about to tell you."

"I haven't agreed to anything." Max put down his cup.

Feldman signaled Jake with his eyes. Jake wordlessly walked behind the desk and unlocked a drawer. He retrieved a glass cylinder four inches in diameter and a foot tall. He placed the vial in front of Max.

Max gasped, his eyes glued to it. He would have stood back up, but Feldman pressed his shoulders. Max looked up at Feldman, who gently nodded.

The bottle was filled with cloudy liquid. A white object was floating in it.

Floating in the liquid was a human left hand, a severed cross section with bone and flesh exposed.

"What is it that you want from me?" Max's voice was still hoarse.

"You heard about the neo-Nazi rally bombing at Dörrenwald two days ago, I'm sure? The *Schwarzes Kreuz* (Black Cross) rally."

Max nodded. Everyone in Germany knew about it. The news had been covering it for days. A bomb had detonated at a rally of the world's largest neo-Nazi group at Dörrenwald, 125 miles west of Berlin. More bombs had gone off after the first explosion, and there had been shooting as well. Sixteen had died, and over fifty were wounded.

An ultra right-wing group, *Schwarzes Kreuz* was gaining support among the young, and had grown to more than seventy thousand members. They were willing to do anything to expel refugees and to stop migrants entering from Africa, the Arab world, and elsewhere. An attack on a refugee detention center in southern Germany a month prior was said to be their work, leaving five dead and thirty wounded. Among the dead were a mother and her three-year-old daughter.

The Dörrenwald bombing was one of the worst acts of terrorism in German history. The fact that a neo-Nazi organization, regarded as a violent terrorist group, was the target of attack was unprecedented.

"Were you the ones behind it?"

"If that were the case, we wouldn't be here now. But we were close by."

The neo-Nazi movement that was rearing its head all over Europe was worrying Jewish communities in Germany, and some speculated the bombing was their plan to wipe it out. Others thought it could be the work of an enemy neo-Nazi organization. Still others believed it marked the revival of a far-left group named *Schwarzer Tiger* (Black Tiger). Rumors were circulating, including that the attack had been a plot by a government at a loss for how to control the movement's meteoric rise. And reports were in that the police had already arrested a number of suspects.

Max had been in Italy at the time, and when he touched down at Berlin Tegel Airport, he'd been surprised by how tight security had become. The airport had been crawling with officers, police dogs, and automatic weapon-toting military personnel. He saw several youths in leather jackets and Mohawks being dragged off with their hands cuffed behind their backs.

"This hand belonged to someone who attended that rally," Feldman said. "The man must have been close to the blast radius. We've no idea where the rest of his body went. We looked in the hospitals the dead were taken to, but we couldn't find him. And the police reports haven't helped, either. Presumably, the rally organizers collected the body. In any case, the situation was out of our hands."

Max pulled his eyes off the vial. "It's got nothing to do with me." He attempted to get up.

"Not so fast," Feldman said, holding him down by the shoulder again, surprisingly powerfully. "I'm sure this will be of interest to you. We looked into this hand's fingerprints and identified whom it belonged to," he continued quietly, never taking his hand off Max's shoulder but relaxing his grip. "It belonged to one Carius Gehlen."

Max looked up at Feldman. "Never heard of him."

For an instant, Feldman's eyes exhibited an odd glint. Max saw that expressionless face of his contort slightly with what looked like anger. Or was it just his imagination? Feldman had already reverted to his usual composure.

"Why did you bring me here?"

Feldman placed a faded sepia-tone photo on the table. Five German military officers in uniform were standing with their arms around each other's shoulders. The Eiffel Tower could be seen in the background. On the right edge of the photo, the date was printed: July 14, 1940. A month after Germany seized Paris. Feldman pointed at one of the people in the photo. "He was a colonel in the Waffen-SS."

Short and stout, the man was glaring at the camera, his chin pulled in and his chest puffed up.

He then placed a second photo on the table for Max to see. It showed a single man in the same uniform striking the same pose. "For a time, he served as the commandant of a concentration camp for Jews in Paris. He would gather up Jews from all over Paris to be sent to camps across Europe. He directed the slaughter of 200,000 people, including children from orphanages and residents of old-age homes. Even months-old babies were killed. All of them were ordered to the camps. To the gas chambers." Feldman's tone was dispassionate and his expression didn't change. He must have had to rattle off these facts countless times. "After the war, he was charged as a war criminal and sentenced to death in absentia during the Nuremberg Trials. The Allies continued to search for him, and we are currently picking up where they left off. Yet he has eluded us to this day."

Max looked up from the photo at Feldman's face. "Are you with the Z Commission?"

The German governmental agency known colloquially as

the Z Commission is a storehouse of publicly available documents concerning Nazi war crimes, which have no statute of limitations. Thanks to the commission's efforts, over ten thousand individuals have been investigated, over seven thousand have been found guilty, and a further twenty thousand are still actively being hunted.

"No. I'm with an organization in Israel."

"Are you an intelligence guy, then? Mossad, is it?"

"There was a time we enjoyed the support of the state, but now we are a civilian organization. With the deterioration of relations with Arab countries, it seems the government can no longer concern itself with chasing Nazi ghosts. But we are getting the full support of Jews around the world."

"So, you're a Nazi hunter?"

Feldman nodded. Max had heard that there was a group out there funded by Jews all over the globe that was still pursuing escaped Nazi war criminals. A chill ran down Max's spine: "Then this hand is a Nazi war criminal's!" he exhaled, glancing at the hand and then the photo.

"I trust you understand now," Max heard him say from above his head.

"But how . . . ," Max's voice turned shrill. His eyes were fixed on the hand.

"This hand is from two days ago. But yes, there's something I'm sure you've already realized. Carius Gehlen would be 111 years old today."

Feldman put a hand on Max's shoulder again. Max didn't want him to notice how he was shaking, so he pulled away and pushed his hand off.

"As you can plainly see, this is the hand of a man in his forties— and his early forties at that. His skin is spotless."

"The fingerprint ID must be wrong," said Max.

"That's what we thought, at first. We ran the cross-check again, and even requested an analysis by a professional. We searched for the detective known as the Fingerprint God, which took some doing, since he retired a decade ago. In the end, it was no error. That is why we need you."

"Are you asking me to examine his DNA?"

Feldman nodded. "When the Allies occupied Germany after the war, they compiled any and all materials relating to those thought to have had a hand in war crimes. Yet Gehlen, like many other high Nazi officials, had disposed of any trace of his past. Fortunately, a portion of the relevant records remained untouched at the Gestapo's French subdivision, including Gehlen's prints and dental impressions. It was likely due to some internal act of betrayal, rather than coincidence. Rising to the upper echelons made you enemies. Things happen when a war is lost. Apart from those records, we couldn't find anything on Gehlen in military or government documents." Feldman sighed and turned to Max. Max saw the profound weariness on his face. "As luck would have it, the man's hair was not lost. Hair and nails from when he was a boy were found in his mother's home."

"How well-preserved are they?"

"Very. There are even hairs with the roots attached. They were kept in a wooden box, so light exposure was minimal. A mother's love is a mother's love. She treated those keepsakes with care."

"You should leave it to a lab, not me. The results will be accurate, and it will take less time. Plus, we wouldn't have had to go through this whole annoying mess."

"No. It has to be you," Feldman's bespectacled eyes shone with determination.

"What exactly is the deal with this hand?"

"That is what we'd like you to discover," he said, without averting his gaze.

Max glared right back at him. "I refuse. It's got nothing to do with me, and I'm not interested."

"You refuse to help a Jew, is that it?" An old man was standing behind Feldman. He seemed to be around the same age, but the furrows in his face were far deeper. "You hate Jews, huh? Well you Yankee pigs make me wanna vomit almost as much as a Kraut does. And they say all Jews care about is money. They've never met Americans!"

"Enough, Simon." Feldman stepped to the man's side and placed a hand on his shoulder in sympathy. Simon's hostile eyes were still trained on Max as he left the room. "Please forgive him. His name is Simon, and he is my comrade who has been at this longer than I have. This discovery has upset him terribly."

"I don't see race or nationality."

"But as long as there are people, there will also be races and nationalities. Personally, I like Americans. They saved us from the hell that was the Nazi regime. As I'm sure you know, many of our fellow Jews live in America. They support us and provide for us. And I'm grateful to America for allowing that." Feldman moved in closer to Max. The fragrance of cigars wafted in the air. "There is a reason you can't refuse."

"If I refuse?"

"You would regret it for the rest of your life."

"What do you mean?"

"You heard what I said."

Max studied the vial. Before he knew it, he'd shut his eyes. The hand floating in the liquid almost seemed like it was beckoning him.

"Can we count on you?"

"On one condition," Max said, before he could stop himself.

"Whatever you desire." Feldman looked slightly relieved.

"I want more info. You're not telling me half of what you know."

"You will know more when the time comes. I know you won't regret it."

A flame began burning in Max's heart, and its heat spread through his body. He might finally get what he longed for! He couldn't help but feel excited. Then he looked at his watch, and gasped. "You are taking me back now, right?"

"Is something wrong?"

"I had plans at seven." It was already past eight.

"We will escort you back."

Jake brought in a thermos-shaped container and carefully put the vial inside it. He then put the container in a canvas bag. Max took the bag and stood up. Jake led him to the building's rear entrance. A different blue car from the one he was taken in was waiting for him on the backstreet.

CHAPTER 2

It was ten minutes to nine by the time Max arrived at TU Berlin's genetic research facility. It was still light out thanks to Germany's summer, and people were out in the streets. The research facility's main entrance was closed, so Max went to the guardroom.

He took the elevator to the eighth floor and walked down the dimly lit hallway toward his office. He felt a heaviness in his chest. The photos that Feldman had shown him and the sight of the hand floating in the vial were seared into his brain.

The heavy bag he carried on his shoulder weighed his whole body down—in more ways than one. He had been doubtful earlier, but the implications were becoming clearer. Max shook his head in an attempt to banish the emotion. The greater the hope, the greater the disappointment. He had gone through that many times before. And above all, he didn't want to think about anything at the moment.

He turned the corner and stopped.

A shadowy figure was squatting by the door. He adjusted the bag on his shoulder and stepped in front of whoever it was. A woman in her early twenties, perhaps a student, was sitting on the floor with her knees bent and both arms hugging her shins. Her head was hanging down. As he drew closer, he noticed the smell of sweat, and could hear she was sleeping. He noted her soft, chestnut-colored hair, the delicate curve of her neck and pale skin. A battered backpack was beside her.

Max shook her lightly by the shoulders. She looked up at him. "Professor," she murmured. She jumped to her feet. She was about as tall as Max, but didn't weigh nearly as much. She was wearing small gold earrings. She had delicate features, and her expressive eyes were open wide. In the dim light, her face could be mistaken for a young boy's.

She took a pen from her pocket and thrust it in front of Max's eyes. "Here's your pen back. I had you sign a book earlier. But then you gave me your pen and rushed off. I called to you, but you didn't hear me. It happened four hours and ten minutes ago." She looked at her watch.

"Thank you very much." He remembered now. He'd been focused on the man with the sedan, so he hadn't gotten a good look at her face.

He unlocked the door and entered, and the woman followed him in without being asked.

"So, you managed to infiltrate the lab," Max said.

Two armed guards stood by the entrance to check after-hours visitors. People without ID cards or appointments were not allowed entry.

Genetic science often led to research that generated huge sums of money. Companies around the world competed for the information, and some were very aggressive about getting their hands on it. Also, there was always the risk that genetic modification could create unknown pathogens and organisms. For all these reasons, TU Berlin's genetic research facility had a vitally important P4 laboratory equipped with the highest level of containment equipment in the event of a biohazard or bioterrorism. Protecting facilities from bioterrorism as well as biohazards counted among their vital functions.

"Thanks to an acquaintance of mine, Dr. Cindy Smith. Do you know her? She's doing neurotransmitter research on the first floor."

Max shook his head no. There were over three hundred researchers working in this institute. He had met a handful of well-known scientists, but the others he knew only in passing. He put the bag on his desk and looked up. She was standing there, staring at him.

"Do you have some other business with me?"

"I . . ." She hurriedly rummaged in her bag for an envelope and fished it out.

Max scanned the document. "Dr. Katarina Lang, eh? Are you the brilliant researcher that Professor August Michaels was telling me about?"

"I don't know whether I'm 'brilliant,' but I am the one who requested the professor's recommendation," she said in fluent English.

"So, it was a young female researcher he was talking about . . ."

"Yes, I *am* a woman. I obtained my degree—"

"Sorry, that came out wrong. I'm just surprised. Professor Michaels used the words 'brilliant researcher.' I heard you completed graduate school as a Pauling Scholarship student and now receive grants from Cosmo Pharmaceutical Research."

"The scholarship ended when I stopped being a student, and the grant money stopped coming in last year."

"You have your degree, and you can get more research grants if you want. Going by your career up till now, I don't think you should be going back to being a research student."

"At present, I'm a researcher in Professor Michaels's laboratory. I heard you knew each other, so I asked for a recommendation. I've been thinking of applying to your lab for some time."

Max put the document on the desk. "First, allow me to apologize for arriving late due to personal matters."

She smiled cheerily. "That's okay; I've been sleep-deprived lately, so it actually helped me to take a little nap."

"Do you have time to spare, Dr. Lang?"

"Yes, I do."

"Could I ask for a helping hand?" Max took the bag and stood up. He left the room and headed for the lab on the same floor. Confused, Katarina followed after him.

"Were you sleeping in front of the door the entire time?"

"I was at the neurotransmitter lab until three hours ago. Cindy and I were in the same year at TU Dresden."

"And then?"

"She left to go on a date at six, so I sat by your door."

"I'm terribly sorry. I just couldn't get away."

"I understand, Professor. You're busy. That's why I waited."

Max inserted his card into the lab door's slot and entered the passcode. Frigid air hit them as they went inside. The room was around 550 square feet, and there were three test benches side by side. He handed her one of the lab coats hanging on the wall.

"You specialized in the study of molecular biology, right, Dr. Lang? And after you graduated, you went on to med school."

"Yes, to the med school at TU Dresden."

"Why did you switch to life science?"

"You graduated from med school too, Professor. Why did you switch to life science?"

Max didn't answer, but walked to one of the test benches and put down the bag. Carefully, he pulled the glass cylinder out of the thermos.

Her eyes widened.

"Any clinical practice?"

"Only when I was an intern."

"Then you should be used to dead bodies. Including dead body *parts*, of course."

She nodded, but he could tell she had been taken by surprise.

"Anybody would get flustered. It's only natural. It's just the two of us in here in the middle of the night, and I just showed you a severed hand."

"I'm not flustered. And you didn't do clinical medicine for that long, either. You've been a researcher for far longer."

Max ignored that remark and retrieved a small bottle from an envelope in his pocket. Inside was a hair.

"It's a DNA sample." He pulled on surgical gloves and extracted the hand from the vial. The pungent odor of the formalin made them grimace. Using a scalpel, he cut off a piece of flesh from the cross section.

"You know how to run a DNA scan, right, Dr. Lang?" he asked, as he dropped the flesh into a test tube.

"Please call me Katya." It seemed as though she'd regained her cool, as she set down her bag and put on the lab coat.

"Extract some DNA from the hair and the bit of hand for me, Katya."

Katya looked nervous as she prepared two 1.5 mL Eppendorf tubes and wrote the names of their contents on their lids. First, she lightly wiped the hair with a Kimwipe soaked in ethanol. Next, she finely cut about one centimeter of the hair root and inserted it into one of the Eppendorfs. She replaced the tip of a Pipetman with the 200 microliter container, and transferred the buffer liquid from the vial to the Eppendorf. Conscious of Max watching her, she was a bit stiff at first, but soon that gave way to practiced motions. Katya efficiently carried out the same procedure with the other scraps of flesh. Max observed.

"Professor Michaels was dead on."

"About what?"

"You really are brilliant."

"It hasn't even been an hour since we met, Professor."

"I can tell from watching how you go through the steps of a basic experiment and from how you handle the equipment. You're top-notch."

The preparations lasted around an hour. They set the test tubes into the DNA sequencer. The computer would do the rest.

"Did you create this DNA identification program too, Professor?" she asked, peering at the computer screen.

"I guided one of my students into making it. These days, we get students who are whizzes with computer stuff."

"It's well-programmed. You must have been an excellent guide." Katya typed quickly, and the screen's display shifted just as fast. DNA analysis is performed by severing a string of DNA with a restriction enzyme, extracting a specific DNA fragment, and employing gel electrophoresis to obtain DNA fingerprinting. By comparing the fingerprints, it is possible to determine whether or not they are the same person, but by combining a sequencer and a computer, it is possible to obtain accuracy rates close to 100 percent. Max had also contributed to the establishment of the method.

They returned to his office where Max placed a cup of coffee he bought at a vending machine in front of Katya. "I'm planning to move out of here next week," he said, scanning the room. There were only a few books left on the bookshelf, and three cardboard boxes were stacked in the corner. On the desk were a laptop and a plastic DNA model on a wooden stand. A plate on the table was engraved with the names of all the staff of TU Berlin and the genetic research facility. It was given to him as a memento for his time in Germany. "Where did you get your degree?"

"In 2002, after I graduated from TU Dresden's med school, I moved on to TU Berlin's biochemistry department. After that, I studied abroad at Stanford and got my PhD there."

"That's why your English is so good."

"My mother is American. My father, who works for a trading company, was sent to New York, where they met and married. I was born in America, and lived there until I was 12."

"How old . . ."

"I'm 28." She took a sip of her coffee. "It's not my fault you mistook me for a student," she said, in response to the surprised look on Max's face. She looked at the DNA figurine. "I came in contact with death, so I gained an interest in life itself. I could cure wounds and diseases through medicine, but no one can evade death forever. In the face of that, is medicine not, in fact, powerless?" She put the paper cup on the table. "You asked why I chose life science. That's the reason I decided to do life science research instead of pursuing medicine."

Max looked at the window, listening.

"Well? Have I passed?"

"When it comes to your skill, I have no qualms. There's just one problem." He spun in his chair to face her. "I'm going to be in America ten days from now."

"I'm aware. I have US citizenship since I was born there."

"Can I ask you to be my assistant for the time being? I'll add 5,000 dollars to your current annual income."

Katya's face lit up. Max got up and proffered his hand. "Sounds like a deal, Katya." Katya hurriedly gripped his hand. "Any questions?"

For a moment, Katya seemed to waver.

"Don't hesitate. Don't be afraid to ask questions."

"Why do you always look so melancholy, Professor?"

Max stopped rifling through his files and looked at her. "Is that how I look? I didn't realize."

"All the students talk about it. They joke your wife probably can't stand it."

"I'll keep that in mind if I ever get married."

"Forgive me, that was rude of me. But my father always said we live to enjoy life, and that fun starts with a smile. I agree with those words."

"Your father must be a happy man. And you're his happy daughter."

Katya noticed a book on the desk. On top of it was a birthday card that read "Wisdom saves lives, but it robs people of their freedom and souls. To my beloved patient." Max's signature was scrawled on the bottom. "Is this a birthday present?" asked Katya. She read the title of the book. "*The Enigma Cipher*. That was the Nazi army's cipher, right? Is one of your patients the type to read books like these?"

"I hired you to be my assistant. Is prying part of your job description?" Max put the card and book into his desk drawer.

"I apologize, but I . . ."

"It will take seven hours for the analysis results to come in. I'm going to be in my hotel until then." Max looked at the clock and put his files in his bag.

"I'll head home. I live with my parents near Hasenheide."

They left the lab. It was late, and few people were on the streets. After seeing Katya off in a taxi, Max walked the three blocks to the hotel where he'd been staying since vacating his apartment.

Max couldn't sleep a wink. He'd gone to bed as soon as he got out of the shower, but the hand in the formalin was floating in his head. And the Nazi in uniform was staring at him. He tossed and turned. Whenever he closed his eyes, the darkness threatened to swallow him. When he was a child, he used to turn all the lights on in his room and cling to his pillow and tremble. At daybreak, he gave in and took a sleeping pill, and finally sank into welcome sleep.

He arrived at the genetic research facility the next morning at 10:05. He still felt the effect of the sleeping pill and was having trouble focusing. His hazy mind reflected on the previous day's events. It was just as that old man said—this all might be a clue to what he had been searching for.

Katya was waiting in front of the facility. Just like the day before, she had on a T-shirt and jeans, along with her beat-up backpack. She was sitting on the stone wall of the flower bed beside the main entrance, eating an apple. When she noticed Max, she smiled with evident surprise, and waved.

Max apologized for his lateness for the second day in a row. They took the elevator to the eighth floor and turned to walk down the hallway. Suddenly, Max was almost knocked to the floor when a man in a lab coat crashed into him. Katya grabbed Max by the arm, and Max reached out his hand to help the man in the lab coat, but he brushed it aside and got back on his feet. Then he grabbed his bag that had fallen to the floor and bolted toward the elevator.

"Guy thinks he can get in some exercise here in the lab." Max watched as the man jabbed repeatedly at the elevator button. He noticed Max and Katya were staring at him, and looked back nervously to see what floor the elevator was on. A muffled noise came from the lab, then a scream, and then the sound of footsteps running down the hallway. A group of men and women in lab coats were rushing toward them. One of the men was a former assistant of Max's.

"What is going on?"

"An explosion! The thermostatic chamber, it blew!" shouted Max's assistant. Blood spilled from between his fingers as he pressed his forehead, and one arm of his lab coat was stained red. "It was that man. He was in the lab!"

Max turned around; the elevator opened at that moment, and Max saw the man enter.

"Hold it!"

The man locked eyes with Max as the doors closed. Max wiped the blood off his assistant's forehead and bound his arm with a handkerchief.

"Any others injured?"

"I'm not sure."

"Contact the medic team, and then call the guards. We've got to catch him!"

"Got it," said a woman in a lab coat, who burst into the nearby laboratory.

Max and Katya hurried to the lab and stopped at the entrance. Shards of glass and plastic lay scattered all over. The thermostatic chamber had been destroyed by the explosion. Glass containers had shattered on the floor. The explosion had been small, but the damage it had done to the lab was considerable. Was this a calculated bombing?

Max and Katya ran toward the DNA sample storage box.

"The vial, it's gone!"

The vacuum flask they'd so carefully placed in the box the night before was nowhere to be found. The DNA test pieces they'd created had all vanished as well.

"The bag that guy was holding . . ." Katya murmured.

Panicked, Max turned on the computer and entered the key. "The data's been deleted. And the sequencer with the sample in it was destroyed!"

Katya checked the nearby equipment. "The spare samples are all gone, too."

"So, all of the samples and all of the data are gone." Max felt weak. A devastating sense of loss came over him. He might just have lost something with no substitute. He held onto a test bench so he wouldn't fall to the floor.

"Professor, I . . ."

"Later. Are there any others who are injured?"

A woman in a lab coat standing in the doorway silently shook her head. Researchers from other rooms filled the hallway, and the guards pushed by them to peer into the lab.

"Don't touch anything. The police are going to be here soon." A guard ordered the assistants out of the room, after they'd gotten a look at the mangled, doorless thermostatic chamber.

"Somebody tossed a grenade in there. More than one, probably. We're getting more and more idiots who love wrecking stuff because of their crazy logic nowadays." The guard was referring to the Dörrenwald bombing. "But this is the work of an amateur. If you throw a bomb into something like this that's as sturdy as a safe, then the explosive power's going to be weaker. The door got blown off, sure, but that's about it. If they really wanted to destroy the place, they should've rolled the grenades elsewhere. Unless they just wanted to destroy the equipment. I used to be armed forces, so I know how explosives work."

He picked up a piece of metal off the floor and showed it to Max. It was the thermostatic chamber door's handle. The aim was clearly to demolish the equipment.

"Right after the explosion, a man in a lab coat got in the elevator and escaped." Max pointed to the assistants looking at them from the entrance. "They saw it."

"I'll notify the authorities." The guard went over to the assistants and made note of their recollection of what the man looked like.

"Professor . . . ," Katya whispered to Max. "I connected the sequencer's storage device to the university intranet. The results of the experiment should be linked up to two different systems. The data should already have been transferred from the facility's server to your computer."

Max grabbed Katya's arm, and they rushed out of the lab.

"When I was back in the States, a computer virus once ruined all of my experiment data. Ever since then, I've made sure to back up my data using more than one storage venue," Katya explained as she ran to keep up with Max.

The second Max entered his office, he turned on his computer and pulled up the file.

"You're the ideal assistant! I'm lucky to have you aboard," Max looked at his screen, which showed strings of the letters A, T, G, and C (adenine, thymine, guanine, and cytosine). Below was a pulse waveform representing each base. It was the results of the DNA analysis. The sequence of these 12 billion base molecules determined all there was to determine in a human being.

Max typed something to arrange two pulse waveforms one above the other.

"The top is the DNA from the hand. The bottom is DNA from the hair."

Katya stared without saying a word. Then she nodded slowly.

"They're a match. That man came to the lab in search of this."

"Of the hand, and of the data."

"The hair and the hand belong to the same person. But what does that mean?"

Max stopped to think.

"I think you should report this to the police."

"No one will believe us." Max could barely believe it himself.

Max felt a sudden sharp pain in his chest. A chaotic mix of fear, hope, impatience, and every other emotion filled his mind. He felt faint.

"Professor! Are you okay?"

He could hear her voice. He struggled to control his mind. It was too soon to despair. He gripped the desk and steadied himself.

"You look awfully pale."

"I'll be fine." Max straightened up.

CHAPTER 3

After 3:00 p.m., Max left the research facility with Katya. The police had questioned them about the explosion, but Max repeated what he'd already told the guards, and didn't mention anything about the hand. It wasn't as though he fully understood the situation himself.

Max and Katya walked toward the hotel. Max planned to give Katya some research materials, specifically a dissertation about research topics in the United States. Max would be back in the States in less than ten days. As they rounded the corner, Max noticed a large gray Mercedes sedan parked across the street. Through the open window, Max saw Feldman's face.

"That's the guy who was waiting in front of the university yesterday." Katya saw Max was looking at the car.

"Wait at the hotel. Just say my name at the front desk and show them this." He wrote the name and address of the hotel and the words "give her the key" on the back of a business card and put it in Katya's hand. Before Katya could say anything, he went over to the car. Jake stepped out of the driver's seat and opened the rear door for him. The car set off the instant Max got in. Feldman was the only one inside.

"Are you unhurt?"

"You know about the bombing at the lab?" His tone was stronger than he'd intended.

"You appear to be fine."

"What's going on? Somebody infiltrated the lab and planted a bomb. The guy ran off with your little gift, too."

"It's truly a shame."

"That's all you've got to say?"

"What were the results of the scan? Surely the results are ready by now. You returned to your hotel at two in the morning." Feldman ignored Max's question. His expression hadn't changed at all.

"I'll tell you when you answer my question."

"Nothing too grave has happened just yet. You and I are both unharmed. We're still alive."

"Some of the lab workers did get injured. One wrong step and it would have been more serious."

"You are on the enemy's hit list now, Professor. I'm afraid we underestimated them. Who could have imagined they would move so quickly? It's our fault this happened," he said, even as he gazed ahead. "Now what about the results?"

"It's a match. Both the hand and the hair belong to Gehlen."

Feldman's shoulders dropped slightly.

"Now it's your turn to answer my questions."

"Wait until we reach the office. This matter is quite complex." Feldman turned silent. His hands clasped in his lap, he was deep in thought.

About ten minutes later, the car reached the back road and stopped behind the building. This is where Max had gotten into the blue sedan to return to the laboratory last time. He went up the stairs into the hallway, and the two men seated in front of the door got up. After confirming Feldman was with him, they took their hands out from under their jackets.

"All of the rooms in this building—which is to say, all six rooms—are for the exclusive use of our organization. Now that we've learned of the explosion at the research facility, we've become more vigilant. The enemy has drawn nearer than we imagined, though we in turn are closing in on the enemy."

Max entered the antique shop's office and sat down on the sofa. Feldman took out a few letter-size photo enlargements from his desk drawer and put them in front of Max.

"This one was taken a few minutes before the bomb went off at the neo-Nazi rally." A group of about ten men and women were standing on the stage. "It looks grainy because this is a magnified version of a picture taken by a small hidden camera. Cameras were forbidden that day. Though everybody in the media sneaked some in anyway."

Feldman pointed to one man, and slid another photo next to it. It was an enlarged photo of the man he was pointing at. It was extremely grainy, but one could make out his face and physique. The man was in his forties, and was standing bolt upright wearing an elegant suit. From his lean and toned body and face, one got the sense he was tough and strong. Next, Feldman slid one of the photos from the day before next to the others. It was the sepia-tone photo of the Nazi soldier in uniform.

"It can't be!" Max was shocked. He had half-expected it, of course, but even when the proof lay before his very eyes, he still couldn't believe it. The color of the photos, the hairstyles, the clothes, and the backgrounds were all different, but they were of the same man, down to his apparent age.

"It's Gehlen. All three of them are Gehlen. What differs is when these photos were taken. 1940, and this year."

"I thought you told me he was over a hundred years old."

"To be exact, 111." Feldman opened a file and read it aloud: "Born in Memmingen, Germany, September 3, 1896. The eldest son of Otto Gehlen, an engineer at a chemical factory, and Anna Gehlen. After graduating from university, he joined the German Army, and then joined the SS as a major. Height six feet, weight 180 pounds, blond. Hitler's ideal example of the German race. He was a cunning and cautious man." Feldman handed Max the file. It described a timeline of major events. "This is everything we've come to learn about

Gehlen. We also compiled as much information as we could on what he did after the war. As a close aide of the Nazi hitman Benchell, they always worked in tandem."

Max stared at the document while Feldman spoke. Eventually, he turned back to the photos. "But how?" Max was at a loss for words. He still couldn't believe it. He picked up the two photos taken right before the explosion and looked at the face again. "There's no way he's any older than 50 here." From the old-fashioned sepia photo and the modern color ones stared the exact same man: firm skin, hair trimmed short, a straight spine. His narrow eyes and faint, thin-lipped smile gave the impression of a man who was as strong-willed as he was brutal.

"We couldn't believe it either, at first. We figured he was either a look-alike or had plastic surgery to disguise himself. But our resident expert found no traces of such a thing. Computer graphics are quite advanced these days. With just one photo, you can construct an accurate 3D model of a person's face. And yet these two individuals had not undergone plastic surgery, nor were they in disguise. To remove all doubt, the fingerprints are a match as well. That is why we wished to meet with you, Professor."

"What's the meaning of all this?" Max muttered to himself, still holding the two photos.

"I, too, would like to know the answer to that question. I know that you already had some inkling when you saw the photos yesterday. Otherwise you wouldn't have agreed to assist us. Or am I mistaken?"

Max's eyes were glued to the photos. "I'm not dreaming, am I?"

"We believe you are the one who can find the answer we are looking for." Feldman stared straight into Max's soul. Then he pulled out more old photos.

All the men in the photos were wearing SS uniforms. Max's eyes fell on one of the photos. In it, dozens of men were lined up in front of the Reichstag. It was some sort of ceremony. The man at the center of the front row had a distinctive moustache, a square chin, and eyes that stared defiantly. He was none other than Adolf Hitler.

Feldman pointed to the man standing right behind Hitler, at the center of the second row. "This man is Reinhard Benchell. He would be 115 today. He was the most faithful executor of Hitler's will." Then in his late forties, he stood a head shorter than the others. "Devious, cruel, ruthless, odious, vile . . . every negative adjective you can think of." Feldman showed him another photo, a magnified photo of Benchell. His moustache resembled Hitler's, but he had a rounder face, and his forehead reached halfway up his balding scalp. He was an unremarkable-looking man with glasses. But something was off about him, too. "His rank then was major general. Compared to him, people like Gehlen come off as saints. He wasn't visible at the front stage of history, but he always reigned as an aide among aides to Hitler. In fact, some historians posit that some of Hitler's crimes against humanity were Benchell's recommendations. The eradication of the Jews, the culling of the mentally handicapped . . . he was a great believer in the supposed superiority of the German people. And yet he never appeared from behind the curtain. That's how devious he was. Eventually he was sentenced to death as a war criminal." Feldman stood beside Max, his eyes fixed on the photos.

Seconds passed in silence. Then Feldman pointed to a man behind Benchell. "Gehlen was Benchell's loyal subordinate. He shadowed him wherever they went. They were like a snake and a scorpion competing with each other for the highest number of kills. One can only wonder which of the two killed the greater number of people, and which was the most brutal of the two. Gehlen had a leather wallet. When Benchell noticed it, Gehlen gave him the wallet and a bag, in return Benchell gave him a lamp shade. Gehlen invited Benchell to a meal. There was a comfortable chair in the room. You know where this is going, surely. You can guess what was stretched over that chair. What the lamp shade and the wallet were made of."

Max turned away.

"That's right. The two were using the skin of Jewish children for their art competition."

A chill ran down Max's spine. "Was Benchell at the rally, too?"

"All sixteen who died at the rally have been identified. That includes Gehlen. But Benchell wasn't among them. It makes sense; he wouldn't have wanted to take the risk of appearing at the rally. But Benchell is out there somewhere. And given that Gehlen did show up at the rally, there's a strong possibility Benchell was close by." Feldman let out a painful breath. "We once captured Benchell. It was in 1956, in Argentina. But as he was being transported to Israel, he killed two guards and escaped. We tracked him down again in 1962, in Europe. But we failed to catch him. Afterward," Feldman stopped himself. He bit his lip and closed his eyes. "Never mind. Let's not dwell on the past."

Feldman pulled out a chair and sank into it. He clasped his hands in front of his chest.

Max stared at the photos. A beautiful woman was standing next to Gehlen on the stage. Unusual for a neo-Nazi rally, she wasn't white. "Who's she?"

"We think she is probably a companion of Gehlen's. We searched the scene, but we couldn't find her. Only one of the corpses was female—a German TV reporter."

"Did you check the hospitals? Even if she survived, she must have been injured."

"We didn't find anybody who could be her. Most of the injured were admitted to a municipal hospital, but some are missing. Many among them don't want to be identified. They have an underground medical facility of their own, you see. They most likely went there."

"But she's standing almost right below where the explosives were planted. No way she survived that."

"Then we'll have to find out what has become of her."

Max stared at the photo again. It was too small to be able to read her expression. Then, a photo was thrust in front of his eyes. It was a magnified photo of the woman. It was grainy and blurry, but her face was clearly visible. She had dark skin, and if her facial features were any indication, she had some Latin American ancestry.

"It's computer processed. We're desperate. We'll do whatever we can," Feldman said quietly. "She's over 30. A little less than five feet, three inches tall and weighs about 110 pounds. There's a small mole on the lower right side of her nose. Her clothes were made in France, and we're searching for the manufacturer now. Two days before the rally, she arrived at Hamburg Airport from Lyon. Gehlen entered the country under the name Gugliermo Tinari and the woman under the name Maria Tinari. Their stated purpose was 'tourism.' Both are Italian nationals."

"Where were they before that?"

"We're looking into that." Feldman put another photo on the table.

"We had complete information on Gehlen. His physique, his personality, his tastes, all of his grades from elementary school to college, his family, relatives, and friends. To think we would find him no different from how he appeared sixty-eight years ago! It's hard to believe he changed much at all—appearance included."

Feldman motioned to Jake to put a DVD into the player. The DVD wasn't very clear. It looked like an open-air theater production. But this was no play. It was a neo-Nazi rally that sparked memories of the Third Reich rallies all those decades ago. A banner reading "The 1st International *Schwarzes Kreuz* Assembly" hung from the stage, and a flag bearing a cross-and-triangle symbol hung on the back wall. The symbol was a stand-in—it is illegal to display swastikas in public places in Germany.

"We recorded footage of the rally with a 500mm telephoto lens. With a little effort, you can make out what they look like."

The shot zoomed in on the group in the center of the stage. It was difficult to make out what they were saying. Feldman drew Max's attention to the person at the center of the screen. It was Gehlen, and he was shaking hands with another man, after which he returned to his seat and kissed the woman.

"Gehlen was shaking hands with *Schwarzes Kreuz* Chairman

Friedrich Heiper. That's Vice-Chairman Erhard laughing beside him. Both died in the explosion."

"How old was Heiper?"

"43."

"He and Gehlen really do look like they're around the same age."

"Pay attention to Gehlen. Unlike me, when his body moves, it moves smoothly. The man is undoubtedly in his forties. You can tell not only by his face and physique, but also by his movements." Feldman glanced Max's way, but Max couldn't take his eyes off the footage.

"At the very least, he's not over a hundred years old."

The video footage was shaky; someone's palm covered the lens, and the video came to an end.

"They spotted the camera and took it from us. Then there was the explosion. In the confusion the photographer managed to recover the camera before getting away."

Max looked up at him. "Are you asking me to help you hunt Nazis?"

"Would such a thing displease you?"

"I'm a scientist. I can't play police investigator, and I certainly can't do what you people do."

"No, but we do need your skills."

"Hardly." Max tried to get up, but Feldman grabbed his shoulder.

"If you recall the incident earlier today, you're already involved. They want you dead. Besides . . ." But he stopped there. He drew in closer. "You can't escape this case." Feldman was staring at Max, eyes blazing with conviction.

Max sat back on the sofa. It was exactly as he said. The faces of the Nazi war criminals were already seared into his mind. He could feel himself losing strength.

"Nazi war criminals . . . they're no concern of mine," Max muttered. "But how can they be so young? They should be over a hundred years old by now, but from what you've shown me, they're clearly in their forties."

"We can't solve that mystery. Only you can. That is why we chose you."

"The hand's been taken. Any other body parts we can use?"

"Obtaining that hand was the best we could do. There were body parts and scraps of flesh from dozens of people, including from the injured, but those remains have already been cremated by local police, due to requests from both *Schwarzes Kreuz* and the bereaved. It's summer, bodies decompose more quickly in the heat, and most of the people who died were *Schwarzes Kreuz* members. They must have pulled strings politically as well. The bastards are making inroads into politics, which was unthinkable just five years ago." Feldman sighed. "The far-right party is taking advantage of the neo-Nazi movement to advance their anti-Semitic, anti-immigrant agenda."

"We must find the woman who was with Gehlen."

Feldman looked at the photos. "That will be difficult, but Jews from all over the world are helping us. We have the financial, political, and grassroots-level assistance of millions. Their hearts and minds are with us, too, of course. But they can't help us on the field," he stated, half to himself. "You will help us, won't you?" Feldman looked at Max.

Before he knew it, Max was nodding.

Max left the office. He refused their offer to drive him to his hotel and took a taxi instead. He wanted to be alone with his thoughts. His head was swimming—had he found what he'd been looking for?

There was heavy traffic. The driver was humming a tune and tapping his fingers on the steering wheel. Max stared blankly at those fingers. By the time he arrived at the hotel it was after six. Three hours had passed since he'd left the research facility. He opened the door to his room. The air inside was different somehow. He almost called Katya's name, but stopped himself. He noticed a bulge in the bed.

Katya was sound asleep. Her chestnut-colored curls covered her forehead, and her bright white teeth peeked from between her parted full lips. Her tanned skin looked sleek and youthful to him. The blanket around her chest moved gently up and down as she breathed. He watched her face as she slept for a while, before sitting on the sofa. He spread a few photos Feldman had given him on the table. Max was now caught up in Feldman's organization. His head started to throb. He closed his eyes and lightly rubbed his temples, and the mass weighing down on his brain receded.

"A woman of mixed Latin American ancestry."

Max looked up, and Katya was standing in front of him. "I think she might be mestizo. I took an ethnology course as an undergraduate. We studied facial feature recognition by region." Katya looked closer.

"Can you tell what country she might be from by her facial features?"

"Brazil, maybe? Could be Chile or Argentina or Colombia. Somewhere in South America, I think."

"A lot of Nazis fled to South America after the war."

Katya picked up the photo of Gehlen in SS uniform. "Professor," her tone changed, and she frowned. "Who was in that car? They were the guys who pulled you into their van on campus, weren't they? And then they asked you for a DNA test."

"They're an Israeli organization. They're hunting Nazi war criminals."

Katya stared intently at the photo.

"I may be an American citizen, but I'm half-German by blood, and I'm proud of that. It's true that the Germany of the past committed crimes against humanity, but modern Germany has wrestled with those sins and is looking toward a brighter future. I was taught it's our duty as Germans to make up for the mistakes of the past and to never make those mistakes again. I grew up in the US until I finished elementary school, but that's how I feel too," said Katya.

Max filled her in on what had happened so far. He told her about Feldman, about the bombing at the neo-Nazi rally, and about the severed hand and the photographs. Katya listened with the occasional sigh, and appeared close to tears.

"Was he a clone?" she asked.

"That was the first possibility I considered. If he was a clone, that explains the DNA match. But if the Gehlen that appeared at the rally was 40 years old, that means he was born forty years ago. DNA manipulation didn't exist then. The double helix structure of DNA was discovered by Watson and Crick in 1953. The world's first clone was Dolly the sheep in 1996. There was no human cloning technology yet."

"But it's clear through these two photos that . . ."

"Say he's a clone. Would their fingerprints be a match?"

"Then how would you explain this?"

"I don't know." Max recalled the hand floating in formalin. The whitish chunk of flesh from the man in that video shared the DNA of a man in a Nazi uniform in the sepia-tone photo. Max shook his head and cleared his mind.

Max opened his laptop and typed in a few commands. The pattern waveforms appeared alongside the four-letter base sequences of A, T, G, and C. The top half of the screen displayed the DNA sequence of cells collected from the hand. Below that was the DNA taken from the hair kept by Gehlen's mother. He carefully examined the two sequences. There was no mistaking it—they were identical. That could mean only one of two things—he was literally the same person, or he was a clone. Had the remnants of the Nazi regime already developed cloning technology so long ago?

"It's like something out of a dream, Professor."

"If this is a dream, it's a nightmare. Or maybe . . ." Feldman's face came to Max's mind. There was something enigmatic about Feldman's expression.

When he felt her warm breath on his cheeks, he looked up to find Katya peering into the screen. Max pulled back slightly and turned off his computer.

• • •

II

LADY OF MYSTERY

CHAPTER 4

He was being sucked into a drifting, spongy mass of black. No—he was that black mass—a hideous, meaningless lump of meat. He existed only to decay with the passage of time until he ceased to exist.

His body was rigid; he couldn't move. He was plummeting down a bottomless pit. Where was he? This was a world he knew well, and the place he feared most. The final destination. The land of the dead.

He was melting. His head and limbs were dissolving into the darkness. His existence was fading as the darkness absorbed him, until, at last, he was annihilated.

He knew this was just a dream, but he couldn't wake himself up. He felt so alone. A vise was clamping down on his heart. The eternal silence that was death was what he dreaded most.

His cellphone rang. By force of will, he pulled his consciousness out of the ocean of darkness and reached for it.

"We found her." Feldman's voice was calm.

"She's alive?" Max sat up in bed. His back and neck were sweaty. He unbuttoned his pajamas while holding the phone to his ear.

"We're heading to her location right now."

"I'm coming too." He looked at the clock. It was 1:15 a.m. He looked out the window, and sure enough, it was still dark.

"Please wait at the office. We'd like you to join us when we question her."

"No, I'm going with you. If you refuse, I won't help you anymore. I'm serious."

"It's too dangerous, Professor."

"The bomb blast should have wounded her. I imagine it'd be a good idea to have a physician like me there."

He could hear Feldman cover the mouthpiece for a few seconds. "Very well. On the condition you do as we say. Is that clear? We'll pick you up in front of the hotel in fifteen minutes. Be careful; I don't know what might happen."

He hung up before Max could reply.

Max threw on some clothes and looked down from the window; the street looked hazy in the glow of the streetlights. Every few minutes a car zoomed at high speed down the road. He grabbed the first aid kit that he always had ready. He wanted to be prepared for minor incisions and sutures.

As soon as he stepped in front of the hotel, a Volkswagen van appeared from around the corner. Jake was in the passenger seat. The sliding door opened, and Max saw Feldman looking at him from one of the backseats. Max got in and the van drove off.

The air was thick with tension. Feldman was staring silently ahead. The van had three rows of seats occupied by six men, including Max. This was the first time he'd seen the two sitting in the very back; both were around forty, with lean but muscular frames.

"Where is she?" he asked Feldman.

"A farmhouse about an hour away."

"Is she wounded?"

"We don't know any specifics."

"Let's do it the legal way this time."

"No matter what transpires, don't interfere."

"That depends on you guys."

"We may be living in the twenty-first century, Professor, but we still face Nazism. And we are Jews. Anything can happen."

Max had no answer to that. Feldman's face was stiff and nervous, and his tone was severe.

Thirty minutes later they were outside the city. They left behind high-rise buildings as they drove by tidy single-family homes on both sides of the road. Then, those disappeared. A rural landscape stretched out before them, although they could only see its silhouette under the dim starlight. Farmhouses dotted the fields.

It was already after 3:00 a.m. A Mercedes sedan was parked by a tree. The van slowed down and parked behind it.

"Please wait here, Professor." Feldman and three members of his entourage got out, leaving Max and the driver inside. After they spoke with the two who had stepped out of the sedan, Feldman returned to the van.

"She's in that farmhouse."

Across the field was a typical German farmhouse with a barn next to the main building.

"There are three guards. She's on the second floor. Wait here with the driver and follow our orders." Feldman walked back to the sedan.

Feldman and Jake, who was carrying a large backpack, the two other middle-aged men, and the two men from the sedan made up a squad of six. They ran to the house in the dark. Max could see that they had on night-vision goggles. The driver was also looking through night-vision goggles to follow their movements. Max quietly opened the sliding door. The driver was too focused on Feldman and the others to notice. Max stepped out of the van with his med kit, snuck behind the van, and crossed the field, approaching Feldman's group. When he glanced behind him, he saw the driver's silhouette, gripping a walkie-talkie. He'd been caught.

Max walked up to Feldman. Feldman grabbed Max's shoulder and stopped him in his tracks. The men ahead of them were crouching by a fence. Max saw someone step out of the door onto the porch. He was in shadow until he went to light his cigarette—he was young, and wore a leather vest over his bare skin. The man next to Max pulled something out of his coat pocket. A handgun. Then he took out a silencer and attached it to the barrel. He aimed at the man on the porch.

"Stop!" Max whispered, clutching the man's arm. He looked at Max and brushed his arm away.

"You promised not to interfere," Feldman hissed in his ear.

"There's no need to kill them."

"We need the woman and will do what it takes!"

Max held up his hand to silence Feldman. The man was no longer on the porch.

At Feldman's command, three men crept along the fence to the back of the house. The others jumped the fence and ran over to the house and up to the doorstep. Max heard the faint sound of metal scraping from the back door, but that soon stopped.

One of Feldman's men removed his goggles and knelt in front of the keyhole. A few minutes later, he turned around and signaled for the rest to come. The door opened without a sound. The room was lit only by a single lightbulb.

Something clattered to the floor in the kitchen.

A voice called from the floor above: "*Was ist los, Hans?*" (What's the matter, Hans?)

Footsteps; someone was coming down the stairs. Max's group hid behind the sofa.

A burly man with a shaved head turned on the lights and strode into the kitchen. Max watched from behind the couch, sweat beading on his forehead.

Max heard a muffled bang. The Nazi convulsed, and his giant frame toppled forward to the floor. Max squeezed his eyes shut; he expected the man's body to make a loud thud. But all he heard was dead silence. He opened his eyes to find one of his comrades holding the skinhead up. He'd gone behind him and stopped him from hitting the floor—and without a second to spare.

The man gently laid the skinhead onto the floor. Max looked at Feldman, but Feldman's expression hadn't changed. He and his men were used to this world.

"One more upstairs," whispered the man who'd shot the skinhead, pointing up.

The young man in the leather vest lay in front of the kitchen sink, blood pouring from his throat, staining the floor.

The assassin put on his goggles and headed up the stairs. Max went to follow, but Feldman grabbed him by the arm.

The wait was suffocating. Then, a thud and a muffled shriek.

"Come," said the man from the second floor.

Max followed Feldman up the stairs and into a dimly lit room. There was a bed by the window, and in that bed was the woman they were searching for.

Max turned away. A woman with short hair and a stern expression lay on her back between the bed and the chair, blood pooling from a hole in her forehead. She'd been killed the instant she'd turned to face her assailant. Her eyes were wide open.

Feldman turned to Max. "You're up, Professor."

The woman in bed was naked above the waist, except for the bandages from her chest to her abdomen.

"Give me some light."

Feldman brought over the lamp from beside the desk.

She was covered with wounds, which meant she'd taken the blast head on. Some of her wounds were full of metal shrapnel. Max checked her pulse and heartbeat. Neither was erratic, but both were weak. He removed the bandaging to find her chest and abdomen covered with blood-soaked gauze. When he peeled off the gauze, he discovered suture traces. Judging by the size of her wounds, her internals were probably damaged as well. She needed an X-ray. It was a miracle she'd survived with injuries like these.

The suturing was crude, but the wounds had already begun to close up.

"What's wrong?" Feldman asked.

"Nothing." Max pulled cardiotonic drugs and antibiotics out of his bag.

"Please hurry. We need to take her to the office."

"Her heart's weak. It's too risky to move her."

One of the men pushed Max away and went to pick her up.

"Go get some plastic wrap from the kitchen," Max said, knowing they were determined to move her.

Max applied disinfected gauze to the wound and wrapped the woman's body in the plastic wrap. "This will close the wound, but move her as gently as possible."

Two men gently lifted the woman from each side and carried her from the room. Jake removed his backpack and took out a black nylon bag. He tossed in all the stuff in the room he could get his hands on. Photo frames, notebooks, books—he opened drawers and rummaged through them. When he finished with the bedroom, he moved on to the next room. One of the men grabbed a suitcase next to the bed. Feldman stood by the door, scanning the room. Then he tapped Max on the shoulder; Max had been staring at the corpse on the floor. Max and Feldman went out into the yard and started walking toward the van. Jake followed them with a full bag.

"What about the corpse?" asked Max.

Feldman barely shrugged.

As soon as they got in the van, it zoomed off, the sedan following behind. The woman was unconscious, sandwiched between the two men in the backseat. Every few minutes she moaned with pain.

"That went unbelievably well. The enemy wasn't expecting us to act so quickly." Feldman put his night-vision goggles in his bag. In that bag, Max caught a glimpse of a gun larger than any handgun. It was a submachine gun.

"We killed three people." Max looked up at Feldman.

"And those who shared those three's ideals killed six million of our compatriots."

"You're no different from the Nazis. This is the kind of wanton murder . . ."

"Let's not debate this at the moment. Let us instead rejoice that we are unharmed, and the operation was successful."

"She needs to be taken to a well-equipped hospital."

"Don't worry, Professor. Just do as you're told." Feldman's tone was unwavering. He closed his mouth and looked away; the discussion was over.

CHAPTER 5

The van veered off the main street into a narrow road, and eventually reached the back entrance of the office. The woman was regaining consciousness, and the gauze under the plastic wrap was red with blood. They carried her to the guest room. She was totally still. Her breathing was shallow and her pulse was weak.

Jake took the contents out of the bag and put them on the table. The men began to examine them. They found two passports and gave them to Feldman.

"Italian passports. They're fakes, but they're good ones."

Feldman inspected the passports under the lamp. "The woman's name is 'Maria Tinari.' It looks as though she's the wife of one 'Gugliermo Tinari.' That means Gehlen and this woman are married." He gave Max the two passports.

The woman claimed she was born in 1971, which would make her 37 years old. The other was definitely a photo of Gehlen. The date of birth listed was December 3, 1964. That would make him 43.

The door to the next room opened, and a plump middle-aged woman came in. She was the first woman among Feldman's allies that Max had seen. She knelt next to the bed and took a syringe out of her bag. She popped the lid off an ampoule and withdrew the liquid with practiced hands.

"What is that?" He tried to read the ampoule label, but it was peeled off.

The woman prepped Maria's arm for the injection. Max tried to stop her, but was restrained from behind. The woman stopped and looked up at Feldman for instructions.

"I'm not trying to kill her. You also want to know the truth, don't you?"

"What's in that syringe? Is it a cardiotonic?"

"It's an analeptic. It's harmless."

"Not when she's like this it's not. It'll put too much strain on her heart."

Feldman signaled the men behind Max with his eyes. They pulled Max away from the woman.

The woman casually pricked Maria's arm; she moaned faintly in response. Her head wriggled for a while, but eventually she opened her eyes. They were dark. Blearily, she looked around before her eyes fell on the woman.

"Maria. That's the name on your passport," Feldman said in German, "but it isn't your real name. What is it?"

Maria's eyes moved to Feldman, and a look of horror dawned on her face. She tried to get up. The men holding Max let go in order to pin Maria down. Feldman stooped down and drew in close to her. "Answer our questions, and we will not harm you. When we're done with you, we will take you to the hospital for treatment," he said in a gentle voice, but her fearful expression didn't change.

Feldman said the same thing in English, and finally in Spanish. Maria didn't respond to any of those languages. She just looked on, as frightened as ever. Seconds passed, and the men grew impatient.

"We are not your enemies. You had nothing to do with the past actions of the man we are looking for, so we have no reason to hate you. Rather, we are allies. I want to help you. I want you to cooperate with us," Feldman said slowly in all three languages.

Maria's breathing slowed slightly, but terror was still written all over her face.

"Who are you?" he asked again.

Maria bit her lip and closed her eyes.

"Let's use more of that drug," croaked an old man in English; Max had met him the first time he'd been brought here.

"Simon, please wait outside." Feldman noticed Max's gaze and stood between the two, concealing Simon behind him. Simon was still looking at the woman.

"Hurry up. Benchell may still be in Europe." Simon pushed Feldman away and stood by the bed. Feldman stepped back in resignation.

"You know Gehlen, right? He's your husband. So where's his friend Benchell?" he asked, grabbing her shoulders. Maria's forehead shone with sweat, and she was breathing hard.

"Stop. Her body can't take it." Max tried to move forward, but once again, someone grabbed his shoulder and pulled him back.

"If you interfere one more time, I'll have to ask you to leave the room." Feldman stopped the men from dragging Max out.

"With wounds like those, she should probably be dead already. If you make her exert herself, she'll die. That is my assessment as a doctor. You need to let her rest for two or three days, and then you can ask her all you like. That would serve your purposes more than recklessly killing her." Max's shoulders were still in the men's grip.

Feldman and Simon muttered to each other. Eventually, Feldman gave the men a look, and they let Max go.

"I'll leave it to you. You have until five o'clock tomorrow morning. Twenty-four hours. After that, we will do it our way." Feldman looked at his watch.

Maria's eyes closed; she was out again. Max took off the plastic wrap and gauze and checked her wounds. "The wound in her abdomen is open and bleeding. You forced her to walk, and this is what you get. She may even have blood in her abdomen. An incision needs to be made so her abdomen can be examined."

"I will arrange for whatever you need."

"I can't operate on her here."

"So, you're a competent surgeon as well?"

Max nodded. "I'll give her emergency treatment for now, and then she has to be transferred to a hospital within twenty-four hours. Can you promise that?"

"Can I question her before we transfer her?"

"I'm going to do everything I can to make that happen."

"Very well." Feldman looked to Simon for his approval, but Simon remained silent.

"Her blood pressure is terribly low." Max looked at her travel insurance card. "She needs a blood transfusion, but we really don't want to be going through red tape for one." Max turned his eyes to the men in the room. They looked at each other. Feldman took off his coat and rolled up his shirtsleeve.

"Any infectious diseases?"

Feldman shook his head.

"One more person," Max said.

At Max's prompting, one of the men stepped forward.

The streetlights shone through the gaps in the curtains. The bedside clock said 4:20 a.m.

"I'm going to call my assistant. I need medical supplies and an assistant's hand. She's a doctor too." Max took out his cellphone from his jacket's inner pocket, but Feldman pointed to the landline phone.

"You can't use your cellphone in this room. It's shielded to prevent wiretapping, so you don't have to worry about being overheard."

Katya picked up after ten rings. "Dr. Knight?" she asked, half-asleep.

Max apologized for the early morning call, and told her how to get the medicine she needed to bring him.

"What's the address?" he asked Feldman.

"We'll pick her up."

He hesitated for a moment, before instructing Katya where to wait. "Dr. Lang will be waiting in front of the research facility. She's a woman, so don't be rough."

Feldman spoke to one of his men in hushed tones. The man nodded and left.

An hour later, Katya came in with a man flanking her on each side. Her face was stiff with fear, but when she saw Max, she looked relieved. She couldn't hide her confusion, though. When Max explained the situation, her face grew even stiffer. She, a German, was now surrounded by Jewish Nazi hunters. Max told Feldman to get everyone out of the room. Simon vociferously refused, but Feldman persuaded him to leave. Now it was only Max, Katya, and Maria in the room. Katya frowned at the sight of the blood in a plastic bag and the blood transfusion tube hanging from a coatrack.

"She's in horrible shape. We can't do anything here."

"We can try our best." Max took out the medical equipment from his bag and instructed Katya to make preparations for the IV drip. Though Maria's blood pressure had managed to recover via the blood transfusions, she was unconscious and terribly weak.

"Raise her legs. I don't want to put any strain on her heart."

Katya folded a blanket and put it under Maria's feet. Max removed the gauze on her abdomen and chest, and examined her wounds again. Her abdomen showed traces of bleeding from the sutures, but the bleeding had almost completely stopped. However, they had no way of knowing how her insides looked without opening her up, and they couldn't examine her chest at all. While her ribs didn't appear to be broken, her lungs might have been damaged.

"Apart from the bleeding," Katya said, "her chest will be fine for now. That's just eyeballing it, though. We need an X-ray to see her internals. All we can do is disinfect her abdomen and re-suture it. But if her internal organs are damaged, the rest is for God to decide."

"I agree with that assessment, except for that bit at the end."

The treatment was completed in about an hour. They opened her sutures halfway to drain the accumulated blood. That alone would ease her suffering a great deal.

The door opened, and Feldman and Simon came in. Impatience was written all over Simon's face.

"This is just an emergency measure. You need to send her to a hospital as soon as possible," Max told Feldman.

They could hear the noise of activity outside. It had gotten light out.

"When can we finally talk to her?"

"If you try it now, then the answer to that question is never. I promise you'll have her by tomorrow morning."

Feldman and Simon talked for a while, but they resigned themselves and left the room.

"You also do clinical work?" Max asked Katya, who was staring at him.

"I wanted to be a doctor at first."

"You are a doctor. A great one."

"But there are some afflictions that just can't be cured, no matter how good a doctor you are. I hit that wall eventually. Just like you." Max sat down and rubbed his eyes.

"You should rest. You didn't sleep last night. Your eyes are bloodshot." Katya checked to see whether the door was closed, and set up the cot that the men had brought.

"But before you go to sleep, please just tell me what the hell's going on."

"Don't ask me anything now. I'll fill you in when the time comes."

"I was awakened by a call at four o'clock in the morning and was blindfolded by mysterious men and taken to a seriously injured woman. Two days ago, you had me run a DNA analysis on a hand that was soaked in formalin in a glass vial. The next day, the laboratory was blown up and the hand was stolen. The explosion caused an assistant to need seven stitches. If I had walked into the lab five minutes earlier, who knows what could've happened? This isn't normal, Professor. All of these things should be reported to the police."

Max was silent. His thoughts were racing too. He was the one who wanted to ask a million questions.

"And this patient?" Katya turned to Maria. "She's not normal."

"Indeed. These wounds were more than enough to kill someone, but she's clearly recovering."

Katya stood up and closed the blinds.

"I'll wait, but only because you want me to, Professor."

"I appreciate that," Max murmured in reply.

"Go to sleep. I'll wake you if anything happens." Katya moved her chair to the side of Maria's bed and sat down.

Max lay down on the cot and closed his eyes. He was tired but stirred up at the same time. When he opened his eyes slightly, he could see Katya's seated silhouette. He didn't hear any noise from the next room. He closed his eyes again. The events of the last few days flowed through his mind. Explosions, a dismembered hand, Nazi war criminals, an SS general—all things that occur in a world that was alien to Max. And they had swooped in on him all at once. *What do I do? There's just no way I can do enough.* Eventually, his consciousness clouded over, and he sank into the realm of dreams.

A noise startled him awake. A shadowy figure was next to the bed, holding a penlight to Maria's face.

"Who . . ."

The shadow jolted. "It's me," came Katya's voice from within the darkness. She was reaching out to check the IV drip. Katya drew closer to whisper to Max. "She's regained consciousness."

Max got up off the cot and went to Maria's bed. He turned on the bedside lamp and took her pulse, which was much stronger than it had been a few hours ago. Her condition had stabilized, thanks to the blood transfusions and intravenous drip. Yet she had recovered so quickly that those alone weren't enough to explain it.

Maria's eyes opened. At first she looked frightened, but when she saw Katya, her expression softened. "Aska . . . ," Maria's lips quivered.

"Are you trying to say something?" Katya put her ear closer to her lips. Maria was barely conscious.

"You shouldn't overdo it," Max said, but the door opened at that moment.

Light flooded into the room, and there stood Simon. At Simon's signal, the men came in and pushed Max and Katya away.

"Stop!" Max shouted.

One of the men pricked Maria's arm with a needle.

"You promised to wait until tomorrow morning. She still hasn't recovered enough." Max tried to stop the man, but couldn't.

"We waited long enough. We can't wait any longer." Simon stepped in front of the bed. Feldman was standing behind him.

"You've been waiting for sixty years. What's a few more hours?"

Maria moaned. Her eyes opened, but her line of sight didn't shift until, slowly, it did. Her lips trembled, but she didn't seem as frightened as before.

"She's back with us," said the man who'd administered the injection.

"And the truth serum?"

"It should already be working."

Feldman signaled to the man to back off, and sat down close to Maria.

"*Wie heißt du?*" he asked her. "What is your name?"

"Dona . . ." Max didn't know whether to classify it as a moan or a murmur.

Feldman looked up at Max and Simon. "You're Dona. Not Maria. Dona," he repeated, just to make sure. "Don't worry, Dona. We're on your side. Don't be afraid to answer our questions."

Dona didn't answer. Her eyes were drifting as she stared up at the ceiling.

"Who taught you German? You do know German, clearly."

"Master . . ." Dona's mouth barely moved.

"Master?" Feldman turned to Simon, who gave him a look that said keep going.

Feldman drew closer to her. "Who is your master?"

"General . . ."

"General?"

"What is your relationship with Gehlen?" asked Simon from behind.

"Master . . ."

"Dona, are you saying you're Gehlen's servant?"

Dona shook her head slightly.

"I . . . wife . . . General Gehlen's wife . . . ," she struggled to speak.

"'General'? What do you mean?"

"Yes . . . General Gehlen. Husband. Master . . . Great man . . ." Her voice was faint and hoarse.

"Gehlen was a colonel in the SS. When did he get promoted!?" Simon leaned forward.

"Quiet," Feldman said. "How old is he?"

"I don't know . . . not that old."

"How old are you?"

"I don't know . . . I'm not that old . . ."

"Where did you meet him?"

"My . . . village . . ."

"Where is the village?"

"Far . . . past the sea . . . in the forest . . ."

"Where!?"

Dona's breathing became rough. Her face contorted with pain.

"Enough!" Max shouted. "She's at her limit." The hand on his arm squeezed, and Max's face contorted as well.

"Where is the village? Europe?"

Dona shook her head slightly.

"Africa?"

Dona closed her eyes. She stopped moving.

"Is it America? South America?"

Her eyelids moved.

"Where in South America? Argentina?"

Again, her bleary eyes drifted skyward.

"Chile? Peru? Colombia?" Simon said from behind. But they couldn't read anything from Dona's expression.

"Brazil?"

Her eyes suddenly stopped swimming.

"Brazil it is."

"Brazil?" asked Feldman, just to make sure, and Dona nodded faintly.

"And we'd been searching Argentina and Chile," Simon said to no one in particular. "Where in Brazil?"

"Jungle . . . deep, deep jungle . . ."

Feldman turned to look at Simon. It was clear to see how excited he was. Simon put a hand on Feldman's shoulder, and Simon and Feldman switched places.

"Uaupes, Codajás, Óbidos, Goiás?" Simon rattled off some place names, but Dona didn't respond.

"Flowing river . . . big river. Deep, deep inside . . ."

"The Amazon?"

"Place where no one come. For long, long time, no one come."

"What was Gehlen doing in such a place?"

"Suddenly . . . soldiers came . . . people with guns . . ."

"How many people. Ten? Twenty?"

Dona shook her head. "More . . ."

"Thirty people?"

"More . . ."

The men looked at each other. Dona unclenched her hand.

"Fifty people?"

"First time . . . I see so many people . . ."

"Is that the first time you saw white people?"

"Long ago . . . before I was born, there were some. Most stayed in the village, and died there."

"What kind of white people were they?"

"They came to spread word of God. They built houses and lived there. They worked with the villagers . . . the whites who got married . . . my dad, my mom . . . taught their children their language and letters . . ."

"Sounds just like the Jesuits," said a voice from behind.

"When was all this?" asked Max leaning forward. "A hundred years ago? Two hundred?"

"Long ago . . . so, so long ago . . ." Dona's voice was fading.

"What a bunch of . . ." muttered one of the men.

"Tell us about the large group of white people that came to the village." Simon pushed Max back and grabbed Dona's shoulders. Her eyes opened slightly.

"Thirty-four whites . . . twenty Brazilians . . . they brought many things with them."

"What kind of whites?"

"Gold hair, brown hair, blue eyes, all wearing the same clothes. Black clothes. Long boots . . ."

"Nazis," Simon said, his voice quivering. "And SS at that. Some that escaped abroad ended up there. Were there no women among them?"

"No. All were men. Young men . . ."

The room was dead silent; everyone strained their ears to make out Dona's faint voice. Max could swear he could hear his own heartbeat.

"What happened to those men?"

"The whites ordered the Brazilians . . . they started building big houses. They recruited us, too . . ."

"Big houses? What kind of houses?"

"Big houses . . . with many beds . . ."

"Dorms," said one of the men. "They wanted to make it their new base."

"The things they brought . . . they brought to the building . . . we couldn't enter. We couldn't even get close . . ." Dona closed her eyes.

"When was this?" Max heard himself ask.

"Long time passed . . . Everything changed. The Brazilians who brought the things . . . they died soon after. The number of whites became smaller and smaller . . ." She was breathing easier now. Her speech was becoming smoother. Yet they still couldn't hear her very well.

"Did anyone else come?"

"Whites . . . after years and years, a few left, then came back. From then on, the whites left many times per year . . . many Brazilians would . . . come with things. Many things . . ."

"So, they had contact with the outside world," said a voice from behind.

Dona closed her eyes again.

"And then?" asked Simon.

But Dona's mouth didn't open.

"Answer me!" Simon shouted.

"Get the exact place out of her," Feldman said.

"Where did you live in Brazil?"

Dona's lips were shaking. She took a slow breath.

"What was the biggest town nearby?"

"There is no town . . . the village . . . in the jungle . . . flowing

river, people's bodies . . . big red flowers blooming . . . eating people . . ."
Her voice gradually tapered off.

"She's dead," someone muttered.

Simon looked back. Feldman signaled the man holding
Max with his eyes, and he relaxed his grip. Max bent over the bed,
took her pulse, and put a stethoscope to her chest. Her heartbeat
had stopped. Then he pressed firmly on the center of her chest,
once, twice, three times, four times . . . he listened through the
stethoscope again; her heart beat anew. "Her pulse is weak. Needs a
cardiotonic."

Katya took out a syringe and an ampoule from her bag. Max
pricked Dona's chest with the needle.

"The name of the village!" asked Simon, leaning forward.

"Deep, deep forest." Dona moved her mouth feebly, but they
couldn't hear her.

Simon grabbed Dona's shoulders and put an ear to her mouth.

"Stop! Do you want her to die?" Max said quietly but urgently.
He pushed Simon's arms off Dona. Simon was breathing hard, his
shoulders rising and falling with each breath; he was worked up. The
man behind Max put a hand on Max's shoulder, but Feldman waved
at him to stop.

"Will you will let us handle this?"

"I told you, tomorrow morning."

Feldman signaled the men behind him to leave the room. He
put a hand on Simon's back and got him to his feet; together, they
strode out the door. Only Max, Katya, and Dona remained in the
room. Dona lost consciousness, and her breathing grew erratic.

"Those people, I swear. They're no different from those thugs."
Katya looked at the door.

"They're just anxious. She did say she's the wife of a Nazi war
criminal."

"I understand most of what's going on, but this poor woman's
wounds . . . they're not the ones who did that to her, are they?"

"She was a victim of the Dörrenwald explosion. And don't worry, I'm confused, too."

"I know. I just pray that our actions aren't aiding and abetting a crime." Katya sat in a chair by the bed and looked at Max.

"It's three o'clock. I'll sit here and look after her until the evening. Go get some rest."

Max lay down on the cot. A heavy sensation spread throughout his body, and his head began to hurt. He closed his eyes and tried to clear his thoughts, but Dona's words kept swirling in his mind. It was all so contrary to the history he'd known. But there had to be something that tied the details of Dona's account together.

He could feel Katya staring at him within the dimly lit room. For some reason, it provided him with a sense of comfort he hadn't felt in a long time. Before long, he dozed off.

CHAPTER 6

When he woke up, the rays that had been shining through the blinds had disappeared. The bedside lamp cast the room in dim light. Katya was asleep and she was breathing audibly but softly, her upper body leaning against the foot of the bed.

Max got up, and took Dona's pulse and checked her breathing. Katya's eyes opened.

Just then, the lights went on, and a man entered carrying a tray filled with two identical meals: potato and leek soup, bangers and mash, and coffee. After placing the tray on the table, he walked over to Dona.

"She's still in critical condition. Don't even think about talking to her yet," Max said.

The man frowned a little, but said nothing and left the room. Katya got to her feet and shot Max a worried look.

"She's all right. She's sleeping soundly," he whispered.

Katya put her hand on Dona's forehead and looked surprised.

THE GENE OF LIFE

"Her fever's down, and her pulse is normal. Her resilience is unbelievable."

"She'll wake up before long." Max took a sip of coffee. It cleared the fog in his mind, and he grew more alert.

Katya sat beside him. "Her name is Dona, right? Is what Dona said true? Did Nazi war criminals really manage to escape to Brazil? The war ended sixty-three years ago. It happened before she was born. But she talked about those events as though she'd witnessed them with her own two eyes," she whispered, leaning closer to him.

"All we know for sure is that something happened in the village she used to live in."

"Is that what those guys are looking into?"

"They're hunting war criminals. And that's what her husband, Gehlen, is."

"The General, right? But if he were really a Nazi war criminal, he'd be ancient by now."

"He'd be 111."

"If Gehlen's her husband, then . . ." Katya stared at Dona.

Dona was 37 according to her passport, and her complexion fit that age. She didn't have any gray hair, or missing teeth. And while her voice was hoarse, it was not the voice of an elderly woman. She perhaps seemed a little more mature than 37, but her given date of birth was not implausible.

It was past ten in the evening. "Professor . . ."

Max turned to look at Dona; she was staring at them.

"Don't worry. We're on your side. We won't make you talk more than you should."

"But there's tons I want to ask her."

Dona looked at each of them in turn. Katya gripped her hand, and little by little, the fear in her eyes faded.

"What were the buildings like? The buildings that the whites made the Brazilians build?"

Dona closed her eyes and reflected for a long time until, at last, she began to slowly speak again: "A big building . . . more than a hundred paces long. There was a big machine inside. It made electricity . . . there were tools that let people see things closer . . . thin glass cylinders . . . and they all wore white coats."

"Microscopes and test tubes. A laboratory?" Katya asked.

"Is there anything else you noticed?"

"We got our blood taken once a week. But that was so long ago. Now they almost never take my blood."

"What kind of man is Gehlen?"

"A kind man. He treated my family very well. He gave us food and cigarettes and drink. That's why I . . ."

"This is an SS officer we're talking about," Katya whispered in Max's ear. "He must've done horrific things."

"Sometimes he was scary . . . he would hit me and the children sometimes, he would get drunk . . . he was afraid of something, was dreaming . . ." Dona's voice quivered with excitement, but her words ended there. Tears welled in her eyes.

"That's okay, you can stop there." Katya clenched her hand again. "Talk about something else. What kind of people were there?"

"First there were a lot of young men. Many died. They died in agony . . . fitful with fevered nightmares . . ."

"There are people who survived, too, right?" Katya asked.

"A tall man with eyeglasses. A scary man. Everyone was afraid of him. The exact opposite of the whites that came in the past, the whites that came to transmit God's voice . . ."

"Dona, how old are you?" Max interrupted.

"I'm . . ."

Just then, a loud bang came from downstairs, then shouting. Max went to the door. They heard an explosion, then gunfire. Max jumped back as he heard heavy footsteps running up the stairs. The door swung open, and Feldman rushed in. His face was tense, and he was seething. Max had never seen Feldman like this. He held a gun.

"How is she?"

"She's come to."

"There's a door beside the window in the next room. It's connected to the fire escape. Take the woman and run," Feldman said. He took a magazine from his pocket and loaded his gun.

"What happened?"

"A raid by the enemy. They've come to take her back."

Dona sat up; she was watching them.

"Hurry!" Feldman gave Max a car key and pointed to the door to the next room. "There's a car waiting at the bottom of the fire escape. Protect her."

"What about you?"

"I'll keep the enemy at bay." He trained his gun on the door.

Gunfire intensified. Men shouted clipped orders at each other. Given Feldman's instructions, it was clear the enemy had the overwhelming advantage.

"Go! They'll be coming up here soon."

One of the men rushed in. It was Simon. He held a submachine gun, and was bleeding from his forehead and arm. He turned to face the door, but he staggered and fell to one knee. Max offered a hand, but Simon brushed it aside and got up under his own power.

"Get Benchell's location out of her. Kill the bastard no matter what it takes," wheezed Simon, who gripped Max's shoulder. Then he took a handgun from his belt and put it in his hand.

Max lifted Dona out of bed. Katya held her up from the opposite side. They entered the next room, opened the door by the window, and stepped onto the fire escape. Looking down, they spotted a BMW sedan parked on a narrow path. Feldman and his group had prepared for an attack like this. Max and Katya supported Dona and went down the stairs with her in their arms. The gunfire above grew even fiercer. The three got in the car. In the rearview mirror, they saw a group of people on the landing of the fire escape pointing at them and yelling.

Max thought about Feldman, Simon, and their group, but he cast off the distraction and hit the gas. The engine roared, and they barreled down the lane to the main street.

Just as Max and Katya sped past Feldman Antique Dealers, several men dashed out of the building and into two cars parked out front. They hurriedly started the engines and made shrill U-turns in pursuit of Max and Katya's vehicle.

Max took a left at the first intersection. He looked in the rearview mirror; Dona was unconscious and resting her head on Katya's shoulder.

"How's she doing?"

"You're a doctor, aren't you? We're making a seriously wounded patient with a weak heart exert herself." Katya was peering into Dona's face.

The car zoomed through nighttime Berlin. There was no one else in sight, except for the occasional car going in the opposite direction.

"Where are we going?" asked Katya.

"We're going back to the research facility."

"They're here!" Katya looked back.

Their headlights were drawing closer. Max slammed down the accelerator.

"Where's the police station!?"

"In the opposite direction!"

That pair of headlights was soon joined by another. A loud crack broke the rear window. Katya screamed. "They're firing at us!"

In the rearview mirror, Max saw Katya duck and pull Dona down. Bullets were glancing off the car, but they couldn't hear the shots. The enemy was using silencers.

"They're trying to kill us!"

"Just keep as low as possible!" He pushed the accelerator down even more.

Their bodies were pressed against the seats, and the roar of the engine surged. Each time he turned the wheel, the screeching of the tires resounded through the night. Katya held onto her seat belt, trying not to scream. "Were you a racecar driver before you turned to science!?"

"I seriously considered it for a time. Thought I'd choose a life on the edge!"

"Why do we have to get killed like this!?"

"Ask them, not me!" He turned right, and their bodies swayed left. They soon left the business district, and the streetscape changed. There were almost no other cars on the road now, and the buildings were spaced farther apart. The headlights pursuing them had disappeared.

"Something's wrong with Dona!"

Max slowed down.

"She's been shot! In the back!"

There was a high wall ahead. It was a closed-off factory. Max slowed and turned off the lights. Everything went dark. They drove along the wall and came across a broken gate. They slowly entered the factory, which cast a deep shadow upon the large, empty grounds. Max backed the car between the buildings. He turned off the engine, and all was quiet. All they heard were cars going down the highway in the distance. Their eyes adjusted, and the shadow of the factory approached from both sides like phantoms. Max turned on his penlight and checked the backseat.

"The bullet penetrated her chest." Katya was pressing down on Dona's chest with a handkerchief, which was already soaked red.

Max leaned over and put his hand on Dona's neck. "Her pulse is weak. It's almost totally gone."

Dona's eyes opened. "Aska . . . my . . ." She was barely audible.

"What are you trying to say?"

"As . . . ka . . ."

"You're saying 'Aska,' right?"

Dona nodded slightly. "In Domba . . ."

"Domba?"

"My . . . village . . . fourteen—"

Max stretched out an arm and put a hand to her neck again. Her pulse . . . it was gone.

"She's dead, isn't she," Katya sobbed.

Suddenly, a white light blinded them. They closed their eyes and covered their faces. The inside of the car was as bright as day from the headlights of the car stopped directly in front of them.

Three shots echoed in the factory. The silencers had been removed—intimidation shots.

"Get out of the car," a voice ordered them. "All we want is the woman. If you don't come out before a minute passes, your car will be full of holes."

"Dona's already dead," Katya said, her voice trembling.

"Thirty seconds left!" the man yelled.

"What do we do?" Katya asked.

Max was thinking.

"Ten seconds!"

"Come in front." Max unfastened Katya's seat belt. Katya jumped to Max's side.

"Put your seat belt on and duck down."

Max braked and revved the engine. Then he stuck his arm out the window and fired at a headlight. He stepped on the accelerator the moment the light went out. He could smell the tires burn as they screeched. The car burst forward, and shrieks of surprise and anger flew through the air. The car rocked violently. Max's seat belt dug into his chest, and they heard metal dent and glass shatter. He shifted into reverse, pushed down on the accelerator, and swerved. He backed up about a hundred yards and the gunfire picked up.

"Head down!"

Bullets pierced the car. The car blasted through the factory toward the main gate, only to find a new pair of headlights coming at them. Max swerved, but they were rammed from behind, changing the car's direction. Part of the backseat caved in, and Dona's body fell under the seat. Another car crashed into their side.

"I can't steer!"

The car flipped diagonally and slid with only two tires on the ground.

"We're going to crash!" Katya shouted, but as soon as she did, they slammed against a concrete wall.

"Run!"

Max undid his seat belt and opened the door. Katya's head was hanging. Everything reeked of gas. Max shook her by the shoulders and her eyes squinted open. Her forehead was bleeding. She reached for the door handle, but her seat belt kept her in place. She moved her left arm to undo her seat belt and grimaced; her arm was covered in blood.

"Are you okay!?"

"My arm! It won't move."

Max jumped out and went to the passenger side. Katya's seat belt was jammed. The stench of gas was getting worse. Max quickly removed his pocketknife from his pants pocket and cut her free. "Go ahead of me!" Max tried to open the rear door, but it was mangled from the collision and he couldn't open it.

"Get away! The car's leaking gas!" Katya shouted.

Max pried the door open. Dona's body was sandwiched between the body of the car and the seats. He pulled with all his might, but her corpse wouldn't budge. Then the hood caught on fire. The driver's seat burned, illuminating their surroundings.

"She's already dead!" Katya grasped Max's jacket and tried to drag him away from the car.

The flames spread to the backseats, and heat and smoke enveloped Max. Dona's body was right in front of him. Max desperately reached out for her.

"Do you want to die, too!?" Katya shouted as she clung to Max. Max put some distance between him and the car.

Suddenly, a pillar of fire flared, and the car exploded. The blast flung them to the ground. For a second or two, they were dazed. The flames engulfed the car. The smell of burning gasoline and chemicals was overwhelming. Max opened his eyes. Katya was on top of him. She had leapt to shield him.

"Are you okay!?"

"I don't know." She got up and pulled Max to his feet.

Inside the flaming wreckage was Dona. Perhaps the answer he had been seeking was there.

"I need her!" Max groaned.

In a corner of the lot, the car that had rammed into them was ablaze. Its leaking gasoline created a sea of fire. Two men got out of the car and staggered toward them. All that was left of the car within the inferno was its frame.

"Let's go!" Katya held Max in her arms and started walking away.

The roaring flames lit up the area as bright as day. A car came from the gate, and they heard gunfire behind them. Max and Katya ran toward the factory building, the sound of the car's engine getting closer and closer. Katya tripped and fell. Max lifted her up. With a screech of tires, the car stopped so close it almost touched them.

"Get in!" It was Jake, poking his head out the window.

The rear doors were open. Max pushed Katya inside, and when they were both in their seats, the car took off. They looked back to find the other car was still burning.

"Dona . . . ," Max groaned. Katya grasped his hand.

"Are you okay, Professor?" Feldman was sitting next to them.

"What do you think?"

"Where's the woman?"

"Everything's gone."

Feldman sighed. He stared ahead and remained silent. Moments later, a rumbling explosion. They closed their eyes, but flashes of light danced at the backs of their eyelids.

"Dona, I as good as killed her myself. If only I hadn't pushed her so—"

"She was already dead," Katya said. "You checked for yourself, Professor." She put an arm around his shoulders. She closed her eyes

and leaned in. He could feel her powerful heartbeat, and it helped him
to gradually calm down.

They drove out of the factory.

"The neo-Nazis attacked us so they could take her," Feldman
said.

"Wrong," Max spat out. "It was to kill her."

Katya's body twitched.

"If they'd wanted to just take her back, they wouldn't have acted
this recklessly. Their mission was to kill her."

Feldman didn't reply.

"If you hadn't kidnapped her, she wouldn't have died."

"No. They never intended to nurse her back to health to begin
with. At that farmhouse, they were waiting for orders. They couldn't
take her out of the country with those wounds. They would have killed
her eventually. That they didn't kill her immediately only shows how
valuable she was to them. All they did was let her live a little longer."

"Pure conjecture," Max snapped. "Plus, I find it hard to believe
you intended to save her."

Katya opened her eyes and stared at Max with a shocked
expression.

"In any case, we underestimated them. They must have predicted
an attack. And they were lightning quick to act. She must have been
terribly important to them." Feldman said.

"Or they didn't want to hand her to us." Max said.

"We're back to square one now," Feldman muttered half to
himself.

An uncomfortable silence came over the car as it continued
down the dusky roads.

"Simon died," mumbled Feldman. "He was my last comrade.
We'd been fellow fighters since the end of the war. Sixty-three long
years."

"Do you want me to cry you a river?"

"He was the eldest son of a wealthy jeweler in Berlin. He had a

younger sister and brother, so they were a family of five. He had many
Gentile friends, too. But one of those friends tipped the Nazis off to
their shop. His parents and brother were taken to Auschwitz and killed.
He and his sister managed to survive. They were sent to a medical
facility." Feldman heaved a sigh. "But not as patients. They were sent
there as guinea pigs."

Katya stiffened.

"They were twins. The Nazis must have seen them as valuable
test subjects. And so they were sterilized. They surgically removed the
genitalia of a thirteen-year-old boy. His sister died three days after
Allied Forces freed them. She had mentally deteriorated by that point.
One wonders what they did to her at the camp."

The car went silent.

"That doesn't mean you can break the law," Max said. "We're
living in the twenty-first century, and this is a civilized country. It's not
Nazi Germany, and it's not Prohibition-era Chicago. In the few days
I've known you, how many people have died? Ten? More than ten, I'm
sure. Who are the people that attacked us? They're not just your average
thugs, that's for sure."

"They're well-organized. They acquire intel quickly, and they're
accustomed to using weapons."

"Yes, but who are they?"

"We don't know, either."

"You people are hiding something."

Once again, the car went silent. All they could hear was the hum
of the engine.

"Did she tell you anything?" Feldman asked.

Katya glanced at Max.

"She wasn't in pain. The fact she died while unconscious was a
blessing."

Feldman said nothing. He closed his lips tight and stared
intensely ahead.

They were driving back into the city.

"Let's look for a hotel somewhere," Feldman said, the thought having just occurred to him.

"Take us to the research facility. After that, we will never see each other again."

"They might come after you."

"What they're after are that horrid hand and Dona. The hand, they've already taken, and Dona's no longer with us. They've got no business with us now."

"Just be careful. Whenever you're on the phone, walking around town, driving, or doing anything else. Wiretapping and shadowing are not the sole province of TV shows and movies."

"I've already experienced more than I bargained for."

"I pray you and the young lady are able to return to lives of peace," Feldman said, albeit a little halfheartedly. Then he ordered Jake to go to the research facility.

They arrived at the research facility in about ten minutes. Max and Katya stepped out of the car. Feldman rolled down the window and was about to say something, but Max turned his back on him and walked away with Katya. Jake started the car back up without another word from Feldman.

"Are you really okay with leaving things like that?" asked Katya as she watched the car drive off.

Max just kept walking.

The guard looked surprised when he saw them, but then he smiled and winked, and opened the door for them. He apparently thought Max was looking after a drunk Katya. The two staggered into the building.

"Take your jacket off." Max retrieved a first aid kit from his locker. Katya did as she was told. Her jacket and blouse were torn and blood-soaked. A bullet had grazed her.

"This jacket's done for, huh? Damn, I liked it," Katya's voice wavered.

"It's my fault. I'll get you a new one."

"After what's just happened I might not look thrilled, but trust me, that makes me very happy."

She drew in her lips and grimaced when Max dabbed her shoulder with antiseptic.

"Shouldn't we report this to the police?"

"Do what you want," Max said curtly, as he bandaged her shoulder.

"Thank you for rescuing me from the car, by the way," she said, having just recalled what happened. "Do you always carry a knife?"

"Ever since I was in the Boy Scouts. My father gave it to me the first time I left for camp."

"It's pretty handy. I want one now, too."

"Better not. These days, it'll get you in trouble at airport security."

The wound wasn't as bad as it looked. With some disinfecting and an injection of antibiotics, she would be fine.

"It'll scar a little, but there shouldn't be any problem with your shoulder otherwise. And the scar won't make you any less attractive, so, it shouldn't give you any trouble." Max wiped away the blood and dirt from her cheek.

"You could've phrased that better."

"It's the truth."

Katya put on her torn jacket as she watched Max wipe the blood off his fingers with gauze.

"I'm sorry. I'm just tired."

"Me too." There were dark bags under her eyes.

"I knew we should've gone to a hotel. We need some rest, someplace comfortable."

"It's not too late for that." Katya stared at Max.

Max felt a flush of heat, but it disappeared as soon as it came. "I'll get you home." He pulled out his cellphone and called a taxi.

CHAPTER 7

German could be heard in the empty room, but the words were difficult to make out over the static and high volume distorting the speaker's
voice. Next to the DNA figurine on Max's desk was a digital recorder
smaller than his cellphone.

Max listened with his elbows on the desk and his chin in his
hands. His arms and back were starting to hurt. Two hours had passed.
Most of the conversation had been drilled into his head, but what those
words meant was as elusive as a mayfly drifting in the sunlight. If he
were being honest with himself, he did understand. It was just that the
knowledge he had accumulated up until now was getting in the way. In
order to acknowledge the reality of it all, he needed time, perseverance,
a flexible mind, and the courage to break the chains of common sense.

Three days had passed since the incident.

He stood up and walked to the window. The street was empty.
It was ten to midnight. He stretched; his joints were so stiff he could
practically hear them creaking. After staring outside for a while, he
returned to his seat.

A knock on the door. It opened, and Max rushed to stop the
recorder's playback. Katya came in carrying some data sheets.

"You're still here?"

"The results of the gene analysis are in. It's just as you said,
Professor—No. 5 of Chromosome 7 and No. 9 of Chromosome 11 are
abnormal. The base sequences indicate unique genetic information."
Katya put the papers on the desk and looked at the recorder. "But
without more to go on, I have no idea what those genes mean. But you
must; otherwise, how could you be so calm?"

"Is that how I look?"

"At the very least, you don't look too pressed for time."

Max smiled a little, and looked away from her.

"What is this data?" she asked. "I think you could stand to
tell me."

"I'd like you to wait just a little longer."

"I'm tired of hearing that, Professor."

Max rifled through two, three pages. He'd already seen the data hundreds, no, thousands of times.

Katya started fiddling with the DNA figurine. "DNA . . . I don't think a toy like this determines everything about a person. When I said I wanted to be a doctor, my parents got angry. My family faints at the sight of blood. They wanted me to be a musician or a poet. They thought that the child of music-loving parents would also love music. And not because of their genetics, but through the family's soul— through the shared will of God and mankind. I think it's not our genes that control our fate, but rather our wills."

"Getting past God's whims, the vagaries of our births, isn't that straightforward. That said, I . . ." Max's tone had gotten suddenly harsh.

"I didn't mean it like that . . ."

"How's your wound?" Max changed the subject, ashamed of himself for raising his voice.

Katya rotated her arm in reply. In the three days since she had been injured, new skin covered the wound on her shoulder, and she'd returned to normal emotionally as well—but only on the surface.

The day after the incident, newspapers stated that several people died in a shootout at an old factory site in the suburbs due to infighting among rogue neo-Nazis. Did the Berlin police really come to that conclusion, or did Feldman pull some political strings? Either way was fine by Max. The attack on Feldman Antique Dealers was blamed on a robbery. The truth behind both cases was buried. They had far more power than Max had imagined. Which also meant that neither Max's nor Katya's name came up in the investigations.

"Don't go overboard with that arm."

"You're a fantastic doctor, too, Professor."

"It was only skin-deep. Used to be any parent could've done much the same. In fact, a dog or cat could've licked it clean."

"Are you comparing me to a cat or dog?"

He knew her wound still hurt. Otherwise she wouldn't be grimacing. But for some reason, he couldn't summon words of sympathy.

"Just take the compliment. I'm calling you an excellent doctor." Katya scanned the bare room; most of the stuff had already been taken out, giving the room a drab air. "Five days left, right?"

As their plans stood now, Katya was going to leave for the US before Max, and get their laboratory organized. Max would take a trip around Africa, after a transfer in France, and return to the US in ten days—the trip he'd planned six months before. He'd visit a number of universities and laboratories and meet researchers. When he'd made those plans he was looking forward to the trip, but now it just felt like a detour.

"Any concerns going forward?" Max asked Katya.

"I'm looking forward to returning to the country I spent half of my life in. I was in California until two years ago."

"Oh, right. I almost forgot. You're a US citizen."

"Coffee?" She smiled, looking his way.

Max averted his eyes. She was so cheery and full of life; he was afraid he'd develop feelings for her. But he also knew that it was already too late. He nodded, and Katya left the room.

He pressed a button on the recorder, and the same indistinct mumbling played.

Five minutes later, Katya returned with two cups of coffee.

"Are you still listening to that, Professor? I must say, I'm surprised you were recording what Dona said."

"I just happened to have the recorder in my pocket. It starts recording when it detects a voice." Max always kept it in his jacket's inside pocket so he could record ideas or reminders.

Katya put the cup in front of him and took a sip from her own. "Have you discovered anything new?"

"This Dona woman was over a hundred years old. Or at least—" Max stopped himself, shaking his head. "Her husband, Gehlen, would be 111."

"Do you believe what she said? It was just her being delusional, wasn't it? Because I don't think she was deliberately lying."

"I think she was in her right mind. She was Gehlen's wife."

"Then we're losing it."

"She called him General Gehlen. Even though he'd been a colonel."

"Gehlen must have lied to her, thinking she had no way of knowing the truth."

"Over sixty years have passed since the war ended. More than enough time for a colonel to rise to the rank of general."

Katya sighed, exasperated. "Who promoted him, then? Hitler's Nazi Party isn't exactly around anymore."

Max stared at his cup, thinking.

"Let's just forget about all this. It's past us now." Katya tried to put her cup on the desk, but she frowned in pain. "It's true there's a lot to dissect, but it doesn't have anything to do with us. Unless there's still something on your mind?" she asked, turning to face him.

"Domba. She said the word 'Domba.'"

"The name of the village Dona used to live in." Katya sat on the desk and started fiddling with the DNA figurine once again.

"It sounds like it could be a village in Brazil, but I couldn't find a village by that name."

"I tried searching for it on the internet, but nothing came up," Katya said.

"Aska . . . ," blurted Max.

"Couldn't find a place in Brazil named Aska, either. There's an Asuka in Japan, but I don't think it's related. You looked into it, too, right, Professor?" Katya shrugged. "Considering what Dona said, both she and Gehlen are over a hundred years old, despite looking younger. Research concerning aging is progressing; free radicals damage the proteins and genes in cells, and that's what causes our bodies to change over time. The enzyme that defends against free radicals and the enzyme that repairs the damage have been identified, and that knowledge is being incorporated into modern medical treatments. Have they been undergoing the latest anti-aging treatments?"

"That can't be," Max said. "We're talking apples and oranges; there's a fundamentally different mechanism at play between slowing aging down and turning it off altogether."

"That's just not possible for modern medicine to achieve. And it doesn't make sense physiologically."

"It's not possible for modern medicine, no . . . ," Max repeated, half to himself.

An ambulance siren blared outside, growing louder and louder until it reached the research facility. Katya got up and looked out the window; Max stood beside her. Red lights lit up the darkness as the siren pierced the silence.

"It's the building across from us. Paramedics are entering with a stretch . . ."

Katya's voice suddenly faded away. Chills ran down Max's spine, and his body stiffened. Pressure built up in his head as his vision turned dark and his mind went blank. He staggered away from the window. The last thing he saw was Katya's face; he couldn't hear what she was saying.

"Professor, what happened?" Katya was using a penlight to check his pupils.

He woke up lying on a sofa, his shirt buttons undone. He struggled to sit up. This was his first seizure in a year. He'd been driving the last time it happened. He'd just exited the freeway when his chest started feeling tight. He pulled over and waited for the attack to subside. The fact that he'd been driving slowly saved his life. The next day, he had a thorough checkup, but they couldn't find anything wrong with him. Or rather, modern medicine couldn't.

"It's nothing. Just a little vertigo."

"You're sweating like crazy, Professor. And you were shaking, too." Katya took out a handkerchief and wiped his forehead.

Max brushed her hand aside and stood up. He swayed on his feet and grabbed Katya's shoulder to keep himself up. "Sorry."

"Your face is white."

"You should go home." Max let go of her shoulder and stretched his muscles.

"I'll go get ready." Katya looked a little bewildered, but she returned to her room.

When she came back, they left the laboratory together. The ambulance had already left. All that hung over the streets in the dead of night was silence. There was no traffic, apart from the occasional car zooming along the highway.

After five minutes, there was no sign any taxis would come.

"I'm heading for the station." Max started walking.

"Professor . . ." Katya followed him. "Who is Alex? You called out his name earlier. And you seemed so distraught . . ."

Max froze, but only for a moment. He walked away without a word. Katya hastened after him.

They left the main road and turned down a side street, their footsteps echoing in the silence. But they quickly noticed the number of footsteps had audibly increased—three men were tailing them. Max took a furtive look behind them. One was a skinhead, another had a Mohawk, and the third had shoulder-length hair, and all three were wearing leather vests and studded boots. They looked like they were still just kids. Under the streetlights, their shadows overlapped on the asphalt. Katya drew closer to Max.

The boy with the Mohawk leapt in front of them. Max and Katya stopped in their tracks.

"Lend a guy some money, wouldya, old man?"

The skinhead smiled as he approached from the side. "You could give us her instead, if you like," he said, appraising Katya.

Katya clung to Max.

"How about neither," Max replied.

The three lowlifes looked each other in the eyes. The long-haired boy grabbed Katya's arm. Max pushed his arm away and hid Katya behind him.

"You got a death wish or something, fucker?" The skinhead held a knife.

"Stop this nonsense!" Katya yelled, but she was shivering.

"I'm American," Max said. "If a thug like you stabs a foreign national, let's just say the headlines will be a little different. The police will stake their names on finding the culprits. Are you ready for the consequences?"

The skinhead put the knife to Max's throat.

"Isn't it past your bedtimes?" Max said. "Why don't you scurry home and tuck in for the night?"

"You're dead!" the skinhead said, but he sounded a little afraid. Max's composure unnerved the gang.

"Cutting flesh with a knife always feels gratifying," said Max, staring at the skinhead. "I'm a doctor—a pro at cutting people up. Slit the skin and muscle in one go. Everyone has different fat levels, so for people with more fat on their bones, you're going to have to twist the knife when you slice them. And you should avoid hitting bone. It's way too hard for an amateur."

The skinhead looked at his friends on either side of him, his eyes pleading for help.

"You going to stab me in the gut with that knife, or in the chest? If you want a sure kill, you aim for an artery. All you need's a nick, and the blood will go flying. The side of the neck is prime real estate. But be careful—blood can spray for a good meter. It'll get all over you if you stay where you are. Look, stab me right here!" Max shouted, putting a hand on the side of his neck. "Do it now! I haven't got all night."

He took a half step closer, and the knife's tip sank through his bleeding skin. The skinhead hurriedly withdrew the knife.

"Don't hesitate. Stab me with all your strength and gouge it out."
Max grabbed the skinhead's hand and brought the knife to the side of
his neck. The skinhead resisted. The long-haired boy bashed Max in the
head, forcing him to let go of the skinhead's arm. Max staggered and
hit his back against a building.

"Stop or I'll call the police!" Katya shouted, rushing over to Max.

"Dude's nuts!" The skinhead was breathing heavily.

"Let's get the hell out of here." The guy with the Mohawk pulled
the skinhead away by the arm, and the three ran toward the main street.

"You're bleeding." Katya got out a handkerchief and put it on
the back of his neck.

"They're high school kids. They haven't got the guts to kill."

"They could've gotten swept up in the heat of the moment.
You were lucky you got off this lightly, that's all. Don't be so reckless."
Katya's voice was trembling, her eyes tearing. "Please, please value your
life more. You were chosen by God, Professor."

"You're right. God did choose me. He chose me for . . ." He
stared at Katya.

He could see his eyes reflected in Katya's wide-open eyes.
Something akin to anger was in those eyes, but behind them, a deep
sadness. Katya closed her eyes and turned her face away.

"I'm sorry," he said quietly, walking away.

Katya ran after him. "Don't you believe in God?"

"I'm not that gullible!" Max spat, quickening his pace.

CHAPTER 8

The sky was bright blue and cloudless, which wasn't often the case during summer in Germany. The autobahn wove through the mountains
like the gently curving backbone of a powerful dragon. Hitler had this
road built to double as an emergency runway for military aircraft, and
it served as an important traffic route for the postwar recovery. To this

day, it stood as a symbol of Germany. Even in the new millennium, the autobahn made it so that the nation could not escape from the legacy of the Nazi regime.

Max drove his Porsche due west. He listened to the radio over the rhythm of the air-cooled engine, while the speedometer hovered around 80 mph.

"Neo-Nazi rallies were held in various regions . . . the bullets found at the scene indicate sniper rifles were used . . . since the bombing, the authorities have been waiting watchfully . . . with the robust support of the far-right . . . depending on the future trends of nations of the EU, the United States, too, may soon . . . the German government is holding an emergency parliamentary . . ."

Max turned it off, leaving him with only the hum of the engine. He pushed down the accelerator in order to shake off the black lumps that had accumulated in his head since the events of that day. He was on his way to Wittenfurt, 125 miles from Berlin. His last lecture in Germany would be at the University of Wittenfurt at 4:00 p.m. The talk would be about telomeres, which determine the number of times cells divide, as well as cell suicide, or apoptosis.

His cellphone rang. He slowed down to 60 mph and took the phone out of his chest pocket.

"Swing right. There's a large trailer 200 yards behind. It's going 100 per hour."

Max looked from side to side.

"Don't take your eyes off the road," came the calm voice. "Switch to the right lane and slow down more. Go around 50 per hour."

It was Feldman. Max checked the rearview mirror, and saw the large trailer in the distance. It was approaching at dizzying speeds.

"Is it the enemy?"

"No, it's just a runaway trailer. But if I said nothing while your life was in danger, the world would bear a grudge against me."

Max sped up to 100 mph.

"My, my, Professor. You're wobbling left and right. Eyes on

the road. Now, I'm waiting at a restaurant named 'Das blaue Dach.' You can see it on the hill to your right. As the name suggests, it's the building with the blue roof. It's ten minutes from where you are."

"What do you want with me?"

"Just thought I'd invite you for a spot of tea."

"I told you I didn't want to see you again."

"Don't be so mean. I just want to engage in some small talk."

"And I just want to forget about it. About everything surrounding that incident."

"Do you see it?" Feldman said, ignoring Max's words.

Max strained his eyes, and sure enough, there it was. The blue rooftop at the top of the hill. "Please leave me alone."

"I'm sure you're not uninterested, Professor. In fact, I'm sure you can't pass this up—all this time, the word 'why' has been weighing down on you." Feldman's voice was brimming with confidence.

The Porsche slowed down. Max's foot on the accelerator relaxed of its own accord.

"Excellent. Swing right. It's the trailer."

Max swerved right. The trailer roared past. The car swayed in its wake. Max was clenching the wheel.

"It'd be best if we drop this call. In any case, I'll be here, waiting. Please drive safe. I would hate it if the world resented me." Click.

The restaurant was less than a mile away. Contrary to his inclinations, Max slowed down and turned into a side road leading to the restaurant.

The eye-catching roof aside, the restaurant had a subdued mountain-lodge feel. Max stood at the entrance and spotted Feldman sitting by the window with the best view. He was looking at Max. Max walked closer, and Feldman lowered his head to indicate the seat across from him. Large binoculars were placed at the edge of the table. Feldman called the waitress, and ordered himself another cup of tea and Max some coffee.

"You like coffee, correct?"

"You came to this restaurant on an afternoon stroll, and saw me coincidentally pass by while you took in the scenery. That'll be our story."

"I just happened to learn you were headed for Wittenfurt. And so I got the urge to go, too. I love this road, too. I drive down it from time to time."

"Sure, with your binoculars and everything."

"They're Israeli military issue. You can see a penny 500 yards away." He picked up the binoculars.

"I need to get to the university by 4:00 p.m. I don't have time for idle chitchat."

"Then let's make this brief." Feldman fixed his gaze on him and took a Lufthansa ticket out of a large envelope and put it on the table. "This is for a flight from Berlin–Tegel to Manaus via São Paulo. Charter planes are available from Manaus. We'll take a helicopter to the small village of Boyas and then drive to Umabes. From there we paddle a kayak and then walk. A full day's journey will take us to a small village in the Amazonian north—to Domba."

"Where did you hear that name?"

Feldman ignored his question, and unfolded a map of South America and placed it on the table. A nameless point in northern Brazil had been marked in red.

The waitress came with their drinks. Feldman took his tea and made sure to savor its aroma before taking a sip. Max looked away; it was the first time he noticed that part of the middle finger of Feldman's left hand past the first knuckle joint was missing. In addition, the nails of his thumb and pointer finger were deformed.

"Approximately 450 miles southwest of the Guiana Highlands, close to the border between Colombia and Peru, as well as to what is known as the Amazon headwaters. It's even deeper than the Amazon Reserve, where even the Brazilian National Indian Foundation hasn't set foot. The population and culture of the people that live there are unknown. There's no official record of the place from the Indio Union either. Neither poachers nor rubber collectors have entered, and no specifics are available. As difficult to believe as it may be, the village has been left behind by the twenty-first century. The Brazilian government calls it a special reserve to distinguish it from traditional reserves. There's a possibility it was left isolated on purpose."

"Where did you dig all that up?"

"I told you, didn't I? Our information network is worldwide. I haven't spent all of my time simply mourning that woman's death." Feldman stared at Max, and through his eyes, Feldman exhibited, as he occasionally did, the darkness and the astuteness that enabled him to see through to people's hearts.

Max looked at the map.

"South America is where many Nazi remnants ended up fleeing. Since before the war, the Nazis have aided in the birth and continued existence of a large number of right-wing governments in South America. There were many devotees of Hitler in Argentina, Bolivia, and Chile. They poured immense amounts of money that they stole from all over Europe and from the Jewish people into those nations. It's said that as many as 250,000 men and women disappeared from Germany shortly after the war. At Hitler's behest, they fled to South America to build the Fourth Reich. Where exactly did they disappear to? We still don't know. There's a plethora of mysteries surrounding the Nazis to this day." Feldman heaved a deep sigh. Then he fixed his eyes on Max again. "We've made our preparations. We would like you to accompany us there, Professor."

"Are you saying you're going, too?"

Feldman stayed silent for a while. "Thirty years ago, I ventured into the mountains of Chile and the rainforests of Argentina and Peru. In order to hunt some Nazis, of course. I know full well how fearsome and unforgiving the jungles can be. Besides . . ." He stared at his fingers, which were splayed on the table. His hand was gnarly, rough, and discolored. The golden hairs between the wrinkles shone in the sunlight. "I'm getting on in years," he murmured forlornly.

"I would be a liability. Jake will go. I sent your equipment and clothing to your hotel."

"It's not as though I've agreed to your proposal."

"But you haven't turned it down, either. You will go. It's your destiny."

Max looked out the window. The road stretched on like a winding white serpent. From the distance, the cars going down the road looked like toys. He turned the word 'destiny' over in his mind.

"We'll finish making all of the preparations in two days' time. All you need to do is go to the airport with your personal luggage. The main thing you need to do to prepare is steel yourself for what's to come. I'll allow you to bring your assistant with you if necessary. That energetic young woman will do well, even in the Amazon."

"She wasn't sent to me by your organization, was she? Otherwise, how did you know the name 'Domba'?"

"How silly of you to think we would send someone to spy on you. We wouldn't ever do something so pointless." The gentleness that had been in his gaze moments ago was now gone; in his eyes lurked the ruthless intensity of a Nazi hunter. He placed a photo in front of Max.

"Reinhard Benchell. The man Simon asked you to find and kill." He pulled off his scarf; a reddish-brown scar about an inch and a half wide went down from the back of his neck to his collarbone. "That man, he put a burning piece of firewood to the neck of a ten-year-old boy, laughing all the while." Feldman leaned forward to show him his neck. A fragrant cigar smell wafted through the air.

Max was at a loss for words.

The waitress was whispering to the man at the counter, their faces very close together, watching them.

"I told you about him, about Benchell, right?" Feldman straightened himself up, as though embarrassed by that moment of passion, and wrapped the scarf back around his neck. "After eluding capture in Europe, he was found in a hotel near Rio de Janeiro in 1972 and shot dead in a gun battle. In 1987, he was shot while cruising off the coast of Miami. He got shot twice in the heart. Nine years earlier, in 1978, we found him again in the suburbs of Milan. That time, he'd evidently died in a car crash. Our agent crushed him with a truck, and his car blew up. The burnt corpse was identified." After Feldman regained his cool, he took a number of deep breaths.

"What do you mean?"

"The first man had his fingerprints flattened. Photos just before his death showed that he was right-handed, though the genuine article is left-handed. The man shot in Miami was an alcoholic and addicted to drugs. His face and physique were Benchell's. In the car crash, the body burned up, and he was unidentified at that time. Recently, however, the body was revealed to have been a fake. Some of his organs were cryopreserved, and this was discovered through DNA analysis."

"So, they were all . . ."

"Impostors, yes. And each time, eyewitnesses testified it was, in fact, Benchell. He hasn't come out in the open since then. He is a cautious man." Feldman heaved a deep sigh. "I want to catch this man before I die. I want to bring him to Israel and have him face trial. If I fail to, then the souls of the six million Jews he helped exterminate will never know true peace. And neither will Simon's," he glowered at Max. "You said you only have so much time left. Three or four years."

Max's face went white. *How does he—*

"Your days are numbered, too. Surely, there must be things you need to do to ensure you live on, Professor. Now then, the time is now, Professor. But don't be too hasty—slow and steady wins the race, as they say." He checked his watch, and pushed the envelope toward him that contained the ticket and the map.

Max found himself taking the envelope. Then he reached for the check, but Feldman grabbed his hand. Feldman's hand was deformed and bony, but vaguely warm, and as strong as ever.

Max returned to the lab past ten that night. He stood at the entrance, turned on the lights, and scanned the room. Slowly, he stepped inside.

His eyes passed from the ceiling to the walls, to the bookshelves, to the desk, to the computers, to the lamp. He felt around the underside of the tables, but there was nothing. He carefully checked the desk, the chairs, above the bookshelves, under the lamps.

A half hour passed. He wondered whether he'd been mistaken. *No, we're talking about an intelligence agency that operates on a global scale. They'll be using some method I could never even dream of. They caught wind of Domba's name and location.*

He was about to give up when his eyes fell on the DNA figure on the desk. He picked it up and examined it. It was just over a foot tall. The double helix was beautiful in its elegant simplicity, and it contained endless mysteries and wonders.

He looked at the other side of the teak stand. Nothing looked out of the ordinary about the screwed-on back cover. He removed the back cover with his pocketknife, and a one-cubic-inch chip with a battery was affixed to the hollow cavity. A bug. He carefully removed it and threw it in the garbage chute at the end of the hallway. Now all Feldman and his people would hear was the occasional sound of garbage being dropped in.

Perhaps there were more bugs around, but he couldn't bring himself to care. They had already analyzed the recordings concerning Dona. That's how they'd known where Domba is. They'd also learned of the word 'Aska,' but Feldman didn't mention it or ask about it. That meant he knew more about Aska than Max did. Most importantly, Max had made up his mind.

Max turned on the computer and ran a search on Nazism. Millions of search results appeared. He narrowed the search to "Schutzstaffel officers," in search of a single name—a man whose existence he had never even spared a thought for until a few days ago. Reinhard Benchell. He was a short, stout, round-faced man looking tranquilly at the camera. Max couldn't imagine what lay behind those eyes. Beyond that gentle mask was a world that normal people couldn't fathom.

He checked the time and turned off the computer. He picked up the landline and dialed Katya's extension; he knew she was still at the lab. Sure enough, when she came to Max she had her lab coat on, with a doughnut in her right hand and a cup of coffee in her left.

She washed down some doughnut with some coffee. "I thought you said you'd be going straight back to the hotel."

"Is that what you're having for dinner?"

"This is an hors d'oeuvre. I'll be having dinner later."

"Let's talk over dinner."

"But I'm still . . ."

Max put a finger to her lips. He took the cup and the rest of the doughnut from Katya's hands and placed them on the desk. He'd removed one wiretap, but he still wasn't comfortable discussing things here.

The two left the research facility and found a late-night restaurant nearby. Max told her how he'd encountered Feldman on the way to Wittenfurt, and what Feldman had said. Katya listened as she robotically brought spaghetti to her mouth. Occasionally, she drank from her glass of Coke with an indifferent air.

"You're against it," Max said.

"You have other things to do, Professor."

"Exploring the Amazon is something I've always wanted to do. All boys picture themselves as intrepid explorers at some point."

"Not satisfied with the jungle adventure in Disneyland?" Katya's hand stopped in midair, and she stared at him. "Why are you so obsessed with hunting Nazis, Professor?"

"I'm not. I just want to know more about Dona." He searched for the right words, his eyes drifting to the dark night outside. He couldn't find the words to explain it.

"What Dona said is weighing on my mind as well. But don't you have more important work to do?"

"You have no intention of going?"

"That's not what I said. I just want to know the real reason you're going."

"Just wait a little longer, and I'll tell you."

"You've already made up your mind to go, haven't you?"

"How can you be so sure?"

"If you hadn't, you wouldn't be talking to me."

"I want you to come with me as my assistant. You're the only one who understands what's happened so far."

Katya twisted her spaghetti around her fork. "Is that the only reason?"

"You're good at what you do."

"But there must be loads of people who are even better."

"I'm asking you, Katya. I need you."

"You should've said that from the get-go." She brought the pasta to her lips.

After their meal, they returned to the lab and began preparing. Katya seemed to be having fun as she traced the map according to Max's explanation. Max created a list of equipment to bring with them.

"Two microscopes, one mass spectrometer, two computers. Are you planning to build a lab in the middle of the uncharted wilds, Professor?" asked Katya, reading through the list.

"That's Stage 2."

"Don't you need a DNA sequencer?" she said, despairingly. The sequencer being used at present was the size of a washing machine.

"UNIX created a suitcase-sized one. I'll ask Feldman about getting one."

"What exactly are you expecting to uncover, Professor? I doubt you would be interrupting your research and bringing all of this huge equipment to the depths of the Amazon if you didn't see any prospects in this trek."

"I was going to visit Africa before returning to the US. I've simply replaced Africa with South America."

"I'm coming with you, and it's because you've deemed me a worthy research collaborator. Don't you think it's time you told me at least a little more?"

Max waved her over and turned on his laptop; the screen flickered, and the results of the DNA analysis appeared. Katya stared at the text intently.

"Look at No. 12 of Chromosome 8."

Katya traced the base pair sequence on the screen with her finger. "I've never seen anything like it before." Her eyes were glued to the screen. "Why is this?"

"This DNA was collected from Dona."

"From the blood that soaked the gauze you used to treat her."

Max nodded. Katya brought up Gehlen's DNA sequence, which was collected from the tissues in his hand. Then she put the two sequences side by side.

"They're the same," she muttered while staring at the display. "What does this mean?"

"I don't know either. Dona and Gehlen lived to be over a hundred while retaining their youth. There must be something out there that'll help us solve this mystery. The only base sequence that's different is the one that imparts the anti-arteriosclerosis effect. I want to look into that some more."

Max turned off his laptop. Katya was silently staring at the now blank screen. Max glanced at the DNA figurine on his desk. He already knew what Dona's DNA implied, but he didn't know what lay in store for him were he to pursue this trail. He had to go to the Amazon to find out. And yet, he was running out of time.

Max checked his list of equipment again, in an attempt to shake off the mounting anxiety. He felt Katya's eyes on him. Then he heard a light sigh, followed by the sound of the door opening and closing.

● ● ●

III

——

THE JUNGLE

CHAPTER 9

The dense green forest stretched below them. A river wove through it like a crack in a coffee mug, glinting in the sunlight.

"So, this is the virgin Amazonian forest," Katya said, her forehead pressed against the window of the plane. "And that must be the Amazon River."

Max and Katya had left Berlin during the night, transferred in São Paulo and were headed for Manaus.

"The river with the most water in the world," Max said. "It starts where the Negro and Solimões rivers meet, about five miles downstream from Manaus. If you include all of the tributaries, it is more than 4,000 miles long by the time it reaches the Atlantic Ocean. It's 200 miles wide at its mouth."

"It's like a giant carpet of green. And, it's the planet's conscience." Katya sighed.

"Some trees there are over a hundred feet high. It's the last vast rainforest on Earth."

"We're in uncharted territory. It feels like the Earth started here."

"There's no such thing as uncharted territory anymore. Every inch of the planet is now part of an economic machine. The Amazon is like a promising diamond mine. Ever since anticancer plant roots were discovered there, all the biotech companies have been sending their researchers."

Katya looked down.

"They collect plants, insects, soil samples . . . ," Max continued. "It's a treasure trove of new species. There are endless numbers of bacteria in the soil. They bring them back to their labs, cultivate them and analyze them, looking for molecular structures and genes that will make them money. As a result, the rainforest is disappearing."

"Is the Brazilian government doing anything to stop it?" Katya turned to look at him. There was a red mark on her forehead from the window frame.

"They've banned the removal of animals and plants. But human greed knows no bounds. People think that rules are made to be broken. Poachers and plant hunters, some sent by multinational corporations, take what they want, pretending to be tourists. Then there are the people who collect as a hobby. Some botanists say that the forests along the Amazon River have been shaped by human hands."

"Shaped by humans? This forest? I don't believe it." Katya put her forehead to the window again.

"About 15 million species have been identified. It was thought that no new species were left to be found in the Amazon, but when a French researcher was able to look down at the canopy from the air, he found tons of new species. Now they think there are three times as many species in the Amazon alone."

"When did you learn that?"

"Last night. I read it on *National Geographic*'s website."

"Has civilization reached where we are going?"

"I didn't find much about it. Most of the Amazon has been surveyed, but one area seems to have remained untouched."

"Near the Venezuelan border?"

"Expedition teams and media people have been there. We're going a few hundred miles south. It's not clear why, but the Brazilian government hasn't surveyed that region. And it's cut off from development pipelines, too."

"Must be the Nazis . . ."

"In their heyday the Nazis had their hands in the governments of Argentina, Chile, and Brazil. There's a good chance they're still exerting their influence." Max retrieved a folder from his backpack. Inside were five pages he'd printed out, entitled "The Fourth Reich."

"Can I read it?"

"That's why I brought it."

He handed it to her, and while she seemed to hesitate for a moment, she put it on her lap and started reading.

The car left Teafair and we drove for three hours on a bumpy road less than ten feet wide. It wound through an undeveloped stretch of jungle, and I didn't know where it would end. Looking at the virgin forest all around, it was strange that there was even a road like this. I knew we were near the border of either Colombia or Brazil.

We'd had enough. It was hot, dusty, and the humidity was unbearable. Our shirts were drenched with sweat, and our mouths were gritty with sand. It was like hell on Earth.

All five of us started to think this was all just a big farce.

It seemed the rumor I heard a week before in a bar in Cusco was nonsense. No one would divulge something like that just for some booze. We were angry with ourselves for going all that way on the ramblings of some dirty drunk.

That man, Tom Douglas, showed up while we were playing poker.

"Buy me a drink," he said, dressed in frayed work clothes and reeking of booze. We refused. Douglas said he'd tell us about the City of Gold if we gave him a drink. The name was Estancia.

One of my mates put down his cards and looked up at him. That was the beginning of our little excursion.

It began to rain. The downpour was so heavy our windshield was a miniature waterfall, and the wipers were completely useless. We couldn't see ten meters in front of us. About an hour later, the squall suddenly stopped.

"Whose viewpoint is this from?" Katya looked at Max.

"A self-proclaimed explorer. It's an interview from a magazine by an American journalist. I found it online last night."

Katya's eyes fell on the file once again.

After the rains stopped it got a little cooler, but the air was still 100 percent humidity. It was awful; it was so damp that when we wrung out our clothes, water actually dripped out. We were the only organisms unhappy about the moisture, though. The trees on either side of us, and the creatures inhabiting them, were all flourishing.

Finally we agreed to turn back if, after another half hour, we didn't find anything. Then, all of a sudden, there it was.

"I see the town," our Indigenous Brazilian said.

We couldn't believe our eyes. After climbing a gentle slope, we saw it. A real town! White roofs surrounded by gaps of green. There were twenty, maybe thirty houses, and a white road cutting through the center. This was the "city of gold and jewels" that drunk spoke of. Our hearts soared!

The bumpy dirt road suddenly gave way to pavement about twenty feet wide. On both sides were beautiful European-style houses with front yards. I couldn't believe I was still in the virgin Amazonian rainforest. But we didn't see a single resident. The car rolled along slowly. The road went on for hundreds of yards, and at the end of it was a European-style mansion surrounded by stone walls more than seven feet high. We got out of the car and walked up to the iron gate. It was locked, but we could see inside through a gap in the steel fence. A driveway lead up to the mansion, and the surrounding area was blanketed by a well-maintained lawn. There was even a fountain in the center.

We clung to the steel fence and gazed at the grounds. We heard cars stop behind us. When we turned around we saw three jeeps surrounded by muscular, gun-toting blond men in black clothes. They looked stern, and looked like they could be German, but what removed all doubt was their swastika armbands. It felt like we'd stepped back in time. We showed them our passports and the Amazon research permit from the governor. They talked among themselves, and went back to the jeep to talk into their walkie-talkies. One of them removed his machine gun's safety and pointed it at us. We were all scared for our lives. If they killed us and threw us into the jungle, no one would ever know. We'd be devoured by the animals, rot, and return to the soil. Our lives were in their hands.

Nearly an hour later, we were separated and put into two jeeps. One of them drove the car we came in. We were dropped off about two hours away from the town.

"That town is private property, as recognized by the Peruvian government. Forget everything you saw. If you're ever spotted around there again, there's no guarantee you'll come out alive," said a man who was probably their leader, and then they let us go.

They returned our cameras after they removed the film.

We drove all night and finally reached a small town at dawn. It had all happened in a few hours, and afterward, it felt like I'd been dreaming. Maybe it was actually a dream. A town suddenly appearing in the jungle after a fierce rainstorm? There's no evidence that town exists. But we did see it. Estancia, a European-style town in northern Peru, and the site of the Fourth Reich. When I close my eyes, I can still see the beautiful town that appeared in the deepest depths of the Amazon."

Katya put the folder back on her lap. "The new Nazi city, I've heard of it. But I thought it was just a rumor, or a story in some novel."

"This account should be taken with a grain of salt. The reporter who interviewed him wrote that it might've been an illusion born of one too many coca leaves. It seems there are a lot of stories like this in South America, and they usually mention hidden Nazi treasures, too."

"So was Domba a town the Nazis created?"

"I don't know. All we know is that Gehlen is Dona's husband, and that Dona was from that village. Even if that's true, we don't have any proof."

"Maybe Feldman knows the truth."

"I'm sure he knows some of it. Just not all of it. If he knew the whole truth, he wouldn't have pulled us into this."

"We should have met with the self-proclaimed explorer before we got on the plane. Maybe he knows something about Domba, too."

"To do that we'd have had to find his tomb. A few days after he met with the reporter, he was found floating in a river in Peru with a swastika-shaped wound on his chest. He must've been made an example of—though I don't know if that's true."

"We will be arriving at Manaus in thirty minutes," said the cabin attendant in Spanish. "We are experiencing some turbulence. Please fasten your seat belts." The message was repeated in Portuguese and English.

Katya gave the folder back to Max. "Damn. This was my first time flying first class. I wanted to enjoy it for a little longer." She put on her seat belt.

Max reclined in his seat, feeling a dull pain in the back of his head that had been there ever since he decided to go to the Amazon. He was too afraid to dwell on what that pain could be. He closed his eyes. The plane was beginning to dip down. Below lay the city of Manaus.

Max and Katya arrived at Eduardo Gomes International. The airport was crowded with people of all skin colors. Many were of mixed ancestry, from Indigenous to Black to white to Asian to some combination thereof. The atmosphere in this diverse city was friendly and lively; they could feel life was, in a way, simpler here than what they were used to.

"We're finally in Brazil!" Katya grabbed their luggage while Max looked around absentmindedly.

The second they exited the building and stepped under the cloudless blue sky, they felt the merciless heat bearing down on them.

"Did you enjoy the flight?" Jake asked, with an affable smile. Instead of his usual suit and tie, he had on a safari jacket and work boots—not exactly the image of a Nazi hunter. He looked more like a cheery American tourist. He started walking, and said, "Usually people travel the Amazon by going along the rivers with Cessna floatplanes, but with our luggage in mind, I chartered some helicopters. Helicopters are also easier to land. Actually, the Brazilian Air Force is doing us a favor."

At one end of the airport, two midsize helicopters were on standby for them.

"Here's our guide, Bocaiúva."

Bocaiúva had dark brown skin, a grumpy-looking face, curly black hair, and sharp eyes. He was wearing shorts and sandals. He was about five feet, three inches tall, and his body was thin and lithe, like a piece of wire. But not just any wire—he was like piano wire. His muscles were lean, without an ounce of fat. He was the opposite of Jake.

"We leave in two hours." Bocaiúva spoke in accented but perfectly fluent English.

Two Indigenous porters were loading their luggage onto the chopper. Jake said that their supplies, food, and equipment weighed nearly 700 pounds.

Max inspected the equipment Feldman had sent them.

"There's even a battery-powered cooler," said Katya.

"Shame we can't take some beer with us."

Katya opened the lid. Inside the cooler were empty cases for blood collection.

"It's a state-of-the art cooler that uses liquid nitrogen," said Max, as he examined the binoculars. "Blood or cells can be preserved in a culturable state for three days."

Feldman had prepared all of the equipment that Max had asked for: portable DNA sequencers, blood sampling devices, storage containers, everything. And they were all the latest, most cutting-edge versions. It would normally have taken months to get it all. The organization behind Feldman had to be huge.

All together, they were a party of nine. Jake had two assistants, the man in his thirties and the man in his forties that Max had seen a few times at Feldman's office. As for the native Brazilian contingent, Bocaiúva was joined by three porters, who were from a village near the Amazon River Basin.

"Bocaiúva did well to find helpers. Even the Indigenous people dislike going into the back regions—especially the region where we're headed," Jake said, as Max watched the porters carry their luggage.

They entered a restaurant inside the airport as the rest of their things were loaded onto the chopper.

"Check if everyone has all their shots," Max told Jake. "Measles, polio, the flu . . ."

"Before I left Germany, the professor forced me to get all of them in one go," Katya said, listening beside him. "I spent half the next day in bed. A little cold isn't going to stop me, though."

"The shots aren't for our sakes," Max said, "but to protect the villagers from the contagions carried by us so-called civilized people. We're going to a place that's isolated from the world we live in. There were once nine million Indigenous Amazonians. Now there are only two hundred thousand. Europeans slaughtered a good number of them, but it was the infectious diseases that wiped out most of them."

"All things I'm aware of," Jake said, before turning to Katya. "The Brazilian government recently enacted some laws. I mean, the flu has wiped out whole villages. First, we'll take the choppers to a village near Boyas. From there, we have a half-day car ride to Umabes, where we switch to kayaks for another half day of travel. After that, it's a day's walk to Domba."

"Domba wasn't on any map I saw."

"It might not be an official name. On the map, it's just a point in the middle of the rainforest. And it must be small, since the Cessna pilots couldn't spot it. Indigenous villages are usually guarded by government rangers. They have issues with food and medical treatment. There is no record of Domba. Even the Protection Agency officials knew nothing. Somebody must be pulling strings to prevent organizations and individuals from intervening."

Bocaiúva called them over. The chopper was ready.

As they headed for the chopper, Jake whispered to Max, "Domba's existence could just be a rumor. All we have to go on is a satellite image from NASA. Our experts say they found something in the jungle. To me, that 'something' looks like a scratch or a mark on a photo. But I'll try to find the place. This is all we can rely on." He took a device not unlike a miniature radio from his pocket. "It's a GPS." He flipped its switch, showing it off like a toy.

They left in the two helicopters and flew upstream along the Amazon River. Pockmarks of red earth—Indigenous settlements—dotted the dense jungle. After about two hours, the helicopters landed in a small clearing. The "village" was only a few huts along the river.

As they unloaded their luggage, a group of Indigenous children gathered to stare at them. They were all barefoot, with black hair, dark eyes, and brown skin.

Jake quickly made his way through the children and headed to the lavatory. When he exited, he had a weary look. He'd had an upset stomach since they left, and he looked pale during the chopper ride. It was a sign of the toll the trip would take on their bodies and minds. It had only just begun.

"This place was inaccessible by helicopter until just last year," Bocaiúva explained, as he observed the children surrounding them and watching them from a distance. "We used to have to walk from

Manaus. It was a three-day trip. That's why there's still some nature here. And the children still enjoy their traditional way of life. But soon they'll be wearing sneakers, listening to the radio, and begging travelers for things."

"Are there still unknown villages around here?" Katya asked him.

"Don't know. I'd never heard of Domba, either. I'm just taking you to the place in the picture," he replied in a less than friendly voice.

"We found out about the village," Jake said, watching Max's reaction, "when we combed through NASA satellite and aerial photographs to search for the place Dona described. It's the fruit of modern science. Not that any of us has actually entered the village. You can consider us true pioneers."

"Hold on," Katya lowered her voice and looked at Max. "Dona spoke German and lived in Europe. Gehlen must have traveled all over Europe. I don't think they could have lived in such a remote area."

Max took out his notebook and jotted something down.

One of the porters walked over to Bocaiúva. "We're ready."

They were divided into two pickup trucks. As they drove off, Katya opened the book Max gave her on the plane, entitled *The Flow of the Amazon*. It was about the native flora and fauna.

The unpaved road along the river was flanked by jungle, just like the road to Estancia. They were rumbling through towering walls of green, the trucks bouncing and jostling as they went. Dust roiled like smoke behind them. There was no way anyone could read a book like that; Katya gave up and closed it.

They arrived at Umabes a little after 5:00 p.m. The "village" was a collection of ten huts in cleared grassland. They were in the backcountry now. The villagers wore T-shirts and jeans. Half were barefoot. They shot curious looks at the party, but they didn't come near.

That night they stayed in a hut on the dock. They hung hammocks in a building that looked like a garage with a dirt floor.

Bocaiúva checked for snakes, scorpions, and venomous insects. Katya sprinkled pesticides throughout the hut.

"You're still going to get tortured by insects tonight," Bocaiúva said.

"This is a special insecticide meant for Amazonian mosquitoes," said Katya. "A friend told me I should bring it if I don't want my face to get red and swollen."

"You sprayed enough to kill a person, never mind bugs," Max said.

"Do you know the number one killer in the Amazon?"

"Yes. People. I think people are the deadliest and most evil creatures on Earth, let alone the Amazon. If the world ever falls to ruin, it will have been because humans once walked it."

"Do you have some kind of grudge against humanity, Professor?"

"Homo sapiens is the only species stupid enough to destroy its own habitat. And the only species with boundless appetites beyond just reproduction."

Katya sighed. "All right then, what's the second most dangerous?"

"I can't think of any. The impact of the number one deadliest species is too great. Other species don't cause more harm than what's necessary for their survival."

"It's mosquitoes, Professor. Not crocodiles or piranhas or venomous snakes. By morning they'll have eaten you alive."

"Did you learn that on the web?"

"No, a friend told me."

Katya was right. They hung up mosquito nets, but they were awakened several times by mosquitoes that got through the gaps. Each time, Katya's swatter dispensed the invader. Once, Max put his tongue to the mark left behind by the insect that was squashed in the dark—it tasted strongly of iron.

The temperature dropped as the night went on. Max got up and threw on a windbreaker but was still cold.

The next day everyone woke up at dawn. Everyone but Bocaiúva and the porters had bloodshot eyes and had been bitten by mosquitoes all over their bodies, including their faces. Around the red, swollen rashes, there were crushed mosquito corpses and splotches of blood. Jake had applied anti-itch cream and insect repellent; he looked miserable. Anyone who got near him was hit with a whiff of the strange odor of the two mixed together.

A river flowed in front of the hut. It was one of the tributaries of the Negro River, whose black, muddy, calm waters cut across the Amazon for more than six hundred miles.

A few Indigenous people were waiting on the riverbank. They lived in a nearby village and they were going to take them to the next dock. From that point on, they would have to rely on Bocaiúva's experience and Jake's GPS.

Three kayaks with outboard motors were floating next to each other. They split into groups, with Max, Katya, and Bocaiúva sharing one.

"Don't put your hands in the water," Bocaiúva told the others.

"If you're worried about piranhas, they don't come up to the surface." Katya paddled her hands in the water contentedly.

Bocaiúva pointed to the side. A few yards away, a footlong red and black creature was floating.

"It's a snake. If it bites your hand, then we'll have no choice but to amputate before the venom circulates."

Katya hurriedly took her hands out.

"There are also leeches and nematodes. Nematodes enter the body through any orifice and feast on your insides, down to your organs and brain matter."

Katya raised her hands above her chest. Her face went pale.

They had lunch as they floated. The outboard motor buzzed as if to intimidate the dense jungle on both sides of the river. When the sun began to hang on the treetops to the west, they arrived at the pier, which was nothing more than a few wooden planks in a row. There was no sign of people living in the area. Max stood on the pier and looked at the river and the forest surrounding it. The virgin forest, which stopped at the very edge of the water, stood high and dense, as if to rebuff intruding humans.

The porters gathered around the kayaks. The Indigenous people navigating the kayaks pointed to the forest upstream and said something in a language Max didn't understand. The porters were nodding and listening; judging by their expressions, they were afraid.

"What are they saying?" Max asked Bocaiúva.

"They're talking about the forest, the people, the animals and plants. And about the gods and evil spirits," he replied nonchalantly, before instructing the porters to unload quickly.

After their things were unloaded, the kayaks returned to their village.

"From here, we walk. Our destination is thirty miles away." Bocaiúva pulled out a machete that was more than a foot long and peered into the jungle.

"How long will it take?"

"I don't know. It's my first time going down this path."

With Bocaiúva in the lead, they started walking into the lush virgin forest. He hacked away at branches and vines in their way. The sunlight and the scents of the forest and soil wrapped around the party like a choking miasma. Their hiking shoes sank into the spongy mulch.

"Be careful where you step," Katya said. "Leeches can get at you through the gaps in your socks. The leeches around these parts rend your flesh and enter your blood vessels to reach the heart."

"Another tidbit from the web?"

"No, this was something my old friend told me, too."

Meanwhile, Bocaiúva and the porters kept hacking a trail. The branches and leaves that hit their heads and faces were full of venomous insects and mites. Jake screamed each time one hit him.

"There are venomous snakes, venomous spiders, and more here. Don't touch them, don't step on them, and don't get close to them.

Pay attention to where you're walking so others don't have to do it for you." Bocaiúva pointed to a black and yellow spider on a leaf.

"Then I have no choice but to stand still," Jake blubbered.

"Humans are the outsiders here. They are beings of little significance. The protagonists are the jungle and the flora and fauna that live there. Keep that in mind if you don't want to die." They felt the truth in Bocaiúva's words.

The tangle of vines continued on like an endless maze. Trees over a hundred feet high blocked the light and trapped in moisture; Max could almost swear they were confined under a huge dome.

They were sweating buckets. Their sweat formed a film on their skin that attracted insects even more.

"The humidity is 100 percent," Katya said. "I wouldn't be surprised if water came oozing out of the air." Katya stopped, wiped her sweat, and sprayed her whole body with insect repellent again.

"Zero appetite is great for dieting, but I'm thirsty." Jake took out a water bottle and drank from it.

His diarrhea hadn't abated, and every time they took a break, he squatted away from the others. His face and body had changed over the last few days.

"Bocaiúva said that if you drink too much, you just get tired."

"I know, but my body won't listen to me."

The moisture didn't evaporate, instead becoming another coating of sweat. They felt sticky all over, and had a sensation that insects were crawling all over them. Max looked up; the branches and leaves of the broadleaf trees were layered, and he felt like a prisoner in a green cage.

"Even America is outmatched here," said Katya. "NASA's satellites were only able to take photos of leaves."

"The village has been found. The Brazilian government has also allowed us to visit," Jake argued, but it sounded like excuses to them.

"What if it's not a village, but rather something that looks like a village? Also, permits are one-sided. You used your connections to get a signature on a document. That doesn't mean the villagers are going to welcome us. We don't even know if the village actually exists. Did they use infrared to find the village?"

"It was something like that."

"A few years ago," Max said as he walked, "four corpses were found downstream of the river we just went up."

"What did they die from?"

"Impossible to tell. The corpses were rotten and fish-eaten. They were researchers and guards at a German pharmaceutical company."

"Run!" shouted Bocaiúva as he swung his machete. The porters followed him, pushing their way through the branches as they ran.

From overhead, a shower of avocado-sized bluish-black masses rained down on them. The screams of Jake and his assistants echoed through the trees. Max's group ducked down and got out of the avocado shower.

Katya shrieked. Max checked under her shirt collar and found a two-inch-long leech on her neck. Max tried to get it off with a knife.

"If you take it off wrong, a piece of it will sneak into her body!" Bocaiúva pushed Max away and pushed a lit cigarette into it instead.

Now the back of Katya's neck was swollen, reddish purple, and bleeding. Bocaiúva looked around and cut a three-foot-tall tree at the roots. He grasped the opening he'd created in the tree with his fingers, then grabbed Katya's neck and bent it closer. When he let go of the tree, clear water began to flow from the trunk. He washed Katya's neck with the water, and told her to drink if she wanted to.

"Cold, delicious water." She was hesitant, but kept drinking anyway.

"Shippo de Agua—the 'water tree,'" Max said.

Bocaiúva nodded, as he drank from it too.

"Is that also from *National Geographic*, Professor?"

"It seems that the Amazon is full of God's grace—as well as the Devil's traps."

Jake and his assistants were breathing heavily as they sat.

"We'll be in leech territory for a while yet."

Everyone jumped up as if Bocaiúva's words had lit a fire under them. They kept walking for almost two hours without stopping until Bocaiúva motioned for them to pass through the tunnel he had cut through the trees.

Suddenly, the view opened up.

Max stood there, speechless. Katya was staring beside him, as captivated as he was. Before them lay a huge trunk; it looked like a boulder, and it was more than fifteen feet in diameter. The upper part was hidden behind the surrounding trees. The trunk, covered in moss and ivy, crept over the earth like a huge living creature. Thick branches hung overhead, and thousands, no, tens of thousands of smaller branches covered completely by leaves jutted out from them, making for a single, gigantic life-form.

"It's a Samauma tree," Bocaiúva said, looking up at the green giant. "I've never seen such a huge tree. It must be 300 to 400 years old."

Jake and his assistants stood around gaping at the tree as well.

"God's tree," murmured Katya.

The calm of the forest began drifting in the air, alongside hints of night.

"We'll make camp here today." Bocaiúva set down his backpack by the tree.

The porters came together and talked, shooting glances at Max and the group.

The next morning, they woke to the sound of Bocaiúva's voice. The porters were nowhere to be found. Jake was making a fuss about chasing after them, but Bocaiúva didn't appear fazed in the least.

"They only took their own portions of the food. Our destination is a day away. As long as we each take some of the luggage, we'll get there." Bocaiúva had seen this coming.

"What do we do on the return trip? I won't have any strength left," Jake was beside himself.

"You gringos always worry about pointless things. The gods of the forest will guide us. We humans have only to obey," Bocaiúva said matter-of-factly as he began dividing up the luggage.

As soon as they finished breakfast, they were on the move. They walked single file without a word. Jake kept checking the GPS and the map. By noon they encountered a spring that formed a small pond. When Bocaiúva said they could take a break, they all sat down at the base of a tree. They were drenched in sweat. All of a sudden they heard screaming and yelling. They looked over at the spring; a dark mass had formed in the air. Bocaiúva grabbed the jacket he'd just taken off and rushed over.

"Blackflies!" Jake exclaimed.

One of the assistants was shirtless in the water and the blackflies swarmed him. Bocaiúva tried to slap the flies away, but the black cloud clung to him. Max took a smoke bomb from out of his backpack and lit it. It blew white smoke, which enveloped the man and drove the swarm away. A few minutes later, the assistant got out of the water; he was red and swollen all over. Bocaiúva applied an ink-like salve he'd brought along. It reeked of ammonia.

"It's a quick remedy the people here make from bat guano—bat excrement. The swelling will go down in half a day. Next time, if you don't want to die, stay still and hold your breath. Also, get it into your heads that in this forest, humans are outsiders."

The assistant couldn't even open his mouth. He just grimaced and endured the smell.

They ate lunch and set off once again. The burden on each of them grew since they now had to carry the assistant's things. It was all they could do just to keep putting one foot in front of the other. The sun was beginning to sink. Jake had been hurrying along, relying on the walking stick Bocaiúva had made him, but he was falling behind. Max asked him if he was all right, but Jake was breathing heavily; he couldn't even speak. Unable to stand by and watch, Bocaiúva took Jake's load. Max kept soldiering on; Katya was keeping pace behind him.

A fallen tree blocked the way. Katya lost her footing and was about to fall when Max held out his hand. "First time doing fieldwork?" he asked.

"I didn't know it was necessary. I thought all we needed to do was to stay in our sterilized rooms and familiarize ourselves with microscopes, computers, cells, and blood."

"You're half-right."

"When I was at Stanford, a biologist friend of mine did fieldwork all the time. He'd go to the Himalayas or Africa in search of undiscovered microbes or plants. He even went to the Amazon. He invited me to come with him, but I turned him down."

"I'm sure your friend was an outstanding scientist."

"He was only able to graduate because I started writing his papers."

"You're a good friend."

"If he'd been held back a year, that was another year I'd have had to look after him. Besides, we were engaged."

Max stumbled over himself for a second. "When are you getting married?"

"We were engaged. Past tense. We broke it off."

"You got tired of writing his reports for him?"

"I realized he hated studying. He's the type of guy that likes using his body over his mind." Katya's breathing became unsteady. "One of the species he was always hunting was human females. He collected and researched them enthusiastically. The only things he exceeded me in were his physical strength and his insatiable spirit of inquiry with regard to new species."

"That's the most important quality for basic research."

"The problem is he directed those rare talents only to the bedroom," said Katya, as she swatted her neck. A mosquito died with a bloody splat. "You're used to mountain treks, aren't you, Professor?"

"Ever since high school. The last time was when I was in tenth grade. I went camping with my dad."

"That sounds fun. You didn't go again after that?"

"He died on the last day of camp."

"I'm so sorry!"

"No need to apologize. He committed suicide. When I woke up in the morning, I saw my dad wasn't in bed beside me. I went to the lake, and there he was, floating in it."

"How do you know it was suicide?"

"Because he was mentally weak," Max said quietly. Then he picked up the pace, as if to deny her any follow-up. She chased after him.

CHAPTER 10

Bocaiúva held up his hand, signaling them to stop.

The sun was shining through the gaps in the trees, and they suddenly came upon a small clearing with about ten huts. The walls and roofs were made of palm tree leaves, blending in with the trees behind them. No wonder this tiny village, enclosed by towering trees, couldn't be spotted by helicopter. There was no sign of people. Two skinny dogs watched them. One hut was a little bigger than the others.

"Is this Domba?" Max asked Jake without taking his eyes off the clearing.

Jake hurriedly took out his GPS and map to check. Bocaiúva motioned to Jake to stay put and entered the clearing. Max took a step forward. Katya came to his side and grabbed his arm; she was shivering.

Before they knew it, they were surrounded by partially naked men and women, all about five feet tall, with black hair, dark eyes, and glistening brown skin. The men held small bows, but they looked like toys. They were barefoot and barely covered by cloth around their waists. They were expressionless apart from their harsh eyes.

Katya trembled. Max hugged her to him, and told her with his eyes to look behind the men with bows. There were children behind the adults. They had their arms folded, and stared at them with piercing eyes. They looked stern, but there was no hostility there. Katya felt relieved, but her face quickly turned fearful. A group of men filed out of a hut wielding bows nearly twice their height.

"They're holding spears," said Katya.

"They're blowpipes. They're not for fighting. These people are hunters."

"Leave this to me," Jake said, who was trying to seem cool under fire, but he'd turned pale, and his voice was quivering. "I have the government-issued permit."

Max's gaze remained fixed on the men walking toward them. Their chests were proudly puffed out, and they radiated dignity. They stopped about five yards away.

"*Não somos inimigos,*" Bocaiúva addressed the man at the head of the group. "We are not enemies."

They didn't reply. It wasn't likely they'd understood what he said.

"*Nosotros no somos enemigos,*" he repeated.

Still no response. A man at the center came closer. He sized them up one by one. Katya clenched Max's arm tighter.

"*Bist du der Anführer?*" he asked Max. "Are you the leader here?"

Everyone looked at the man. He spoke with a bit of an accent, but his German was clear.

"*Nein,*" said Max, pointing at Jake.

Jake hurried to show him the government-issued documents, explaining how they'd been granted permission in São Paulo to trace the Amazon River to its source. The man ignored this and directed his piercing stare back at Max. Dozens of villagers now had them surrounded.

"*Ich bin Davi,*" he said.

They were taken to a hut at the edge of the clearing. The walls and roof were made of palm leaves woven into wooden frames. It was dim and empty inside, the sun trickling in from the entrance the only source of light. They were hit by the heady aroma of herbs.

"Why German?" Jake asked Max. "I mean, if they don't speak Portuguese, you'd think they'd speak Spanish."

"Consider it proof we're closer to your objective. Dona spoke German, too. Nazi war criminals fled to this village and taught them their language. Only then does this make any sense."

"And yet there's no evidence of that whatsoever." Jake scanned the inside of the hut. Small dried flowers hung on the walls and their scent wafted through the room. There were stakes for hanging hammocks and a few earthenware vessels. One of the assistants checked them, but they were empty.

"The Indigenous people of the Amazon live in huts and spend their days more or less nude. The men are hunters, and the women gatherers. They're simple and friendly. That's what all the literature says about them. It never mentioned anything about them speaking German," Katya said.

Max put down his backpack and sat on it.

"It's not exactly a five-star guesthouse," Jake said as he wiped his sweat, "but it's comforting that they've accepted us."

"Feldman didn't have something arranged?" Max asked.

"He negotiated with the Brazilian government. That's why we were able to get this far. But his influence didn't reach this village. There are supervisors for preserves, but none in this area. It seems they want to leave the nature here untouched."

"If you ask me," Katya said, "the government doesn't think there's a village here."

Jake had nothing to say to that.

"It seems like they're used to visitors from outside," said Max, "white people included. They don't seem to be scared or hostile."

"Maybe they have contact with poachers. I hear that pharmaceutical companies are sneaking in. Meaning that no Indigenous people are completely isolated, not even here."

"Did you notice the few mixed-blood people? I think around half of them have Caucasian ancestry. Their features and skin tones are different from other Indigenous Amazonians. Dona was obviously mixed race, too. The villagers here—"

Bocaiúva beckoned to them, pointing to the base of the pillar. "I figure this has something to do with what you're looking for." There were knife marks there—in the shape of a swastika.

"It could just be a scratch," Jake said, frightened by the implications.

"Is this a Nazi guesthouse?"

The light coming through the entrance was blocked before Katya could finish that sentence; Davi appeared with a few other men. Jake's face tensed up.

"What did you come to this village to do?" Davi asked politely.

"We are investigating the headwaters of the Amazon River. Geography, wildlife, and plants. We would appreciate it if you would let us stay here for a while," Jake said, trying to put up a bold front, but his voice was high-pitched and trembling.

Davi stood with his arms folded, but nodded slowly.

"Do you know this woman?" Max showed him a picture. It was a magnification of Dona's passport photo. "Her name is Dona. She was with a white man."

"She isn't of this village," Davi said without expression; he'd glanced at the photo for a second before looking away.

"She told me where this village is."

"Villagers never leave the village," said Davi, without looking at the picture again.

"Does the word 'Aska' mean anything? Could it be the name of a place, or a person? Maybe a plant?"

Davi shook his head, his expression unchanging. Meanwhile, villagers had gathered at the entrance and were peering inside. "You can use this hut while you're here. Get out when you're done. May your travels be safe." As Davi went to the door, the peering faces disappeared all at once.

"He's lying," whispered Katya. "Dona is definitely from this village. Some of the women look a lot like her."

"Note he didn't say he doesn't know her. All he said was she wasn't 'of this village.' Maybe she's not really a 'villager' anymore."

"That's equivocation."

"But it's still not a lie."

Katya looked at Max as if she wanted to say something, but she stopped herself.

The hammocks were hung up according to Bocaiúva's instructions.

"Hey, no mosquitoes," said Katya.

"The smell of the herbs must be keeping them away."

"We've secured ourselves a place to sleep. But that is one strong smell." Jake crinkled his nose.

Max breathed it in. It was intense, but not unpleasant. If one got used to it, he could imagine it becoming relaxing.

When the sun went down, the temperature plunged. The cries of countless creatures keened from the jungle.

"The forest speaks," muttered Bocaiúva, who was staring at the doorway.

The moonlight shining through the entrance lit the hut's interior. After finishing their meals, everyone got into their hammocks. Snoring began immediately all around. For the first time in days, no mosquitoes were torturing them. The peacefulness of the clearing surrounded by jungle, combined with the smell of the herbs, had a calming effect on them.

Max was exhausted, but he couldn't fall asleep. He could sense Katya turning over in her sleep. When he closed his eyes and listened to the voice of the forest, a wondrous peace wrapped over him. Eventually, he was lulled into a deep sleep.

The next morning, Max was unpacking in front of the hut when Jake came up to him.

"Professor, you're free to begin your investigation whenever you like. Mr. Feldman asked us to accommodate you to the greatest extent possible."

"What will you three be doing?"

"Looking for Nazi war criminals. It's what we came here to do." Jake pointed at the edge of the village, where Bocaiúva and the assistants were standing. "We spotted something suspicious in the satellite photos, so that's where we'll look first."

"Estancia, I take it?"

"Traces of Nazis." Jake replied.

"Can I come?"

"I don't mind at all, Professor. In fact, it'd be reassuring if you did. Considering . . ."

Jake watched the circle of villagers staring at them. Clearly, Jake was uncomfortable.

They set out, with Bocaiúva at the head. As soon as they stepped out of the village, they were surrounded by trees and were disoriented. The damp rainforest air enveloped them as mosquitoes and horseflies swarmed them. The smell of the trees and mulch was enough to gag them. The deeper they ventured, the thicker the air became. Katya had her mosquito-net hat on, hiding her expression.

After about twenty minutes, Bocaiúva stopped. He turned around and shouted.

What looked like a building could be made out between hundred-foot-tall trees. They entered a wide open space and stood there, stunned. Giant buildings in the middle of nowhere! Three one-story wooden buildings had been built side by side. The whole site was around sixty-five feet wide and a hundred feet long. Surrounded by jutting branches, twisted vines, and tall trees, it had become a part of the jungle.

The buildings were dilapidated. The walls were rotten and covered by vines; nature was reclaiming them. The place would be tough to spot even with incredibly high-resolution satellite photos.

Max got closer to one of the buildings.

"This must be Estancia," Katya said, her eyes on the building.

"This is one section of Estancia," Jake said, comparing it against the photo. He had a grave look on his face. "Did you read about it in a book? Or did someone tell you about it? The Fourth Reich, I mean. Estancia, it's the legacy of the Nazis. Nazi fugitives created German-style towns all over South America, and tried to form a German ministate. They had schools, factories, even hospitals. They educated themselves and conducted research while looking for an opportunity to come back into power. Some even claim UFO sightings were actually new Nazi weapons, but those are just rumors or urban legends."

"This place is the Fourth Reich?" Katya asked. "Doesn't seem all that glorious."

"No, but this is just a small section of it."

"This is more like a haunted house. Nobody's lived here for decades."

"But the fact they'd build this way out here is something," said Max. "And more than sixty years ago, too. They must've needed vast amounts of money, time, and labor."

Max walked around the building searching for a door, while Katya and Jake followed. Half of the windows were covered in vines, and most of the glass was shattered.

"There must be an airfield somewhere around here. There's no way they could've manually lugged all the equipment and materials they needed to construct these buildings."

Jake nodded, but they weren't able to find it in the satellite photos.

The door handle was rusted and broken. Max jumped back as the door fell open when he pulled it; the hinge had corroded. The interior was surprisingly well-lit, the stench of rotten wood and mold notwithstanding.

"Watch your step. The floor's rotten," Max said, as he stood in the entrance.

When he shifted his weight onto the wood floor, it bent and creaked. The beams of the ceiling were exposed, and shafts of light shone down through big gaps in the roof. There was a hallway running through the center of the building, with rooms lining both sides of it. The doors to half of those rooms were off, and the walls had holes in them. Max entered the first room.

"It's a laboratory." Katya came up behind him.

Katya squeezed Max's arm. Her body was stiff, and the blood had drained from her face. Max followed her line of sight, and saw a long striped creature about six inches in diameter on the floor.

"It's an anaconda!" she gasped. The giant snake slithered toward them. "Professor!"

"We shouldn't move."

The snake stopped a few yards away from them and raised its head. Then it slowly slithered across the floor and left through a gap in the floorboards. Jake let out the breath he'd been holding. Max gingerly stepped forward. He looked into the hole where the snake had gone, but all he could see was the black soil beneath the floor. Jake and the other men followed him with nervous looks on their faces.

The sun shone through the broken windows and holes in the ceiling. The room was covered in white dust. Old bottles lined the shelves on one wall. Test tubes and drug bottles were scattered on a row of wooden desks. Max picked up a piece of paper buried in dust. He blew the dust off, and though the ink on the discolored page was faded, it was still partially legible.

"It's in German," Katya said. They could make out words like *Zelle* (cell), *Experiment* (experiment), *Wiederholung* (repetition), *Menschen* (people). "There's even a microscope." She went to the desk by the window, where there was a large optical microscope. She tried to work it, but it was too rusty. It would have been a cutting-edge microscope sixty years ago.

"We're going to inspect the building over there," Jake said. "You stay here and take a good look around, Professor, and try to figure out what they were doing here."

"There are a lot of test tubes and petri dishes." Katya walked around the room. "Conical flasks, pipettes, and a constant-temperature incubator. There's even what looks like a shaker, an extremely old-school shaker. If this is a Nazi laboratory, then they were definitely researching bacteriological weapons."

"With this much equipment they could do a lot more, too. But you're right; bacterial cultivation and cell division were at the core of their research."

"All the equipment is pretty old. Which makes sense if it were the Nazis who brought this stuff here."

"But not everything here is sixty years old."

Katya looked at him.

"One is still in use at smaller colleges." Max squatted in front of a spectroscope, a device used to identify a substance's composition. It was, at most, twenty years old, yet it was rusted, and there were no signs it had been used for very long.

"Which must mean that research was conducted here for at least that long," Katya said.

Max stepped in front of the constant-temperature incubator, which allowed cells to proliferate in a controlled environment. He opened its door; several petri dishes with brown masses lined the bottom of the device. "The Nazis were researching biochemistry here."

"No way!" Katya said.

"Does this look like a brewery or bread factory to you? Biochemistry first came to light twenty or thirty years prior. Before then, they examined cells by means of biology. Yet they clearly had been working with biochemistry in this laboratory." Max explained. "They weren't necessarily doing biochemistry as far back as sixty or so years ago. But they were doing it up to when they abandoned this place.

We're talking fifteen to twenty years ago. This equipment was probably still working. But the humidity made it rust faster than normal."

They moved on to the next room, which was clearly an operating room. There were four operating tables. One had stirrups attached for obstetrics and gynecology. Next to it were several rusted surgical lights. There were clumps of rust on the tables—surgical knives. Metal petri dishes, forceps, tweezers, Gosset abdominal wall retractors . . . Max picked up a bent wire to examine it. It was a suturing needle.

Max looked away; remnants of leather belts were attached to the surgical tables. *That must be what they'd used to strap their "patients" down. The Nazis had experimented on living people in the concentration camps in Europe. Had they picked up where they left off in this operating room?*

"Professor," Katya was crouching in front of a refrigerator-like box.

Max went to see. There were injection solutions inside ampoules.

"Some are labeled morphine," Katya said, carefully taking out the case of ampoules. "The unlabeled ones, they're broken. At least the patients weren't conscious." She put the case back.

Max opened a door in the corner of the room that led into a narrow passage, lined on each side by two rooms closed off by iron bars. Inside each cramped ten-square-foot cell were crude wooden bunk beds. "It's a prison."

Katya stifled a scream. There were weighted shackles on the floor. Inside those shackles were lower-leg and ankle bones. The rest must have been taken by jungle beasts or mice over the years.

Max took her by the arm and left the room. "Do you want to wait outside?"

"Don't leave me alone." Katya gripped his arm tightly.

Together, they moved to the next room. One step inside, and their breaths caught. A hundred or so jars lined the shelves built into the walls. A specimen room. The jars were about a foot tall, and just as wide. A dried-up black clump was stuck to the bottom of each.

"Professor . . ." She gripped his arm harder still. She was looking at a jar full of yellowish alcohol. Something whitish was floating inside. "That looks like a section of some animal's internal organs."

"And humans are animals, too." Max thought of the operating room, and judging by the way Katya's hands were shaking, she had come to the same conclusion.

Max felt pressure in his chest, and his heart was pounding. What was floating in that jar was a four- or five-month-old fetus. It had discernible limbs, and it was curled up with its eyes closed, as though deep in thought. Katya was staring at it too. Neither said a word.

Suddenly, Max felt something hot come up his throat. He ran to a corner of the room. His stomach contracted, and his mouth filled with a sour-tasting liquid. He doubled over and vomited. After his stomach was empty he calmed down. Katya was stroking his back.

"Time to revoke my doctor card, huh."

Katya wiped his mouth with her handkerchief. "It means you're only human."

They left the building. Stepping outside felt like crossing into a separate dimension. Max kept taking deep breaths. His heart rate was reverting to normal. He looked up at the sky; he felt like he was looking at it from the bottom of a pit. The sun's rays bore down on them from a hole in the canopy.

The door to the next building was open. After a moment's hesitation, they entered. Just like the lab building, it reeked of mold. Close to a dozen doors lined a narrow corridor. One of the doors in front of them swung open; Katya clung to Max—it was Jake.

"What are you doing?" Jake asked.

"There could still be snakes around."

"This building was probably for the commissioned officers. There's a mess hall and a shower room on the other side. The third building appears to have been for the soldiers and the Indigenous people."

Max entered a small room furnished with a bed and a desk. A chair without legs lay on the floor, and the window contained no glass, allowing vines to creep along the walls. The room was full of dust and cobwebs, hinting at how much time had passed.

"Professor Knight!" Jake shouted.

They stepped outside. He was calling them from behind the building, and they walked toward his voice. Jake and the others were looking at the satellite photos and pointing beyond the tangle of trees and vines. Jake showed them a photo. It was grayscale, and all it showed was the forest—no village, no buildings. The trees that concealed the ground were too tall for the satellites to see past.

"A specialist determined that there were signs a space had been cleared. And sure enough, you can see it's a different color here," he said, pointing. Max hadn't noticed before, but now he saw that spot had a slightly different tone.

"Is that the remaining bit of Estancia ?"

"It's around two hundred yards south of here. We'll check it out shortly."

Max nodded.

Behind the buildings was an overgrown road about seven feet wide. It was covered in weeds that reached their waists. They walked through it with Bocaiúva at the head, slashing at the branches and vines stretching from both sides. Eventually they arrived at an open area. Just like the trio of buildings, it was concealed by trees. From the air, it would look like nothing more than a rift in the forest.

"It's an airfield," Jake said.

"A *former* airfield," Max said.

The grassland area was about ten yards wide and one hundred twenty yards long, bordered by tall plants and bushes. One wouldn't be able to tell it used to be an airfield without anything else to go on.

"Little wonder the eyes in the sky couldn't pick this up. It looks no different from empty wilderness," said Max.

"It was well-made. Without ultrahigh-resolution satellite photos, no one would ever find it from the air."

"It must have been twice as big before. Give it a few more years and this whole area will be virgin forest again."

"This is more than enough for takeoff and landing for a JU-55," Jake said, as he glanced at the photo and the open area in turn.

"JU-55?"

"A midsize Nazi transport plane developed just before the end of the war. It has a maximum load capacity of twenty tons, a breakthrough at the time. They used this airfield to bring in people and materials."

"That's how they built those three buildings. But to what end?"

"To create the Fourth Reich, and realize their march back to power."

"Oh stop. This is the twenty-first century."

"But this place is frozen in time."

"This is the Nazi legacy? Everything's a ghost of the past."

"Even now, a helicopter could easily land here." Max pointed toward the clearing.

Max could tell Jake and the others all came to the same conclusion. There were no shrubs in the center, only weeds and undergrowth. The shrubs had been cleared away by human hands, and not all that long ago—a few months prior at most.

They stood there for a long time.

Jake and his assistants set about taking pictures and measuring the old airfield. Max and Katya returned to the lab building.

"Are you okay?" Katya looked at Max with a worried expression.

Max nodded.

They entered the laboratory and opened the desk drawers. Most were empty, but they found a few discolored notebooks. They were experiment records, but there was nothing in them about fetuses or about surgeries conducted on humans. Rather, they had to do with cell division in plants.

Katya was flipping through the pages of one of them. "I can't imagine Nazi scientists were researching botany."

"Either they took the rest away or destroyed them."

"Which is to say they started doing their research elsewhere. Either that, or . . ."

Max was thinking it over.

"Are you being possessed by Nazi ghosts, too, Professor? What do you gain from looking into any of this? I understand collecting blood samples from the villagers, but . . ."

"You ventured out to the depths of the Amazon with me because you believed there was something here. Everything here means something. The inviolable law of fieldwork—in nature, nothing is pointless."

After looking through the lab for an hour they went back outside. The sun was beginning to set. They were exhausted, and not just from physical exertion. Mental fatigue had a way of affecting the body.

All of a sudden it got dark. Black clouds obscured what little they could see of the sky through the trees. Huge drops pelted down on them, and they hurried under the trees for cover. Protected by the dense canopy, they didn't get the least bit wet, as if the rain was just an illusion.

They leaned against each other and watched the rainforest haze over. A half hour passed without any sign of the downpour letting up. They started walking; the village was due east. The jungle was so dark now that they half-believed it was already sundown. All they heard was the splash of the raindrops on the leaves.

There was no change in scenery no matter where they looked. They were surrounded by trees and more trees, and the ground was a soft mix of mulch and water. Their hiking boots were full of water, and it splashed out at their ankles with every step. There was no sense of progress.

"We're lost," Katya said.

"Someone's watching us," Max said, scanning their surroundings. That was the feeling he had.

"Is this any time to make jokes?" Katya drew closer to him.

An hour had already passed since they'd started walking. The rain had only increased, and the rainforest became one big wet blur. They were truly lost.

"We should wait out the rain somewhere."

The water level was rising. It had already reached above their ankles.

"Be careful. There's a river or swamp nearby. That's where all this water's coming from," Max said.

Katya screamed. Max turned to look her way, but she was gone.

"KATYA! WHERE ARE YOU!?" But the rain drowned him out.

"Help!!!"

"WHERE ARE YOU!?" He rushed over to the source of her voice.

A muddy deluge rushed past. The water was rising above his knees. He spotted an open space in the tangle of trees a few yards away. Katya's head was bobbing up and down in the water. The rain had swelled a stream. Katya hadn't been washed away because something was holding her in place. She struggled to bend backward and keep her head above water and breathe. Max was about to step into the water before he stopped himself. He could get sucked in, too, and they'd both be swept away.

"Careful!" Katya shouted. "The ground falls away with a steep drop!" She swallowed water and started to choke.

"Don't let go! I'll get you out of there!"

He stretched out his hand, but couldn't reach her. He couldn't see any branches or footholds. Max wiped his face with his palm; it was raining so hard he could barely breathe. Katya went under. Max stepped into the stream. He lost his balance and his legs swayed. Just when he was about to fall, he spotted a vine and grabbed it. He leaned forward while holding onto the vine and grabbed Katya by the arm. He lifted her up with all his strength. Katya paddled through the water and gulped in air while coughing up water.

They noticed a little girl standing nearby. She was holding onto a vine hanging from a huge tree.

"That girl's come to the rescue!" Max said.

Katya looked at the girl, who was staring at them. She was fourteen or fifteen. Her skin was tan, her hair was reddish brown, and she had big, dark blue eyes. She looked like she had Caucasian blood in her.

Katya reached out and gripped the little girl's hand. The girl looked up with a shy smile.

Just as suddenly as it began, the darkness lifted, as did the rain, and all that was left was the gurgling water winding through the undergrowth.

"Storm's over." Moments ago, the forest had been too dark and misty to see more than a few yards, once again it was transformed into a world of lush green. "Do you know the way to the village?" he asked, gesturing as he spoke.

The girl thought a moment before nodding and walking off. The three wove their way through the trees as large drops fell from the leaves. After about a half hour, the entrance to the village come into view. Before they knew it, the girl was gone.

A few hours later, Jake and the rest returned as well, exhausted and dripping.

"Three buildings, an airfield, and German-speaking villagers," Jake said. "That's plenty of evidence Nazis were here, but they're not here anymore. And we don't have any leads as to where they ran off to yet. We'll search again tomorrow. With this much evidence, we should find something." He dug into his meal and shortly after, fell into his hammock.

Max couldn't sleep at all. The snoring from the huts was worse than the sound of the jungle at night.

"Thank you so much, Professor," came Katya's voice from the next hammock over. "You jumped into the water for me."

"If that girl hadn't been there, would we still be alive?"

"We never asked her name. I'll look for her tomorrow."

When he closed his eyes, he saw the girl's face. She was clearly different from the other villagers they had seen.

"Can I ask you something?" Katya said. "You have your doctor's license, so why did you end up going down the research path instead? It's the same question you asked me the day we met."

Silence.

"When I was a kid," Max said, "I wanted to be a football player. That was before I realized I lacked the talent." A small sigh. "Everyone's got their own talents. And everyone has things they must accomplish. People have no choice but to live complicated, interconnected lives."

"That's not what I asked, Professor," she said softly. "What I want to know is . . ."

"You should go to sleep. More jungle awaits us tomorrow."

The silence that followed lasted for a while, until, at last, he heard her dozing breath. Max closed his eyes again. Now he saw Katya's fair face, but soon enough, he drifted into a deep sleep.

CHAPTER 11

Max woke up to the voices of children. There was no one in the other hammocks.

The voices were coming from outside. He could hear Katya's voice as well. Max got down from his hammock and went out. The sudden brightness made him dizzy. Katya was surrounded by children. A few other people and a few dogs were also in the clearing.

"The children brought it here," Katya said. Her surgical-gloved hands were bloody, and she held a fishhook-shaped sewing needle. "Their little pet must have gotten attacked by wild animals."

A foot-and-a-half-long capybara lay in front of her. It didn't have the energy to run, but just moved its head from side to side. The giant rodents were a valuable source of protein for the Indigenous Amazonians.

"You're just prolonging its suffering," Max said, shaking his head. Its belly was torn, exposing its organs.

"How could I just let it be?"

"It should be euthanized."

"I'm not a fan of euthanasia," Katya asserted firmly, pushing its entrails back in and resuming her stitches. Her skill and dexterity were a match for any expert surgeon's. "I studied medicine in order to save lives, and I'm researching life science in order to know more about the mysteries of life," she muttered to herself, but clearly Max was meant to overhear. She finished stitching in ten minutes. "There. That should do it. Let's just let it rest. Here, a good luck charm." She took off her red scarf and tied it around the capybara's neck.

"Your skills are wasted on veterinary surgery."

"Tania. The girl's name is Tania." Katya stood up and pointed to the girl holding down the capybara's legs. "I thanked her earlier, but she doesn't seem to understand me. Asking her name was all I could get across."

The girl from the day before looked at Max and smiled bashfully.

"Where are Jake and the others?"

"They left about an hour ago. They lose their minds whenever Nazis come up."

"Which, from their viewpoint, is totally understandable."

When they spotted Max, the dogs began to bark, and a villager raised a hand and said something. The chattering children took the capybara away, leaving Tania behind. Max asked Tania where the Nazi buildings were. Tania just stared at him.

"It's no use asking her," said Katya. "She doesn't understand a word you're saying."

"I want to go to the place from yesterday. There are three big buildings. They were built by the Nazis." Max drew three buildings and a swastika on the ground. "Please take me there."

Tania looked like she was thinking. Then she started walking toward the jungle. They walked through the dense treescape for around a half hour, but there were no buildings in sight.

"This is a different path from yesterday," Max said. "And I don't think this is a shortcut, either."

"You're right; the village with the buildings wasn't this far."

"Where is she taking us?"

Tania just kept walking. Max grabbed Tania's shoulders, and she stopped and turned to face him. Fear flashed across her face.

"Don't get rough!" Katya pulled her away and hugged her.

"I'm not going to. I just want to know where we're going."

"Let's trust her. She saved our lives yesterday!" She gently stroked Tania's hair and gave her an affectionate push on the back. "Go on. We'll follow."

"I have a feeling we're going to get lost again."

"But today we have the best guide we could ask for."

"Another rainstorm!" They looked up, but while they heard the sound of the rain, the drops hadn't reached them yet. The leaves were acting as umbrellas. "Let's hope it won't be as bad as yesterday."

Tania walked along unconcerned. Then she stopped, and stared straight ahead. Max and Katya looked in the same direction. What they saw stopped them in their tracks—a plank among the trees, with a mark that was fading away—a swastika.

Though now covered with shrubs, they could tell that this place had been cleared of vegetation long ago. As they looked around they found more planks. Max pushed his way through the bushes, and suddenly he saw more than endless trees. He saw a clearing with overgrown grass, misted over in the rain, with more than forty cross-shaped headstones lined up in rows. This was a graveyard.

Max stepped into the rainy cemetery, and Katya cautiously followed.

"Karl Heinberg, 1918–1962," Katya read. "Albert Schneider, Otto Mronz—they must be the Germans who fled to this village! We have to tell Jake and the rest as soon as we can."

Max tried to use drawings to explain to Tania, who was standing by the entrance to the graveyard, about the three Nazi buildings, and that Jake and the rest were there. Tania stared silently at Max's crude illustrations.

"The fat old man is over here. Bring me over to him," said Katya, gesticulating.

Tania nodded, took Katya by the hand, and entered a part of the jungle opposite from where they'd just arrived.

The storm had passed, giving way to the sun's harsh rays. Max walked around the headstones in this secret graveyard where no one ever came to pay their respects. Here lay those who had escaped the hunters the world sent for them. What they had done could never be excused, but Max wondered how they felt, dying in a jungle so far from their homes.

"Over here!" said Katya.

He followed her and Tania, and a very short-of-breath Jake appeared alongside the other men. His face and hair were dripping wet, and his shirt was clinging to his body. He raised a hand in Max's direction as he hyperventilated. Then he entered the graveyard, and crouched down to inspect each of the headstones. "Reinhard Benchell," he said, reading a faded inscription. He couldn't hide his swell of emotion. "There's one here for Gehlen, too! 'Died August 19, 1978'," he read, tracing the epitaph with a finger. "That's thirty-six years ago."

"So, they did die," said Katya. "And past the age of 80. They lived for a relatively long time."

"Then explain that hand. The fingerprints and DNA were a match. How could it have belonged to anyone but Gehlen himself?"

"It was a clone. They were making clones here. There's no other explanation."

"Clones, in the '70s? They hadn't even analyzed the human genome yet."

"What other explanation could there be? Granted, back then they . . ."

Katya stopped there. She just couldn't account for it, and neither could Max. He was confused. *Calm down. Something must have happened. There must be a scientific explanation. There must be an explanation that makes sense,* Max repeated in his head.

"We know for sure they were doing genetics research."

"That equipment made that crystal clear," Katya said.

"Someone must have continued their research and used the left-behind DNA of Benchell and Gehlen to make their clones."

Katya didn't reply. Max hadn't said it because he thought it was true. He just couldn't think of another plausible scenario.

Jake took pictures of each decaying headstone with his video camera, and his assistants copied their inscriptions. Max and Katya walked between them as they read the inscriptions. Max froze in front of one headstone in particular. "Dr. Otto Gerhard."

Katya stared at Max.

"He was said to be Dr. Mengele's right hand."

"That Nazi scientist? The one they called the Angel of Death?"

Max nodded.

"Looks like he came here, too. And then he died."

Jake joined up with them. He was pale. "They're all dead. There are forty-eight graves. Thirty-four of the war criminals we've been hunting are buried here," he said.

"For all we know, those tombstones could be fakes," Max said. "It was you guys who doubted Hitler's corpse was real. You're not going to dig them up and examine them?"

"We'll start tomorrow," Jake replied. "We'll examine their bones, their teeth, what they were buried with, and if we can, their DNA. We'd like you to lend us a hand, Professor."

Katya stared intently at the headstones. The sun was soon blocked by the trees, and the air was turning cool while silence fell. The jungle's nighttime transformation had begun.

"Let's wrap it up for today," came Bocaiúva's deep voice.

After dinner they had nothing to do but think. They were all still in shock over their discoveries that day.

Max went outside. The village was quiet, the villagers were already asleep. He heard the occasional cries of the birds and beasts as they tried to intimidate each other. He sat on a log in front of the hut. The moon was shining in the center of the sky, which was filled with stars. Just the moonlight alone was surprisingly bright.

"This night sky is too beautiful to miss by sleeping." He turned around, to find Katya standing there. "But the mosquitoes will eat you alive by morning," she added as she sprayed him with insect repellent.

The chemical smell spread through the air. One spray was enough to fell quite a few bugs. She sprayed Max's whole body before sitting down next to him. "It's so quiet. Almost as though no one's here."

"When the sun goes down, we sleep, and when the sun rises, we wake up. People are a part of nature, and everything we do falls in sync with its flow."

"Life is supposed to be that way. But we're running against that. We're trying to take advantage of all twenty-four hours in the day. And that definitely comes back to bite us one way or another."

"We have been culled by natural selection and evolved, all within the bounds of nature."

"If Darwin knew what we get up to today, he'd be shocked. The theory of evolution itself has changed. Natural selection no longer applies to humans."

"That just means a new theory of evolution will rise to take the place of the old."

"A body that can withstand chemical substances," Katya said, "a stress-free psyche, a giant braincase of a head, and barely functional arms and legs. That's where we're headed. And we could live longer if we got rid of our emotions. Soon we won't even need reproductive organs, or gender differences. We'll have virtual sex and create offspring from clones. The brain will be everything. Just thinking about it makes me shudder."

"But in the larger cosmos, that doesn't matter. In the eyes of the universe, we might just be some accident of nature born in a far-flung corner—just a little dust and nothing more."

"Even beings made of dust have a right to exist. You don't know what it's like to be insignificant, Professor. You've always basked in the brightness of the sun."

Max laughed at Katya's words. "Your career is nothing to sneeze at, either. You've written quite a few papers already. When I was your age, I hadn't published a third of what you have."

"But when you were my age, everyone in the world of science already knew your name. The quality of work isn't measured only in the number of papers. Your discoveries are featured in textbooks. Those who aspire to life science read your papers and follow the path you walked."

"But does any of that matter?"

"It's important," she said with conviction. "I said you were chosen by God when those thugs attacked us in Germany. You got angry."

"I wasn't angry."

"Don't lie. I think you were."

"Why did you come to this jungle? Don't say it was because I asked."

"It interested me. One can't do much in a lab alone." Katya thought silently for a while. "The truth is," she added, "I was interested in the actions you take. Something of tremendous significance must be behind the actions of a man with a track record as impressive as yours— something someone like me can't fathom. Why did you come all the way out here, Professor? And please don't say it just interested you."

"It's getting chilly out there," he said, ignoring her words as he zipped up his sweatshirt. "But there are still plenty of mosquitoes and blackflies around."

"Okay. I get it. I'm an assistant who forced you to hire me. I won't ask any more." Katya shivered and leaned toward Max. "Now I know the Amazon gets cold, even though it's near the Equator."

"You should thank your roommate. We were close to freezing to death in the rainforest." She'd brought a thick sweatshirt because of his advice.

"Former roommate. Now he's just a friend," she said, with a hint of sadness. "Can I ask you a question?"

"Is this picking up where you left off last night?"

"Will you ever get married?"

"Do you think I have that kind of time?"

"Time has nothing to do with it."

"Time is an important factor. People live on borrowed time."

The two silently gazed at the sky for a while. Max felt the warmth of Katya's soft skin.

"You're thinking about that laboratory, aren't you?" asked Katya.

"What were the Nazis doing there?" Max said.

"Viruses, biological weapons, iron-bar cells, operating tables with leather belts—it's scary to think about, but the villagers don't seem scared. They seem indifferent."

"Maybe they've forgotten the horrors. The research building was used more than twenty years ago, but when I try to imagine the research Dr. Gerhard was doing there—" Max swallowed his words, hesitant to say more.

"There were four operating tables," said Katya. "And an examination table with stirrups."

"Did they do the same thing they did in Auschwitz?"

"Human experimentation . . ."

Max thought about what Feldman told him about Simon and his twin sister, as well as Feldman's neck scar and missing fingertip.

The Nazis were merciless even toward women and children. "The Nazi doctor Mengele was said to have made soap using the fat of slaughtered Jews, and lamp shades from human skin."

"Some of the equipment we found had to do with biological experiments, and at the cellular level."

"Bacterial or viral cultures. They could make biological weapons and infect people. Was the dry black lump in the jar once part of someone's body?"

It suddenly grew dark. The moon was gone. Raindrops pelted them, and they hurried back into the hut. The snoring from the hammocks that were lined up in the dark was as loud as the pouring rain. Max got into his hammock. The rain pounded violently on the roof. Max closed his eyes and listened.

The next morning, Max called out to Jake, who was about to go back to the graves. "I want to collect blood samples from the villagers."

"I don't think that's in the cards," he replied, staring at him like that was obvious. "Are you just going to say 'give me your blood'? They'll think we are some kind of vampires from hell. They might shoot us with poison darts and burn us alive. And right after we established friendly relations, too. So please, Professor, don't ruin our historic discovery by causing trouble."

"They just need to be shown respect and gratitude."

Max surveyed their food piled up in the corner of the hut. Most of their rations were meals like noodles, soup, and vegetables, but there were also cans of corned beef and meats. There were also snacks like chocolates and cookies.

"Don't push our luck. We have enough food to last six people for five days. Taking into account the way back, we're close to running out as it is. Besides, I don't think that's going to work on them."

"We won't know until we try. Didn't Feldman tell you to 'accommodate me to the greatest extent'?" Max took a few cans of corned beef and some chocolate from a box.

"Are you planning to trek through the jungle without anything to eat on our way back?"

"I can eat fish, birds, insects, the same things they eat. And if that bothers you, I'll just become a vegetarian."

"I can't say I like either idea."

"Just think, if we do things my way, we might actually find what we're looking for."

"We've already found what we were looking for. Now we can finally free ourselves from the nightmare of the twentieth century."

"But we still need to do this, just to make sure."

Max stared at Jake until he gave in, sighing, as he looked up at the ceiling.

"I'll let you give away half of it. If it all disappears, we'll have a mutiny on our hands. I'm already dieting enough," he added before going back outside.

Max also left the hut.

"Professor!" Katya was sitting on a log in front of the hut, Tania beside her. "Tania's the village chief's daughter. She and Davi live together, just the two of them."

"Are you sure she's not his granddaughter? Davi's over seventy years old. Or do you mean to say . . ." He didn't want to entertain the thought that the two were married.

"She calls Davi 'Vater.'"

"So she does speak German?"

"Just that one word. I don't think it's her native language."

Max looked at Tania and had a thought. "Could we maybe take a sample of her blood?"

"You want to take samples from the kids first? Not sure I agree."

Katya shrugged and turned to face her. Then she crouched down and gripped her little hands. "We don't want to hurt you. We just want your help."

Tania stared at Katya with quizzical eyes. In the meantime, more children had formed a circle around the three.

"We'll only be taking a tiny little bit of your blood. And it won't hurt, promise. I always disinfect, and I never use the same needle. You will be helping science." She stretched out her arms and faced the other children. A desperate gambit.

The kids whispered and sniggered among each other. Tania got to her feet and headed for the hut.

"It's no use. They don't understand us."

"It's not like you to give up so easily. Put yourself in their place. How would you feel if a stranger popped up out of nowhere asking for your blood?"

"I wouldn't be thrilled about it."

"I'd think an evil spirit was coming for me. And I'd try to drive it off. We need a quicker, easier—"

"Say no more. These people are plain and unaffected. I especially like the children. The kids in America and Germany try to act all mature. The kids here are a million times more natural and human, chasing after mice and climbing up hundred-foot-tall trees without a care in the world."

"That's just another way to be."

The kids were kicking up a commotion, pointing at Katya and talking. Tania approached her with a coconut-half container.

"What's this?" Katya squatted down next to her.

The coconut half contained a red liquid. It was the crushed fruits of some tree. Tania put a finger in the liquid and drew a line on Katya's forehead. The other kids cheered joyfully.

"What is this?" Katya took a mirror out of her bag, and almost shrieked.

Tania also applied the red liquid to her own forehead. Each of the kids took turns dipping their fingers, tracing some pattern on Katya's head, and then tracing it on their own. At some point, the women from the village also gathered around.

"You've finally been recognized by your comrades. You are the kids' boss now," said Max, stifling a laugh.

"But—"

"This must be a ritual among the children. I'm sure it washes right off."

"That's not the issue," she said, on the verge of tears.

The women surrounding them were also laughing.

With Katya's help, Max began collecting blood from the villagers, giving them food and chocolate in exchange. At the same time, they conducted interviews. They asked for their names by pointing at themselves, saying their own names, and then pointing at them. Katya jotted down their approximate ages, heights, weights, and physical characteristics. Surprisingly, they didn't object to the shots. Each silently offered their arm and watched as the needle punctured their skin and drew their blood. Perhaps this was not their first time. He asked a mother with her child if she had ever seen a syringe, but she just stared at the needle tip expressionlessly. Blood collection proceeded more smoothly than expected, and by evening they'd been able to take blood samples of around half of the population.

"Analyzing the blood of fifty-seven people here is going to be impossible," Katya said, as she sorted the samples and data.

"Just collecting the samples is enough for now. We'll analyze them when we get back." Max was peering into a microscope.

"The interviews are the real problem. Davi can't be the only German-speaker, can he?"

"They're being modest. They won't flaunt their education. That's how they've been able to live here undisturbed all this time."

"Please don't make fun, Professor. I'm being serious."

"We could always learn their language, you know."

"I'm tired. Opening cans is hard labor."

"Even if that's all we'll learn through this, that alone's a considerable find."

"They're really eating the stuff with relish. I feel warm and fuzzy inside just watching," she said, as she observed a bunch of villagers gathering in a corner of the village, eating chocolate and cans of corned beef.

"A unique combination, to be sure, but it looks like those flavors aren't unfamiliar to them."

"You're saying they've had whatever food the Nazis gave them."

Max nodded silently.

Jake's group returned. His assistants were each carrying a full bag.

"These are the pairs of glasses, teeth, and uniform scraps of thirty-two people. We also found notebooks and photos. But they're all very old. Some fall apart at the touch. Grave robbing is not easy."

"What about Benchell and Gehlen's personal belongings?"

"All we found was their skeletons with their uniforms on, and they were deteriorated. Maybe because of the humidity?"

"And the teeth?"

"Care to see?" He took a smaller bag from the big bag and shook it in front of Max.

"Unfortunately, I'm not a dentist."

"We'll be finished robbing their graves in two days."

"Will you be able to finally settle the score that way?"

"I hope so, Professor," Jake said with a fatigued look, peering down at the bag full of teeth. His expression radiated equal parts relief and anxiety.

The next day, while Jake's group was out exhuming, they continued their blood sample collection and interviews with the villagers. The interviews didn't go all that smoothly. For one, nobody knew their date of birth. There were no calendars in the village, and no paper. They had to rely on their own judgment.

They woke up at sunrise and went to sleep at sunset. The women prepared the meals and dug up potatoes in the fields. Women also extracted starch from the potatoes. The men went hunting in groups with bows and blowpipes, but all they'd managed to bring back in three days was a single spider monkey.

The village was isolated from civilization. It made sense for the remnants of the Nazis to flee to such a place, and yet at the same time, they couldn't help but wonder why.

That evening, Max sat on the log in front of the hut, looking at the village. Katya was beside him. When the sun went down, the light disappeared quickly, as the village was surrounded by trees. Scant light shone through the dense canopy onto the clearing.

"They're tough customers," said Katya, watching the villagers who continued about their lives as if nothing had happened. "There are obviously people who understand German besides just Davi. Like the older men. The younger women seem to speak it, too, but they pretend they don't for some reason. What can they possibly be thinking?"

"I don't think they're hiding it. I think they just don't want to get involved."

"In any case, they must have learned German from the Nazis. Maybe Tania too."

None of them mentioned the arrival of the Nazis in the village. Mentioning Dona and Gehlen's names did nothing but elicit suspicious looks. And yet there were traces of Nazi activity here.

"Have you noticed the number of kids is increasing?"

"They must've come out from hiding."

At first there were only a few children in sight, but now there were more than ten.

"We're going about this all wrong. Drawing them in with food is basically bartering in blood. And all we're giving them is a can of corned beef and a piece of chocolate. We're swindling them."

"Is there any other way?"

"If we took the time to persuade them, I'm sure we'd get through to them."

"We haven't got that kind of time."

"What's the point of doing this? The Nazi war criminals we were looking for are already dead. Is it our job to collect blood from the villagers?" Katya slammed her interview notebook on her lap.

"They're rustic, innocent, and not poisoned by civilized society. But I barely even know their names. No one knows their date of birth. They don't even know what day it is today, because they have no need to," Katya said. "Benchell, Gehlen, the owner of that hand. Their clones may be physically identical, but that doesn't mean their minds are identical. I think it's unreasonable to punish them even if they are former Nazis. It wasn't the clones that committed those crimes. What is the point of examining the villagers? You could examine the lab building in the same amount of time and get a hundred times more to go off of."

Katya took a breath. "Your eyes are bloodshot. You woke up in the middle of the night and looked into the microscope all through the night, didn't you?" She was glaring at him. "You're looking for something. Please tell me what it is. I can tell by looking at you that you're hiding something. That you're suffering alone. It's only been a short time since I met you but I came all the way out here with you. It's time you put some faith in me."

Max gently averted his eyes. "Even I'm not sure what will come of this."

"But you do have an idea. Otherwise, I . . ." Sweat coated Katya's forehead.

"Ninety-nine percent of research is monotonous and boring. Everyone dreams of the remaining one percent, but the majority never get there."

"What are you looking for, Professor? Please tell me that much."

"I want you to wait a little longer."

Max stood up and turned to the forest surrounding the village. The silhouettes of the trees floated in the now colorless air.

What I'm looking for—I know full well what that is. And at last, I'm beginning to see a small light at the end of the tunnel. But that light felt so fragile, he was scared speaking it aloud would cause it to vanish.

"It's quiet. It's like being taken into the forest." Katya sighed. The sun had set, and there were no people in the clearing. All sound disappeared, and the silence pressed in from the wild. The huts were lined up in their modest rows, and inside people were doing what they had done for thousands of years, and were now trying to fall asleep.

"People have lived this way since ancient times. This may be what we are all meant to be like."

"Their lifestyle is too far removed from mine," Katya said.

The sky was as black as ink. The stars were shining as if someone had tossed a handful of golden sand into the heavens.

"It's strange, if you think about it," she continued. "Civilization is just around the corner. Satellites are taking pictures, and radio waves are zipping by from all over the world. Why don't they adopt civilization? They could go into town if they wanted to."

"They've lived this way for hundreds, no, thousands of years. Just as Inuit are no longer Inuit when they abandon hunting, they would lose their identities if they were to leave this place. They can only live here. Just like the Nazis, who couldn't live outside of civilization, met their ends here."

Max thought again of the grass-covered tombstones. He felt a heavy leaden mass inside, which swelled and spread throughout his body.

"What's wrong?" said Katya, puzzled.

"Jake and the rest ought to be back soon. As representatives of civilization, they've been out working this whole time. Let's prepare them some food."

Max went up the stairs. Katya was about to say something, but decided against it and came to Max's side instead.

CHAPTER 12

When he woke up the next morning, people were gathering in the clearing. Max stood in front of the hut. "What's going on?" he asked Bocaiúva, who was watching the villagers.

"The soothsayer is performing his prayers." Bocaiúva looked at one of the huts. Dozens of villagers were sitting in front of it, and a monotonous sound similar to a beast's roar could be heard from inside. "Davi's daughter appears to be ill."

Villagers entered the hut by turns. As Max approached, the villagers who had gathered split off to the sides to open the way. There were so many in the hut it was almost overflowing. Tania lay in the center of the dimly lit dwelling, and Davi traced lines across Tania's body with feathers in red, yellow, and blue.

"He's also the medicine man," Bocaiúva whispered from behind. Next to him, Katya was listening.

"Let me examine her."

Davi stopped and turned to face Max. Max pushed his way through the villagers to Tania, and Katya followed him. He knelt in front of Tania, took her pulse and palpated. Then he took out a penlight to examine her pupillary light reflex. Tania curled up and groaned.

"What are the symptoms?"

"She says her stomach's been upset for two days. Last night, she had a fever and nausea."

Max recalled when they first met Tania in the jungle. She didn't appear to be suffering at all. Tania's face contorted when her abdomen was pressed; it hurt.

"It's appendicitis. There's a chance she has peritonitis, and it's also possible that her inflamed appendix ruptured. She needs surgery, and fast," he told Katya behind him.

"Surgery is impossible here," Katya said. "It's dim and far from sterilized, to say nothing of the heat and humidity. It would be infection central. And we have no surgical tools anyway."

"I know." Max injected painkillers and instructed the villagers to cool her abdomen before going outside. When they returned to the hut, Jake and his assistants looked at Max with anxious faces. Max didn't know what to say.

"Are you a doctor?" came a sudden voice. Max looked in its direction, and there stood Davi.

Max nodded.

"Do the surgery." His gravitas as village chief had given way to naked pleading and fear of the creeping shadow threatening to take his daughter away from him. Max explained that surgery would be difficult under the conditions.

Davi was listening silently. Surprisingly, he understood what Max had told him. He opened his mouth as if to say something, but instead he left the hut. Max took out his medical bag and examined the equipment. It wasn't usually a difficult operation, but it was still impossible to operate in the hut.

"Professor, you can't be serious. If she has peritonitis, she'll need an extensive laparotomy. And we don't have the surgical tools."

Max arranged his surgical tools on a vinyl sheet laid on the floor. "Do you carry these with you everywhere you go?" asked Katya, stunned .

"Not always. But it sure is lucky I happened to this time."

"Do you have a lot of experience as a clinician?"

"Only about a year's worth, after I graduated. Beyond that, I just learned by imitating."

"It's too dangerous. If Tania were to die, then—"

"Davi understands the meaning of surgery. Including the dangers. Yet he asked me to do it anyway."

"We don't have enough gauze or bandages, and we don't have rubbing alcohol or distilled water. How do we anesthetize her?"

"If we leave her like this, she'll die for sure."

"But if she dies during surgery?"

"We'll use the operating table in the lab building. Go get people to clean it. Rinse the floor and walls with water and disinfect the operating table with boiling water."

"That horrid, filth-ridden place? We don't have enough surgical tools."

"No, but we have an excellent surgeon and assistant." Max turned to Katya.

"The assistant for this appendectomy has only done it once."

"This will be your second."

"What do you do about the anesthesia? The morphine we have won't cut it. Wait, you don't mean for us to use the lab building's . . ."

"It's worth checking out."

"They're past their expiration dates."

"The inflammation is widespread. At this rate, there's no telling what shape she'll be in tomorrow. You know that," Max said.

"I'll help. Give me your orders." Bocaiúva was standing at the entrance of the hut. From behind him, children were peering inside.

"We'll help, too." Jake and his assistants offered. Katya sighed and stood up with the surgical tools.

"Everyone, hurry up!" she said, leading the group out of the hut.

"Get as many people as you can to bring the water to the lab building. Then make a stretcher to carry the girl," Max told Jake, who had been about to follow Katya. Then Max headed for Davi's hut. An hour later, Jake and Bocaiúva came with the villagers holding a makeshift stretcher composed of a hammock stretched over two logs. Tania was on the stretcher, carried by the villagers. Tania's forehead was drenched with sweat, and she was gritting her teeth. She must have been in blinding pain, but she didn't let a single moan escape her lips. Children with worried faces followed the group.

The operating table had been cleaned and covered with vinyl sheets, made from cutting up the tarps they'd brought in place of tents. In a corner of the room, hot water was boiling on a stove. The surgical tools were disinfected with the boiling water and placed on the operating table. Suddenly, the table became brighter.

"What's this?"

"A substitute for surgical lights," Katya said, adjusting the light. She had attached a battery-powered lamp to a rusty stand and made a reflector from aluminum foil.

"It seems I've got a magician for an assistant."

"I'm good with my hands. And I have many other special skills besides. I'll show them to you soon."

"Is humility one of them?"

"Isn't it more attractive when women keep some things to themselves?"

"You're more than attractive enough as you are."

They all left the room except Bocaiúva and Davi. Bocaiúva was standing in front of the door with his arms crossed, watching over the room. Davi sat in a corner, closed his eyes, and muttered something.

"It's just not usable." Katya held up a morphine ampoule, which she had taken out of the storage case. The otherwise clear liquid was a little turbid.

"We've got no choice but to use whatever morphine we've on hand," said Max, who was not shocked by this turn of events.

"It's just not enough."

"Use this." Davi handed them a wooden tube. As soon as she removed the stopper, Katya frowned. It gave off a strong pungent odor and contained brown liquid.

"If she drinks this, she will stay asleep."

"What we don't know about could be dangerous," Katya whispered in Max's ear.

"It must be a soporific drug, that's all."

"If there are side effects—"

"Do you want me to perform a laparotomy without anesthesia?"

Tania's eyes squinted open, and she stared at them. She had to be in agony, but she didn't make a sound or shed a single tear. Max poured the liquid into Tania's mouth. Tania's eyes darted as though searching for something, but soon her eyes closed.

"What about her pulse and breathing?"

"They're on the low side, but it's okay. She doesn't seem to be conscious."

Katya looked into her eyes with a penlight.

"Starting surgery." Max took a scalpel.

"We can't make distilled water, so I boiled water and filtered it through gauze." Katya disinfected the girl's abdomen with alcohol.

"Actually," Max said as he took the scalpel to Tania's abdomen, "this is my second-ever peritonitis surgery, too." Max carefully carried the scalpel forward. "I've formed a gene therapy team with a medical faculty professor."

"I heard you don't do clinical work."

"I received a letter that said that if I couldn't save him, the whole world would reel from the loss. And that if I could save him, I'd have the right to ask him for anything."

"Was this letter from some country's president, or a sultan or something?"

"It was from a spoiled brat from New York."

"Did you save him?"

"He's physically well, but that mind of his is beyond my control."

Tania's blood had pus in it. The purulent appendix had ruptured, causing complete peritonitis.

"This is pretty bad," said Max. He tried to wipe it off with gauze, but blood and pus spread throughout her abdomen.

Katya handed him a tube. "I'll suck it out."

Max turned his eyes to Katya. He saw her give a nod, and inserted the tip of the tube into Tania's abdomen. Katya sucked out the blood and pus. Davi's deep-voiced incantation filled the room.

The operation was over in about two hours.

"Disinfect your mouth immediately."

"The alcohol's all gone."

Bocaiúva came to the rescue with a small flask he drank from occasionally. "A drink for the heroes. Drink it all!"

When Katya gargled, the smell of whiskey spread throughout the room. "If I ever need surgery in the future, I'm going to ask you to do it," she said cheerfully, her voice high-pitched with excitement and nervous tension. "You're incredible."

"And I'd like you to operate on me. And I'm not just flattering you, I mean it." Max took the flask from Katya and took a sip.

"Professor, you have a wonderful smile."

With the help of Jake and the others, Tania was moved to a bed brought in from the building next door. Tania slept quietly, her expression calm and peaceful. Her pulse and breathing were normal.

"She'll wake up tomorrow morning. She just needs to rest a while," Max told Davi, who was anxiously standing beside the bed, looking at Tania.

"I want to take her home. Evil spirits live here." Davi looked around the room. His prior calm disappeared, and he was clearly frightened. "The spirits will get her!" he said, his voice shaking as he touched the bed.

"Stop! Do you want to kill her?" Katya grabbed Davi's arm and took it off the bed. He was terrified. They could hear voices outside the building.

"The villagers are upset. They want to take her home," Bocaiúva said as he walked into the room.

Max gave it some thought. "We have no choice but to let her sleep here all day today. Don't worry, I'll be here with her. Tell them that I'll take her back to the village tomorrow if she's up for it."

"But, Professor . . ."

Max shot Katya a glance: *Don't say a word.*

Davi returned to the village with the villagers, mumbling incantations under his breath.

Max and Katya stayed with Tania all night. The lamp dimly lit Tania's face. "She's a pretty girl," Katya whispered. She had deep-set eyes and a straight nose. Her skin was tanned by the sun, but without that tan, it was probably closer to white than brown.

"She's got Caucasian blood in her," said Max, who was cleaning the surgical tools. "She's an enigma. I think I see a little Asian in her, too."

Katya looked at Max and Tania in turn.

"That's just being human. If you trace the origins of humanity, the closest common female ancestor of modern humans was 'Mitochondrial Eve,' one hundred sixty thousand years ago. Different races, same origins, same genes."

"When it comes to anthropology, I'm not quite up to speed."

"I don't like that stubborn and sarcastic streak of yours, Professor," Katya said as she gazed at Tania's face. "I read *The Origin of Life* when I was in college. I didn't quite understand it, but I got the sense it was more a book full of love and compassion for human beings rather than a science book. The mysteries of life, the beauty of humanity—I felt the vastness of the universe. Life, people, the cosmos, everyone is connected in one big circle. And then there's the meaning of life. I interpreted your book as a poem praising everything in the world. I saw your picture on the back of the book and thought to myself, so that's the person who wrote this book. That's why," Katya looked up and stared at Max, "that's why I was surprised when you said you don't believe in God. I thought that you had a great affinity for the spiritual."

Max said nothing as he cleaned the surgical tools. Katya watched Tania for a while and then got into a hammock prepared by Bocaiúva. Max lay down in a sleeping bag next to the bed.

The moonlight shone through the hole in the ceiling. Max couldn't believe he was in a Nazi operating room. He was overcome with fatigue. He tried to think about the future. He tried to focus his thoughts, but couldn't. The fatigue was always there to sweep away his consciousness like a quiet wave.

He woke up to a faint noise. He opened his eyes and saw a black shadow staring at him. He smelled sweat and felt warm breath on his face, but he didn't dislike it. They had a delightful sweetness to them that shook loose what had been sealed in his body.

"You're . . ."

Soft lips silenced that sentence. Time stopped and all the voices of the forest disappeared. The room was still and silent. The shadow's lips slowly pulled away as though waiting for Max to take the next step, and she put her cheek to his. Seconds passed.

"I must be dreaming." Max gently pushed the shadow away. Now wasn't the time.

The shadow stared at Max for a long time, then returned to the hammock in resignation. Max closed his eyes. He felt relaxed and satisfied. It had been decades since he felt this relieved. Eventually, he was pulled into a peaceful sleep.

"Professor!"

He jumped at Katya's subdued voice. The sun hadn't risen yet, and the room was dim.

Katya hung over Tania. Max pushed Katya away and put his hand on Tania's neck. Her pulse was powerful.

"What is this?" Katya looked surprised.

Tania opened her eyes. She looked quizzically at Max, but soon saw Katya and smiled.

"Her resilience is awe-inspiring," Max said quietly. He took off the gauze and saw the wound was already covered with thin skin. By the time the sun rose, the anesthesia had worn off, and she was conscious. Tania smiled, and when Katya gripped her hand, she gripped back. She looked meaningfully at Katya. Perhaps Tania knew it was Katya who had sucked away the blood and pus.

Katya's eyes met Max's for a moment. She seemed sad, but then she seemed cheerful, as if nothing had happened. Max began to think that what happened last night was just a dream. He was sure of it.

That evening they brought Tania to the hut. People from all over the village came to carry the stretcher.

The whole village celebrated that night. Villagers gathered in a hut that was their version of an assembly hall, and talked and ate. Max, Katya, and the others were invited as guests. Children came over to touch them and put their hands under their shirts. The hut was full of laughter.

When their dinner was taken out of the pot, Katya shrieked—it was a boiled monkey, served shaved and whole. It was purplish-red and puffy, and it was steaming. The villagers picked it apart. Arms, legs, torso—they cut off the meat and ate their fill.

"We've been recognized as allies and companions," Max told Katya, who'd turned away and closed her eyes. "They're treating us to a feast, and to their best hospitality. It'd be rude not to eat it. It's really no different from steamed turkey or steak."

"I'm happy just appreciating the thought behind it. I'm already full."

"Once, at a Japanese restaurant, I ate some live shrimp. It was still moving in my mouth, but I bit into it anyway. I also had sashimi with the heads still attached. It was twitching even after getting sliced."

"Stop! If you say any more, I'll vomit right here. As a doctor, you should know how the body reacts to that kind of thing." Katya had turned pale.

"Well, I think we shouldn't snub their act of good will."

"I'm fine with just this," she said, sipping from the soup that one of the children brought her.

"Is that soup Chinese food to you?" Max pointed at the children with his eyes; the capybara's head was in their midst. A red scarf was wrapped around it.

"For them, death is nothing special. It's just a necessary step to nurture the lives to come."

"I don't regret what I did. I just did what needed to be done," she murmured as she stared at the oily liquid.

Davi offered him a coconut-shell cup. The cloudy liquid inside gave off a strong odor.

"It's fermented nuts." Max brought it to Katya's nose.

"I'll pass." She turned away, not even looking at it.

Max drank it all up in one go. "If this were served in a crystal glass, this would be thought of as three-star cuisine."

Davi was looking on happily.

"I definitely want to know how to make it," said Max.

"You don't know? They ferment the nuts. Using saliva," she said, frowning. "So says my former housemate."

Max choked a little.

The banquet lasted until midnight. Max returned to the hut and sat on the log. He was so exhausted, he felt like he could melt into it. Light was still glowing from the assembly hut. Katya sat down next to Max, holding a coffee cup in each hand; Max took one. The smell was comforting.

Max took a sip. "Noticed anything about the villagers?"

"There are few girls. The ratio of boys to girls is seven to one, out of fourteen kids. Not a big enough sample size, but it's certainly odd."

"And yet when it comes to the adults, there are overwhelmingly more women than men. The older the age group, the more the ratio skews female."

"Maybe something happened to this village in the last few decades? A war? Maybe the adult men died. And the girls died as babies or in their teens? Either that, or . . ." Katya paused for a few seconds. "Maybe the girls didn't die. Maybe they were taken."

Max recalled the operating room and the cells in the lab building.

"But Jake said all the tombs belonged to Nazi soldiers and German civilians. No Indigenous people."

"Couldn't that be for religious reasons? The villagers' graves may be elsewhere."

They heard footsteps, and when they looked up, a shadow was looking down at them. Max hugged Katya, who was about to scream. The short man who looked like a dignified statue against the jungle backdrop was none other than Davi. He sat down between Max and Katya. He had a faintly sweet scent about him, and it wasn't booze. Max had smelled that smell before somewhere.

"A long time ago," began Davi, "when I was younger than the girl you saved, many white men came, and made the brown men carry their bags."

"Dona told us about them, remember?" said Katya.

"The white men asked our fathers whether we would fight or obey. If we obeyed, they wouldn't harm us. Our fathers talked among each other and concluded the white men were too strong to fight. They had sticks that could shoot fire and weapons that could blow away our homes. The villagers chose to obey to survive." Davi sighed deeply. "The men took villagers to the forest, where they ordered them to cut down trees and mow the grass. Our fathers cut down the trees and cut the grass continually."

"The clearing with those buildings, right?"

"The place was swallowed by the forest, and no longer exists."

"It's the airplane runway. That's the first thing the Nazis had them make."

"On the night of the fifth day of cutting the trees in the forest, our fathers were told to line up trees on the long and wide road that they made and spark a fire. A big metal bird flew down sounding like thunder."

"A plane," said Katya quietly.

"Men dressed in black came out from the belly of the bird. They were allies of the men who had passed through the forest. They ordered us to carry the things that the bird spit out."

"What kind of things?"

"Some were big and some were small. They were in wooden boxes and couldn't be seen."

"And then what?"

"The iron bird came over and over, spitting out men and their things before flying off again." Davi closed his eyes to reach the depths of his memories. "There was a big tattoo on the metal bird's body." He traced it on the ground with the tip of his cane.

"A swastika," Max muttered.

"Many were young men, and friendly. They taught us their words, gave us new food, and healed our injuries and illnesses. They stabbed needles into our arms and cut our stomachs, just like you did."

"That's why you asked me to perform Tania's surgery. You already knew about injections and surgeries."

"They built three buildings using the materials carried in by the steel bird. We helped them, but we were forbidden to approach them once they were built."

"The lab building and the two lodging houses."

"Ever since those buildings were created, villagers went missing. They would come back two or three days later, but without remembering anything."

"Were they anesthetized, I wonder?" Katya turned to Max, who nodded.

"Did all the missing people come back?"

"Most of them came back, but some didn't."

"Were they men or women?"

"Women."

"How old were they?"

"I don't know. Young women. Some children and babies, too." Max said no more.

"Do you now know what they were doing in the lab building?" asked Katya.

"We couldn't get close. When we did, that was what they hated the most. They were kind the rest of the time. Sometimes we were called to help build roads, to draw water from the river, or to carry the things the metal bird spit out. And each time, they . . ." Davi trailed off; he was staring vacantly at the sky. Eventually: "We lived the same way as before."

"Did they ever request anything else of you?" asked Max, but Davi turned his eyes to the jungle and did not answer. Seconds passed.

"We offered up our blood," said Davi undramatically.

"Blood?"

"They used the tools with the needles attached that you use to draw blood."

"So that's why they weren't afraid of injections," Katya said, turning to Max. "They didn't even ask what we were doing, despite us taking their blood. Also, I doubt the Nazis were doing a blood drive."

"Maybe it was a blood drive, only one meant to prolong their own lives," Max muttered.

"There was a homeothermic incubator and a shaker in the lab. They were trying to make some kind of blood serum."

"Probably."

"But to what end? They obviously weren't trying to create a pharmaceutical company."

"It's possible," Max said expressionlessly. "When did they disappear?"

"Dozens of rainy seasons ago. When I was still about the same age as your male companion."

"Jake, he must mean," said Katya. "If Jake's over forty, and Davi's about seventy, then that would make it about thirty years ago. I wasn't born yet."

The old man ruminated for a long time. "Sometimes, even after they left the place, some men would come to the village."

"But it doesn't look like the airfield has been used in a long time," said Katya.

"The bird wasn't as big as the one before. It was like a hummingbird. It descended from the sky."

"A helicopter," said Katya. "Did it come to the village?"

Davi shook his head. "The trees around it are too tall. It's like falling into a hole."

"There was a spot in the middle of the airfield without shrubs," said Katya. "That's where it landed."

"What were they doing here? That lab building hasn't been used for more than a decade."

"They wanted our children—babies born that year." Davi was staring at the dark forest.

"Babies?" asked Katya.

"Yes. It was always babies."

"Boys or girls?"

"At first it was both, but lately, only baby girls."

"'Lately? Are they still coming?"

"They came on the day of the full moon three moons ago."

"Three months ago?" Max exhaled deeply.

"Why just hand them over? Their parents don't resist?"

The old man silently looked up at the sky. Max got the feeling he saw a shadow in his eyes. Katya also noticed it, and turned away from Davi.

"One mother refused. The men brought a drink that night. We drank it. The next morning, the mother and baby were gone."

"They must have spiked it," said Katya.

"What happened to the baby?" asked Max.

"Some have come back. Some haven't. All we can do is pray."

Max's heart started pounding. He took deep breaths to calm down.

"So that's why there weren't any babies when we came," said Katya. "The villagers hid them."

"What else did they do?"

"Gather women and take blood and urine. Whenever they were with child, they examined them using a method we don't know."

"Pregnancy tests."

"The pit of hell sent the Devil's envoys on the full of the moon," Katya muttered.

"More like the Devil himself," said Max.

At that, the three fell silent.

Max's mind was swimming with questions, but they just refused to come out of his mouth. He bit his lips in frustration.

Davi stood up quietly.

"I still have questions."

"I've talked enough."

Max grabbed Davi's arm. His arm was slender and dry. Davi gently slipped from Max's grip and returned to his hut. Max and Katya sat there in silence. The waning gibbous moon illuminated the square.

"So, it's drugs," Max sighed. "The Nazis enslaved the villagers with drugs."

"What makes you think it's drugs?"

"There was an injection mark on his arm. He's not horribly addicted, but he's been hitting it for years. And some of that drug was also in the drink he gave Tania before her surgery."

Katya sighed.

"He's hiding something."

"Dona?"

"Something more substantial."

They sat silently for a long time. The assembly hut's lights were on, but the voices had gone silent. The village was wrapped in a serene hush.

"Feel like digging up some graves?" said Max. "I want to see who was buried in them."

"Nazis, no?" Katya was staring at Max.

"Not the Nazi graves. The villagers'."

"Please don't disturb their graves, Professor."

"I'm going to search for them tomorrow."

"Do you have a place in mind?"

"No, but I think near the river."

"On what basis?"

"The villagers have a special attachment to the forest, the earth, and the water. They don't want to be thirsty in death."

The wind blew in from the forest. Max took a deep breath, and detected a familiar scent. It was what he'd smelled on Davi.

"I'm going to go check on Tania." Max stood up and walked toward Davi's hut.

———

CHAPTER 13

The next morning, Max and Katya went to Davi's hut to see how Tania was doing. When Tania sensed their presence, she opened her eyes. Her wound had almost closed. Her pulse and blood pressure were normal.

"Is this some kind of miracle?" Katya asked. She couldn't hide her surprise. "God has blessed her."

"I told you I don't believe in God."

"We need to examine her blood, her cells—everything."

"But only after she recovers her strength."

Max and Katya went into the woods looking for the villagers' tombs. They asked the villagers where they were, but they all just gave them strange looks.

"I wish they could at least tell us where the graves are."

"Their graveyard is a sacred place. They don't want to tell outsiders about it."

"They must think you'll dig them up, like Jake."

"That is what I'm going to do."

They had to find the graveyard by the end of that day. They were leaving the next morning. They walked along the river for two hours, even though they were afraid to walk through the jungle alone. The towering trees and lush foliage continued in every direction. Mosquitoes and blackflies followed them, and leeches fell on them. Bocaiúva had warned them to watch for vipers.

"They can't be this far away."

"If only that girl were with us." Katya's shirt was sticking to her sweaty body. The rainforest was a maze without a guide. Even if they walked for an hour, they might only travel for less than half a mile.

Max stopped. He picked up on a faint sound through the thick canopy. He looked up, but he couldn't see the sky through the layers upon layers of leaves. The sound passed overhead and disappeared toward the village.

"That was a helicopter, wasn't it?" Katya asked Max. "Is it landing in that airfield? Are they Nazi remnants or friends of Feldman's?"

Max turned back. Katya ran after him. "Professor!"

After about thirty minutes, Katya grabbed Max's shoulder.

They heard gunfire, and not handguns, but the rapid fire of automatic rifles—along with people screaming.

"Hurry!" Max shook off Katya's arm and started running. They could smell something burning, a strong smell. Gasoline, and . . .

Max ran faster. Katya's breathing became labored and she began to lag. The gunfire stopped, but the smell got stronger as they approached the village. Smoke was blowing toward them. Then they heard a helicopter in the air. The whirring rose sharply, before disappearing to the east.

Max stood at the entrance of the village, or rather what used to be the village. The huts had been razed, and their wooden frames were smoldering. Katya reached Max and gasped. Dozens of bodies were stacked up like firewood in the center of the clearing, and a massive fire was issuing black smoke. The stench was horrible. They had been sprinkled with flammable chemicals.

"Genocide," came a quiet voice from behind.

Max turned around, to find Jake with Bocaiúva and the others. His face was stained with soot; his clothes were torn. Dark red smears of blood streaked his face and arms.

"What happened to you?!"

"They attacked out of nowhere," Jake said, stunned. "We were looking at the graves one last time when I heard a helicopter, and I followed the sound to the airfield. It was a UH-1 that landed there—a troop transport chopper the US used in Vietnam. Now South American communist guerrillas are using them. When we arrived, we saw the pilot and a guard with an automatic rifle. Then we heard gunfire from the village, and hurried back to it. Ten or so men gathered the villagers in the center of the clearing, fired their guns and killed. Then they set the huts on fire and threw the corpses into them. We didn't have any weapons. We dashed back into the jungle and hid." Jake's shoulders began to tremble, and he was tearing up.

"The men who came back from hunting are now the bodies burning in the clearing. It all happened so quickly. It took less than thirty minutes."

Max entered the clearing. The flames were getting more and more intense.

"Put out the fire!"

Katya was about to run, but Max held her back.

"Leave it. There's no water and we can't bury them." The flames were spreading over the pile of bodies. He saw black lumps in it, and they looked more like charred dolls than people.

"What about Tania?" Katya asked Jake.

"I don't know. They burned down the huts using something like napalm. They didn't even look inside. They threw the villagers they'd killed into the flames. And then, that girl, she's probably . . ." He turned to the jungle. Smoke was rising above the trees from the lab building. "The buildings were also destroyed and set on fire. They turned everything to ash."

The three stared at the smoke, saying nothing.

"The samples we collected are also in flames," said Jake. "If they had spotted us, we would've been killed, too." He was trembling.

Max turned to the smoldering corpses. He knew there were corpses in the razed huts, too. They were piles of charcoal and ash obscured in plumes of smoke.

Almost an hour later, Jake finally calmed down.

"They were dressed in camo. All of them were men around thirty. They were planning to massacre them all from the very beginning. They didn't even say anything. They just murdered them all in cold blood." Jake was grimacing, and he'd begun to sob.

"Who were they? Do you have any idea?"

"I'd know who they were if they attacked us, but they attacked the villagers." Jake turned his attention to the bodies of the villagers. Their carbonized shapes could be seen through the flames and smoke.

"They were so innocent! I can't believe what I'm seeing! What did these people do to deserve this horror?" Tears streaked Katya's cheeks as she stood still and gazed at the fire. She was staring at a pair of little legs. Bocaiúva pushed them into the flames using a tree branch.

"If they'd known about us, we'd be dead, too," Max said, as he scanned the area. "We need to leave, and fast. We don't know when they'll be back."

"We don't have any food or equipment, Professor. What do you want us to do?"

"Call a chopper. You have a satellite phone, and you know the location of the village. We also know for sure it can be reached by chopper. And I know Feldman's on standby someplace not too far from this corner of the world."

"I don't want to use it if I can avoid it. We don't know who's listening in."

"Then what did you bring it for?"

"As a last-resort trump card."

"Look!" Max shouted, pointing to the pile of still-smoking bodies in the center of the clearing. "Now is the time."

Jake hesitated, then shrugged and called one of his assistants, ordering him to take the satellite phone out of his backpack. The assistant pulled out a laptop-sized bag and assembled an antenna.

"I'm not thrilled about this because I'm sure someone is listening. Both enemies and allies included," said Jake.

Jake was referring to the satellite communication system "Echelon." Five English-speaking countries (including the US, the UK, and Canada) intercept and automatically analyze millions of communications per hour in order to advance their military and economic interests. Did Feldman's organization have any connection to it?

"Beats dying a dog's death in the Amazonian hinterland."

"Mr. Feldman will surely look the other way," Jake said, resignedly.

The assistant put the receiver to his ear and pushed the button. "It's not going through," he said, while adjusting the antenna pointed at the sky. When he switched to speakerphone, they heard a tremendous sound; he hurriedly lowered the volume.

"It's a state-of-the-art device, but you get that sometimes. It has to receive transmissions from satellites that are like little specks flying through space and send radio waves back." The assistant was moving the antenna around, but it wasn't going through.

"Let me do it." Katya pushed the assistant away and sat down in front of the satellite phone. Her face was patchy with tears and dirt. She adjusted the angle of the antenna and worked the buttons and dial with practiced hands. "It's difficult to reach a satellite. But there's a trick to it. It should work now." She gave Jake the receiver.

Jake looked dubious, but he took it and pushed the button. "Well, I'll be damned." He winked at her, turned his back, and started talking into it.

Max went to the remains of the hut where he'd left his luggage. The hut had been burned to the ground, leaving only ash and charred support posts. All the samples they'd collected had been in there. All that remained of them was whatever samples each had packed in their backpacks.

"It's just a lump of metal now." Katya pulled the heat-deformed storage box out of the ashes. She hesitated to open it; it contained the blood of fifty-seven villagers.

"A rescue helicopter will come for us in three hours. Please hurry up and get ready," Jake said. "The village has been destroyed. And a whole race has disappeared from the earth. Which is exactly what the Nazis wanted." Jake's voice was full of anger. Just when the sun was about to go down, they heard the whir of rotors from the south.

• • •

IV

THE SECRET

CHAPTER 14

By the next afternoon, Max and Katya were headed to the US from São Paulo International. Max insisted they go back right away.

As he sat in a first-class seat provided by Feldman, Max read from a newspaper he had bought in the airport. "Colombian left-wing guerrillas crossed the border and slaughtered the inhabitants of an Indigenous Brazilian village. There were no survivors." The attack on the village had made the news, but it was treated as a minor story, to be forgotten in a few days.

"Did Feldman's group feed that information to the press?"

"It was the Nazis that killed them. This article's not worth reading. Feldman's group wants the world to know Nazis are still out there, while the Nazis want everyone to think they're gone. The government says they'll investigate, but doesn't say when. They'll probably never send anyone."

"The media were quick to believe this cover-up."

"Nazis still have power in South America. They fed the story to higher-ups of the government and the media. The world isn't concerned about the death of some Indigenous Amazonians." Max folded up the newspaper and jammed it in the seat pouch in front.

"And Tania died, too . . . ," Katya murmured.

It was evening when they touched down in San Francisco. They rented a car at the airport and headed for Allon, sixty miles east of San Francisco. The city was home to genetics labs and research branches of universities. It had become known as Gene Valley, since Silicon Valley was right next door. It was past six; and the sun was setting when they arrived at the Institute of Genetics, a research facility of the California Institute of Technology.

"There it is." Max pointed ahead with his eyes.

A modern building stood against the sinking sun. At the center of the expansive lawn stood a DNA double helix sculpture, with a stainless steel sign reading California Institute of Technology Genetic Research Laboratory.

"It's the country's top genetic research facility. It's about nine square miles, with three stories and a basement. It has twelve genetics-related laboratories, specializing in things like biochemistry and molecular biology. Two Nobel laureates and three Nobel Prize candidates work there."

"And you're also in the running for the prize!"

"It was built twelve years ago with what was then the latest equipment, but it's already outdated. The usefulness of the P4-level labs has gone down, and the equipment for information processing is outdated, too. The director is trying to get it rebuilt, but I have no idea where its future's headed."

They stopped in front of the main entrance. Two armed guards were sitting in the security room.

"Welcome back, Professor!" said an older security guard as Max stepped outside.

As protocol demanded, Max was asked to show his ID, and the guard called human resources to confirm his identity. It took close to twenty minutes to get clearance.

"I made you a temporary ID. The PIN is the same as before. It will take three days for your assistant's to be ready." The security guard handed him a magnetic card. "You're important, Professor! If anyone else had been gone for a year, it'd take them half a day to pass through. Starting next month, they'll have a new system. You know, the one that scans your eyes." The guard gestured as though looking through binoculars.

They drove through the grounds.

"There are always security guards at the main entrance 24/7, and also at two points in the building. Whenever somebody enters or exits the lab, they need to use their card and PIN, and it's recorded. The alarm system's connected to both the security room and the local police, so if something goes wrong, they'll rush here in minutes."

"I noticed the guards are armed. They're much more serious than at European universities."

"This is the center of genetic science not just in the US but in the world, and it's a treasure trove of genes. Cells from all over the world are collected and frozen, and DNA data is also stored here. It's sort of like the federal bank of pharmaceutical companies."

They drove to the back of the building. There were still dozens of cars in the lot. Max parked far in the back, next to a Mercedes convertible with the top up. He took out his keys, opened the Mercedes door, and loaded his luggage. Katya, holding her backpack, looked on with suspicion.

"It's my car," Max said. "I'm friends with a car nut in the lab; I asked him to keep an eye on it for me, which he agreed to as long as he was allowed to drive it."

The cafeteria was closed, but they bought sandwiches and coffee from a vending machine and headed to the lab. On the way there, ten or so researchers called out to greet Max, hoping to shake his hand.

They entered the building with the card and PIN the guard gave him, and stepped into a space like a hotel lobby. At the center was a reception desk flanked by two guards.

"Assistant Professor Dr. Warren managed the lab while I was gone. I called him last night to tell him I was back. I can use the lab right away."

Max's room was at the back of the first floor. He inserted his card into the door's slit.

"I'm a tenured professor here. That's my official position. But I don't have students. I have no obligation to teach," Max said. "All I have to do is submit a research report twice a year. This year's budget is $2 million. Half a million is provided by the university. The rest comes from foundations and companies. Some is donations, some is collaborative research. Tomes Foundation, the Foundation for the Promotion of Science in California, Magnifique Pharmaceuticals, Unimac Pharmaceutical Company, the list goes on. Their contributions range from ten thousand to hundreds of thousands of dollars— including contributions from Europe and Asia. Your salary also comes from that well of funding."

The room was furnished with a large desk, with a sofa and a table in front of it. The wall on the right had built-in bookshelves. Max put his luggage down, took two lab coats out of a locker, and handed one to Katya.

"Good thing you're the same size as me."

"What are we going to do here, Professor?"

"We came here to do some research, didn't we?"

Holding the cooler box he'd taken out of his backpack, he headed for the experiment room on the same floor. The door had a sign with a strand of DNA, and *Welcome to Our Lab* in fancy cursive underneath. Max inserted the card and opened the door.

Katya stood still at the threshold.

"Researchers here for the first time always freeze at the door," he smiled back at Katya.

"I'm nervous. This is one of the best genetic laboratories in the world."

"It's more a sacred place. The mysteries of life are unraveled here. What is a gene? What is life? What does it mean to be human? When those answers are found, there are more mysteries to solve: Why do humans exist? Where do humans come from and where are they headed? Why are humans human? The meaning behind humanity's existence may finally be discovered."

Max took Katya's hand and brought her inside. Devices were lined up on shelves: carbon dioxide incubators, constant temperature incubators, optical microscopes, electron microscopes, and at the back were two benches.

"Can you use the micromanipulator?"

Katya nodded. The device, used for nucleus replacement and removal, operated extremely thin needles and pipettes while looking at the monitor of an inverted microscope. It was also used to adhere sperm to an egg during artificial insemination.

"Next door's a P3 lab. The P4 lab is on the second floor. But experiments for 90 percent of the things I'm involved in can be done here."

"Are you doing dangerous experiments that would need P4-level safeties?"

P4-level laboratories deal with highly contagious killer microorganisms such as the Ebola virus, the Marburg virus, and the variola virus. P4-level safeties are also necessary when unknown microorganisms might result from genetic modification.

"Nature loves and nurtures us humans, but we are always trying to step out of the pen nature placed us in. When we cross that line, we need protection. That's our responsibility as humans—and the policy of the director, Dr. Tom Owens."

Katya silently scanned the room. Eventually, she turned to Max: "What are you planning to do?"

"A basic experiment any student could do."

"You said the same thing back in Germany when you showed me that hand."

Max took the case out of the freezer box. It contained a reddish frozen scrap of flesh.

"When did you . . . ?"

"These were too good to let them return to the soil of the Amazon."

"It's Tania's appendix, isn't it?" Katya muttered.

"Tania was such an incredible little girl. So, so special. She's Aska!"

"Her? Aska? But everyone called her Tania."

"You saw how fast she healed. I'm sure she was Dona's daughter."

"But the names don't match."

"She was also Gehlen's daughter. Think about it. Nazis value blood purity and claim that the German race is superior. Would he have been allowed to raise a child with the blood of an Indigenous Amazonian? She was probably given to Davi, the village chief, and 'Vater' is what they call whoever raises children. And in return, Davi, he . . ." Max's scowled. The Nazis took advantage of the weaknesses of the human spirit and destroyed souls. "Aska was raised by Davi under the name Tania."

"Why was Dona with Gehlen to begin with? Why did he take Dona as his wife?"

"There was a reason they were together."

"What reason?"

"I don't know yet. I'm trying to figure it out."

"Tania was Aska. And Aska was Dona and Gehlen's daughter —so that's why you wanted to hurry home so fast." Katya stared at the frozen pieces of appendix.

Max nodded, carefully placing the scraps on a glass slide and putting it under the microscope.

"Keep the rest of the cells in saline. I want to check the cell division process, the DNA, everything," Max said, looking into the microscope.

Katya followed Max's instructions.

"I managed to get these here just in time." Max turned on the display screen linked to the microscope.

Dyed cells were projected on the screen. Each one was lively and vigorously pulsating.

"They're normal cells."

"I'd like to split these up."

While paying close attention to sterilization, she created a culture medium and implanted the cells, after which she began detecting the DNA. Meanwhile, Max continued to silently operate the microscope.

"What's in these cells?" she stopped to ask, disgruntled. "What are you looking for? You already know what you expect to find, why won't you tell me? I ran myself ragged and nearly died in that village."

Max didn't react.

"You want me to wait? Fine! I'll wait!" She resumed detecting the DNA.

When they finished setting all the samples, it was past one in the morning. But even that late, they heard voices in the hallway. Some of the rooms were still lit.

They went back to Max's room.

"You look tired," Max said, taking off his lab coat.

Her face was pale, and she had dark circles under her eyes. Her lips were dry and chapped.

"I thought that when we got back from the Amazon, I'd at least get to go home the next day. I didn't expect I'd go straight from the airport to the lab and start the experiment immediately."

"A day later and the cells would've died."

"I'm not complaining. I'm just surprised."

"You can stay at my house tonight." Max stood up with his luggage in his hand.

The Mercedes went down a quiet residential street. On both sides of the wide road, the streetlights cast long palm-tree-shaped shadows.

The car stopped in front of a neatly kept home set atop a hill. They got out of the car and walked toward the house. The landscaped garden was well-lit, and Katya was drawn to the fenced-in pool.

"Is anyone here?" said Katya anxiously.

"It's managed by a security company."

They opened the front door into a sparsely furnished living room. A vase full of flowers was on the table, and that day's newspaper next to it.

Katya came to a stop. "Someone's here . . . a woman."

Max read the card next to the vase. "Welcome home! —Nancy."

"Are there any hotels nearby? Please call me a taxi."

Max gave her a look. "Nancy comes two days a week to clean."

"She's very talented. Look how spotless everything is."

"She likes things neat and clean. It's a hundred times cleaner than I'd have left it."

Max brought Katya to the guest room on the second floor before he went into his study. A pile of mail was on the desk. Once a month his secretary had sorted his mail, and sent what was important to him in Germany. The rest was here waiting for him. He communicated with most friends and business contacts by email, but some snail mail still had to be dealt with.

He sat at the desk and opened some of the letters, but he could feel his energy draining away. He'd been hit by this sinking feeling more and more often. His body would go slack, and he felt if he closed his eyes he could be pulled into a deep sleep—the kind of sleep one didn't wake up from.

He pulled himself together and went back to the letters. An envelope caught his eye. The sender was "California Memorial Hospital." Inside he found a copy of a medical record and a concise letter. He didn't need to read the letter's contents. The salient bit was: "Nothing abnormal detected." But those three words meant that whatever was wrong was getting worse.

He sighed and rubbed between his eyes. During his stay in

Germany, he hadn't gotten any results either. There was some hope left in the Amazonian jungle, but he didn't have much time left. He leaned on his desk and closed his eyes, and exhaustion overcame him. Dark gray clouds gathered in the back of his brain, jamming the gears of his thinking. He knew what it was, but the solution was still shrouded in darkness.

Suddenly, tremors ran all over his body. He wrapped his arms around his torso and tried desperately to endure it, but the shaking didn't stop. He broke out in a cold sweat, and an indescribable fear and loneliness rose up from the depths of his soul. *Someone . . . anyone . . .*

He stood up and staggered out of his study.

The guest room was quiet. Light from outdoors shone through the curtains, and his bed was a silhouette against it. He approached the bed. Katya had her eyes closed but wasn't sleeping. He felt her hot breath. He clenched his trembling fists and stared at her. Unbearable emotions overflowed from deep within him. Fear, loneliness, lust. No, it was a more powerful impulse than that. He craved life itself. There was no way he could stop his emotions.

He hugged her.

"No . . . Stop . . . ," she gasped, turning her face away from him.

Max willed strength into his arms. Katya's body stiffened. Max began unbuttoning her pajamas. Her skin was warm and soft, her body brimming with youth. There was no doubt in his mind—it was pure life energy.

Max hugged her with all his might. Their moist, wet skin touched, and her cells, full of life force, assimilated into his body. Max's tremors gradually disappeared, as if Katya was absorbing them.

The words slipped out of his mouth: "I'm scared . . ."

Katya's body relaxed.

When Max came to, he had his head down on the desk in his study. Bright shafts of light were pushing through the gaps in the curtains.

There was a blanket on his back, and the lights he'd never turned off himself were off. The clock on the wall said eight.

Max heard a knock and his door opened.

Max staggered as he tried to stand. The same oppressive weights were holding his body down from the inside, and he couldn't gather the strength—the usual effect of his seizures. He couldn't remember half of what had happened, and he was still on the border between dreams and reality. But he remembered last night.

"Good morning, Max! Welcome back!"

Seconds after the door of the study opened, he was squeezed tight, his cheek subjected to a rain of kisses.

"Thank you. It's all exactly like I left it a year ago."

"The souvenirs were wonderful, especially the sausage and wine. It arrived two weeks ago." Nancy stopped and looked at him suspiciously, only to break into a big smile. "So, that's how it is." Nancy let go of him and pointed a finger for him to see. Max turned around; Katya was standing at the door.

"You should've let me know in advance! There's so much I need to prepare now. Especially myself, emotionally!" she admonished him, but couldn't hide her joy. "You're so young and pretty!" Nancy wrapped her arm around Katya.

"That's Dr. Katarina Lang. She's a brilliant life scientist with a degree from Stanford. And she's my assistant. I'd like her to stay here until she finds a place to live. Though, of course, that's up to her."

Katya tried to smile, but it was an exceedingly faint smile.

"She's my most formidable rival as well. She is a talented and ambitious scientist who's gunning for a Nobel Prize."

Nancy was visibly unconvinced.

"Could you please make breakfast for us in about ten minutes? The lab is waiting for us!"

"You never change." Nancy smiled back and went to the kitchen.

Katya stood there without saying anything. Max was about

to open his mouth, but didn't. He didn't know what to say, and he knew nothing he said would be right. They were staring at each other silently.

"I . . . you . . ."

Katya looked away and went back to her room. Meanwhile, Nancy could be heard singing in the kitchen.

Max was silent in the driver's seat.

Katya hadn't said a word during breakfast. The false smile she'd shown to Nancy made Max's heart turn to ice. Even after she got in the car, she looked out the window away from Max.

"I'm ashamed of myself," said Max.

Katya said nothing.

"Even if you leave, or you sue me, I won't object. To me, you're—"

"Professor, I . . ." She swallowed her words, and wiped the corners of her eyes with a finger. Then she put that hand out the window to feel the wind.

"I'm a weak man. Sometimes I'm struck by a fear so deep that I can't control myself. When I'm alone, I just endure it. And I've been alone all this time. But last night, I was with you."

"All you did was give me a goodnight kiss. You didn't do anything else." Katya turned to Max. She was trying to smile, but all she did was curve her lips in an odd way.

"Can I take that as a sign of forgiveness? I won't do that ever again—"

"Nancy is a lovely person and a beautiful woman," she said, trying to sound sunny and failing miserably.

"She is an excellent housekeeper."

"How old is she?"

"She says time stopped when she hit 50. That is, when her husband died in a plane crash. Her oldest son, who was 20 at the time, got married, and his kid's going to junior high now. He's a history of science professor at Berkeley. She's also her son's student. She's much more knowledgeable about science than I am. It's been eight years since she started coming to my house."

"That's why she knows all about you."

"She thinks she does. My favorite food, my favorite clothes. What time I get up and what time I go to bed. My habits, my type, but so what? It's impossible to know everything there is to know about someone. I don't even know myself."

"Sometimes there are things others notice about you that you don't see yourself."

"For example?"

"You're ridiculously confident, stubborn, and hard to please. None of which you have any idea about."

Max just kept driving.

"Plus," Katya thought for a while, "you have some kind of major secret."

Max froze for a moment. A Cadillac passed by and honked at him.

"Careful on the road. My life's just beginning." Katya refastened her seat belt.

When they arrived at the lab it was past ten o'clock.

"Let's introduce you to everyone." He took Katya to the cafeteria. Suits, blazers, T-shirts and jeans—there were more than ten scientists, dressed from formal to casual.

Remarks came from every which way.

"Are you single?"

"Any hobbies?"

"Are you interested in making new genes? Can I help you out?"

"I'd like to get to know you."

"She's my assistant. And she's under contract stating she can't accept any other jobs." Max grabbed Katya's arm and left the cafeteria. "Bunch of juvenile idiots . . ."

"They're all world-class researchers. I've read dissertations by nearly all of them." Katya's face was stiff with nervous tension.

"The slogan of the institute is *Enjoy life, for it is both beautiful and short*. And that's a consequence of the genetic information incorporated into the genes of all living things," said Max in order to ease her tension, but Katya's face remained stiff.

"Don't be nervous. Everyone here's just a normal guy."

"If there were drugs that could enhance my scientific talent, I'd take them, even if it ended up shaving years from my life."

Max stopped and stared at Katya. He had a serious look on his face. "Don't even joke about shortening your own life."

"You'll never understand how I feel, Professor."

Max didn't answer and began walking.

When he reached his office, he heard the phone ringing inside. He hurried to pick up, listening silently at first, and then he said, "It shouldn't take that long to decode the DNA. All you've got to do is extract it and run it through the sequencer!" A pause. "Just tell them to hurry up!" He slammed down the receiver.

"That was the lab. It seems the genetic analysis I asked for last night is going to take all day. I should've had you do it."

"You're being awfully pushy, Professor. Almost as though something's standing over you."

"This is just my pace!" he shouted, out of an intense surge of emotion that quickly turned into regret. "I'm sorry I yelled. Sometimes I can't control myself."

"We need to take it easy. It was the same story in Germany and the Amazon. Science isn't going to run away from us."

"But time waits for no man," muttered Max. He put on a lab coat and headed to the lab.

CHAPTER 15

That Saturday afternoon, two days later, Max left home alone. Katya had been out since the morning.

He drove south from San Francisco, pushing down the accelerator until the car reached a cruising speed of 60 mph. He'd been on the road for over an hour when he changed freeways. The Pacific was on his right, and on top of a small hill in front of him, a white building like a pigeon spreading its wings came into view. He exited the freeway and turned onto a road leading to the building.

As he entered the parking lot, he saw a red Toyota climbing the hill in the rearview mirror. He'd noticed it several times. He could see the driver; a woman with a yellow scarf wrapped around her head and dark sunglasses. Her profile looked familiar. Max got out of the car with a bouquet and a small box. He crossed a large, park-like garden toward the building. At the front was a block of granite that read CALIFORNIA MEMORIAL HOSPITAL. He entered and stood behind a tall plant in the corner of the hall. Max's reflection showed in the window. A puffy face from lack of sleep, red swollen eyes, and a tired expression. Anybody would want to look away from a man in that sorry state. After a few minutes, the woman in the yellow scarf strolled in.

Max went to up her. "When did you change jobs to private eye?" he said quietly.

She looked surprised, "I just want to know about you, Professor."

Max felt a deep melancholy. It was different from anger or sadness. It was part despair, part resignation. Max grabbed Katya's arm and quickened his pace. Katya resisted for a moment, but soon relaxed. They crossed the hall to the elevator and went up to the third floor. As they walked down the hallway, the nurses passing by flashed them friendly smiles. Max greeted them; this was a familiar place for him. Katya's face softened.

They stopped in front of a room and opened the door without knocking. It was clean and well-maintained, with a slight disinfectant odor. A man was in a wheelchair in the sun, his back to them. Max approached him and gently put his hand on his shoulder. Then Max turned to Katya, who was standing at the entrance, and motioned for her to come in.

"Don't be afraid to look. He's not shy or ashamed at all." He turned the wheelchair toward Katya. She tried to hide the horror that came over her.

Liver spots on the man's scalp could be seen through his sparse white hair, and his face was creased with deep wrinkles. Tears were leaking out the corners of his eyes, and strings of drool streaked down his chin from his half-open mouth. The arms poking out of his short-sleeved pajamas were bony, and his dry skin was full of blemishes. The ugliness of old age radiated through his flaky, emaciated form. Max stood beside the old man and stared at Katya.

"This is my older brother, Alex."

Katya's expression turned to shock.

"Today's his birthday. He's 44 years old—nine years older than me."

The hollow eyes of a decrepit old man were staring at her. They were a stagnant yellow, and she didn't think he could see. He looked like he could be Max's grandfather at the youngest. "Werner syndrome," Katya murmured.

Werner syndrome begins during puberty or adolescence, and it causes aging to progress more rapidly than normal. Hair falls out and turns gray, and the skin wrinkles and ages. Illnesses associated with old age also appear, such as cataracts, diabetes, and heart disease. It's caused by a genetic defect, and the gene that causes it, the SW gene, was discovered in 1996.

"It's similar to Werner syndrome, but not quite." Max took a tissue from the table and wiped Alex's mouth.

"There are more than a dozen types of progeria, but this one is different. Symptoms suddenly appear after the age of 40. For my brother, they manifested at the age of 42. For my father, it happened at age 43. He committed suicide the following year. I heard that my grandfather was 41 years old. In the first year of the disease, the sufferer ages ten years, twenty more years during the second year, and thirty more years during the third year. The rate of aging accelerates. No one has survived after year three. Brain defects begin within two years of the onset of illness. The progression is slow, but dementia is inevitable," Max told her plainly, as a doctor might describe a patient's clinical condition. Katya's eyes were glued to the wheelchair. "My brother was a talented attorney. He graduated from Berkeley Law School at the top of his class and worked for a law firm in Los Angeles. But now he doesn't even remember his own name, or my face, for that matter." Max put his hand on his brother's white head and looked into his face.

"It's unprecedented in the world. There were some similar cases, but the cause and cure are unknown. What's certain is that it's hereditary and only appears in men over the age of 40. And that they're sure to die within three years."

"Then, Professor, you . . ."

Max nodded. "I'm 35 years and 6 months old. I only have four years and change left before it's my turn."

Katya's face was pale and her fingertips were trembling. "What are the treatment options?"

"It's not looking great. I've scrutinized my brother's genes. But given that it's an unprecedented form of progeria, there's not much to compare them to. I managed to get my hands on my father's and grandfather's genes, as they were born and raised in the US. I traveled to London and several other towns to get my great-grandfather's genes. I wanted to look into my ancestors' medical history. My great-grandfather immigrated to the US from the UK. But I couldn't find his house or any relatives in London, thanks to the Blitz."

Katya looked down. The Blitz ("lightning" in German) was a huge air raid on London by German troops during World War II. Katya looked up and stared at Max with fight in her eyes.

"What are the similarities to Hutchinson-Gilford syndrome, Cockayne syndrome, Down syndrome?"

"We examined all cases of progeria. Each has similarities and differences to this case." Max put his hand on his brother's shoulder. "In some cases, the causative genes have been identified, but there's still no treatment. Everything has been tried. In this case, we haven't even identified the causative genes."

"That's why you went to Germany."

"I wanted to look at it from a different angle. I thought that mulling it over in a different place and discussing the issue with different people might lead to new ideas."

"You were looking at the genes of centenarians, too. I saw it in a file on the computer."

"I thought I might hit on something by comparing the genes with the DNA of the long-lived—people who lived past 100. They're in the exact opposite position, after all."

"Then you found out about Gehlen and Dona . . ." Katya nodded, convinced.

"Carius Gehlen, Reinhard Benchell, and Dona. They are not clones. They are the original Gehlen and Benchell—who have been running from Nazi hunters for sixty-three years. Somehow they've retained their youth. They've found the road to immortality."

Katya's eyes widened.

"Those are the facts, and there must be a cause. If some are forced to age many times faster than normal, it makes sense others may age at a fraction of the rate normal people age," Max said confidently, and stared at Katya. Katya looked bewildered. "Gehlen and Dona died in that bombing, but if that didn't happen, they would have lived on for decades to come. No—if they didn't die by an accident or illness, they would have lived for hundreds of years. I'm sure Benchell is alive somewhere—and that he hasn't aged a bit."

"Then the graves in Domba are fake."

"They erased all evidence of their survival. That was why they slaughtered the villagers and destroyed the village." Max walked by the window and looked down at the garden.

He thought of the mound of charred black lumps in the smoldering flames in that clearing surrounded by jungle. He closed his eyes and let the nausea pass.

"The key lies in that village," Katya said, picking up Max's train of thought. "And now you think the key is in the cells of the girl who lived there."

"Yes, you saw that amazing resilience. I'm convinced that girl was Aska. The child with Gehlen and Dona's blood, the daughter who holds the key to the miracle we need," he stammered, taking in deep breaths.

Some patients were basking in the sun on the grassy hill. A place where life and death live together. It was a peaceful scene and, at the same time, a scene of desolation.

"So, did you learn anything?" Katya asked. "You got the results of the genetic analysis the night before yesterday."

"The repetitive junk sequences matched. Dona and Aska are definitely mother and daughter. Also . . . ," he exhaled faintly, "the telomeres at both ends of her chromosome are several times longer than those in normal people." Max turned around and looked at Katya.

"But that alone can't be proof of longevity." Katya looked confused and sat in a chair next to the bed. "Certainly, the length of telomeres can increase the number of cell divisions. They could be beyond thirty to sixty times of the Hayflick limit. In fact, there have been cases where giving telomerase to human cells has increased the life span by more than four times. However, even if cell division increases, DNA damage caused by free radicals will eventually cause normal cells to turn cancerous."

"There's next to no damage in Aska's DNA. There's also an unusually high amount of antioxidant enzyme secretion. In addition . . ." Max stared at Katya. "Her telomerase is different from everyone else's."

Katya's expression grew even more serious.

"Aska's telomerase not only prevents telomere loss, but it may also repair DNA damage. Or maybe other genes are what's preventing the cell damage. There's probably also some difference with respect to her embryonic stem (ES) cells. Not that I know what that difference is." Max muttered the last few words under his breath.

"We know that telomerase is an enzyme that prevents telomeres from shortening as a result of cell division and that cancer cells repeat division indefinitely by producing telomerase. That's why they're called 'immortal cells.' However, telomerase does not have an effect on most adult cells and only functions during the fetal stage, reproductive cell production, and stem cell division."

Max's brother moaned and looked up at them. Max stood in front of him and stared at his face. There was a long silence between them. Max quietly nodded and wiped the tears from the corners of the old man's eyes with his fingertip. They "communicated" by staring at each other.

"If you discover the relationship between Dona, Aska, Gehlen, and Benchell, you may discover a possible treatment," Katya said, trying to lighten the suffocating atmosphere.

Max didn't answer. He had sought that miracle since he saw that disembodied hand in Germany, and he had yet to find it.

The door opened, and a nurse came in.

"It's examination time. Please go see the doctor. He said he's ready to talk to you." The nurse smiled brightly at Max.

"I want you to come with me," Max told Katya.

"But I . . ."

"I chose you as my research partner, and as my partner, you need to get a grasp of the symptoms you are studying."

Katya stared at Max and nodded.

Max led Katya into one of the examination rooms. A middle-aged doctor with an easygoing air looked at Max and stood. The doctor shook hands with him, and then turned to Katya.

"This is my brother's physician, Dr. George Hamilton," Max said.

"This is Dr. Katarina Lang, and she's my research partner. She's a physician as well, and a life scientist. I'm looking forward to her help in the future."

Dr. Hamilton took out a folder with medical records and CT scans, and put it on his desk. "His dementia is progressing faster than expected," he said, showing them a CT scan of Alex's brain.

Max stared intently at the film inserted in the Schaukasten light box. "How are you treating him?"

"As we discussed last time, we're administering a combination of immunosuppressive drugs and hormone therapy. We expect to see results, but even if it can slow the progression a little, it won't help him on a fundamental level." Max looked at the medical record. "If he continues to age at the current rate, we'll have to face the problem of infectious diseases, since his immune system will be significantly weakened. It's more or less the same as AIDS. But the rate at which he ages is accelerating. In a few months, he'll need to be transferred to a sterilized room."

And if that were to happen, Max would no longer be able to come into direct contact with Alex.

"Since maintaining his physical fitness is the best treatment, I'll avoid relying on drugs as much as possible, as they may cause side effects."

"I leave it to you, Doctor." Max bowed his head, stood up, and headed for the door.

"Professor Knight," called Hamilton. "He seems to have entered the hospital again."

"Something the matter?" Max's expression changed slightly.

"Physically, you could say he's completely recovered. Mentally, on the other hand . . ."

"That's his problem."

"Did you keep in touch with him while you were in Germany?"

"I remembered his birthday."

"He really wants to talk to you. He only relaxes his guard around you. He trusts you."

"He just wants to show me what he can do."

"But that's just another way he expresses his affection for you, Professor."

Max tilted his head to the side and gave it some thought, but didn't say anything. They left the examination room.

"Who was he talking about?"

"An old patient of ours. Dr. Hamilton was my old research collaborator."

Max hurried to the elevator, and Katya followed. They were silent as they left the hospital and walked toward the garden. The bright sun beat down on them, but the sea breeze was refreshing.

"Since my brother was hospitalized two years ago, I'd been seeing Dr. Hamilton once a month to discuss treatments. Today is my first time seeing him in a year."

"I'm sorry for following you. First I went to the car dealer. When I came back to show you the car, you were just leaving. So I just followed. I knew it was wrong."

"I would've had to tell you at some point anyway." Max signaled for Katya to sit on the bench. "I think I already told you my father committed suicide when I was 16."

Katya nodded.

"My father was weak. He was afraid of what was coming. But my brother hasn't succumbed. On the night of my father's funeral, he and I promised that from then on, we would fight. This is our battle—and one we can't afford to lose. My brother worked himself half to death. He attended college and worked at the same time. He decided to become a lawyer so he could make money quickly. He made money and invested it in my education. Thanks to my brother's help, I was able to concentrate on my studies. I studied hard, because my life depended on it. We have to find a cure, and break this hereditary chain of misery."

Max watched as a young man and a teenage girl pushed an old man's wheelchair up a hill. "You said you quit being a doctor and chose life science because of your interest in 'life itself.' I became a doctor to save myself and my brother. When I realized that medicine doesn't have an answer I switched to life science."

Katya's eyes were fixed on him.

"When he got older and knew that the illness would begin soon, my brother told me he refused to commit suicide. He told me to research his body, and find a way to live on. To find what causes this abominable disease, and make it a thing of the past. And he said if I can't, my body should be available to my kids so that they can keep fighting this battle."

Restless, Max stood up, then sat down again. "I couldn't save my brother. I might not be able to save myself, either. But I don't care what Alex says, I'm not having kids. I can't stand the idea of my kids suffering the way we have." He continued, muttering quietly, "My brother placed all his chips on me. And he lost that wager. I was helpless."

"I'm sorry for prying. I had no idea."

"It's nothing to be sorry for. It's not a secret. It's just a personal matter that's got nothing to do with anybody. And now you happen to know. That's all."

"Don't be so dismissive of it."

"It's the truth. The unavoidable reality."

"There's something I have to apologize for." Katya's eyes were glued to Max. "I'm a research fellow at Cosmo Pharmaceuticals." She averted her gaze and searched for words. "I really wanted to get a degree from an American university, and I needed a scholarship. I managed to get the Pauling Scholarship starting my second year. Until then, I was under a scholarship from Cosmo Pharmaceuticals. Ever since then, I've had a working relationship with Cosmo."

Cosmo Pharmaceuticals was a major company, headquartered in Munich, that had expanded globally. Their research and technology were among the highest in the world, and their facilities attracted the best researchers.

"I know. I checked your work history."

"And you hired me anyway?"

"I'm more convinced that was the right call with each passing day. Med school isn't cheap. And I went to graduate school on a scholarship. I don't see a problem."

"After graduating, I had to work for Cosmo for a while."

"That's no crime."

"But my contract with the company hasn't ended." Katya looked at Max. "Professor Michaels was a research advisor at Cosmo. I asked him for a letter of recommendation. He doesn't know anything, but Cosmo contracted me to find out what you're researching. Just knowing what you're working on in advance is valuable to them."

Max looked up at the hospital ward. It stood imposingly against the blue sky above.

"But that's not the only reason I came to you, Professor." Katya's voice was trembling, and after a long pause, she spoke once again. "The year I entered graduate school, I wrote a research paper on the relationship between embryonic stem cells and genes."

"I remember writing one, too."

"I'd been sitting on the idea since I was an undergrad. When the perfect experimental method came to me, and I started preparing, you published your dissertation. And it laid out the same technique."

"I can't tell you how many times I've felt similarly stymied. But I took those setbacks as inspiration to keep going."

"It's not that simple for me." Katya sighed. "Don't rush, but keep trying. Life is deep and short, but beautiful."

"I remember those words. That's what I told a graduate student when I was selecting a dissertation for *Nature*. His idea was unique, but the proposed experimental process was too involved."

"This is the letter you sent me."

Katya took her wallet out of her pocket and retrieved a carefully folded piece of paper.

"If I remember correctly, that proposal came to me from a male student."

"That was an upperclassman in the doctoral program I was in. My name was third on the list after my professor's, but the idea was mine."

"I sent a message because I thought you had promise."

"I dreamed of working with you, Professor." Katya's glance returned to Max. "Are you surprised?"

"I am surprised."

"You don't look it."

"I got the feeling you weren't just a researcher. A scientist with your skills and track record wouldn't need to be an assistant. Besides, I don't know any other life scientists that know their way around a satellite phone. I have a favor to ask." Max turned to face her. "I want you to help me." He gripped her hands. "You're brilliant and brave. And you understand me. I want you to take over my research when my symptoms manifest themselves, and my brain begins to be affected. Use me as research material."

"You're so strong, and kind." Katya said under her breath. "I wouldn't be up to it, Professor. I'd go crazy."

She reached out and gripped his hand.

Katya was the first to leave the hospital, after she said no to Max's dinner invitation.

Max went back to the lab after eleven that evening. The lights were still on in the experiment room, and he saw a shadowed figure bending over a microscope. The figure looked up.

"It's just as you said, Professor. Aska's cells are strangely slow to divide. Her telomeres are several times longer than normal, and I'm seeing telomerase secretions, too. The telomerase definitely needs analyzing. It's clearly different from your standard telomerase." Perhaps from excitement, Katya was blushing.

"Her cells can divide several times, no, dozens more times than usual." The two screens showed the results of Aska's cell and gene analyses. "But telomeres only matter for dividing cells such as skin and hair. I think non-dividing cells like internal organs including the heart have more of an impact on life span. We need to examine her brain neurons, myocardial cells, and muscle cells. Along with her reproductive cells," she continued in hushed tones.

"It could be," Max said, "that all of Aska's cells might develop into various organs based on the genetic information like embryonic stem cells."

She gave him an incredulous look. "But she wasn't an embryo." Max and Katya knew ES cells worked only when the fertilized egg begins to proliferate.

"If Aska's cells act like ES cells, in her body, telomerase caused innumerable cell divisions, and special ES cells constantly replaced old cells with new cells. Eternal life." Max shook his head as if to rub out those last two words. "The human body is full of mysteries. Only 5 percent of our DNA is used as genes. The remaining 95 percent is meaningless. But the percentage of Aska's DNA that's non-junk is 8 to 9 percent. It could even be in the double digits. It's still undeciphered, but there's no question there's something there."

"Benchell and his men must have found a way to get at those genes," Katya said. "That's how they were able to stay that young even over the age of 100 . . ." She suddenly looked up. "Cell transplants. The babies were stolen from Domba for bone marrow transplants."

"I came to the same conclusion. The Nazis transplanted those special cells into themselves."

"If you try the same thing against your disease, it might work!"

"But there are no donors. And there's nothing I can do about that."

"If we find Aska . . ." Katya swallowed that sentence. She pictured the charred bodies in the village. There was no way Aska had survived.

"That village, cut off from the outside world, was a breeding ground for those with special genes. And the Nazis knew that."

"Why didn't they transport them to a controlled environment? They were hiding them from the Nazi hunters, but it was still too dangerous to keep them in the middle of the jungle."

"They must have thought so, too. There had to be a better place to continue their research. Even if they hid in America, it would've been less dangerous than the Amazon."

Katya nodded.

"Years ago, in an attempt to 'civilize' a village in the deep Amazon, they slapped clothes and shoes on the people, and brought in electricity. The gave them wheat, corn, and beef. In a year, the number of villagers decreased by half. At the time, they didn't understand why."

Katya's eyes were glued to Max.

"Their bodies were built for life in the Amazon, isolated from the outside world. Their genes made them that way."

"What about Dona? She was in Europe."

"They didn't die immediately upon contact with 'civilization.' Things go out of whack more gradually than that. Plus, there are differences between individuals and across age groups. Dona was over 100 years old. She was Gehlen's wife for many years. Maybe she was able to adapt to a new environment. Either that, or . . ." He couldn't think of what to say after that.

"But, Professor, if that village was a 'breeding ground,' why did Benchell have all the villagers killed? They were carriers of the genes they needed. Benchell and his gang owe their extended youth to them." Katya turned to the display. "It must mean they were no longer needed."

Max slowly nodded in reply. "They found another way to get those cells. They found a way to extend their life spans and avoid aging without relying on the villagers." Those words hung ominously in the room.

"That's so scary." Katya's lips quivered.

"But we're just guessing."

"I can't think of anything else it could possibly be."

"Maybe Hitler's Reich is rising again, just like Feldman said."

"Aska has to be alive. I so want to believe she is," she murmured.

Max enlarged the microscope image. The cells spread to fill the entire screen, as if they were trying to tell him something. The cells, which retained their vibrant coloration, were still dividing. For a long time, the two stared at the pulsing cells.

They christened Aska's cells "A cells," and the research unraveling her genes continued.

CHAPTER 16

When Max and Katya entered the lab building lobby, Dr. Phillips, another of the leading Nobel Prize candidates, put his hand on Max's shoulder and spoke into his ear: "You've got to tell me where you got those cells. I hear they're really something else. Telomeres many times longer than normal? Wow."

"Are you talking about planarians, or Drosophilidae flies?"

"Let's team up, Max! I have military contacts. I can snag us all the funding. I'll scrounge up a cool million by next week."

Max removed Phillips's hand.

"Culture the stuff and you're sitting on a gold mine. Sell it to pharmaceutical companies or research facilities. We're talking seven digit figures, easy. Let's start a company together."

He winked at Katya as he spoke. Katya frowned and turned aside.

"I mean, they're human cells. Let's make some clones. You know, bring them while they're in an embryonic state to a country where human cloning research isn't banned. Though to be honest, I wouldn't mind doing it here, either."

"Keep dreaming."

"All right, forget the company. How about we just collaborate on the research? I'll be in charge of the cloning. I can't wait to see what kind of freaks come out of it. You just have to donate the cells to me. They hand out Nobels to research teams, too."

"If it's mouse or fly cells you want, I can give you some today. Cockroaches are showing great potential, too."

Phillips shrugged and got on the elevator. Katya motioned to Max to start walking.

"Unbelievable," said Katya, scowling. "Talk about the ugly American."

"How did info about our A cells leak?" asked Max.

"Information is too open around here. We should copy a corporation's example. From now on, I'll do the DNA extraction and testing myself."

A week had passed since they visited the hospital. Katya never mentioned Alex, yet the sight of his damaged body was seared indelibly into both of their brains.

Associate Professor Warren paid Max a visit, with a letter in his hand. He looked at Katya, and then turned to Max. He seemed to want Katya to excuse herself, and she was about to, but Max stopped her.

"Anything you need to tell me, you say in front of her," said Max. "She is my research partner."

Warren put the letter on his desk. "It's from the Tomes Foundation."

Max picked up the letter.

"What's going on? I don't get it," Warren asked.

Max read it silently.

"Bad news?" Katya asked Warren.

"It's a notice of termination of the research grant, in the amount of $400,000. That's 20 percent of the lab's annual budget. It's going to wreak havoc on us."

Max put the letter down. "When I published the report last week, they said they were fairly happy with the results."

"Foundation officials said it wasn't because of the research results, but rather a financial issue on their end, but I've heard an environmental NGO, Green Lands, is cozying up to Mr. Tomes. They're at the forefront of the anti-genetically-modified-organism (anti-GMO) movement."

"Our research doesn't have anything to do with GMOs." Max picked up the phone and asked the secretary to get the Tomes Foundation on the line and said he'd like to talk to its director, George Tomes. He nodded along for a while, before hanging up without a word. "Looks like Tomes is in Europe. Though they were being pretty evasive."

"Is there something he doesn't want to discuss with you?" Warren said, not exactly thrilled by this.

"I'll do something about it. Keep it a secret from the other researchers for now."

"Please do," Warren said as he left the room.

Max mulled it over. "Maybe this is a warning."

"No way! A warning from whom? Over what?"

"We were attacked in both Germany and Domba. We could easily have been killed. The enemy Feldman is chasing is now trying to crush us."

"And that enemy is a Nazi war criminal hated the world over. Why would the Tomes Foundation be helping him?"

"They've survived for more than sixty years because the world doesn't unanimously hate them. There are still followers of Nazism all over the world."

"So you're saying George Tomes is a Nazi sympathizer?"

"He's not. I know him well. But I'm sure there are people who can put pressure on him. The richest people in the world have their own issues. The fact he didn't call me directly means he knows something he knows I won't like."

"I'm not sure I understand."

"There are so many things out there that we don't understand. Our world is full of mysteries," he said, more to convince himself, and patted Katya on the shoulder.

Before the week ended, five foundations and companies had cut off their research grants. Some contacted the facility by phone, and some by mail. They all tried to sever ties in a businesslike fashion, emphasizing that it was due to internal financial circumstances, and not because of the quality of the research. The lab's funding for the next fiscal year was slashed by $900,000 within a week. It was a giant blow to the institute.

The following Monday morning when they entered the cafeteria, all eyes were on Max. Max raised his hand in greeting, and was met with awkward smiles and averted eyes.

"Did something happen?" Katya asked.

"You're asking me?"

"Then ask them." Katya watched as researchers avoided Max. A researcher tapped Max on the shoulder and put a local newspaper in his hands.

"The world is really mysterious. That's why it's fun."

He arched his eyebrows and shrugged before walking off.

BEHIND THE GLORY

Beside the headline was a photo of Max about the size of a business card. He skimmed the article, then silently left the cafeteria. Katya chased after him.

"Is it that mysterious?" Katya asked when they were back in their room.

Max put the newspaper on his desk. THE REAL FACE OF MAX KNIGHT, WORLD-RENOWNED BIOLOGIST, read the headline subhead. The article was about his high school arrest history, drunk driving, and violence.

"Is it true?"

"It's ancient history."

"So, they're just the ghosts of your past from twenty years ago?" she said, looking up from the article.

"That's not the world's opinion."

"But why did you do all that?"

"How was your high school experience? You're beautiful, intelligent, and in perfect health. You must have been the center of attention at school. The future was always rosy for you. You probably had a blast." Max put his hands on the desk and closed his eyes. "Try to see it through my eyes. Out of nowhere, my dad's hair turns gray and starts falling out. His body starts getting wrinkly, and veins appear all over his now-spotty skin. My mother was confused and afraid. She left home six months later. No one could blame her. In our hearts, we wanted to avoid him, too. We were afraid of him. He was like an avatar of old age and death—of what humans fear."

Max looked up at Katya. "But it was my father who suffered the most. In addition to his accelerated aging, everyone was afraid of him, and he was left to rot by his loved ones. So, he chose to die. That was the beginning of my high school life." The blood drained from Max's face. Katya looked away. "What really ruined me was how the universe suddenly decided to take away everything that made me. All through elementary and junior high, I was going to be a football player. I was the star player of Little League, too. Think about how I felt when I realized I no longer had a future. Where would I be ten, twenty years down the line? Close to death, that's what." Max's voice was trembling.

"No matter what I did, I wondered whether there was any point to it. At first, I was just afraid of death. Then I went wild and was reckless." Max looked off into the distance. "I wandered around the city and got some weed. I never took harder drugs, but I was close. I got into fights over money, and did other dangerous stuff. That was when I got arrested for drunk driving, and was tried in court for battery." Max's hands were shaking. Katya gripped his hands.

"When you came to my room, you . . ."

"No. It wasn't like that. I just wanted to hold you. For some reason, my heart feels at ease when I'm with you. It feels like a hole in my heart is getting filled up."

Max took a few deep breaths. Gradually, he calmed down.

"It was my brother who saved me. Alex picked me up at the police station and brought me straight to the lake where our father committed suicide. He dragged me into the lake and said if I couldn't keep the promise we made on the night of our father's funeral, then we should just follow in his footsteps then and there. We'd only live to 40 anyway, right? If I couldn't get a hold of myself, the only thing in my future was a miserable death. My brother is a far greater man than I ever was. I vowed to save him—and myself in the process." Max looked up at Katya. "I studied hard after that. I swore I'd never touch a football again. I'd figure out what killed our father and grandfather. And my brother and I will live on."

"What happened to your mom?"

"She remarried and is living out East."

Katya sighed and threw the newspaper in the trash.

That afternoon, Max got a surprise visit from the lab's director, Dr. Thomas Owens. When he entered the room, Director Owens sat down and looked up at Max. His long white hair and beard gave him the air of a mild-mannered old man. The eyes behind those thick lenses, however, were sharp enough to pierce the soul. While he hadn't won a Nobel himself, he counted two winners among his protégés. He was retired from research and focused on the institute's daily operations. His personality and approach to science earned him the respect and support of researchers all over the world—as well as the moniker of "the Conscience of the Science World."

He had an uncanny insight as to what was ahead. When everyone had their sights set on IT, he predicted that the twenty-first century would be the era of the genome, and set out to establish a genetic research institute. He was appointed its first director, gathered leading researchers, and made the institute the core of the genetics world. Now he hoped to reinforce the institute's status by making state-of-the art updates.

There was a letter on the desk. Director Owens told Max to read it. There was no return address. He'd expected this, but his hands trembled all the same.

"It's an anonymous letter, and it arrived at my doorstep. I could have thrown it away, but I figured I'd better show it to you," Owens said, his tone as gentle as his expression.

The letter mentioned one of Max's high school classmates. "I remember a girl named Annie Jones. I heard she moved to New York after graduating, but that was a long time ago."

"Did anything this letter says actually happen?"

According to the letter, she'd had an abortion during high school, and she swore the baby was Max's. She claimed the abortion left her unable to get pregnant, and that her life was a misery. She also wrote in detail about Max's unfaithfulness and acts of violence.

"No. I never dated her, and haven't spoken to her since high school."

"Would you like to report this to the police, or sue her for defamation?"

"Just throw it away, please."

"That's all I need to hear." The director stood up and took the letter back from him.

"I'm going to keep it, though. There seems to be trouble brewing around you. We may need to give it to the police."

Max thanked Director Owens and walked him to the door. Max's hand was on the doorknob, when,

"Professor Knight."

Max halted and looked back.

"Do you remember about fifteen years ago? You were my student."

"Yes, I do."

"Do you remember that math problem?" Owens said, with a distant look. "I always asked that problem in the first class of the school year. I'd let the freshmen agonize over it for two hours. I never thought they'd be able to solve a high-level math problem of that caliber. I meant it as a reminder that college is about challenging yourself intellectually, and tackling the questions of the day."

Owen smiled faintly as he reminisced. "Thirty minutes in, the classroom was dead silent. I could almost choke on the youthful enthusiasm. I liked that moment. But one student was looking out the window. I walked over to reprimand him, but when I stood behind him, I was stunned. Not only was there a solution written neatly on the page, but even more surprisingly, that solution was perfect. That was the first time that had ever happened. That student was you." Owens stared at Max. His eyes shone with compassion and kindness. "You have my thanks."

Max looked at Dr. Owens, taken aback.

"It was only after I met you that I understood the importance of teaching, and how much fun it could be. You absorbed my knowledge and skills like a sponge. You were the best student I ever had." Dr. Owens smiled at Max. "I have great expectations for your talent, and I greatly respect your scientific spirit, a respect that goes beyond teacher and student. I believe in you, and I plan to defend you no matter what. I think your brain is this institute's treasure—no, the world's." Owens laughed. "That math problem was the same one my mentor asked me to solve during my first year at Caltech. Actually, I couldn't solve it then. I finally solved it six months later." Owens waved goodbye. Max thanked him, and smiled at him in appreciation.

The next evening, Katya drove Max home in the Mercedes. She offered to drive because she could see Max was racking his brain. She stopped a block away; several cars were parked in front of the house. A large minivan was from a TV station. They were waiting for him.

"They've finally got me cornered." Max got out of the passenger seat and stuck a newspaper in front of Katya.

"A 'mysterious female housemate'? Does that mean me?"

"I don't think it means Nancy." Katya looked at the newspaper article and the cars parked in front of the house.

The article included photos of Max and Katya entering the house and of them in the car. Depending on the viewer, they could be interpreted as either pulling each other by the arms, or hugging and kissing each other.

"Expert timing," she commented. "I wonder when they took these. They were definitely using a telephoto lens from far away; look at how grainy they are."

"First they cut our funding, now we get paparazzi? Talk about getting kicked while we're down."

Max told her about the letter that had been delivered to the director.

"Any idea what any of that is about?" she asked.

"I did have a girlfriend, and I may have gone a little too far," he said quietly, sighing. "Remember when I said I was taken in by the police over a fight? And I can't count how many times I got a ticket for a traffic violation. Have you ever broken the law?" His voice had gotten louder. "But nothing like what that letter said happened. As far as I can remember, anyway." Max pulled the newspaper from Katya's hand.

"Relax, Professor. I know you aren't a saint. I know you're a scientist, not some televangelist selling a squeaky clean image to the world. If there's nothing you feel guilty about, then there's nothing to be afraid of." Katya started the car. "Ready?"

"I'm ready when you are."

A reporter pointed to the Mercedes and said something to a man with a TV camera.

"I changed my mind," Katya said. "This is too much for me."

She backed up and veered into a side street. They could see the press chasing after them in the rearview mirror. Katya pushed down on the accelerator.

That night, they stayed at a hotel downtown.

When Max and Katya entered the lab together next morning, Dr. Phillips approached them.

"Aren't you supposed to be at university administration right about now?" he laughed while looking at the clock. "The director should already be headed there."

"What are you talking about?"

"Isn't it your inquiry hearing?"

Max hurried to his room and called Director Owens. Max asked about the inquiry and was told it was just about to begin.

"I told you to leave it all to me, didn't I?" Owens said, in his typical calm and even cadence.

"But . . ."

"You're 35 years old, if I remember correctly. Well, I'm 62 and feel the ticking of my clock. Do I really want to just keep managing the facility? Is that all I want to do with the rest of my life? Maybe it's time to plant new seeds. When it comes to ideas, you young people won't beat me quite yet," he laughed.

"Are you saying you're stepping down as director?"

"I might, depending on how the wind blows. But it's not because of you." The tone of his voice had changed.

"I don't hate teaching or running the facility. I believe it's as meaningful a vocation as research is. In fact, it may suit me better. And I was able to raise a life scientist par excellence in you. I will defend you even if it ruins me. But please forgive me if I lack the power. Only God can decide where my path will lead me now." Before Max could think of what to say, Owens had hung up.

For a minute he just stood there, the receiver still in hand. Katya was beside him, giving him a worried look.

"I've hurt a lot of people," he said, after hanging up the phone.

"Don't feel bad!"

"I was naive. They're ruthless enough to slaughter a whole village of people. I can't believe it didn't occur to me how easily they'd cut the facility's funding and manipulate the media."

"I'm going to stick by you, even if I'm not paid. But please have me stay home for the time being."

The door opened, and Warren leapt in, newspaper in hand.

"They put out a corrected article in this irresponsible gossip rag they call a newspaper. It was on TV, too. They don't exactly put out corrections every day, you know. Either they saw the light, or somebody had friends in high places pull some strings. In any case, the inquiry hearing's been called off."

The door opened, and this time the secretary appeared. "You have a call from a representative of Theodor Roemheld of the Roemheld Foundation. She wants to talk to you directly, Dr. Knight. Please pick up the phone now."

"Another sponsor cutting all funding?" Warren's smile vanished from his face.

Max pressed the extension button and picked up the receiver.

"Roemheld's one of the world's leading foundations, with headquarters in New York," explained Warren under his breath to Katya, "It was founded by Theodor Roemheld. He began an IT company, made a fortune, and retired at 45. He's funded dozens of research institutes and universities around the world. But it's weird. The Roemheld Foundation never gave us any funding in the past."

Max put down the phone. "It's about funding research. In the next few days, Roemheld's secretary will come to negotiate contract terms."

"How much we talking?"

"$900,000."

Warren sighed. "I didn't know you knew Roemheld."

"I don't. This was our first time speaking. I spoke with Mrs.

Catherine Roemheld. She was doing business on his behalf, but she introduced herself as his wife."

"That's the exact amount of money we lost. And I don't think that can be a coincidence."

Max was thinking.

"I'll go tell all the staff. Once they hear about this I guarantee the other donors will take back their cancellations. We'll be getting enough funding to rival the national budget! Get me an electron microscope and a new sequencer, if you don't mind. Phew, I can finally sleep easy!" said Warren.

"This is Feldman's handiwork." Max looked up. "Theodor Roemheld is Jewish. Feldman pulled the strings."

"He has that kind of power?" Katya asked.

"Jews share a hatred of the Nazis. Plus, Feldman said he has support from around the world."

"He must have felt guilty. He's the one who got you into all of this."

"I did everything of my own free will. I have no regrets."

"So, Jewish money beat the Nazis."

Suddenly, Max's body seized up, and something hot ran up his throat. Max pulled out a handkerchief and held his mouth closed.

"What's wrong?" asked Katya, looking on anxiously.

"Nothing," he rasped, but his heart was pounding. As if to dampen his joy, the same heavy, oppressive clumps of lead flowed back into his mind. They grew denser as they metastasized, pulsating. He took deep breath after deep breath, and began to feel better.

"We may just be dancing in the palms of their hands," Max muttered, and turned on his computer. On the screen, the familiar DNA sequence and waveform that had already been seared into his eyes appeared.

———

CHAPTER 17

That Saturday, Max and Katya were in the experiment room. It was already past 11:00 p.m. Red emergency lights illuminated the silent corridor.

The experiment room—where everything he did when he was a student took place. Max had started his days there, eaten there, and slept there.

He looked up from the microscope. In a corner of the room, Katya set cell samples into the constant temperature incubator.

Then it shook.

There was a rumbling boom. The floor rose up a few inches. Max felt a powerful blow to his back, and was thrown against the wall. Dull pain spread through his whole body.

The room was completely dark; the power was out. He tried to get up, but a stabbing pain in his back sent him right back down.

"Katya!"

No reply.

"Are you okay? Answer me!"

Nothing.

After a few seconds, the pain subsided. He grabbed a fallen shelf for leverage and managed to get up. Fine particles flowed into his mouth and nose, along with the smell of burnt chemicals. He stumbled to the desk in the dark, careful of the holes in the floor, groped for the drawers, and found the flashlight. The room was shrouded in smoke and dust from the collapsed floor and walls. In the scant light he could see that the floor in the center of the experiment room was gone.

"Katya! Where are you?!"

The corner of the room where Katya had been was buried in debris. He weaved through fallen shelves and shattered equipment to the spot where the constant temperature incubator had been. He could see a lab coat in the gap between a shelf and the floor. He put the flashlight down and lifted the shelf with all his strength. He thrust his arm in the gap and felt around for her. She was moving. She was alive. Using an iron pipe that had clattered to the floor as a lever, he raised the shelf further, then pulled out Katya's body. Max picked her up and carried her out to the corridor. Half of the corridor floor had collapsed along the wall, and he could see fire from the bottom of the hole.

A shaft of light moved beyond the shroud of dust. It was a flashlight.

"Over here!" Max shouted.

"The emergency exit won't open!" the guard shouted, coughing as he ran from the emergency exit. "Go to the main exit!"

Just then, flames shot up from the hole in the floor. Max ran back to the room in a hurry as the sprinklers went on. He tore a piece of cloth off a lab coat and wet it to cover Katya's face, then dashed through the smoke toward the main exit. In the lobby they passed firefighters on their way in.

Max grabbed one of them by the arm. "What happened!?"

"There was an explosion underground."

"Is anyone injured?"

"Three that we know of. They've been taken to the university hospital."

"Is anyone else still here?"

"We're going to find out now."

Outside the building, there was a mass of parked fire trucks, ambulances, and police cars.

"Stay away from the building," blared a police megaphone. "There could be more explosions." Officers pushed back the crowd that had begun to gather.

Katya was waking up. A paramedic tried to take her into an ambulance, but she refused.

"Why?"

Max stood there, stunned. Katya's question echoed in his otherwise blank head. There was a strange odor in the air, a mix of burnt chemicals, plastics, organic matter, and more. From the building's wreckage, white fumes that could be smoke, or perhaps dust, rose to the sky.

The next day, newspaper headlines sounded the alarm.

START OF GLOBAL BIO-WAR?
WORLD WAR III BREWS OVER GENES
LEADING-EDGE AMERICAN BIO-LAB TARGETED

That afternoon, the fire department and the police began their inspections. The bomb had detonated under Max's experiment room. Of the twenty-seven lab rooms on the first and second floors, the one that had sustained the most damage was Max's. The adjacent cell storage room and equipment warehouse were also partially destroyed. The power to the cell storage room was out for half a day, and all the frozen samples were now useless.

The center of the floor had collapsed underground, and the heat of the fire almost completely destroyed the computer data. Miraculously, the other experiment rooms had suffered little to no damage.

"Several bombs were set in the basement," explained one of the firefighters. "Looks like there were also fire-starting explosives such as napalm. Whoever's behind this seems to have broken into the lab disguised as someone inspecting the air-conditioning system. A few security guards have corroborated that. They knew the inspection was scheduled Saturday night. The car the bomber drove and the uniform he wore weren't fakes, and the maintenance company reported the theft. When a guard called the company, he was told they'd dispatched the worker. The company's switchboard was evidently tampered with, so that any call made to the company would be redirected to the bomber." The firefighter closed his memo pad.

A plainclothes detective was standing by the firefighter. "The hit was meticulously planned. The criminal's car carried a few pounds of explosives into the building's basement service entrance. He used the latest plastic explosives, too, and the time bomb was an elaborate IC-based bomb. They're not easy to get. It was set on an underground pipe, and it was like a napalm bomb, basically. Think of it like a time bomb filled with combustibles to deliberately start a fire. It was set to go off a few minutes after the first explosion. Destroy the place, then burn it down. This was the work of a terrorist organization, no doubt about it. Still remember the Oklahoma City bombing. One hundred sixty-eight people killed, five hundred or so injured." The detective was looking into the hole opened by the explosion, but turned to Max. "It's like they were aiming for your room specifically."

"Then they could've just set those bombs in the experiment room itself."

"It's hard to get inside the lab. You can't enter without a card and PIN. But all you have to do to get to the basement is pretend to be with a company they do business with. Makes sense, doesn't it?" the detective said matter-of-factly, "it happened at midnight on a Saturday. That's why there were zero deaths, unbelievably enough. Only five people got injured, and one of them's a guard who fell down the stairs. Usually, the kill count of an explosion on this scale is in the double digits. It couldn't be clearer they were only aiming to destroy the facility."

Max looked at the hole. Bent and dented steel girders were poking out from the concrete, and they could see the underground parking lot in between the gaps. The stench of burnt plastic and rubber was still hanging in the air.

The detective scowled. "Any idea who did this?"

Max didn't know how to reply.

"It's possible a rival lab did this to delay your research, wouldn't you say? There's got to be a lot of competition when it comes to genetic research. I hear there's money in it."

"We're scientists, not barbarians. This attack has set back the whole world's genetic research by a few years," he said, the words coming fiercer than he'd anticipated.

"Which I'm sure loads of people are thrilled about," pressed the detective. "What about an environmental group? Like, say, Green Lands. The extremist group that opposes biotechnology. The police haven't gone public with it yet, but they have declared their intent to turn to crime. Don't trespass into God's realm, they say. Though you'll forgive a scientific illiterate like me for thinking they've got a point."

"Yeah, well, sometimes God's whims cause outrageous suffering. Should we just sit down and take our licks? Maybe people have a right to fight against God's cruel jokes."

The detective was taken aback by Max's outburst.

The investigation was over, and Max drove home.

"The bombing was laser-focused to destroy my experiment room," Max said.

"You're being paranoid, Professor. Where the bombs were placed was pure chance. You heard what the police said: it was an act of terrorism against biotechnology."

"Is that what you honestly believe?"

Katya didn't answer.

"They wiped away one of mankind's treasures," he groaned.

"The institute stored one hundred seventy-five thousand items of genetic information and research data, the result of decades of research by eighty-seven researchers. People's lifelong research, their blood, sweat, and tears—all gone."

"But no one died. And that's a miracle. As long as we're alive, we can continue researching." Katya gently put her hand on Max's shoulder.

"This may be my opportunity to call it quits. The idea we humans can bend life to our will is just hubris."

"That sounds like what the Nazis are doing, not us."

"Are you telling me to fight the Nazis? That's what spurred them to develop the atom bomb."

"You have to fulfill that promise to your brother."

"It's like Medusa's blood," he muttered.

"Medusa, as in the Gorgon?"

"Medusa's blood was so cursed that when it hit the ground, it spawned venomous snakes. Maybe I should just die and take my cursed blood down with me."

"But Medusa's blood also gave birth to Pegasus—a beautiful white horse that flies through the sky," Katya said.

"In any case, this bombing is my responsibility."

With that, Max kept quiet and drove down the road. Katya also was silent.

The summer sun was shining down on the Californian vista.

That evening, Max was in his study at home. He had barely slept since the bombing, as he'd been swamped with drawing up the documents he had to submit to the university and the state. His head was swimming; he had no idea what to do, and he no longer even had a grasp on what was unfolding. The only thing keeping him going was his sense of responsibility regarding the laboratory.

Suddenly, he heard a clattering noise. He looked up to find the door to the study open and a man standing there. A tall, strong, well-built man.

"Joe?" Max said.

"Your front door was unlocked. And your security's off, too. This may be a good neighborhood, but you're being careless, particularly at a time like this."

"I just don't care anymore."

"You went through a nasty experience. I sympathize." Feldman walked over to him unhurriedly. "This is how they do things."

"Why are they destroying my research?"

"Because your research got to the heart of their operation. This was a warning. Next time, they'll take your life. I take that back— they were aiming for your life. You're a lucky man, Professor," Feldman said coolly. He took a seat on the sofa in front of the desk. The not unpleasant aroma of cigars wafted faintly. It stirred in Max a strange sense of nostalgia.

Feldman continued. "What did you discover? Would you be so kind as to inform us?"

"Are you telling me your syndicate doesn't already know?"

"We have a general idea, but even that's just the conjecture of laymen. I may have intelligence men and dealers of destruction for allies, but I don't know any pro-life scientists."

"I can't continue my research anymore. Everything's gone. I've got nothing left."

Feldman sighed. "Professor . . ." He tapped himself on the head. "You still have it all right here. And the world's greatest intellect. Data and specimens are mere matter. You have something here that is more valuable. You have wisdom and creativity. No supercomputer or library or laboratory can top your mind. I'll add a third—courage. You ventured into the depths of the Amazon and came back with something to show for it." Feldman was calm, but what he'd said, he'd said with passion.

"Did you pressure the newspaper to publish those corrections about that 'scandal' article? Are you the one who pulled strings with Theodor Roemheld?"

"I was gathering evidence corroborating Jake's report, and investigating what sort of organization attacked Domba," Feldman said, his tone reverting to calm. His reply evaded the question. "Unfortunately, we still haven't reached any conclusions. About a dozen white people were wearing the same camouflage uniform as the left-wing guerrillas of neighboring countries. The copter they were in was a medium-sized UH-1 transport copter. UH-1s are used by the US military to transport soldiers. And they were armed with Kalashnikovs. When they rounded up the inhabitants, they shot them indiscriminately. That's all we know."

"That's all the info you need to identify them. That, and

familiarity with the lay of the land. There must be a base nearby. The incident didn't get much international attention, they blamed it on guerrillas. This group must have sway with Brazil's government," Max said as Feldman listened silently.

"In our world, we can't act based on assumptions. The higher-ups aren't so brave."

"There's somebody higher up than you?"

"An organization that gives us money and manpower."

"Are they able to catch the guys that blew up the lab?"

"I fight because I believe they can."

"In that case, send me to them. I'll negotiate with them myself." After witnessing the violence at the farmhouse and the lab, and the firefight at the old factory site, he knew this wasn't a war he could wage alone.

"Professor," Feldman fixed his eyes on Max, "that's not your concern. Leave those sorts of things to us. Besides, you're still hiding something. Tell us everything you know. Our organization won't cave in to them, either." Feldman placed the newspaper he'd been holding in front of Max.

The paper's headline jumped out at him: IS EVIL UPON US AGAIN? FAR-RIGHT PARTIES GAIN POWER ACROSS EUROPE. The article detailed how France's far-right party had gained power in the recent election. In celebration, neo-Nazis were holding rallies all over the continent.

"It's got nothing to do with me."

"That's what everybody says, Professor. And that's how the world's tragedies happen."

"So, the ends justify the means? They still haven't caught the Dörrenwald bombers. Neo-Nazis aren't the only ones who are violent. I think your organization was more than capable," Max said.

Feldman lowered his eyes and paused to think. After a moment, he looked up and stared at Max.

"I like you, Professor. I respect you. I want your cooperation.

I believe mutual trust comes from a relationship where neither party keeps secrets."

"I knew it. That bombing was done by you guys."

"It happened because of the recklessness of Simon and his subordinates. After Simon's death, a Galil sniper rifle was found in his apartment. Galils are Israeli guns. Semtex, a plastic explosive, was found there, too. It must have been left over from the bombing. The organization itself had nothing to do with it. Simon simply hated Nazism with every fiber of his being." Feldman's voice shook. "Cancer had spread throughout his body. I told you how the Nazis experimented on him. They bathed his body in radiation, supposedly to learn about the connection between radiation and sterilization. And then, those Nazi scum took his . . . he knew he was dying, so he took action. He wanted vengeance on Gehlen and Benchell while he still drew breath."

Feldman looked down and said nothing. Max stood up and pulled a DVD out from between two books on the shelf. He inserted it into his laptop, and an image appeared. Aska's vermiform appendix, video of cell division, and the results of the DNA analysis also showed on screen. Then Max appeared, speaking about the telomeres and telomerase in Aska's A-cells, and about embryonic stem cells.

Feldman stared at the screen. The video ended, and Max turned the computer off, but Feldman continued to think. Soon the sunlight disappeared, and the room turned dark.

"Benchell's alive," murmured Feldman. "And they're going to stay alive indefinitely. We can't let that happen." His hands were shaking.

"God let them live," Max said.

"God wouldn't do that. They cheated God!" he said, glaring up at him. "I don't mind selling my soul if it means I can kill him with my own two hands." For a moment, hatred flashed across his face. But just as suddenly, his characteristic calm returned.

"What are they trying to accomplish?"

"That's what we're trying to find out."

"If you ask me, you've got both an organization that can oppose them, and the passion."

"Many are skeptical about digging up the ghosts of the past." Feldman sighed, before steeling his face. "Can I have that DVD?"

"No. This is just conjecture on my part. We'll be gathering the scientific proof from here on out."

Feldman nodded weakly. "Something is starting to move on the world stage. I can feel it. Neo-Nazi activities around the world are getting more forceful and more energetic. Given that, Benchell really must be alive."

"I said everything I know. It's your turn now. You're hiding something."

"I can't say anything for now. We need time. We're looking into their objectives, their base of operations, their funding, their connections. Please wait a little longer. All I can say is that they're on the move. And that I will need your help to stop them." Feldman heaved a deep sigh. "Hitler was extensively psychoanalyzed. He was calm and cautious. He was also cunning. Otherwise, he wouldn't have survived so long. He used body doubles, and always had escape routes planned. On paper, he committed suicide, shooting himself with a pistol on April 30, 1945, in an underground bunker, and was doused with petrol and burned to death along with his wife. But there's no evidence to support that story."

"Who are you looking for, *Hitler*?"

"Perhaps."

A long pause. Feldman was walking aimlessly in the darkness. Max suddenly had a thought: *This is the ghosts' resurrection.*

"The Fourth Reich is coming back," Feldman said from the shadows.

"The Fourth Reich?"

"The empire they plan to create in the wake of Hitler's Germany."

"No! It can't happen!"

Feldman pushed the newspaper at Max. "The signs are here, and all over the globe, too. The stirrings of the neo-Nazis, the criticisms against Jewish organizations, and the gathering strength of right-wing groups. Some are even trying to justify Hitler's crimes. I don't think all of it is about creating the Fourth Reich, but the world is moving in a dangerous direction."

"Where's Jake?"

"In Europe. France, Germany, Italy. After he returned from Brazil, he's been flying all around. We're not playing. And all this calls for communing with God as well."

Max frowned, and his head began to ache. His body grew heavy, and something that felt like tar stuck inside him. He closed his eyes and massaged between his brows. By the time he opened his eyes, Feldman was gone, and the door thunked to a close behind him.

The comeback of the Fourth Reich. That dreaded empire's name echoed ominously in his mind.

● ● ●

V

THE LABORATORY

CHAPTER 18

A week had passed since the bombing. With the help of university administration and the state government, the institute was repaired ahead of schedule. All new research equipment had been brought in as well. Dr. Owens played a central role, working not just for the US but for all the world to see that the facility was ready for new research.

Researchers had lost heartbreaking amounts of data, materials, and samples, but they were pleased with the initiative to rebuild. Dr. Owens tapped his wide network of contacts and planned a new laboratory complex with all the latest equipment and facilities—and in record time, too.

Since Max's experiment room was the most heavily damaged, he had to move to another building temporarily. Most of the equipment had been destroyed, along with most of the test pieces and cell samples they'd stored, and what little of it was left was too damaged to use.

Despite it all, their research resumed, owing in large part to Katya's dedication, and her words of advice and encouragement.

Aska's "A cells" were lost in the bombing and fire. All the genetic data in the experiment room's computers were lost, too, but luckily Katya had made a copy on her computer, so they were able to pick up where they'd left off.

Max wrote up a report on the damages for university administration. It was already past five in the afternoon. He had been typing away for more than three hours, and he was sick of the monotony.

Before leaving for the cafeteria, he checked his mail. Mixed in among the messages was an email with an attachment from an unspecified sender with a hidden address. Afraid it could be a virus, Max was about to delete it when he noticed the Star of David in the subject line. It had to be from Feldman.

Under the heading AZTEC RESEARCH INSTITUTE, there was an overview of the company. Capital stock of 37 million USD. Eighty employees. Research mainly revolved around genetic engineering. Genetically modified crops of various vegetables and fruits produced and patented. $57 million in funding last year. La Cruz, California—probably where the company was located. That was all the email contained.

He remembered what Feldman had told him: "We're not playing around here." Something stood out from the company overview, and he knew Feldman had sent it to him because it had popped out at him, too. Max sat back down and typed for an additional three hours, as he placed a number of calls. When he looked out the window, it was dark out.

He printed a few documents and left the room to head home. He passed in front of the lab; the lights were on. He gently opened the door and went in. Somebody was in front of the computer. It was Katya. Ever since she'd met Max's brother at California Memorial Hospital and learned of Max's illness, she'd devoted herself to researching it. All she could do was analyze what data hadn't been lost. It wasn't uncommon for the lights to be on in the room until sunrise.

"What's that?" Max asked, looking at the screen over Katya's shoulder.

Katya turned around; her expression went from surprise to relief.

"The results of Alex's genetic analysis. It was included in the data you were given."

"Anything new?"

"It's as you said. Without DNA to compare it to, there can be no progress. We still need to look more closely into Aska's cells and genes."

"Aska isn't with us."

"I'm sure she's alive. They wouldn't ever kill her."

Max pulled a chair over and sat next to Katya. "Ever heard of Aztec Labs?"

Katya thought a moment, but shook her head.

"It's a private research institute that conducts research on genetic modification."

"I've never heard of it. They're not associated with other companies, and their research article publication output must be pretty low. But there are so many genetics startups these days. Where is it located?"

"It's in La Cruz, a small town north of San Diego. It was a fisherman's town five years ago before the labs were built. I don't know much more than that."

"So, what makes you bring it up?"

"I got an email about it. Probably courtesy of Feldman."

"Why did he email you about it?"

"He says he's got friends all over the world. He probably got a tip from a member or ally of a global-scale Jewish organization. That means they've got a worldwide information network."

"Did you check online?"

"Couldn't find anything. I contacted the city authorities about it, but they only gave me a rough idea." Max handed Katya a few sheets of paper. "Publicly available information about the city."

"It's a midsize research institute," she said, rifling through.

"But it's strange that there isn't anything online about a lab complex of this size. That must be intentional. Also, they have too little capital stock compared to their research expenses."

"I think it mainly deals with genetically modified plants."

"Annual research funding, 57 million. That is a big figure. They're either doing really high-level research, or they hold one or more juicy patents. No sales or settlement reports here."

"Most of the administrative costs are covered by venture capital, which is to say, donations."

"It's the 'Aztec Foundation.' Did you look into that?" Katya was skimming through the text.

"Their headquarters are in Paris, but whether that's the real story is unclear. It's weird for a French foundation to be funding an American business venture."

"There's always a lot of government involvement when it comes to this kind of research institute. It requires a lot of licensing and permits. If you contact the government agencies, you might be able to uncover a fair bit."

"I contacted the CDC and was told that it was out of their jurisdiction. Aztec Labs has a P4 lab but doesn't deal with infectious viruses or bacteria. Their research is limited to the field of genetics. I was told their main activities involved the development of genetically modified plants and pharmaceuticals. The CDC didn't have much of any data for me, either."

"Then is it under the jurisdiction of the FDA or WHO?"

"I called both of them. None of them have any info. I asked a friend of mine in government, too, but he didn't know much, either. Aztec can't be doing anything substantial."

"A laboratory full of secrets. They did a hell of a job getting licensed like that. And continuing to operate," Katya said.

"The work of politicians, no doubt. And not your average politicians, either. Unless you're close to the governor or president, you don't have that much authority. Maybe we should leave it to Feldman."

Katya swiveled her chair back toward the computer and began pounding on the keyboard even faster.

"I tried access into the lab's computers, but the security's too strict. It's the same in every lab."

Katya ignored Max's words and kept typing.

"I'm not trying to hack them. I'm looking at companies and organizations that do business with bio-related laboratories. We may just learn something."

"Is that possible?"

"I'm looking up companies and organizations that might be relevant. I've pulled up a list of trade partners for companies that supply the chemicals, drugs, and equipment necessary to conduct genetics research." The company names took up the entire screen. Katya sighed.

"There are hundreds of companies. I'd give up if I were you."

"It's a million times more likely to turn something up than doing nothing. Now let's look up computer suppliers. Supercomputers are a must for detailed gene analysis and for determining the molecular structure of purified proteins. The government knows where all supercomputer delivery destinations are."

Max shrugged.

"Wow!" Katya leaned closer to the screen.

"They have the world's fastest supercomputer, IBM Roadrunner. Two of them, in fact. And one unit costs $100 million."

"Are they doing genetic analysis or determining molecular structure? Or both?"

Katya started typing faster.

"What did you uncover this time?"

"I was wondering if we could break into the supercomputer. They would definitely be connected to universities and other research facilities."

"It'd certainly be more efficient that way."

"But that's not the case. Their computer network is completely insular. They must really hate the idea of outside interference. Even though they would still be protected by multiple layers of security even if they were connected to an outside establishment." Katya's fingers danced across the keyboard like a pianist.

"You're a woman of many talents," Max said, chasing Katya's fingertips with his eyes.

"I admire a different talent more."

"I know a young man who said he'd conquer the world using his computer. And I have half a mind to believe him now."

"He's half right. But don't you think conquering people's hearts is a more attractive prospect than conquering the world?"

Max stood behind Katya, watching the rapidly changing screen. He sighed and left the room. He returned to his office and took out a sheet of Aska's genetic information from his bag.

Two hours passed. A knock on the door, and in came Katya. She had an inches-thick stack of papers, which she placed in front of Max. "This is a list of medicines that Aztec Labs has purchased from companies that it's done business with in the past year. No matter how insular the company tries to be, it can't do everything on its own. Aztec Labs is a good customer in the eyes of pharmaceutical companies and equipment suppliers. I don't think this covers everything, so this isn't exhaustive."

Max scanned the list.

"Extraction buffers, DTT, Endim solution, primer, phenol, chloroform, isoamyl alcohol, marker, Eppendorf tubes, Kimwipes, micropipettes, vortex mixes—all indispensable purchases for genetics researchers."

"How about twelve spectroscopes?"

"Twelve is a lot. They're doing genetic research in there for sure."

"That adds up to a lot of money, but the amount of corporate income of the lab itself is less than 20 percent of the total income. The rest is funded by the Aztec Foundation. It doesn't make sense in the eyes of a corporation."

"That's too big a figure to cover just through donations. It's just research without a real business behind it." Max thought for a while.

"We should leave it to Feldman. We can't handle it anymore."

"But as things stand, I think Aska must still be . . ." Katya looked away from Max, searching for the right words.

"Are you saying Aska's at those labs?"

"It's possible. We have to find her! Her cells and genes will lead us to new discoveries. Besides . . ." She shot him a pleading look. "Aska saved my life when I was about to drown. Now it's my turn to return the favor."

"Guess we've got no choice but to go there," Max muttered, glancing at the stack of papers.

CHAPTER 19

Two days later, Max and Katya headed for La Cruz. They took a flight from San Francisco to San Diego, rented a car at the airport, and drove north on the freeway. They zoomed along the coastline, the Pacific sparkling in the sunshine to their left. The Mexican border lay a mere twelve miles to the south.

According to a brochure they'd found at the airport, La Cruz was a resort area, and a small country town of around five thousand people. It had a yacht harbor, and tourists went fishing and diving there as well.

Aztec Labs and the University of California's Marine Research Institute were shown on the map. The two laboratories were north of the town, facing the sea.

"It's pretty around here." Katya stared happily at the water.

They were enjoying the picture-perfect California landscape.

The water was dark blue, and the skies azure. Rolling hills sculpted the land opposite the ocean. They saw a few windsurfing sails in bright primary colors.

After an hour's ride from San Diego, they arrived at La Cruz. They parked near a U-shaped motel at the entrance to town. The motel had about forty rooms, a pool at the center, and a big parking lot around it. It seemed large for such a small town.

At the front desk sat an old man with a stubbly beard reading a fishing magazine.

"We'd like two rooms next to each other, please."

The man cast a sharp glance at Max, then turned his eyes to Katya. "The beds are king-size. Big enough for two to sleep in. Plus, it'll be cheaper if you share a room. I'm not here to rip you off."

"But we'll each be more comfortable alone," said Max.

The man shrugged and got their keys. He pointed to both wings of the motel: "Sorry, we're full up with people staying here to fish or dive. You won't be near each other, but you won't be so far you need a car."

Katya was standing silently behind Max, who paid and took the keys.

"Can you direct me to Aztec Labs? I think it's around six or so miles from here."

The man froze for a moment, before returning to his chair as though he hadn't missed a beat. "Those labs don't really mix with the folks here. They just pay their taxes and keep to themselves. And let me tell you, the company pays a lot in taxes."

"Where do all the employees and researchers live?"

"All the way over at the private beach. They've got a huge site over there, with their own apartment buildings and everything. I hear they've got a restaurant, a supermarket, and a hospital. Don't know if they've got a school, on account of how I've never seen any kids around there. 'Course, I never bump into lab folks in town, so I wouldn't know."

The word "Estancia" sprang to Max's mind. Katya gave him a look which told him she was thinking the same thing.

"Ever been there?"

"No way. They're researching genetics and bio stuff. Rumor has it they're whipping up Frankenstein's monster over there."

"We're talking about a P4-level laboratory. There must have been public hearings before construction was approved."

"Look, I'm not really that interested. I'm not afraid of biohazards, and the town loves having a company that pays a fortune in taxes. What's it to me what they get up to?" Then he went back to his magazine. This conversation was over.

Max grabbed Katya's bags and headed for her room.

"Can I come to your room later?" Katya said, as she took her bags and her room key off his hands.

After about ten minutes, she came back. Max was looking at the guidebook he'd taken from the reception counter. Nothing about Aztec Labs in it, either.

"The guy's lying. He knew P4 laboratories come with the risk of biohazards. Not many people know that. He understands the danger level. The labs were built five years ago. I read that there was a big opposition movement when construction started. And then the protesters were suddenly in favor."

"Are you saying the residents were bought off?"

"Absolutely. Look how swanky this motel is for a town this size."

After a few minutes rest, they got in the car and headed for the coast. The road had four lanes, but there were few cars. Two large trucks with AZTEC logos passed.

"I think this road was built specifically for the labs," Katya said.

"Around five miles ahead, there's the California University Marine Research Labs and a campground. The campground's been around since before Aztec Labs was built," Max said as he eyed the trucks.

A building surrounded by a white fence was visible on the hilly coastline. Three box-shaped buildings stood in a vast lot.

"There it is. Aztec Labs." Max pointed at it with his eyes.

"It's bigger than I imagined."

"It's on a mile-long private beach. And it's off limits."

They turned onto a road that continued along a wall. Max slowed to a crawl.

"Can't make out anything beyond the wall," Katya said, her face to the car window.

Max stopped the car. The wall was nearly ten feet tall, but it gave way to a fence protected by barbed wire. Inside, they could see a lawn, with an unobstructed view except for a few trees. The buildings were about two hundred yards away.

"Watch, the fence is probably electrified," she said.

Max pointed at a sign on the fence. PRIVATE PROPERTY, NO TRESPASSING, then ELECTRIFIED in red letters.

"I get security being tight, but I've never heard of a private business electrifying the fence. Think about the liability headaches. This can't be just an ordinary genetic research lab," she said, looking up. The security camera on top of the fence was pointed at their car.

They slowly went around the perimeter; after a few minutes, they hit a dead end—and a cliff.

In the rearview mirror, he saw a Hummer coming closer. There was nowhere to run; they were backed against the cliff, below was the sea.

"I'm going to pretend we got lost." Max took the map and spread it out over the steering wheel.

Two guards with blue short-sleeved uniforms came out of the Hummer. They were about six feet tall, blond and lean. They looked like they could be German. They had their hands at their holsters.

The driver sat behind the steering wheel without moving, his eyes on Max and Katya.

"Hello, could you tell me how to get to the Marine Research Labs?" Max showed the map to the man who was peering at him through the window. Both of the labs were by the shore, so this cover made sense. One might think this road led to both.

The two men stood back and talked in low voices, never taking their eyes off them. One came back. "Go back about two miles. Then take the narrow road at the fork and go straight down it until you get there," he said cordially.

Max revved the engine.

"They must be standing guard 24/7," Katya said. She looked in the rearview mirror.

"An electrified fence, surveillance cameras, and armed guards. These labs must really hate visitors."

The Hummer followed them about a hundred feet behind. Max pushed down on the accelerator.

They stopped by the harbor before returning to the motel. About thirty yachts were moored. Most were open-sea cruisers, some were forty-foot class. It was a beautiful harbor that one wouldn't expect to find in such a small port town. At the other end of the bay a few miles away were a few white buildings. It was Aztec.

"There doesn't appear to be any fence on the sea side," Katya said, looking at the labs.

They walked along the harbor. A dive shop was at the end. A young man in his early twenties with coconut-colored skin was connecting an air tank to a compressor.

"Can we dive here?" Katya asked him.

"What else do you think there is to do? The sea and the sky are all this place has. C'mon, I'll show you some sharks mating. For you, I'll knock the price down to two hundred bucks a day, equipment rental included," he said cheerfully. He was clearly checking her out.

"I haven't seen sharks mating, but I did see whales mating, once."

"You've dived before?"

"I just said I saw whales mating."

"Name's Al." Al wiped his right hand on his pants and extended it to Max and then Katya. "How about I take you exploring? There's a sunken ship. I'll charge a hundred bucks per person. It's romantic."

"Do you go out to sea every day?"

"Yep, except for when there's a storm, but that's only a few days out of the year at most."

"You go out to the laboratory, too, right?" Katya pointed to Aztec Labs.

"We pass through open sea."

"Did you happen to see a girl over on the laboratory grounds? She's 14 or 15, and looks half-white, half-Indigenous Brazilian."

"The chief of police told me not to get anywhere near the labs. The year the labs opened, I was on a date at the private beach and got caught by a security guard. A bunch of big rough guys with guns came and cuffed me. Luckily, a friend saw it happen and told the chief. The chief came around and got me out of there. He's a distant relative of mine, the chief."

"But have you seen that girl?"

"No, I haven't. I've never seen a single female over there, let alone a girl. If you ask me, that place is a gay commune," said Al, shrugging.

"What's it like inside the laboratory? They brought you in there, right?"

"I wasn't exactly able to soak in the sights. Keep this between us, but I almost wet myself in there. Plus, my date dumped me," he replied. "So, uhh, I was put in a room with a desk and a chair. It smelled like a hospital. I hate that smell. Made me feel like they were going to chop me up like in some horror movie. Actually . . . ," he paused a little. "They blindfolded me when they walked me down the hall, but I did catch a glimpse of something. There was new-looking equipment, and it looked really clean. Everybody had a lab coat on. I figured they must all be really smart. That's a laboratory for you, right? But the mood in there was just off. Everyone was like a robot, no expressions. Bad vibes, man, bad vibes."

"I wonder if we can enter from the sea." Katya turned her eyes to the air tank.

"The tidal current is fast, especially by the labs. Every year, a handful of people get caught up in the current and die. Somebody died just last month." Al stopped tying the rope to the air tank and looked at Katya.

"You can't dive off the cape, right?" Katya asked.

"Last year, two divers went out to search for a sunken ship, and washed ashore on the lab's private beach."

"Did they say anything? About the institute, I mean."

"Dead men tell no tales. They got hit by the waves and by hungry fish; the corpses looked awful."

"So, they drowned before washing ashore?"

"That's what the officers who picked up the bodies said. It seems like they definitely drowned, according to the coroner, but I have no idea where."

"Where can people go diving in that area?"

"Anywhere as long as it's away from the bay, but that's only if you have a professional guide that knows what they're doing. It's a great area; Baja California's right next door, and the ocean is just endless. Diving is the best sea sport there is."

"Where do you live?"

"The second floor of the boathouse. Come anytime. I'm open twenty-four hours a day."

Ignoring Al's words, Katya squinted at the laboratory with her arms crossed. The sun was setting. Its light dyed the ocean blood red.

Max and Katya found a beachside restaurant that looked appetizing. It was situated on a piece of land that jutted out into the sea adjacent to the harbor. They sat by the window and looked out onto a yacht right below them. They could hear the sound of the waves. A light on the yacht's mast cast a bluish-white reflection on the water.

An array of illuminations shone at the other side of the bay—the glow of Aztec Labs. They heard the occasional firecracker going off from the harbor.

They ordered oysters, crab, and a half bottle of white wine. The waiter lit the candles on the tables around them.

Katya looked back at the sea. "We need to hurry."

"We still have time. Four years and six months' worth of it," Max said, as he cracked a crab leg.

"That's all the time we have."

"That's more than enough time for science to make discoveries and progress."

"They've been researching a cancer cure for more than a century, and still haven't found one. We don't even have a cure for the common cold. We have drugs to extend the lives of AIDS patients, but not a real remedy. And what about diabetes? We can only treat symptoms."

"We eradicated smallpox. Polio is no longer a threat if you just take the vaccine. And we've discovered a few cancer-related genes."

"But now we have hospital-acquired infections that are resistant to antibiotics. We have new dreaded diseases like Ebola and Marburg hemorrhagic fever to contend with. And tuberculosis is back in circulation, too."

"We've pinned down the underlying cause of Alzheimer's."

"But we have no idea when we'll come up with a cure for it."

"I'm sure I won't live to see it."

"You don't believe we can make rapid progress?"

"I believe in breakthroughs, too. That's why I'm taking my sweet time eating this crab."

They exchanged glances and smiled, but their smiles were tinged with sadness.

The smile immediately disappeared from Max's face. "Life traded immortality for evolution. The ring-shaped DNA of things like E. coli and prokaryotes without mitochondria contains no telomeres, and so they're virtually immortal organisms that can undergo cell division pretty much indefinitely. The DNA of eukaryotes like yeast fungus which have nuclei, on the other hand, is linear in shape, with telomeres at their ends. Because their DNA is linear, they can reproduce and combine two strands of DNA, allowing for more diverse offspring. Biological sex also contributes to the diversification of genetics, enabling living things to evolve."

"Death is a by-product of our ancestors choosing evolution." Katya averted her gaze. "How bittersweet," she added quietly.

"When I was in elementary school, I'd wake up in the middle of the night and stare into the darkness. I felt like I was getting sucked into it. I thought that darkness was death itself, and that death was eternal nothingness. The irrevocable loss of the self. But what is that eternal sleep? No one can say that they've experienced it. But we all will, eventually. I was afraid of eternity. I could barely stand that fear. So I'd jump out of bed and go to my desk. Keeping busy was my salvation," Max looked out to sea, then turned to Katya and asked, "What do you think death is?"

"I was taught that death is the irreversible stoppage of an organism's consciousness and bodily functions."

"I want to hear your thoughts on the matter."

"I don't know. I mean, I never really want to think about it."

"You're an atheist, too. Those who don't believe in God usually either fear death or don't think about it."

Katya froze, a forkful of crab at her lips. She tilted her head and gave it some thought. "I think serenity will come one day for all of us. The moment we're released from suffering and sadness. And it won't take longer than a moment."

"Eternity in a moment? You might be right. The moment we will never wake up from. But it's that moment of serenity I'm afraid of. It means I lose my conscious self, never to experience anything ever again."

"Everyone needs to accept that moment will come. How much a person lived isn't measured in time. You've lived a pretty full life, don't you think? Shakespeare died at 52, and Mozart at 35, and yet the world is still fascinated by them. The mathematician Évariste Galois died at 20, and he solved a problem that had stood for centuries. People are born to die. The second they're brought into this world, they begin their march toward death."

"Accepting the inevitability of death is a bitter pill to swallow, and at times I look at my brother and think this is our destiny. Whether we humans live or die isn't that big a deal after all."

"When I first read your papers, I got a sense of the beauty and mystery of life. The more transient something is, the more precious it is. Some say life is like the briefest twinkle of a star. And some say that flash of light is actually eternity. Stars disappear in tens of billions of years. A human life is like the birth and death of a star. It's all part of the workings of an eternal universe." Katya breathed a soft sigh. "Max, you can see eternity in a fleeting moment."

"I'm just a weak and inexperienced fellow scientist."

"You are my . . ." Katya stopped there. The red flames of the candles danced in her eyes.

A woman in white robes sat near them and started strumming a harp, which resonated with a clear and relaxing tone.

Katya continued. "But the loss of death isn't experienced by the dead. It's experienced by the family, friends, and sometimes even society. I want you to be alive."

"I believe in science. But I also know science has its limits. And I know the truth. That's my burden to bear."

"Everything is up to God. We may not be aware of it, but God's will works through all things."

"God's will," he repeated. "Imagine me, the boy who feared the shadow of death. While my friends discussed the future, I was all alone trembling, thinking of my death. Have you ever truly contemplated the reality of death?"

"All I know is that I want to save you. I want you to live on." Katya stared at him intently. "I want you by my side. To that end, I'll . . ."

Max found himself looking away. Her gaze was so earnest it scared him. "Let's wrap up this pointless discussion."

"People live in order to enjoy life."

"Good drink, good food, beautiful music, and beautiful women," Max sang.

The harp performance continued. The two locked eyes for a while.

"Something must be going on at Aztec Labs," Katya said, as she watched the lights shining across the water.

"We could get there by sea," she said.

Max stuck a crab leg in front of Katya. "Hey, if it's possible for these guys . . ."

The candle flames gave her face a rosy glow. Max gently reached out his hand and put it on hers. He could feel her warmth.

It was past ten by the time they reached the motel. Their eyes met briefly before they each walked back to their own rooms.

CHAPTER 20

When Max awoke the next morning, it was already bright outside. He went to the window and looked at Katya's room, but the curtains were still drawn. He quickly got dressed and headed for her room. He knocked. No answer. He pressed his ear against the door. No signs of her. He took out his cellphone and called her, but it went to voicemail.

When Max tried reception, the man at the counter was reading a fishing magazine, same as the day before.

"Excuse me, have you seen the woman I was with yesterday?"

He looked up from his magazine and smirked. "The young lady called a cab and left around three hours ago. But she didn't check out," he said. Then his eyes fell right back on the magazine.

"Do you know where she went?"

"It's in a conscientious motel manager's job description not to divulge customer's private information," he winked, suggestively.

Max drove to the harbor. He had a bad feeling. He thought that Katya seemed a little distracted the night before. *I should have been more attentive.* The unease in his chest swelled.

There were few people in the port. He ran along the harbor. Several yachts were being loaded with cargo, preparing for departure. He asked the boatmen whether they had seen a woman matching the description he gave them, but they all said no.

He then headed for the diving school they'd gone to the day before. When he arrived, Al was just leaving the boathouse.

"Would you happen to know where the woman who was with—"

"I was just about to go see you," Al said. "Katya asked me to. She came here at around six in the morning to rent a full set of diving gear. Said she wanted to dive early in the morning."

"Where did she go?"

"She's near the labs. I took her there by boat. She asked me to take video." Al took out a video camera from the bag he was holding. It was Katya's. "She told me to take it to you in case she didn't come back after two hours."

Max played the video. Katya was smiling at the camera. She struck a pose, and then dove into the water. She stayed at the surface for a while to get a feel for the currents, but then the camera caught her getting carried off. She waved her hands and submerged.

"I tried to stop her," Al said, watching the video from the side. "I told her it was a bad idea."

Max pressed Fast Forward. Fifteen minutes of video later, a figure rose to the surface near the beach, and started swimming toward the shore. He fast-forwarded some more; five minutes of video later, Katya had reached the sand, and she was staggering as she walked. A number of guards appeared. They apprehended her and led her off to the buildings.

"She said she wanted to take her chances. That was pretty impressive, too, how she managed to swim through that current," Al said. "Gave me three hundred bucks to take her," he added under his breath. "That lady wanted to go to the labs from the start. If I didn't take her there, she would've gone on her own, which would've ended way worse."

"Did she say anything else?"

"She asked me if it's possible to reach the beach if she got swept in the current."

"And what did you tell her?"

"I told her she'd drown before she got there," he said, shaking his head. "But she made it. Alive. Pretty impressive," he repeated. "She told me to keep the camera running until she reached the beach. She's got guts. It's almost a waste she wasn't born a guy. For real though, what's going on in those labs?"

Max stopped the playback. "Where are the officers that detained you stationed?"

"You won't say a peep about me, right?"

Al entered the boathouse and drew a map on the back of a diving application form. Max took the camera with him to the car.

At the police station, a young policeman was reading a magazine as he leaned against the counter; it looked like he had time to waste.

"A woman washed up on the Aztec Labs beach and hasn't come back. She was with me, and I want to get her back."

"Are you sure?" The policeman looked up from the magazine, visibly annoyed. "That place is off limits. You can't just stroll right in."

"She was diving nearby, and got swept away by the tide."

"It's a no diving area."

"We didn't know that."

"Then your companion is probably—"

"Can you call the chief?"

The officer's expression changed. "The chief is busy!"

"There's no time to waste," Max said, the tone of his voice rising. "I know she reached the Aztec Labs beach, and I also know that the institute's guards took her inside."

"Got any proof?"

"I have a video." Max thrust the video camera in his direction.

The policeman made no attempt to conceal his discomfort and stared at Max. "If your friend ended up trespassing, you can't complain if she got shot dead."

"Which is why you haven't got time to waste."

"Aztec Labs and the beaches around it are privately owned."

"Just call the chief already."

"I said he was busy."

The clock on the wall said 11:30 a.m. Going by the time stamp on the video, almost three hours had passed since Katya was taken inside. Max took out his cellphone and pressed a button. The young policeman watched silently.

"Who is this?" came a grumpy voice Max was very familiar with. The person who had answered, who was three time zones away on the East Coast, had picked up the phone before it could ring a third time. This is around the time he gets himself some coffee and doughnuts, Max thought.

"It's Max, Max Knight."

With that, his tone was no longer so grumpy. "Where are you now?"

Max could picture the man's face—a complex mixture of joy, confusion, and unease. "It's a town called La Cruz. It's near San Diego."

"Never heard of it," he replied dismissively.

"Could you do me a favor?"

"There's something you need me for?"

While Max was talking, the officer was listening, the tip of his pen on his nose. But the faint smirk on his face gradually disappeared.

"Could you give me this place's number?"

The officer gave Max the number, and Max repeated it to the man on the phone. The officer looked tense as he stared at the phone on the desk. Before long, it started ringing. The policeman glanced at Max before picking it up.

"Please, just a moment, sir. I will call him in right away, sir," he said, polite to a fault. He rushed into the back room. Less than ten seconds later, he came back with a middle-aged police officer.

"This is Chief Brian," the young policeman told Max.

"If this is a false alarm, he'll get tossed into lockup, and you'll be spending your career doing night shifts driving around town."

The chief stared at Max as he muttered something and picked up the receiver. Several other officers had appeared, and they looked amused. The chief nodded for a while, but his face gradually stiffened.

The chief hung up. "Get the boys and dispatch five cars!" he yelled, shaking his head.

The young policeman froze in amazement.

"What are you waiting for!?"

He hurried out of there.

The chief frowned and turned to Max. "Mayor Jefford's ordered me to accommodate you to the fullest. I'm heading to the labs now, so if you would, please come with me. Personally, I'm not quite convinced," he spat contemptuously; though he was being accommodating, his look of displeasure was clear. Sixteen uniformed police officers, including the chief, piled into the squad cars and headed for the laboratory. They stopped in front of the mass of steel that was the gate. When Max and the chief stepped out of their car, a security guard rushed out to meet them.

"This morning a young woman washed up on the Labs' private beach. We'd like to take her to the hospital immediately," Max told the guard. The chief crossed his arms and glared at Max and the guard in turn.

The guard saw the chief and the officers lined up and hurriedly picked up the walkie-talkie at his waist. Immediately, several men in suits came out of the building.

"A man in a fishing boat saw a woman who drifted ashore on the Labs' beach get rescued by the workers here. She's with me. I'd like to see her as soon as possible," Max stated firmly. Next to him, the chief was listening with a stern look.

"I haven't received any such report," said one of the suits. "Maybe there's been some kind of mistake?"

"A diver was caught in a current and washed ashore on the Labs' private beach. You helped her. That's all. The second she's back with me, everything is settled," Max said.

The men looked at each other with confused expressions.

"There's video of one of your guards helping her into the lab. That woman is my friend. You saved her. You have my thanks." Max looked at the chief. "I'm telling the truth, right, chief?"

The chief nodded with his chin slightly lowered and his eyes on Max.

"A moment, please. I'll go look into it," said one of the men, who hurried to the guardroom and picked up the receiver. He was back a few minutes later. "A woman was taken to safety this morning, and she's being treated at the infirmary. I'll get her for you right away."

After around ten minutes, Katya was brought out, supported by a man in a lab coat on either side. She was wearing a white gown. Her unsteady gait made it clear how weak she felt. She stood in front of Max, but her eyes lacked focus, and she was hanging her head.

"She ended up drinking a lot of seawater. She was agitated, so our doctors gave her sedatives. She'll be back to normal in a few hours," explained one of the suits, who gave Max a bag of diving equipment, an air tank, and a wetsuit. Max thanked him, and loaded them into the police car.

Max and Katya were driven back to the motel.

"Please make this be the last time I have to bail you out." The chief grabbed Max's arm as he was about to get out. "I don't want any trouble with Aztec. Four years ago, we were driving down bumpy one-way roads." He let go of Max's arm, but didn't stop glaring at him as he pointed behind himself with a thumb. "You saw the port, didn't you? It used to be a wharf for smelly fishing boats. And now it's full of yachts. We've even got a fancy restaurant down there now."

"So, in other words, no defying the town's benefactors."

"I don't want the higher-ups complaining to me, and Aztec Labs certainly doesn't mind this arrangement. That company gives us huge amounts of money in taxes, and they also donate to the town and the city. They've got permission from the state and from DC, and they pass the state's environmental standards. There haven't been any issues since the place got built."

"What are you trying to say?"

"I want you to leave town tomorrow. You're more liable to cause trouble around here than they are. Or that's what my gut's telling me."

Max nodded and got out of the car. Meanwhile, an officer drove Max's car into the motel parking lot.

Max began walking, holding Katya up, when the chief poked his head out of the car window. "By the way—who exactly are you?"

"We're just tourists. Tourists who will be out of here by tomorrow. We won't bother you again."

"You ain't just a tourist. Not many tourists know presidential aides." The chief spat at Max's feet. "The aide called the governor, and the governor called the mayor. Apparently, the aide told them to send in the National Guard if I wasn't up to the job. He must've meant business, threatening me like that."

"Next time I see him, I'll tell him he made La Cruz's chief of police none too happy."

The chief spat at him again before ordering the driver to pull out.

Max took Katya to her room and helped her to the bed. She opened her eyes and tried to focus on him. She still seemed sluggish.

"Don't do something that stupid ever again."

"What was stupid about what I did? I know what's important to me." She tried sitting up, but frowned and lay down again. Her body wasn't cooperating.

"So waltzing into the Labs to get captured was important to you?"

"But I'm back. I knew you'd save me," she wheezed.

"It just happened to work out. Stop being unreasonable."

"I'm not being unreasonable. I'm . . ." Katya stopped speaking. She teared up as she stared at him.

"Why didn't you talk to me first?"

"I knew you'd be against it."

Max put a hand on Katya's back. She shuddered a little.

"I really want to find Aska," she said. "If we examine her, we can find some new clues. Otherwise, you'll—"

"Stop talking."

"I want you to live, Professor." Katya turned away from Max. Tears rolled down her cheeks.

Max bought coffee from a vending machine and gave it to Katya.

"Aztec is no ordinary laboratory." Katya struggled to get up and reach for her wetsuit and diving gear.

"Don't exert yourself."

"I had a digital camera for underwater photography. I seized a window of opportunity and snapped several photos before those sedatives hit." The camera was with the diving equipment, but all the data had been erased. Katya closed her eyes and paused to think. Eventually, she opened her eyes and started retracing her memories aloud:

"I was taken to the building by the sea. The medical office had facilities similar to those of a large hospital. They have operating rooms and CT scanning equipment. There were several doctors there, too. It's a fairly large facility. Also . . ." She put a hand to her head. "A man in the medical office was talking about a girl."

"Was it Aska?"

"I don't know. I did hear the word 'daughter.' He said the girl left the lab last week. She was a 'substitute for her mother.'" She exhaled a faint breath. Her face was pale and her breathing faster.

"You can tell me more tomorrow." Max took Katya by the shoulder and gently laid her down.

"Why did the police come? So many officers, too," Katya said.

"If I'd gone to the Lab by myself, they wouldn't have let me in. And you would have been in even more danger."

"That chief didn't look happy to be there."

"I pulled some strings with a friend. I was roommates with presidential aide George Anderson in college."

"You were just roommates?"

"He was a good guy, and he had his talents, but those talents were never very well-rounded. When it came to math and physics, he was no more competent than a particularly unintelligent high schooler. I can't believe he made it into Caltech. He said he was at the top of his class in high school, but at Caltech, that doesn't quite cut it."

"I feel bad for the guy."

"I wrote most of his reports. He only graduated thanks to me."

"That's fraud!"

"It's the same story as your former boyfriend. He just didn't have the talent for science. Just like I don't have the talent for politics. Now he's one of the brains behind the United States."

"Then he should've chosen the major that actually suited him."

"Unfortunately, he only realized his predicament when it was too late to start over."

"Well," Katya looked forlorn. "I understand how he feels."

"I really can't see you as the type who would. He was just bullshitting his way up."

"He was lucky. He woke up from his delusions and returned to reality. You'd never understand what he went through."

"You need to go to sleep." Max put his hand on Katya's forehead to make sure she had no fever, and gently touched her cheeks with his fingertips before getting back up.

"Don't go." Katya grabbed Max's hand.

———

CHAPTER 21

Max stirred with the distinct feeling something was off. He'd fallen asleep sitting beside Katya's bed. He looked at her, she was sleeping peacefully. Then he realized his phone was vibrating in his pants pocket. According to the phone, it was two in the morning.

"Listen to me, and don't interrupt," came a woman's hushed voice.

"Who is this?"

"An ally. Look out the window. Don't turn on the light."

He went to the window.

Looking through the gap in the curtains, he spotted a car parked next to the pool. He saw the dark figures of several people inside.

"You need to leave the room as soon as possible."

Max hesitated for a moment, then he shook Katya by the shoulders. Katya's eyes squinted open.

"We need to pack up and leave, now." He put a hand on her mouth. Katya looked surprised, but got up without saying anything. She moved slowly, but the drugs seemed to have worn off considerably.

Max went to the window again. Several people were getting out of the car.

"When I give the cue, vacate the room and go toward the parking lot. A blue Ford is on the north side. I'm in the driver's seat," she said, her voice charged with tension.

"Are you telling me to just trust you?"

"If you want to live."

"Who gave you my number?"

"Your friend."

"Give me a name."

"Hurry up!"

"When you give me a name."

"Mr. Feldman."

Max looked behind him. Katya had changed clothes, and was standing with her backpack.

"Follow me." Max unchained the door. "It's the blue Ford on the right side of the exit."

The people who'd stepped out of their car were walking toward Max's room.

"Hold it!"

A shadow was crouching in front of Max's room, unlocking the door.

The door opened, and the shadow gave a signal to the men behind him.

"They're in your room now! Hurry up out of there!"

Max left the room, supporting Katya's body and stealing across the parking lot as they headed for the exit.

The blue Ford was parked right where the woman on the phone had said. Max opened the back door and pushed Katya in. As soon as they got in, the group that had entered Max's room rushed out and started toward Katya's room.

The woman quickly turned the key in the ignition. Looking back as they left the motel, Max saw the men hollering and running toward the car. By the time they reached the road, they were hit by the screeching of tires and the furious roar of the engine.

"Where are we going?"

The woman sped up. When she floored it, they were thrown violently against their seats.

"They're gaining on us!" Katya shouted.

Suddenly the rear window shattered.

"They're firing at us!" Max grabbed Katya's head and ducked. "Go to the police station."

"They're in the opposite direction," the woman shouted.

The car lights grew closer to them. Katya clung to Max.

The sound of bullets ricocheting off the car rang in their ears.

After each shot, Katya clung even harder. The car zigzagged and bumped up against a telephone pole. Somehow, the Ford made it out of town, and zoomed along the coastline.

"Faster!" Max yelled, while looking behind him. The enemy was gaining on them. Their headlights blinded him.

"There's a sheer drop on this side," the woman said, "and below that is the sea." She pushed down the accelerator anyway, and the car sped up.

The headlights gradually receded, but bullets continued to hit the car.

"Turn off the lights! They're aiming for our taillights!"

"That'd be suicide!"

"It's either that, or getting shot to death, or driving off a cliff, so pick your poison."

"Open the backpack on the passenger seat."

Max took the backpack and opened it. In it he found night-vision goggles—the same type Feldman and company had when they abducted Dona. Max gave her the goggles; she grabbed them and expertly strapped them on. A few seconds later, the lights went out and darkness swallowed the world ahead of them. The gunshots stopped and the lights behind them receded farther still. Their pursuers had lost their target. Moments later, however, the gunfire started again. They could still see the Ford by their own headlights.

"Shoot back! There's a gun in the bag!" the woman shouted.

Max found a handgun at the bottom. He aimed through the smashed rear window at the car's lights and pulled the trigger.

It took a few shots before sparks flew—one of the lights went out. The remaining lights fell farther back, but soon the distance closed again. The whir of a helicopter hovered above.

"They've got a chopper now." Max squatted to scan the sky, but all he saw was darkness.

Katya screamed as the last of the rear window shattered. Gunfire lit up the sky. Bullet holes peppered the ground lit by their pursuers' headlights.

"Duck!" Max shouted. "They're shooting from the sky, too."

The headlights behind them suddenly went dark. Then there was a loud screech, shouting, and a crash. Max checked the rearview mirror and saw orange flames.

The woman slowed down and turned on the headlights.

"Turn them off!" Max shouted. He stuck his head out the window to scan the skies. The helicopter dropped lower and passed thunderously overhead. The car stopped. "Don't stop! There's a chopper!"

But the woman didn't reply. Max looked at the driver's seat; the woman was breathing hard with her face on the steering wheel. Max got out of the car with his gun. The wreckage of the car that had been following them burned about fifty yards away. A pillar of flame towered higher, and then there was a deafening boom.

All of a sudden, the copter was above their heads.

They were buffeted by the strong wind from the rotors. The pilot blinked the red lights and dipped lower still. Max went back to the car and shook the woman's shoulders, but she didn't move, her head still on the wheel. The helicopter landed on a hill about twenty yards away. Max pointed his gun at it.

"Don't shoot! It's me," shouted a man against the whir of the rotors. The door opened, as a man ducked, holding his hat to his head. Tall, impeccably dressed, gray hair—it was Feldman. As he walked toward the burning car, Max ran up to him.

The fire was dying down, but flames still shot out from the edges of the car's dented hood. They saw two charred figures in the driver's seat and passenger's seat. From the backseat, a man thrust his arm out the window at Feldman. Feldman's arm shot up, and a gunshot rang out. The man's eyes were wide open; he screamed something to Feldman. It sounded to Max like "You're . . ." Another gunshot, and the man's arm fell.

Max stopped and stared at Feldman with blank amazement.

Feldman took the gun from Max's clenched hand before walking to the car and getting into the passenger seat. The woman sat up and gripped the wheel. Max got in the backseat and reached out to a shaking Katya and hugged her to him. The driver said nothing and started the car.

"What are you doing here?"

Ignoring Max's words, Feldman glowered at the darkness before them. Meanwhile, the chopper hovered above like a mother bird watching over her chicks.

They drove for almost an hour on the late-night freeway. The helicopter flying overhead disappeared. Feldman folded his arms and stared silently ahead. The landscape changed, and they were now driving through the business district of a small town. They turned onto a back road and stopped in front of an old building. Feldman signaled for the two of them to get out.

Together they entered one of the building's offices. The second the door closed, Feldman turned on them: "If I hadn't made it there in time, you'd be dead." Max had never seen him look so angry. Feldman took in deep breath after deep breath to control his rage.

A woman came in holding two paper cups of coffee. It was the woman who had been driving. She appeared to be Hispanic. She was very beautiful, in her thirties with long, black hair and dark eyes, and she had an intelligent look about her.

The woman gave the cups to Max and Katya, then came back with two more cups. She handed one to Feldman.

"This is Ms. Ryan. She's the person you owe your lives to."

She smiled faintly as they thanked her.

"She is an ally of ours. She was looking into Aztec Labs, and she happened to be there when a questionable car left the complex. You two should really thank your lucky stars. Without her, you would certainly have been killed." Feldman's tone had already returned to his usual calm.

"We are incredibly lucky," Max said. "Lucky that both of you came to save us. And for that we thank you. But you're lying. She was watching us, not Aztec Labs. I saw her car parked in front of the motel last night."

"You're imagining things. Without us, both of you would have died."

"So, how do you know they were going to kill us? Katya came out alive."

"What else could they have possibly wanted? To invite you to dinner?" Feldman raised his voice again.

"Why would anyone want to kill me?"

"I already explained to you—you've struck the enemy where it hurts. You're onto something big. And, you made the first move and marched into enemy territory; that is why they were after you, Professor. You are no longer bystanders. You're neck-deep in a war with this era's Nazis," Feldman said. He put a hand to his neck and turned his head; he was trying his hardest to stay calm.

"What do I know that I shouldn't?" asked Max.

"I also want to know." Feldman sighed and stared at Max. "Please don't attract their attention like that again. You're waking a sleeping dragon."

"Don't speak in metaphors. Just spit it out."

"I meant what I said, Professor."

"How did you know we went to La Cruz?"

"You contacted a presidential aide. That got the governor, the mayor, and the police chief involved. Anybody would think it was suspicious."

"You're listening in on their calls?"

"Heavens, no! I have no intention of making an enemy out of America. Wiretapping isn't the only way to gather information."

Feldman looked at Max. "It's as I told you, Professor. We are professionals, as is the enemy. But in this, you are an amateur. Just as I can't understand the work you do, you can't understand the work we do. Nor is that necessary. It's better if we stay in our own areas of expertise and cooperate." Feldman gave him an earnest look.

"The human mind is tenacious, and yours is particularly so. The flesh, however, is weak. Our bodies can be easily crushed. To kill a person, just pull your trigger finger a millimeter. That's all it takes to destroy body and mind alike."

"What are you trying to say?"

"I'm saying they'd kill you as soon as they'd kill a mosquito," Feldman said without changing his expression.

"Stop it!" They turned around; Katya was staring at Max and Feldman. "Stop arguing! We were almost killed! In just a single day, so many people died. How many were in that car? Three? Four?!" She shouted as she violently shook her head.

"I've had enough of this! In Domba, all the villagers ended up dead! Children, adults, old people, everyone. They were shot and burned right in front of us! When will the killing end? And yet here you are, fighting. Enough is enough!" Tears ran down Katya's cheeks.

Max and Feldman were speechless. Ms. Ryan sat next to Katya and hugged her shoulders.

"Katya heard them talking about the girl in the lab. Maybe she's the girl that disappeared from Domba," Max said.

Ms. Ryan froze. "A mixed race fourteen- to fifteen-year-old Indigenous girl with Caucasian blood. They called her 'daughter.'"

"You know the girl?"

"Yes. She was at the lab until a few days ago. A vendor guy who comes to the cafeteria told me he saw a girl in a wheelchair."

"Why didn't you report back to me sooner?" The color left Feldman's face.

"I only heard about her yesterday morning. And after that, I had to watch him," Ms. Ryan glared at Max.

"Where is she now?"

"I heard they took a boat to Mexico."

"You didn't see it yourself?"

"The vendor guy did. He said he saw them take her on a cruiser, and that he remembered it because she was the first girl he'd ever seen there."

"She's alive! Aska's alive!" Katya murmured.

"Where in Mexico did they take her? She may have all the answers we're looking for," Max said.

"I'll have them look into it immediately." Feldman stood up, patted Ms. Ryan on the shoulder, and went to the next room.

That night, Katya lay in bed, silently facing the wall. Max tried to start a conversation, but she wouldn't turn to face him. When he put his hand on her shoulder, he could feel her trembling. He had no idea what to do; he stayed for a while, but eventually gave up and went to the next room.

In the morning, Feldman entered the room where Max was sleeping. It was only six, but it was already bright outside. Max sat up in bed, and Feldman handed him a cup of coffee. The warm scent spread through the room. Feldman's eyes were bloodshot, and had heavy bags under them. He moved slowly, and it was clear that he hadn't slept last night. He pulled a chair next to the bed and sat down before taking a sip. "Two days ago, a girl and three men left the airport in Mexico City for Europe."

"Where in Europe?" Max asked.

"Rome."

"Rome?"

"Yes, and they're most likely headed for the Vatican," he said with confidence.

"The Vatican?" Max muttered. He remembered what Feldman had told him when he was at Max's home: This calls for communing with God.

"Is this the fruits of Jake's investigation?"

Before Feldman could reply, there was a knock on the door, and Ms. Ryan came in. She smiled at Max, but she looked exhausted. She handed Feldman a thick folder of files and left.

"These are the fruits of his investigation."

"Where is he?"

"Europe. He went from France to Rome. Right now, he's at the Vatican."

The folder contained documents and photos of people and buildings. The photos were grainy, enlarged copies.

"The Aztec Foundation. Their headquarters is in an old building in the backstreets of Paris, with three staff members. We're having trouble figuring out what's behind the organization."

"The foundation has provided Aztec Labs with hundreds of millions of dollars in research funding."

"The source of funding for the foundation is unknown. It's just a front. We've been tracing the flow of money for two months, and finally found the last cashier this morning. It was the Vatican." Feldman heaved a sigh.

The door opened, and Katya walked in. Max nodded to her to sit on the bed. He gave her the coffee cup he'd been holding. Katya inhaled the welcome smell.

"You mean the Vatican is paying the Labs through the Aztec Foundation?"

Feldman nodded. "Do you know the history between the Vatican and the Nazis?"

"I'm not a historian."

Feldman paused to collect his thoughts. Slowly, he spoke: "Before World War II, the Vatican's greatest enemy was communism, which rejected religion, and the Soviet Union was encroaching upon Europe. If left unchecked, the whole of Europe would turn Red. The Vatican thought that the only country that could fight with the Soviet Union was Germany, which was dominated by Hitler and the Nazi party." He took a deep breath before continuing. "There was also a Nazi-friendly priest within the Vatican." Feldman took a photo from the file and placed it on the table. "Father Artyom Yunov, a Russian-Croatian priest." In the photo, a man in vestments was gazing coolly at the camera.

His wavy hair covered his forehead, his features were well-proportioned, and he had a faint smile. He resembled more the Hollywood stars of yesteryear than a servant of God.

"He was called '*der gute Pfarrer,*' or 'the Good Father,' and he was the prime example of such priests. At the end of the war, many of the high-ranking Nazi officials and SS executives hunted by the Allies fled to South America with the help of the Vatican. Gehlen and Benchell included." Feldman put the photo on the table and took out a cigar. He breathed in its aroma, cut the cap end with a guillotine cutter, and lit it. Its rich scent filled the air.

"After the war, there was a network of Allied and Jewish agencies all over Europe dedicated to hunting Nazis. And many organizations were created to slip through that net. Odessa, Spider, Rock Gates, Brotherhood, HIGA—through those organizations, many Nazis fled to Europe, West Asia, and South America. But the largest organization to lend them a hand was the Vatican. They say thousands of Nazis were hiding inside the Vatican, at one time," Feldman said matter-of-factly. Max and Katya listened with rapt with attention. "The fleeing Nazis suffered a range of fates. The first thing the US and Soviet troops did when they entered Berlin was hunt down the scientists. Many Nazi scientists were top-notch. Their rocket technology and missile guidance technology far surpassed both countries', and that was clear from the V1 and V2 missiles fired at London before the end of the war. They were even on the verge of developing atom bombs. The main scientist behind Germany's rocket development, Wernher von Braun, was at the top of the list of scientists who were semi-forced to serve the United States and the Soviet Union, on the condition they wouldn't be charged with war crimes. But the Nazis that the Allies wanted were not all scientists. Then the world entered a new war—the Cold War. Many Nazis took advantage of that state of affairs, and sold information and offered their experience to right-wing governments around the world, especially in South America." Feldman's words stabbed deep into Max's spirit like a sharp blade.

"It's like something from out of the dark side of the moon."

"For us, it's just an ongoing fact."

"The Vatican, eh. What exactly is God?"

"He who knows and understands all. He who can do or create anything and everything. A priest is nothing more than a man. God is above man."

"So, why did they bring Aska to Rome?"

"I believe you know why more than we do, Professor," Feldman said.

"Is Benchell still hiding in the Vatican?" Max asked.

"No idea."

"Please save Aska," Katya pleaded, her voice feeble.

"I'm not interested in Nazi war criminals or the Vatican. I just want to save Aska. I need her in order to survive."

"What's so special about this 'Aska' girl?" Feldman asked, frustrated.

"I'm not a god. I don't know everything. But I do know that Aska is the daughter of Dona and Gehlen. She has all the answers."

"We're leaving for Rome today. I hope you will join us, Professor. I have some acquaintances in Rome," Feldman said. "And I don't know what you'll get up to if I leave you here," he added to himself, before getting up.

"We have to hurry," Max whispered to Katya. "Aska may not be able to survive for long away from the Amazon."

Katya gave Max a worried look.

● ● ●

VI

THE VATICAN

CHAPTER 22

They arrived at Leonardo da Vinci Airport around four in the afternoon, and from there took a taxi into Rome. When they entered the city, they were stuck in the typical traffic jam, so it took them more than an hour to reach their hotel near the Pantheon. They gave their names to reception, and Max and Katya ended up in the same room.

"The reservation was so short-notice, this is how it played out," Feldman said with a slight grin. "Or maybe Ms. Ryan did you two a little favor?"

"You and I should be in the same room," said Max.

"When you get to be my age, Professor, having to share a room with someone can be taxing. Please, let an old man be alone for a while." Feldman handed his bag to a bellboy and headed for the elevator.

"I don't mind this arrangement," Katya told Max, who was trying to discuss their options with the desk.

A bellboy was waiting for them with their bags. Max took the keys and started walking. Their room had the subdued elegance of medieval European décor, with light brown wallpaper, two old-fashioned beds, and a teak writing desk. Out the window, they had a view of the roof of St. Peter's Basilica across the Tiber. The sun was tilted westward, and the strong light dyed Rome vermilion.

"A city of stone. I don't like it. It's cold," muttered Max as he soaked in the cityscape.

"I like it. It's like a record of the past. It really makes you aware of the passage of time. So much culture was born here, so much history." Katya got a little closer to him.

"Slaves, gladiators, early Christians—so many people died against their will here." Max stepped away from the window.

Feldman called to tell them he'd be going out, so Max and Katya found a restaurant nearby for dinner. When they returned to their room, they felt awkward. The Italian spoken on TV was too fast for them to follow. They each took a bath, and got into bed a little past ten.

An August night in Rome. The minutes and hours went by quietly. Max had his eyes closed and his back to Katya. It was so still they could hear each other breathe. It made them think of the night they spent in the jungles of Brazil—the night of Aska's surgery.

"Professor . . . ," Katya whispered.

A cool breeze was blowing through the half-open window.

"Can't sleep?"

"Am I not attractive?"

In the moonlight, the room's interior was quite dim.

"Your charms shattered my shield of rationality a long time ago."

"Then why are you refusing to come closer?"

"I'm a coward, Katya. I'm not confident someone as attractive as you would ever choose me."

"I've looked up to you for so long. I can't believe we're together, just the two of us, like this."

"We've only known each other for a few weeks."

"It's been five years and six months. Germany was the third time we'd met. When you lectured at Stanford, I was right in the front row. We also shook hands at a conference at Caltech. I guess you didn't remember me at all."

Silence.

"The reason I took up the offer from the pharmaceutical company is because I wanted to work with you," she murmured.

"Admiration and sexual attraction are two different things."

"You're a man and I'm a woman. It's in our genes to be attracted to one another. You wrote in one of your books that defying that is defying God. Even if it started as admiration, it's not unthinkable for it to turn into sexual attraction."

"I'm afraid of falling in love. I can't stand the thought of passing my suffering on to the next generation."

"Suffering is a sign one's alive. It's better than feeling nothing at all, don't you think?"

Max turned to face her. Katya sat up in bed and turned toward Max. She lifted her arms and pulled off her T-shirt. Her white skin shone in the moonlight. Her shoulders were smooth, and her breasts were perfect.

Max got out of bed and fled for the pale shadows.

The next morning, they awoke to a knock.

Max opened the door, and there stood Feldman.

"I'll be waiting downstairs." With that, Feldman bowed his head with excessive politeness and walked toward the elevator.

It was more than an hour after the time they had agreed to meet. The two hurriedly got dressed and went down to the lobby. Upon spotting them, Feldman cleared his throat inconspicuously, but he didn't say anything.

After a quick breakfast, the three headed for the Vatican. They strolled through Rome and arrived there in around an hour.

They crossed the Sant'Angelo Bridge and entered Via della Conciliazione, which led to St. Peter's Basilica. It was already teeming with people.

Feldman was walking in the lead. He turned to face them: "Try not to get separated."

Katya linked arms with Max as he frantically tried to keep track of Feldman's head above the crowd.

"Is it always like this around here?" Katya asked Feldman as she looked around.

"It's Sunday. There's going to be a papal address."

In the distance, Max saw St. Peter's Basilica, a cathedral held up by huge stone pillars. It was over 445 feet tall, including the cross that topped its dome. The building's sheer majesty was enough to awe even nonbelievers. Was what they sought somewhere inside? A strange chill went down Max's spine.

"We're at the heart of the Vatican city-state," Feldman said, his eyes on the basilica. "This place harbors all that has to do with Catholicism. It covers more than 110 acres, and about nine hundred people reside here. They use the euro, but they have their own passports and postage. They even have a courthouse and a radio station. The pope has dominion over the Vatican, and it's the smallest sovereign nation in the world. The basilica was built where the first Roman bishop, St. Peter, was said to have been martyred and buried by Nero, upside down on a cross. At first the cathedral was in the middle of nowhere, and was used for burials. There's a necropolis under the basilica, full of the remains of martyrs. Eventually, a home for the pope was built nearby, and palaces were added. When a wall with a small spire was built to surround the city-state, the Vatican as we know it was complete."

"And now it's a grand and imposing tourist destination," Max said, scanning the area. There were people from all over the world, and clearly not all of them were devotees.

"Do you dislike religion?" Feldman asked. "I know you have doubts about God's existence."

"Every religion reeks of blood. Christians, Muslims, Buddhists, Hindus . . . countless people have died in the name of God. Even now, blood is being shed all over the world. Can you really call that the work of God?"

"One can't measure life by means of death. Some are dead even though they're still breathing. Sometimes death can inspire life. A death that keeps the will alive is more meaningful to someone than simply persisting. Martyrs died after achieving peace of mind, and victory."

"I just find that whole world inconceivable."

"To tell the truth, I do too," Feldman said with an impassive expression.

The bustle began to subside as tens of thousands of eyes focused on one man, who appeared in the window. It was Pope Benedict XVI. His mic-amplified voice began to reverberate, and a solemn air enveloped the square. As the pope delivered his address, Feldman's eyes were on their surroundings. To the side of the basilica, the roof of the Apostolic Palace, where the pope lived, could be seen.

The address ended in about half an hour, and the crowds began moving once again.

"The Apostolic Palace is closed to the public. Not just anybody can get in," Feldman told Max, who was watching the palace.

"Do you think Aska's in there?"

"I don't know. But I have a feeling that the people who hold all the keys are here. Tonight, my comrade will be getting in touch. Why don't you just enjoy Rome in the meantime?"

"I didn't come here to sightsee," Max said as he looked around.

"Impatience is our greatest enemy. If we make a careless mistake, we could make an enemy out of the whole world. We have to be cautious."

"Aska's here somewhere," muttered Katya, looking from the basilica to the palace.

"Facing the palace to the right is the guard barracks. They used to have their own army, but it was disbanded in 1970 and replaced by Swiss Guards."

"Is that a soldier?" Katya asked, pointing to a guard holding a spear and dressed in Renaissance-style yellow and blue stripes—a uniform said to have been designed by Michelangelo. He didn't look like a soldier who would fare well on a modern battlefield.

"We don't know much about the Vatican's security. Ever since their military was abolished, it's been guarded by private security forces and Swiss Guards. We don't have a clue what weapons they carry. But it's safe to assume that security got much stricter after 1981 when Pope John Paul II was shot."

They entered St. Peter's Basilica, stepping into an enormous, dim space. The dignified construction created a sublime and solemn atmosphere.

"This is the largest church in the world," Feldman said, his voice echoing in the vast space.

Max and Katya followed Feldman around the church. They stopped under the huge cupola designed by Michelangelo that covered the intersection of the church's transept and nave. Feldman looked up at the dome ceiling, then down at the altar beneath it.

"This is the Altar of the Confession, or the Papal Altar. This is where the pope professes his faith."

"I bet any Nazis here would start melting on the spot."

"Thou art Peter," Feldman said as he admired the cupola, "and upon this rock I will build my church. And I will give unto thee the keys of the kingdom of heaven."

"Matthew 16:18-19," said Max.

"It seems faith and knowledge of the faith are two separate things. Those are the words carved around the cupola, translated from the Latin."

"We're at the center of God's domain," murmured Katya. "The ladder leading from the Earth up to heaven."

Faint sunlight shone through the cupola's glass windows, illuminating the altar directly below it, which made it seem even holier.

They left the basilica and stepped out onto the elevated rampart, where they had a view of a huge, round castle—a cylindrical edifice towering above sturdy walls. It was the Castel Sant'Angelo, which had been converted to a museum. Standing at the top was a statue of an angel wielding a sword. Their guidebook said that the angel was trying to sheath the sword, but to Max it looked more like it had unsheathed it. Where was that sword pointed?

"The Vatican and the Nazis—the godly and the demonic. What do they have in common?" Feldman asked.

"They're both obsessed with life and death," Max said. "Or, with the image of death. They both have death at the base of their worldviews."

"I agree," Feldman said, nodding as he glared at the castle.

They entered the castle alongside groups of tourists. After passing through the gate, they were in a courtyard with rusty artillery and cannonballs. They could peer down at the Tiber from a terrace. Far, far away, they could see a hill, the Janiculum.

The elevated passage stretched in the direction of St. Peter's Square and enclosed the Vatican city-state, linking the Vatican and the Castel Sant'Angelo. In the past it had served more than once as an escape route out of the Apostolic Palace for the pope, who was chased out by the emperor. And in the twentieth century, the Nazis used it to escape from the Allies.

After they left the Castel Sant'Angelo, they looked for a restaurant for lunch. They felt surrounded by the harsh rays of the sun, people and cars coming and going, and the frenetic activity of a busy Roman afternoon. They found a restaurant with a table on a terrace. All three stared at the street below.

At the next table, six middle-aged men and women were chatting about the Vatican Museum over beers. They were playing a radio that was broadcasting the news in English: *". . . picked up many seats in the general election . . . far-right parties . . . response to increasing numbers of immigrants and illegal aliens in France and Germany . . . culprits behind the Dörrenwald bombing have yet to be identified, but the police have said they will continue their investigation . . ."*

"What terrible times we live in," Katya said, putting down her wine glass.

"That is why we're hunting Nazis."

"What do you plan to gain here? We didn't come here for the scenery, I imagine," she said, looking at the cityscape.

"Except a corn of wheat fall into the ground and die, it abideth alone: but if it die, it bringeth forth much fruit."

"John 12:24."

"It seems it's true; you really did memorize the entire Bible when you were in elementary school, Professor," Feldman said.

Katya looked at Max.

"Was that in my dossier, too?"

"It was," Feldman nodded.

"Rumors are always at least a little embellished. My mom used to take me to Sunday school, that's all."

"I used to go to church, too," Katya said. "But I've never actually read the Bible."

"I just found the Bible more interesting than the sermons," Max said. "The second I stepped outside church, God would vanish from my mind. I had football waiting for me."

"So, what's the deal with the wheat verse, then?" asked Katya, losing her patience.

"I don't know," Feldman said. "It's part of the message that was sent to me."

Feldman looked down. A red ball had rolled under his seat. Behind him, a girl of four or five was looking at the ball. Then she looked at Feldman. The girl had big dark eyes.

"Hand it back to her," Katya said.

Feldman clumsily picked it up and glanced at Katya.

"Now give it to her."

Feldman looked at the girl and hesitantly held it out for her.

"Thank you." She smiled, and took the ball with embarrassment. A young couple at a table a few feet away were smiling their way.

"Have you never talked to a kid before?" Katya asked.

"I'm a busy man." Feldman watched as the girl's parents held her hands and walked out. "Family, eh . . ."

A taxi stopped nearby, and out stepped Jake wearing a bright-colored jacket. He greeted Max and Katya with his eyes, and whispered something in Feldman's ear.

"I have to go. Rome is a beautiful place; please, you two, enjoy your holiday here." Feldman was about to walk off, but he stopped himself. "Please be back at the hotel by nine," he said, his expression as dead serious as ever. Then he got into the taxi with Jake.

Max and Katya went back to the Vatican and walked around St. Peter's Basilica and Castel Sant'Angelo. The whole city glowed in the summer sunshine, but Max couldn't shake his anxiety, and Katya was constantly checking the time. In the evening, they walked around the street market near Stazione Termini.

"Market's 'mercato' in Italian," Katya said. "I came here with my parents once."

They walked arm in arm. Max was beginning to feel natural and relaxed about it. The events of the night before kept coming back to him, but the reality of what had happened hadn't really sunk in yet. He'd say it was a dream, but the memories of the warmth of Katya's skin and the way she smelled were so vivid.

The market was overflowing with both locals and tourists.

"It's a wonderful city, isn't it?" Katya said. But her expression wasn't cheerful. She just couldn't stop thinking about Aska.

They had more time than they knew what to do with. Max called Feldman's cellphone but it went to voicemail.

They had an early dinner near the Pantheon before they went back to the hotel a little after seven. They asked reception whether Feldman had left them a message, but he hadn't. After each took a bath, they tried watching TV. They called Feldman's room a number of times, but there was no answer. His cellphone still went straight to voicemail.

It was past ten, but Feldman still hadn't been in touch. Max stood in front of the window. The shadow of Castel Sant'Angelo could be seen across the Tiber. To its west lay St. Peter's Square and the Basilica. There was something he wanted there, and when he thought about it, something hot welled up inside him.

"I'm worried," Katya said from behind him.

Those plain, unaffected words soaked into Max's mind. "There's no need to worry. We're in God's domain. And what we're looking at is God's land."

Katya's hand touched Max's. Max gripped it softly, and Katya held his hand strongly. He caught a faint whiff of the scent of her perfume.

"Feldman said all of the answers are in there."

"'All of the answers,' huh. I just want to know about Aska, that's all. I just want her back. If she—" She stopped. Outside the window, the yellow moon was shining in the middle of a blanket of twinkling stars. "What is Feldman planning? I don't think the Vatican's going to open its doors for us without a fuss. The Vatican's hardly going to go public with its Nazi ties, and it's not as though the world's going to put their feet to the fire."

"To Nazi hunters, this is a bridge that needs crossing, which is why Feldman and his group ended up here."

"His work must have reached its final stage. And that means, your objective . . ."

"But Feldman, he . . ." There was something unaccounted for in his heart. He didn't know what it was, but the anxiety that appeared like a sunspot got deeper and darker. It grew to an oppressive mass that spread to his entire body. "I don't know." Then he said no more.

A knock on the door. They opened it. There stood Feldman.

"We're leaving tonight," he said. Max thought Feldman's face looked rather stiff. "You should stay here." He looked at Katya, who was standing beside Max.

"You must be joking! What did I come all the way to Rome for?" said Katya.

"Even we don't know what will happen. This is our first time doing this."

"When did you become so chivalrous? You're letting a woman in on the action?"

"There's no way the Vatican is more dangerous than the jungles were," Max said. "I don't think we're going to get killed in God's own city."

They thought about the grand and solemn atmosphere of the Vatican, where they'd strolled around that day.

Feldman looked at Katya. "Very well, then," he said, nodding. "We are going to meet up with a certain individual."

"A Nazi war criminal?" Max asked.

"He's an important figure. That's all I know. A Vatican insider will guide us."

"A traitor to the Vatican?"

"That, too, I don't know. However, there will always be weak points in any organization. In any case . . ." He searched for the words. "I have a feeling something will come to a close with this mission. Some of the answers that we've been searching for sixty-three years lie inside this place."

"It may just be the beginning," Max said half to himself.

"I'll come get you at midnight. You have time to shower again. I hear the noses of God's servants are quite sensitive."

Feldman patted Katya's shoulder before bowing his head a little and leaving the room.

CHAPTER 23

It was just after midnight. Max and Katya followed Feldman out of the hotel. There were still plenty of people in the streets. Feldman briskly turned into a side street, which was surprisingly empty. Occasionally, a car's headlights on the main road flashed across the buildings, and the street echoed with the sound of the engine.

A black car stopped in front of them. Two priests were inside. The three got in, and one of the priests, a young man in a black cassock, started the car without a word. He was hunched over the steering wheel and kept looking around as he drove. The priest in the passenger seat had on the same vestment. The face they saw in the rearview mirror was a man entering old age with a white beard. He was putting up a calm front, but he was clearly terribly afraid, and that fear was palpable.

"Please wear these." The older priest turned around and handed the three of them black cassocks.

They slowed down. A police car drew up to the side of their car, and a policeman in the passenger seat made eye contact. The face of the priest gripping the wheel grew stiff. The older priest bowed his head a little, and the police car sped up and moved away. For the next twenty minutes, not one of the five said a word.

The car crossed the Ponte Umberto I into the road by the Tiber and stopped in front of Castel Sant'Angelo. The older priest and Max, Katya, and Feldman, all dressed in priestly garb with hoods, stepped out of the car, which drove off. The castle towered over them like a black mountain. Though it looked majestic during the day, by night it radiated an eerie aura. The priest glanced at Max's group, and began to walk. They strode to the other side of the castle until they came to a sturdy door. The priest pushed the door open and ushered the three into a corridor that was dead quiet.

The ceiling was lofty, and the walls had been tinged by the passage of time. It felt as though this space had trapped in the air that people had exhaled in medieval times. None of the warmth they'd felt during the day made it inside. Ever since the castle was built, so much had unfolded here, and vast amounts of blood had been shed. It seemed more like an old fortress where ghosts wandered around than a place of great importance for Roman Catholicism.

The three silently followed the priest. Suddenly, he stopped and forced them behind a pillar. Two guards were walking down the hallway in their direction.

A faint tapping sound; Katya's shoes touched the wall. The guards stopped. They exchanged a few words, and one started to walk toward them. The priest put his index finger to his lips and communicated with his eyes that they were to wait. Then he straightened up and stepped out from behind the pillar. The guards stopped to gaze at him.

Max noticed Feldman's hand held a gun with a silencer. The priest talked to the guards, who pointed in the direction of Max's group and said something. Feldman's arm rose, and he took aim at the guards. Max put his hand on Feldman's gun. Eventually the guards nodded, and they walked down the hallway. After the guards turned a corner, the priest motioned for the three of them to come out. They followed the priest down the empty corridor. The priest stopped in front of a door and knocked three times before making the sign of the cross. No answer came from the other side. The priest gently bowed his head to the three and returned to the hallway. When Max turned the knob, the door opened quietly. A man was standing alone in a dim room. He had on a white gown, and was cradling something in his hands. He stared at them without moving.

Feldman pushed Max and Katya into the room. Flames from candles lit the space, casting a huge shadow on the wall, like a ghost imprisoned in an old castle. The sound of the door closing behind them echoed in the air. As their eyes adjusted, they saw that the man was holding a Bible.

"Are you the one who's going to tell us everything?" Feldman asked, but the man didn't answer.

The room was simple, with white plaster ceiling and walls, no decorations, and furnished with only a wooden bed and desk. It was like they'd been transported to a medieval monastery. Standing next to Max, Katya glanced at the man defiantly.

He flipped a switch, and a faint light illuminated the room, revealing the man's face. Katya grabbed Max's arm. She was trembling.

Max and Feldman gawked at the priest.

"You're . . . ," uttered Feldman in disbelief.

It was as though the object of an image from sixty years prior had slipped through time to the present. He had slightly wavy brown hair, a shapely nose, and firm lips, like an old Hollywood actor. Even in the stark light, he had no wrinkles. His glossy skin shone. Max recalled the photo Feldman had shown him at the office in the town near La Cruz. The man before their eyes was Artyom Yunov.

Father Yunov stood tall and straight. He looked no older than his forties. The man who was over a century old had retained his youth and vigor.

"I'm your—"

Yunov raised his right hand to cut off Feldman. "I've been waiting for this day," he said in a low voice.

Yunov's bluish eyes gazed at Feldman, Max, and Katya in that order. His hair had the faintest traces of white. Max could sense that past his peaceful expression lay a bottomless well of fear and sorrow. Something was lurking within this man's soul—and it was the same feeling Max felt in his own.

CHAPTER 24

Time slowed to a frozen standstill, as the four fell silent for quite a while.

Feldman broke the silence: "We came here because a resident of the old castle told us this is where we could uncover the truth."

"The truth, you say," Yunov said quietly. "I am the truth you seek." He picked up a candlestick and slowly walked over to them. Feldman reached a hand toward his shoulder, but Max grabbed Feldman's arm.

Yunov opened the door and walked through to the hallway. The three followed the white-cassocked priest, crossing the hallway in silence before descending the spiral staircase at its end. It seemed like the staircase might continue all the way down to the center of the Earth, but finally they reached the bottom. Their path was blocked by a thick iron door.

"Where are we?" asked Max.

"The basement of the Castel Sant'Angelo," Feldman said.

Yunov took a key from his pocket and unlocked the door, which opened without a sound, and they were hit by the chill of a narrow brick passageway. Yunov entered without hesitation, and the candle lit up the slimy sheen of the brick walls. The musty air smelled like it was in there since the Middle Ages. It felt like they had been pulled into a realm of darkness, their footsteps echoing eerily against the walls.

"This is a passage secretly constructed by the pope hundreds of years ago," Feldman told Max under his breath.

Yunov clearly knew where he was going. He must have gone down this passage countless times before.

"Where does it lead?"

"That, I don't know."

Eventually, they reached an iron door identical to the previous one. Once again, Yunov took out his key and inserted it into the rusty keyhole. Beyond the door was another staircase. Father Yunov ascended with slow but steady footing. Before long, they reached the Vatican Museum.

Yunov entered the Sistine Chapel, the others following behind. The chapel was brightly lit, the lights that were turned off in the daytime illuminated it even brighter than during the day.

All three of them suddenly stopped. Within this enormous

building, they were hit with the odd illusion that countless people were squirming and wriggling.

The huge fresco that covered the ceiling depicted the works of God, as he created light, the stars, and the moon . . . Adam and Eve . . . and more. The Prophet Jonah, St. Bartholomew, the Virgin Mary, and Christ the Judge stared at the four visitors standing still in their chapel. All around them sprawled the masterwork of Michelangelo.

On the wall behind the altar, the image of the Last Judgment faced them. Seeing it in the still of night with no one else around, the mural created an aura of magnificence that was much more moving than what could be experienced during the day. Max felt chills from neither fear nor admiration. In a word, it was awe.

Yunov approached the altar and knelt. He looked up at the fresco.

Time passed without a word. A few minutes, perhaps it was only a few seconds. But it felt like an eternity, like the flow of time was being sucked into the cosmos and painted in the chapel.

Yunov hung his head and knelt in prayer. The other three remained standing behind him, staring at his back. Max's brain was lulled into the feeling that time had stopped. There was something there, he knew it. And it was beyond what he feared and hated. Something was enfolding him. No, he was being enfolded. He felt a serenity he'd never felt before.

Yunov finished praying, stood up, and turned to face the others. "That's Christ the Judge in the center," he said. His calm, gentle voice sounded young. It echoed in the spacious chapel and all but penetrated it.

Christ the Judge was a young, strong, and bold depiction of the Savior. His right arm was raised as though he was about to strike someone. Beside him, the Virgin Mary averted her gaze and looked downward. Surrounding them were the chosen of God and the transgressors—those who were helped up to heaven, and those who were dragged to hell.

"Perhaps Christ suffered on the cross to obtain eternal youth,"

Yunov said, his eyes on the center of the giant fresco. He stared at it, as though identifying each figure one by one. "St. Peter, St. Bartholomew, and the woman falling to hell . . ." Yunov's voice wavered.

The face of a muscular woman was twisted with dismay and remorse. A devil was gripping her legs, and trying to drag her down to hell. One could practically hear her sobbing and shrieking. Max's mind was overtaken by a peculiar sensation. Until now, death had been what Max feared most. Death had been an ugly, hideous thing, an eternal stretch of nothingness, a boundless darkness. It was twined around Max's body at all times, gnawing at his soul despite never revealing itself, and laughing at Max's trembling body. But now, even though the spectacle before his eyes was not unrelated to his image of death, it rid him of the fear he'd been harboring. Michelangelo's depiction of the horrors of hell and the glories of heaven had captivated him.

"I disobeyed God," Yunov murmured. "After the war, the Vatican hid Nazis. People are not allowed to judge other people; only God can judge. That is what we told ourselves. At times, more than two hundred Nazis stayed here. They escaped abroad through various organizations. And the Vatican helped them do it." He sighed deeply. "I've been acting as a de facto point of contact between the Vatican and Nazis. I didn't turn away Nazis that escaped the Allied Forces."

Feldman took a step toward him.

"We believed that the only ones that could stand up to the encroaching menace of communism were the Nazis. Everything we did, we did in the belief it would protect God's country."

"If that is the case, why hide it?" Feldman said, his words lashing Yunov's back.

"People are not gods. The pope can make mistakes."

"Isn't it the duty of those who serve God to acknowledge and apologize for those mistakes?"

"It was too great a mistake. Great enough to rock the world. Think of the believers who revere the Vatican and follow its commandments." His voice grew slightly shriller. "The Church suppressed it, buried it.

And the world chose not to pursue the matter." Yunov breathed a sigh of relief. Silence fell upon them for a while, until Yunov slowly turned to face them. "I made an even greater mistake," he said, his voice wavering, and tears welling in his eyes. "I was asked to read and decipher ancient Church documents. I found a report from a missionary who had been sent to South America in the eighteenth century. A letter from distant South America written in Latin. I was so absorbed that I forgot to eat or sleep and I lost track of the hour."

Yunov looked up to the ceiling and raised his arms up high. "There is a peculiar race inhabiting his land, as he has by all appearances lived for centuries, and to believe his wondrous condition to be an act of Providence would be justifiable indeed. Embraced by the great earth and the trees, the womenfolk possess the smooth skin of lasses, in addition to their black and lustrous hair. Not only do they boast unimpaired faculties of sight and hearing, but their bodies, brimming with life and beauty, know not aging or wasting away, and verily it is as though God dwells within them. The fountain of life that abides in the bodies of the womenfolk . . . He who drinks of the water of that fountain shall obtain life without death." Yunov's voice grew louder and louder, echoing in the chapel. "The missive made clear that he had discovered a tribe with perennial youth. And the name of that land was Domba. According to the map, it lay near the border between modern-day Brazil, Peru, and Colombia. I reported my discovery to my superiors. But no one put any credence in the account. And that is how that story ought to have come to an end." Yunov dropped his shoulders and took a deep breath.

"But the Nazis believed it, and sent people there," Feldman said.

"Under Hitler's orders, the Nazis sent a team to investigate. Before the team reached a conclusion, the Allies were nearing Berlin, Hitler committed suicide, and Germany capitulated. Their empire had collapsed. But many survived to inherit his will."

"Gehlen, Benchell . . . ," Feldman murmured.

"After the war, the Vatican tried to cut off their relationship with them. But Benchell was cunning and merciless. He took measures to ensure we couldn't escape."

"Did he blackmail the Church?" asked Feldman. "Did he threaten to go public with the Vatican's Nazi link? Or—" Feldman's voice trembled.

"A few within the group of Nazis that fled overseas made another demand. And we couldn't refuse it. We had no choice but to do as they said," Yunov said quietly.

"They demanded research funds," Feldman said.

Yunov nodded. "In return for hiding Nazis, the Vatican received works of art that the Nazis plundered from all over Europe during the war. Many of them fell into the hands of individuals within the Vatican, and were secretly whisked overseas to be sold off. The Nazis then demanded that the vast amount of stolen artwork they owned be turned into money through the Vatican. Then they demanded money of the Vatican directly.

"The Aztec Foundation," Katya said.

Yunov didn't reply. "The Church's reach and financial muscle are vast. We collected money from all over the world, and could transfer it legally to anywhere in the world."

"They made use of that organization and provided funding for Aztec Labs."

"That's another one."

"The Vatican knew about the Nazis' research. Having seen you, how could they not?"

Yunov looked away. "At first, I thought I would decline their offer indefinitely. But I gave into temptation. I sold my soul to the Devil, and acquired eternal life in exchange." Yunov sighed. His clenched fists were trembling. "Something even more fearsome is happening," he continued. "Among the young monks, there are some who think I am God. After all, someone who has obtained eternal life must be

God." He made the sign of the cross and looked up at the altar to the beautiful body of the youthful Christ. "What do you think people who think they've found God on Earth begin to desire?"

"They start to want to be gods themselves," said Max.

Yunov nodded. "The moment they began revering me as 'God,' they began to want to be like me. I asked His Holiness to take my life. But, as someone who serves God, it is not allowed. I'm not even permitted to take my own life."

"I can take your life." Feldman was suddenly holding a gun.

Yunov didn't react to it at all.

Max stood between the two. "This isn't like you. Your mission is to round up Nazis and those who aided them so they can face judgment."

"I can't forgive him. I believe in God as well. I can't stand by a so-called servant of God joining forces with agents of evil. He's a mere pawn now. In God's name, I—"

"Why did you want to speak to us?" Max asked, interrupting Feldman.

"Look." Yunov looked up at the ceiling fresco. "Depicted in this fresco is everything a person can experience: joy, sorrow, anger, compassion, hatred. Life, and yes, death. All of these were bestowed upon humanity by God. Life and death are both a part of us. To lose either would be to stop being human. Both are part of God's plan."

"But you—" *will no longer die.* But Max held his tongue.

"The people I loved, and the people who loved me, and the people who helped me, they're all gone now. Look at what I've become." Yunov turned to them and opened his cassock at the chest using both hands. His skin was as glossy and fair as that of the Christ in the fresco.

"I am no longer the man that God created. I have been molded by the Devil this way, I know that now. Every second I spend in this holy place, I ask where my fate lies."

Yunov looked at the Last Judgment, and raised his arms

overhead. Max saw what he saw: a woman descending to hell in a serpent's clutches.

"Every night I am racked by terror. And I have come to a conclusion: were I to continue living, it would be nothing but torture. One has but one life to live, and a timely death brings that life to a fitting completion. By extending my life, God is punishing me," he said, as he viewed the painting. "I'm already in hell. I must live here for an eternity in isolation, where no one can see me. That is hell. I now fear life and loathe my own existence. I fear and loathe myself. Death is what makes us human. A man who does not die is not a man. What am I?" Yunov heaved a deep sigh.

"What are Benchell and his men trying to do?" Max asked. "They've already wiped out a Brazilian village and the women who were carriers of the gene of life. I'd like you to tell us what you know about Aztec Labs."

"I don't know much," Yunov said. "They simply extended my life, in order to gain control over the Vatican." Yunov paused to think. "I don't know," he added quietly. Then he knelt in prayer once again.

"We know that Aska . . ." Katya added, "that a girl came here. The girl with the gene that gave you your youth. She's mixed white and Indigenous Brazilian, and the daughter of Dona and Gehlen."

Yunov's expression clouded.

"You do know her."

"The ritual. That's what they called it." Yunov closed his eyes, and kept them closed for some time.

"What does that mean?" Max asked.

"They put me to sleep. Probably by injecting me with some anesthetic or soporific drug. And then they conducted some manner of ritual while I was knocked out."

"You mean you don't even know what they did to you?"

Silence.

Yunov's eyes regarded the scene above. The silence lasted for so long that time and space melted together. At last, his eyes rested on a point in the painting, and he spoke: "At one point, years and years ago, they began the ritual without realizing I wasn't unconscious. I fought to remain conscious, and I heard a female voice. I saw her, too. I thought that it was just some dream. But with time, that memory gradually grew clearer, sharper." He shuddered, a fear from long ago rushing back. "I slept face down in bed. The woman was taken in by two men who were holding her by the arms. She was nude. Tanned skin, black hair. She wasn't white."

"That was Aska," Katya said quietly. "Wait, no, it was Dona."

"She lay face down on the sofa beside the bed. And her back, they stuck a needle in my back as well. It didn't hurt. I don't remember what happened after that. When I came to, it was the same as always: I was in bed, and all alone in the room."

"Did you feel strange at all?" Max asked.

"My back felt heavy, but that was overshadowed by the overflowing energy. It was as though new life force entered into my body after each ritual."

"Those were marrow transplants. The Nazis transplanted the bone marrow of the Indigenous woman who possessed the gene of life into you. Until now, they'd used Dona. And this time, they brought her daughter, Aska."

"Where is she?" Katya asked. "Where is Aska?"

"Last night they came. They put me to sleep and conducted the ritual. The person they brought for it may be the person you're looking for."

"Aska . . . ," Katya murmured. "So, where is she?"

"I don't know. I didn't even see her face."

"You're extending your life by draining hers."

"Oh, God . . . please, God . . . ," Yunov moaned.

"Why are they keeping you alive like this, anyway?"

"Because my very existence allows them to manipulate the Vatican. I am what they have wrought—I am living proof of their deeds. Thanks to my presence, the Vatican can't reject their demands," he said, his voice quivering.

"Do you know a town named La Cruz? It's a small town in California."

Father Yunov didn't reply. It was clear he did know of it.

"Is Aska there?"

Still no reply.

"In that town, there is a bioscience laboratory complex named Aztec Labs. Perhaps Aska was taken back there? Please tell us what you know."

Max peered at Yunov's expression, but it was too emotionless to read.

"Tell us!" Katya shouted. "Her whole circle of loved ones got slaughtered. I want to save at least her!"

Yunov slowly got to his feet, and walked toward the chapel's exit.

They came to the veranda of St. Peter's Basilica. Deep darkness shrouded the square below. Max looked out at Rome. Across the Tiber, the lights of the ancient capital's skyline extended as far as he could see.

Suddenly, Max thought he saw a red light. In ancient times, Nero purportedly set fire to the city, indulging in a feast and reciting poetry as he watched from his veranda the people flee from their burning homes. At the Colosseum, slaves would have to fight to survive, and Christians willingly let themselves be eaten by lions in order to be with God. The city of death . . .

Katya's shriek snapped Max back to reality. Yunov was standing on the rail. His arms were outstretched, almost like Christ's on the cross, and he was looking up at the heavens.

"I have committed a sin. And as a servant who fears God, I was about to commit a grave sin. God, show me the path I must follow," he spoke into the darkness. "Those who value their own lives lose it, and those who loathe life in this world live forever. Lord, I return to your bosom." Yunov looked at the three, and grimaced almost imperceptibly. Perhaps he was crying. Perhaps he was smiling.

"No!" Feldman shouted.

"God is eternity. Those are the words that will open every door," Yunov said quietly, before exclaiming: *"Liberate te ex inferis!"*

His white cassock, fluttering in the wind, he vanished from the veranda. Katya screamed.

"His God prohibits taking one's own life," Feldman said. "So, he has sinned in the eyes of his God."

"Fermatevi!" Guards with guns surrounded them. "Stop right there!" the guards shouted.

Feldman thrust his hand in his jacket pocket. He grabbed his gun.

"Put down those guns," said a quiet but forceful voice from behind the guards.

They looked in the voice's direction. Standing in the dim moonlight and guarded by several monks, the man was wearing a white cassock. His expression was gentle, but also vaguely somber, and the tranquil eyes under his head of silver hair were staring at the three of them.

They were frozen in place, as though they'd been tied up with wire. Their eyes were fixed intently on him, and the tension drained from their faces.

The guards lowered their guns and fell back. The man approached them. His eyes radiated love, kindness, and affection; their serenity could engulf even the plants, let alone people and animals.

"The pope . . . ," Katya said.

The pope stared at the darkness where Yunov had stood. "It's over now. Was it all God's will?" His voice carried through the dim light like an echo from the heavens. It contained sorrow, compassion, and the magnanimity to tolerate all.

The pope made the sign of the cross, signaled the guards with his eyes, and returned to the palace.

The guards escorted them out through the exit.

———

CHAPTER 25

Max, Feldman, and Katya sat silently. The lights of Rome shone through the window. Ever since they'd returned to the hotel, they had been drinking whiskey in Feldman's room. Two-thirds of the bottle was already gone, but nobody was drunk. No matter how much they drank, the spectacle of mere hours prior replayed fresh in their minds.

Father Yunov desired eternal life. But in the end, he had come to despise that kind of existence. And he'd put an end to the matter himself. What had life been, in his eyes? What had death been? These questions weighed heavily on Max's heart.

Katya broke the smothering silence. "What were his last words?"

"Liberate te ex inferis," Max said, as he put his glass on the table. "'Save yourself from hell,' in Latin."

"Just as there are those who fear death, there are those who fear life," Feldman said.

"What was he after?" Katya asked.

"If any man serve me, let him follow me; and where I am, there my servant will be also; if anyone serves me, the Father will honor him," Max said quietly. "John 12:26."

"Don't be so cryptic."

"He wanted salvation for his soul," Max said. "Yunov's dying words recited verse 25—the verse following the wheat verse Feldman recited. It refers to salvation. He wanted to be with God. Christ, who serves God, doesn't reside in this world." The image of Yunov standing on the veranda was once again before his eyes.

"Was he able to find salvation, through that act?" Katya asked.

"He made a leap of faith straight into God's bosom. He wasn't concerned with whether he would be accepted. To him, continuing to live was already hellish. He's obtained peace of mind now. Death wasn't suffering to him. It was salvation."

"He jumped on a sudden impulse. I think he just wanted to run from his sins," Feldman said coldly, before draining another glass of whiskey. He grimaced and poured himself another. "Catholicism condemns suicide. His conception of God wouldn't forgive him for choosing death. They even forbid abortions and contraception. He was just a coward. He simply fled his own skin. His guilty conscience was crushing him, and so he took his own life."

"Yeah, that's what suicide is," Katya said.

"Just as we suffered, he should have had to suffer even more."

"He suffered enough. That's why he chose death."

Rome's landscape came into view through the window. Max's thoughts turned to his father. Had death been salvation for him, too? "I hate to have to tell you this, but he simply ceased to be. All of his cells became inert, and so his mind and consciousness became no more. He can no longer feel sadness or anguish or joy; any and all emotion has been extinguished. That may be what can be called 'peace of mind.'"

"According to your conception of science, maybe. But we believe you can't sum it all up with just science. That's why I continue to hunt them down, even in my old age." For a moment, hatred passed over Feldman's face. He took a glass of whiskey and gulped some down in order to dull his mind. "I want to send them to the desolation they deserve." Feldman brought the glass to his lips again, only to change his mind and set it on the table. "If they and I end up in the same place, that's fine by me. So long as I get to bury the Nazis," he said.

Pale in the face, Katya looked at Max. A frigid silence covered the three like a shroud.

"Aska, where are you?" Katya asked suddenly.

"Her role in this is over. I'm sure she's no longer here," said Feldman.

"So, she was taken back to America, is what you're saying," Katya said.

"What is it Father Yunov wanted to say?" Max recalled his last words: "God is eternity. Those are the words that will open every door." His head began to hurt. He just wanted to forget it all and go to sleep. But he knew this wasn't the time for that.

"Who guided us to the Vatican?" Max looked at Feldman, but Feldman didn't reply. "It couldn't have been the pope, could it?"

"It was God's hand at work," Feldman said.

"God, the Vatican, the Nazis . . . are you saying they're all working together?" Katya whispered.

"Gaining control over the Vatican means getting that much closer to standing at the top of the world and ruling everything. Given how graciously the man guided us, he must not have wanted them to ascend to those heights."

"What do you mean?" Katya asked.

"They're trying to rule the world. They've amassed wealth and power. What could be next on their list?" Feldman said. "Hearts and minds. They want to conquer people's hearts and minds. They aim to get hold of the soul of the world." Feldman took his glass and downed its contents.

"Tomorrow I'm going back to the US." Max stood up. "I've got no time left."

Katya followed him out of the room.

● ● ●

VII

TELOMERES

CHAPTER 26

The next day, Max and Katya took a morning flight back to the US. Feldman would head to Israel after finishing his work in Rome. He said he didn't know where he was going from there. Max was silent on the plane. Katya didn't strike up any conversations.

Benchell, Gehlen, Dona, Yunov, and Aska—more than half of them were already dead. Max went over the events of the past few weeks in his mind.

He closed his eyes and tried to sleep, but the familiar swirling darkness invaded the backs of his eyelids. The shadow was clad in death's mantle, and it crept in close and tried to wrap him in its cloak.

"You're sweating, Professor. Are you feeling okay?"

He came to, and found Katya looking at him.

"It's just exhaustion and lack of sleep. Plus an empty stomach. No big deal."

"Don't lie, Professor. You have a fever. I have a doctor's license, too, you know." Katya tried to put a hand on his forehead, but Max brushed it off.

"Sorry. Just leave me to my thoughts."

He thought about the decade before Alex got sick. He started keeping a diary after he turned 30. Body temperature, pulse rate, blood pressure—it was now in Max's desk.

They arrived at San Francisco International Airport after four in the afternoon. The sun was still high in the sky, but it was fading. Max grabbed his luggage, walked with Katya to the exit in silence, rented a car and headed home. As he drove, the reality sank in—this was a battle against time. *And I am determined to defeat the enemy. I will find the parasite lurking within me, and I'll find a way to survive.* Max made this promise to himself as he clutched the wheel.

He ignored Katya's suggestions to stop for dinner somewhere or to buy something to eat, and went straight home. Sandwiches were on the kitchen table. Nancy's doing.

"Nancy knew you were coming home tonight?"

"I called from the airport in Rome."

They ate the sandwiches in silence, then Max went to his study. He had a lot to talk about with Katya, but he couldn't organize his thoughts. What had taken place in the Vatican was too intense.

A pile of envelopes were on his desk.

"It'll take all day to look through those." Katya entered with a coffee cup.

Max could sense Katya's concern, but he didn't know how to respond—and he was frustrated about it.

"Clearing it up in ten minutes is how I survive modern times." Max sorted the mail by the senders' names, and divided the letters into two piles—one on his desk, and the other in the trash. Most were tossed out unopened. He picked up one of the envelopes in the pile on his desk, and stared at it. It was thick, and sealed tight.

"Time for bed," he told Katya, putting it down. "Get some rest. The institute is closed anyway." He stood up and walked Katya to the stairs. She turned to him as if to say something, but climbed the stairs without a word. Max went back to his study. A cool breeze was blowing through the open windows, and silence filled the room. Max looked at the envelope. It was the same envelope that arrived every other month. He took a deep breath and opened it. It contained a DVD. After closing his eyes and clasping his hands in prayer, he inserted it into his computer.

The DNA analysis results, the electron micrograph of the cells, and the test results of the blood sample popped up on screen. There were no abnormalities detected in his white or red blood cell counts, GOT, GPT, gamma GTP. Urinalysis, no protein abnormalities, blood sugar levels—he stopped at the DNA test section. The blood drained from his face.

"It's already started, hasn't it?" came a voice from behind him.

He turned around; Katya was peering at the screen over his shoulder. "Your DNA analysis results and a photomicrograph of your chromosomes. Your telomeres are pretty short. Have your cells begun to age?"

Max turned off the computer. "You didn't say peeping was a hobby of yours in your résumé."

"You don't have any time left."

"My accelerated aging may start earlier than I expected."

Katya reached out to turn it on again and began typing.

"You have three years left."

"I've got one or two years left at best."

"Then we'll have to hurry."

"Hurry and do what? Pray to God?"

"Benchell kept Father Yunov young even over the age of a hundred."

"But now he's dead."

"Sure, but we saw the reality of it with our own eyes. People have successfully kept themselves from aging past their forties. It's undeniable now. And that fact is what's going to save your life."

"By what method?"

Katya sighed. The two gazed at the screen without exchanging another word. The quiet room grew quieter still. An oppressive weight threatened to squash him.

He watched as Katya absorbed the contents of the screen.

A package arrived the following morning, delivered by an employee of the Israeli Embassy. He told Max this was a stop on his way back to Washington, DC, from Italy—which was quite the detour.

"Who's it from?" Max asked, looking at the label. The sender section was blank.

"I just got orders from above, sir."

"What's inside?"

"I didn't go through customs, but I can tell you it's not a bomb." The embassy worker tilted his head and shrugged.

"It passed through without inspection as 'diplomatic luggage,'" the courier said as he turned to walk away.

"This must be from Feldman."

The heavy package contained a cold storage container.

"It's got the blood and bone marrow fluid of Father Yunov." Max read the label.

Katya snatched it from him. "Let's run them through a sequencer right away."

"Only two sequencers in the laboratory are running. And we'll only get our turn a week from now. We'll have to ask the university for a favor."

"Either way, we won't be able to get it done by today."

"Just the paperwork and procedure take a whole day. We could barge in, but I don't want to do that."

"We don't have time to be choosy, Professor." Katya was getting impatient.

She pushed Max away and sat in front of the computer. "First, let's search for genetic laboratories within a three-hour drive. Look, there are twenty-four locations. Now let's narrow our search down to places with high-performance DNA sequencers and supercomputers. Now we're left with four locations. One of them being your lab, then there's the Eoghan Research Institute. Their computers are also connected to Caltech. It's in Cheerton. That's just an hour away."

"Do you know the laboratory?"

"Sort of. Grab your things and let's go. I'll get ready." Katya turned off her computer and ran upstairs.

Katya drove them down to Cheerton, an emerging town between San Francisco and Allon. Though smaller than Allon, it was home to bio-laboratories and bio-startups—it was Bio Valley. It had wide open spaces and roads, landscaped lawns, and row after row of beautiful buildings. It was a scenic, if flat, town, reminiscent of the old Silicon Valley—not unlike Allon.

"You can tell me now," Max said. "What's your stupendous plan?"

"I'm still with Cosmo Pharmaceuticals, and they should still be sending money to my bank account in Germany on the condition I report on your research progress. Eoghan is owned by Cosmo."

"So, it's the branch office of the prince of thieves."

"They told me that it's not illegal if it's just information."

"Sure, if all you did was relay my daily schedule."

Katya didn't answer.

"You know the term 'industrial espionage,' right? That's what you were doing."

"That's how much attention people are paying to you. You're a superstar."

"And you're the one standing guard by the star."

"I already told you what I'm after, Professor." The car sped up.

"I wanted to work alongside you. I wanted to watch your brain work from up close." Katya stared forward, biting her lip.

"Forget about that. You must know by now that my brain is nothing special."

"There it is," Katya said.

Grassy green hills stretched on both sides of the road, and a white building sat in the center. On the lawn stood a sign that read EOGHAN RESEARCH INSTITUTE.

"You're with Cosmo, not with Eoghan," Max said.

Katya took a card out of her pocket. "Cosmo Pharmaceuticals is a multinational company. It has laboratories, factories, and branch offices all over the world. And its employees fly all over the world. Eoghan Research Institute is one of the branches of Cosmo Pharmaceutical's main genetic research institute."

"Does that card work at all of their branches, then?"

"As expected of a Nobel Prize candidate, you're quick on the uptake. This card lets me in and out of Cosmo-related companies, no matter where. Cards range from levels E to A, with level A cards going to top executives. The only place they can't access is the president's office. Level E cardholders can go in and out of the parking lots and restrooms of their designated department. At the head offices, you need both your key card and to pass a fingerprint ID system. In some places, they replaced the key cards with biometric eye scanners."

"What level's your card?"

"It's level B. It was actually level C, but I upgraded it to level B. Unilaterally."

"What's that mean?"

Ignoring Max, Katya parked in the lot. She went to the reception desk, showed her ID, and signed in. Then she brought Max his visitor's name tag and put it on his chest.

"Don't look so furtive," she said. "We're not here to steal anything.

We're just borrowing some equipment, that's all," she whispered as they walked down the corridor.

"Compared to what Cosmo's doing, we might as well be Girl Scouts."

Katya motioned for Max to quiet down and asked an employee where the laboratory was. "First, we extract the DNA from the blood and put it on the sequencer. Then, we head to the supercomputer. That, plus we need to check the cells. Busy busy."

They entered a restroom, where Katya took lab coats from her backpack and handed one to Max. As they exited, they passed some staff. Katya gave them a little nod. Another group walking toward them stopped when they saw Max.

"Forgive me if I'm wrong, but are you Max Knight?" asked a nervous-looking young man in glasses.

Max nodded. The man smiled, but soon his face turned serious.

"When did you arrive here, Professor?"

"Only ten minutes ago."

"I read *On Life and Genes*. I've read all of your papers." He'd relaxed his expression, but his voice was hoarse.

"Thank you. This is a good laboratory. I bet you guys are happy to work here."

"What brings you here?"

"You saw what happened to my lab, didn't you?"

"That's a terrible shame, but it's an honor to meet you."

They each wanted to shake hands with Max. Katya urged him to hurry and started walking. Even as they turned the corner, the group was still looking their way.

"In ten minutes the whole building will know."

"You're the one who said being famous was a good thing."

They walked faster. Katya stopped by a door that said EXAMINATION ROOM. She inserted her card into the slit. The door opened, and they stepped inside.

"I want this DNA extracted and run through the sequencer."

"Fill out these forms and go to reception. The results will come in the day after tomorrow at the earliest. We're full of requests." The young researcher didn't look up from his microscope.

"You heard the man, Professor Knight," Katya said.

The researcher looked up and stared wide-eyed at Max. "You're—"

Max turned to the electron microscope next to him.

"You're Professor Knight, from Caltech!" Immediately the whole room's eyes were on him.

"This is his request. I'm sure you heard what happened to his lab . . ." Katya looked at the researcher's ID. "Dr. Thompson."

"I'll have the results back to you in half an hour. Please, have some coffee while you wait." Thompson received the samples from Katya, but his eyes were on Max.

"Load the results onto a disc, if you could," she told him.

Thompson went into the lab, while continually glancing back at Max. A long-haired man brought them cups of coffee. Someone had already brought two chairs over to them.

"See? Being famous has its perks," Katya said with a sly smile.

While they sat waiting and sipping their coffee, fifteen researchers come over to shake hands with Max, and seven brought Max's book and asked him to sign it.

"I hoped to get this over with before becoming the talk of the building. Looks like that ship has sailed," Katya said, looking out the window. Outside, several researchers had gathered to look at them.

"I think our results are back—and not a second too soon."

Thompson rushed back in, disc in hand.

"Why our laboratory, specifically?"

"Keep this between us, all right? I'd like it if you didn't go telling the world. Management arranged this for us in secret," Max said under his breath.

"Leave it to me. If it's for you, these lips are zipped," Thompson replied, matching Max's volume with a serious frown.

"These test results are a private matter. And I want you to keep the fact I was here to yourselves, too."

"Roger that," he said with a wink.

The whole time, all eyes were on Max, Katya, and Thompson.

"I'd like to borrow a room for a while. Someplace quiet would be nice."

"How about the computer room? Not too many people there. It is a bit cold, though."

"We'll be all right," Katya said.

Thompson led them to the computer room.

"The JSX-3A. It's not quite as high-powered as Aztec's supercomputers, but it's close to the fastest supercomputer in speed. It can analyze the structure of proteins." Katya lowered the blinds and sat in front of the terminal.

"A person's genome is an encyclopedia, and we're about to open it," Katya said, inserting the disc. The DNA sequence appeared on screen. "Father Yunov's DNA. Now we can compare it to Dona's, Aska's, and Gehlen's."

"Hurry up. There's no time."

"Don't get hasty. You want to find out about the purified proteins' composition, too, don't you?" Katya peered at the screen. "This thing has all the latest programs for gene analysis and protein structure analysis." She began to type. Max went to the window and looked out from behind the blinds.

"Hurry. Someone's coming," Max said.

"It's calculating huge amounts of data. Even with this overgrown calculator, it's going to take thirty minutes."

"We haven't got that kind of time."

Katya kept typing. "I set it to send the results to your university folder."

"You know the password?"

"It's not the most secure password if you can guess it in a hundred tries—and I got yours on the second try. The first time, I tried your date of birth. The second time, I tried Alex's. I memorized it when you showed me his medical chart."

"That's an amazing and praiseworthy talent."

"There's no need to envy my paltry talents."

Max came behind Katya and looked at the screen.

"That 'talent' isn't what I wanted at all. You could do it even better if you felt so inclined. But the silly thing is, you're never so inclined."

"You're the one who told me to accept people's compliments," Max said.

"When you were in junior high school, you won the California Math Olympiad. What number did you place nationwide?"

"I never went to the nationals. It coincided with a local football game. The nationwide champion was the girl who placed second in California."

"That's incredibly ironic."

"She became a world champion and won the Fields Medal."

Katya sighed. Max reached out and tried to switch off the unit. Katya grabbed his hand while continuing to type with the other hand.

"Wait, I still need to put in the finishing touch. I need to make sure that once the info makes it to the university, it erases all traces this ever happened. This program is important."

"Now that's a talent I don't have."

They left the computer room.

"There's going to be a huge commotion in five minutes," Katya said in Max's ear, nodding her head to the researchers who were whispering while looking at them.

They left the lab and drove to a McDonald's. It had been over thirty minutes since they set the Eoghan Institute supercomputer to crunch the DNA analysis and purified protein analysis.

As she ate her burger, Katya connected her cell to the laptop she'd taken out of her backpack, and opened the university files. On the screen, the base pairs and their related gene appeared alongside a model of the proteins they'd purified there. The data the supercomputer had crunched had been transferred.

"This is the data re the A cells and Aska's DNA," Katya said.

"No, Father Yunov's data, as extracted by that talented young man."

"What did you find? "

Max pressed a key. The screen split into a top and a bottom segment. "The top is Aska's DNA. The bottom is Father Yunov's."

"They're the same! It makes sense, if the priest had Aska's bone marrow fluid transplanted into him."

Max nodded and took a sip of coffee.

"Then let's extract the DNA of the A cells from the priest's bone marrow fluid, and multiply it via cloning. Then we can transplant it to you."

Max typed some more. As, Ts, Gs and Cs flowed across the screen alongside numbers and images. The two stared in silence.

"Wait!" Katya said. "The X5-6 regions of chromosome 3 are different. So they aren't totally identical, and there are more differences besides. This didn't exist before, though." Katya traced the numbers on the screen with her finger.

"The transplanted bone marrow fluid has changed since it entered the priest's body."

"Tell me in a way I'll understand, Professor."

Max was thinking, his fingers still on the keys until he slowly drew them away.

"A cells are changing even as they extend telomeres, repair chromosomal damage, and repair the cells in other organs. But at the same time, some segment of the genes in A cells is switched on for a short period of time, turning off their proliferative function for a short time."

"So that's why both Yunov and Gehlen had to transplant A cells on a regular basis—and why Gehlen traveled with Dona at his side. You knew about this?"

"I figured that might be the case when I first looked at Gehlen's genes. And now we've proven it." Max turned off her computer. "The genes of A cells have functions that defy our common understanding. They can rejuvenate other cells. But that function can't be maintained for very long. When A cells are taken away from their original body, something happens. There's no question they harbor some other unique properties—including the fact that it's extraordinarily difficult for the bearer to conceive. The ovulation cycle probably lasts ages."

"No way!"

"That's just another way to survive. If they had a kid every year while being that long-lived, their family structures would buckle and the population would explode. If three hundred years is their life expectancy. If we assume they live to three hundred, then they'd have to be three times less fertile than normal."

"So, they only ovulate once every three months?"

"I don't know, but if their bodies evolved for population control, they might be ovulating only once a year. For the Nazis, Aska is a gift that keeps on giving. I bet as kids they age normally until they mature, then they stay young through their ES cells, abnormally long telomeres, and special telomerase capable of repairing genes. It's not so much 'eternal life' as it is extreme longevity. Gehlen and Yunov started transplanting in their late forties and managed to freeze their bodies in time."

"Then why did Benchell have the villagers with such valuable genes killed off?"

"Probably because . . ."

Katya suddenly looked blurry. Max felt his consciousness slipping away. He grabbed the edge of the table to steady himself. Katya watched his face.

Max looked out the window at the cars in the parking lot. A man was reading a newspaper in a blue sedan. It was familiar scenery in the suburbs of California. The seconds ticked by. Gradually, the world came into focus again.

"They learned how to artificially generate cells with the same genetic information as Aska and her people, so they no longer need them." Max didn't use the word "clone." Katya was already aware.

"They have the same DNA as Aska's people? So, they're clones."

"Yes, as has already been done with animals."

"Aztec is applying it to humans."

Max nodded.

"Immortality. Humans have finally achieved their dearest wish."

"But that isn't the Nazis' motivation. They're trying to create the Fourth Reich, the world Hitler dreamed would happen after the Third Reich. And with this breakthrough, that's no longer just a dream. They even tried to wrest control over the Vatican."

"But they failed."

"Next time, they may succeed." Max looked out of the window. He thought about Yunov's youthful appearance. "They're trying to conquer hearts and minds not with military force but by their works— armed with the immortality humans have always craved."

"Are you going to call Feldman?" Katya asked.

"He'll stay in Europe for now. The Americas aren't the only place Nazis fled to."

"He should give up. Sixty-three years. I can't imagine spending all that time chasing Nazis. He could have led a different life."

"It's what he wanted. For him, this is his best life."

"Do you believe that? A life spent hunting people down, capturing them, sometimes killing them. I wouldn't be able to stand it. He'll regret that's what his life amounted to in the end. I wonder what he'll think about when he's at death's door?" She looked at Max, confused.

Max kept looking outside. He was sensitized to the word "death" and Katya knew it.

"Let's go back to Aztec," she said. "There's some research going on over there that might cure you. Aska was definitely taken back there from Rome."

"It's too dangerous. They tried to kill us."

"You only have so long to live, Professor."

"Even if we get inside again, they're not going to show us their research."

Katya met Max's eyes. "It's our only option."

CHAPTER 27

They left McDonald's and Katya began driving them home.

"Have you noticed?" she said, looking in the rearview mirror.

"I noticed five minutes ago. Let's change places." She pulled over, and Max exited the car. Just then, a black Grand Cherokee passed by. There were two middle-aged men in the front seats. Tinted glass hid who was in the back.

"Maybe nothing to do with us?" Katya wondered.

"We can't be sure."

As Max started the car, his cellphone rang.

"Where are you now?" It was Feldman.

"I'm heading home."

"Why not take a little detour? We've heard a strange bunch is waiting for you near your house."

"A strange bunch? Must be your people then?"

"It's not funny, Professor."

"Where are you?"

"I'm in the US. Not even fifty miles away."

Katya pointed to the rearview mirror. The Cherokee was chasing them. The man in the passenger seat held a submachine gun.

"Call me back. Looks like you're not the only strange bunch in town." Max accelerated, and the SUV sped up.

"Is that a handgun the man in the passenger seat is holding?" Katya said.

"It's the type of gun that can shoot way more bullets."

"They don't mind shooting us in the middle of the city?"

"Why don't you ask them." Max stepped on the accelerator. Katya shrieked, as she was slammed back into her seat. Max's cell was ringing again. He put his hand in his pocket and turned it off.

"The light's red. Be careful!" Katya cried.

Max pushed on the accelerator and flew through the traffic lights. Cars honked from all directions, and the screech of brakes filled the air. The Cherokee had stopped at the intersection. Katya clasped her hands, her eyes shut tight. Max turned the first corner and continued.

"You're crazy," Katya said, her gaze fixed forward.

"When our lives are on the line, sure." He kept turning down side roads, and when they were no longer being tailed, they left town. The clear blue sky stretched to the horizon. The Mercedes zoomed down the freeway until the straight desert road turned into a green mountain road.

"Where are we going? Isn't it dangerous to be someplace so isolated?"

"Wasn't it your father who said that life is to be enjoyed?"

"Yeah, when we're not getting chased by gun-toting psychos. I'm really not in the mood right now to enjoy the great outdoors."

After about two hours on the road, there were no more houses in view.

"There aren't any stores past this point." After filling the gas tank, they bought food at the neighboring supermarket.

Once they hit the mountain road, Max put the convertible's top down. The cool air felt great. Katya squinted into the distant mountains. After about another hour, a lake came into view, its blue water shining between the trees.

"This was definitely worth the risk," she said, her words trembling in the wind. A small log cabin was on the lake's shore. Max parked in front.

"My villa. Or rather, my brother's and mine."

The logs were about a foot in diameter, and a deck surrounded the house. A wide window faced the lake, and the living room had a stone fireplace.

After the sun went down, the temperature dropped. Max and Katya sat in front of the fire. The only sound punctuating the silence was the crackle of the flames. It was past eight, and they didn't hear any noise from outside.

"It's quiet." Katya leaned against Max and snaked an arm around his waist. All they could see through the gaps in the curtains was darkness.

"When despair for the world grows in me," Max recited, "and I wake in the night at the least sound in fear of what my life and my children's lives may be, I go and lie down where the wood drake rests in his beauty on the water, and the great heron feeds. I come into the peace of wild things who do not tax their lives with forethought of grief. I come into the presence of still water. And I feel above me the day-blind stars waiting with their light. For a time I rest in the grace of the world, and am free."

"'The Peace of Wild Things' by Wendell Berry," Katya said.

"I guess you didn't spend all of your time studying."

Katya smiled.

"But no matter where I went, I never had any peace of mind. I was only ever dragged forward while cowering in the shadow of death."

They went quiet for a bit, lost in their own thoughts.

"I've told you about my father before," Max said. "When I was a kid, I was afraid of the dark, and of silence. Whenever I closed my eyes to fall asleep, I plunged back into the terror of death coming for me. Of never waking up again. Then I'd jump up and turn on the lights. I'd turn on all the lights in my room, and just keep my eyes open and listen to rock music with my headphones. I was telling myself I was still alive. After two straight days of that, I'd be exhausted. But that was better than the fear of death."

"I wouldn't be able to take it."

"Now imagine how shaken I was when I saw my dad floating on the lake. Just like that, death was no longer so far away. I knew that was the point I'd reach someday, but I'd thought it was still miles away, only to realize it was right in my face. The year after my father died, my brother gave me my father's diary. I kept it on my desk for months. I was too scared to read it. I didn't want to know the details of his misery—or that was the excuse I told myself. I was just scared to face death. One night I started reading it. He'd been scared out of his mind by death, just like me, but his terror was deeper and crueler." Max stared at the fire, as though he were staring into the distant past.

"My father saw his own father die. My grandfather shot himself. Back then no one knew about genes. He was an elite navy man with a bright future, but his illness began at forty. It was a curse. My father found his father in a naval hospital bed bleeding from a hole in the head." Max put a log on the fire. The flames went up, illuminating Katya's face. "I faced setbacks and pushed through them many times. I told myself I didn't want to die defeated like my dad or grandfather." Max turned to the side, pretending to avoid the heat. He didn't want Katya to see his eyes were filled with tears.

"You hear it, right?" he asked. "It's the sound of the waves."

They could hear a faint rhythmic sound above the wind.

"My father died in that lake. It was winter nineteen years ago."

Katya's eyes opened wide. "So, this is where you were camping?"

"I come here once a month but now it's been a year and two months since I've come. My brother always came with me when he was well. But two years ago I started coming here alone. Before the cabin, we used to pitch tents. The two of us built this cabin seven years ago, in memory of our father—that is, to remind ourselves that we will die too. Staying here for the night was a reminder of our determination to fight."

"We already found the key to treating you."

"We know the shape of the key, but we don't know how to forge it, or even where the door is. And even if we find the door, we don't know where that door leads."

"It's okay. Everything will work out."

Katya gently put her arm around Max's neck. Max hugged her tight. He felt a dampness on his lips. It felt full of life. It felt like life itself.

The flames wavered, casting long shadows on the curtains.

The sound of shattering glass and a rumble cut through the air. Max pushed Katya down to the floor. There was a hole in the windowpane facing the lake.

"We're getting shot at!"

Max covered Katya's body. More glass shattered as violent impacts shook the room. Bullets pelted the logs, but they couldn't hear any gunshots. A silenced automatic rifle. They lay down on the floor and waited for the shooting to stop. Eventually, the night was silent once again.

"Stay here." Max tried to crawl to the bedroom, holding the poker that was by the fireplace.

"Don't!" Katya grabbed Max's arm.

"There's a gun in the closet—"

Before Max could finish the sentence, more rounds punched through the walls. Photo frames and vases on the mantelpiece shattered. Katya shrieked and clung to Max. A figure appeared in the window. Max broke free of Katya's arm and ran beside the door with the poker.

The door burst open. A shadowy figure leapt in, and Max hit him with the poker with all his strength. He felt the recoil in his arms, and the man collapsed. A gun with a silencer fell to the floor. Max picked it up and aimed it, but the man was motionless. Max, seeing Katya was about to get up, motioned for her to stay down.

They heard more glass breaking and another man jumped

through the broken window. Katya screamed. He was wearing night-vision goggles and holding an automatic rifle.

"Get down!" Max shouted.

Katya fell to the floor, and Max's gun fired simultaneously. The man fell backward.

The shooting started again. Bullet after silenced bullet ripped through the logs, tearing through the books and figurines on the shelves. Max crawled closer to Katya, hugging her shoulders and hiding behind the sofa. He felt a burning sensation on his left arm.

Suddenly the shooting stopped.

There was a faint creaking noise from the deck. Max picked up his gun. He could sense Katya's trembling.

"He's coming," she said.

"Stay here." Max lifted his hand from Katya's shoulder and moved toward the wall.

He touched his left arm. It felt wet, but he wasn't in pain.

More rounds blasted through the logs. Max repeatedly pulled the trigger, aiming at the darkness outside, but soon the chamber stuck. He'd run out of ammo.

They heard the screech of tires and the braking of several cars. They heard a car door open, and the sounds of multiple people getting out. They heard a mix of footsteps, gunfire, and barked orders. No silencers this time.

Once again, a hush. Now they could hear the sound of the waves. A figure appeared on the deck. Max put down the gun and picked up the poker.

The door flung open, and a man wearing a ski mask and holding an automatic rifle jumped in. He trained his gun on Max. Katya screamed and jumped up. Max pushed Katya away and stood in front of the man. The muzzle was pointed at Max's chest. Max closed his eyes as a shot rang out.

"NO!" Katya's scream rang in his ears.

When he opened his eyes, the gunman toppled toward Max, blood pouring from the holes in his back. A man in night-vision goggles holding an automatic rifle stood in the door. Max took the gun from the fallen man and aimed it at him.

"Don't shoot! It's me!" The man took off his night-vision goggles. It was Feldman.

Just then, the fallen man's eyes opened and looked at Feldman. He tried to speak, and lifted his arm, but Feldman nonchalantly lifted his own arm and pulled the trigger. The man reeled back, and his eyes closed.

"You didn't have to shoot the guy," Max said.

"I know a lot of good souls who died thinking the same."

The beams of flashlights intersected and lit the room. Two men with automatic rifles came in behind Feldman, keeping an eye on the area. Max turned on a large battery-powered lamp. Glass shards and debris were scattered all over the room, and white feathers from the ruined cushions blanketed the floor like snow. Katya squeezed Max's hand. Her eyes were bloodshot.

"You're injured!" she cried, looking at Max's arm.

"It's just a scratch."

Katya sat him down on the sofa and examined his wound.

"I told you not to act on your own." Feldman's tone was uncharacteristically harsh.

"We just came to rest here, that's all."

"I suppose that's fine, if you plan to take the kind of break that lasts forever," Feldman said, as he helped Katya tear off Max's shirtsleeve.

A man came in and raised his right hand toward Max. It was Jake. He gave Feldman a box the size of a cigarette pack.

"This was attached to your car, Professor. It's a transmitter, locatable via GPS.

"Did they set it?"

"It wasn't us. But we did make use of it."

Max told Katya where to find the first aid kit. Feldman signaled for Jake to open the front door to several men in black clothing to start putting the corpses in body bags.

"This is the second time," Feldman said. "What would've happened if we'd arrived a minute later? Work with us a little more, the both of you."

"I'm thankful for your impeccable timing." Max finished treating his wound and put an arm around Katya's shoulders. He could feel her heart pounding.

Max looked around the room. "It looks like a hurricane and a tornado struck at the same time."

"These are people whose ideology revolves around ethnic cleansing. They don't blink at the thought of killing you."

"I'm just a scientist."

"The scientist that knows their secrets."

"You mean Father Yunov's DNA and cells?"

"I bet the results are in by now. What did you find?"

"It was just as he said. He was kept alive by a girl. The priest's cells had Aska's genes integrated into them. Aska's bone marrow cell transplantation increased his telomerase secretion, created unique proteins, and repaired genetic damage. The cells continued to divide without becoming cancerous. That's the secret of his youth. Though it's much more complicated to explain."

"Mightn't this information be useful in treating your own disease, Professor? I sent them to you with that in mind."

Max didn't answer. Jake and the others had finished putting the bodies in bags, and were carrying them out.

"They'll handle it. Nothing happened here. It's just a quiet lakeside vacation house. You enjoyed some time off with a beautiful woman. Unfortunately, you tripped on the stairs and hurt your arm. Accidents happen." Feldman shrugged.

"Why did you come back to the States?"

"I want to protect you, Professor. I am rather fond of you. And, the world needs you. I want you to live longer. I don't want you to die because of a daft little accident." His expression turned harsher as he stared at Max. "And, we are getting closer to Benchell. I can smell it. No matter how many times he changes his face, physique, or voice . . ." He clasped his hands in front of his chest and struggled to keep in his emotions.

Max remembered Feldman's words: *If they and I end up in the same place, that's fine by me. So long as I get to bury the Nazis.*

"There was a problem with Aztec Labs after all." Feldman took a deep breath. He returned to his calm tone of voice.

"I want to get closer, but this is our problem. If an amateur pokes his neck in, his life is over." Feldman looked around. The windowpanes were gone, and all but the bullets that had burrowed into the walls had been cleaned up. "We will be watching tonight. Tomorrow, we'll leave at dawn and get you home. We will provide you with bodyguards at home. Sound reasonable?" Judging by his tone, he wouldn't take no for an answer. Max had no choice but to nod. Feldman yawned conspicuously and left the cabin, massaging the space between his eyes with his fingers.

CHAPTER 28

In the morning Max and Katya returned to Allon, their car sandwiched between Feldman's vehicles. An unfamiliar tinted-glass van was parked in front of the house. When they went in, Nancy greeted Max as if nothing was unusual. But she knew something was up.

That night, Max sat at his computer. On the screen were the results of the DNA analysis from the Eoghan Research Institute. Katya was beside him, staring at the screen with the same frown on her face as Max.

"There is no laboratory or equipment we can use," Katya said. "All we have are DNA and cell samples."

"But sitting around is fruitless."

"I think we should infiltrate Aztec again." Katya pushed Max out of the way and took over, typing away like a jazz pianist. The contents of the screen changed. Katya looked intently at the website she'd pulled up.

"Pacific Construction." Max read. "This is the company that built Aztec Labs, isn't it?"

"Bingo!"

"They should still have blueprints. It was built five years ago."

The screen changed again. For two hours, photos, drawings, specification documents, and price estimates appeared. Katya got up and stretched. There were shadows under her eyes, and fatigue was written on her face.

"Let me do it," Max said.

"You should use your talents for more important things. We each have our own area. This is mine."

"You shouldn't put yourself down. You're more than talented."

"That's what my elementary school teacher used to say. My middle school and high school teachers, too. In the eyes of most, I'm really talented. My teachers, classmates, neighbors, and relatives still believe in me. But no one knows me better than myself. And I know I'm not as talented as you are."

"Talent is for the outside world to appraise. It's not for you yourself to label."

"If I work myself to death, can I leave behind research achievements on your level?"

"It's not impossible," he replied. "New discoveries are 20 percent talent and 50 percent effort."

"What about the remaining 30 percent?"

"The whims of God. Pure luck."

"You're too nice, Professor."

Katya put her finger on Max's lips. Resignation, loneliness—Max could sense them in her smile. He'd experienced those same emotions for different reasons.

Katya slapped herself on the cheeks and turned to her computer again. After an hour, she took her fingers off the keyboard and heaved a sigh.

"There's a record of the construction of Aztec Labs, but there are no documents left."

"The disposal of the plans must have been a condition for the lab's construction. What security company are they using?"

"They have their own security. Former SS and Gestapo officers. Security is their strong point."

Max moved the mouse. After a few clicks, a column of names came up.

"It's a list of Pacific Construction designers. There are probably laboratory designers in this list. Maybe the designer of Aztec Labs has the plans."

"As a designer you wouldn't want to delete your own blueprints, but how do we find who was in charge?"

"Few laboratories can perform genetic manipulation. Aztec has P4 laboratories. You should search for designers who have experience designing P4 laboratories."

She searched for about an hour, but couldn't find anybody matching that description.

"Wait!" she shouted, just as she'd been about to give up. "Maybe they were outsourced!" Katya pulled up a list of outsourced designers. "Daniel Allson. He also designed P4 labs at Stanford University and the University of California, plus some of the major West Coast labs. He's with Allson Design Office. He's the director, too." When Katya searched the office name, dozens of results appeared.

She went to the website. "Director Allson seems to like the limelight." His career history showed photos of him receiving architectural awards, wearing a cowboy hat, kissing golf and fishing trophies. "I know talent and appearance have nothing to do with each other, but here the gap is really wide."

"Look at that photo of him in a yacht race," Max said.

"A guy like that isn't going to ever delete his blueprints." Katya scrolled down the page to read his past work. "No record of Aztec Labs. He deleted it. He kept his promise to destroy the material."

"No," Max said, "he just hasn't got the balls to put it on his website. Would you delete your own paper and data after presenting your thesis? No, especially, if you're proud of them."

"Apples and oranges," said Katya.

"It's just human psychology, and this guy's especially susceptible."

"Maybe we can access the office's directory." Katya sat down again.

Another hour passed. Max brought two cups of coffee, and Katya leaned in close to the screen, tracing the text with a finger.

"This is the one thing I'm better at than you, Professor. I'm inside the network at Allson Architects." Katya took her cup. "Five years ago, he was working with Pacific Construction. Look, it says 'La Cruz Bay Park.' But there is no park by that name around there." With a click, dozens of photos appeared. "Aztec Labs!"

A beautiful lab complex with the sea in the background. The photos chronicled the process of laying the foundation on bare rock and gradually forming the shape of the buildings.

Max typed, the screen changed. The building on the side of the road was a research facility for genetically modified plants.

"Here, the plants are genetically modified and new species of plants are artificially created. This building is the face of the facility."

The middle building, meanwhile, was just an office building.

"There's no sign of the third building, the one by the sea," said Katya.

"It's the same size as the other buildings. Which were you taken to?"

"I don't know which building it was in, but they took me to a medical office. I think it was in the basement. The current was faster than I'd expected, and I'd swallowed way too much seawater. But I have to say, the facilities were top-notch. Comparable to any large hospital.

I looked around while pretending to be unconscious. There was an X-ray machine, a CT scan, and an artificial dialysis machine. All the latest stuff, too."

Max stopped typing. Drawings appeared on the screen. The third building on the sea side. The drawings were detailed, even describing the types of locks on the main doors. "Room layout, size, power distribution equipment, plumbing, everything is special."

"Here. Their secret research is being conducted in this building," Katya said, pointing at the text: "P4, computer room, shower room." She pulled up detailed shots of the interior. "They still have all the blueprints and photos, even the restrooms and the shape of the door keys. I have to thank Director Allson for his pathological meticulousness."

"If his clients ever found out, he'd get shot. And if he ever found out they were Nazis, he'd be scared shitless."

"It's inaccessible by sea." Katya traced the coastline with her fingertips. "I couldn't do it."

"When I was in elementary school, I almost drowned in an Olympic-size pool, so I decided to do athletics and stay away from pools."

"Al from the boathouse says they're watching the ocean by radar. If anybody gets too close, they tell you to keep out through the speakers. No mercy for trespassers." Katya drank her coffee as she typed. "Some of these files are about security." The big-picture blueprint of the complex detailed the locations of surveillance cameras and infrared surveillance devices mounted on the surrounding walls. "It was here that the guards stopped us before," she said, pointing.

Max put a ruler on the blueprint and drew some lines—the effective range of the cameras and infrared surveillance devices. Max's car had definitely been monitored when they were there.

"These surveillance cameras eliminate any potential blind spots."

"These are the basic specifications of the security system he proposed. If these plans were modified by the active-duty Gestapo, then there really is no way to get in."

The two surfed around the architect's website for a while.

"Do we have no choice but to blend in with the food suppliers?"

Katya typed and pointed to the screen. She found the website of the food company that delivered to Aztec Labs. At the beginning of the week, they brought in a week's worth of food.

"So, we suit up as T-bone steaks and sneak in that way, huh? I don't know about you, but cabbage suits me better."

"Don't be silly. Is there no other way?"

"It's as Feldman said—we are not professional spies."

"So, you just want to rot and die? Even if that means breaking your promise to your brother?" Katya said.

"I have never once forgotten about my brother."

"I'm sorry."

Max mulled it over. Chiseled into his mind was the image of a wheelchair-bound Alex staring at his own impending death. "Let's call it a night. I'm sure Alex will forgive me for getting some sleep."

He turned off the computer and went to the window. Vans were parked across the street. Were they protecting or watching them?

Katya was about to say something, but instead she stood up with her own computer in her hand.

Max sat looking out the window. It was a quiet residential area, with no sounds of passing cars. Bright lights illuminated the road, making the grass look greener and the walls whiter. It was after two in the morning. He turned to the desk, picked up the phone, and dialed. After the thirteenth ring, the other end picked up—just like old times. And, the voice on the other end didn't say, "Hello?" This was just like old times.

"It's me."

"Is that you, Doctor? I'm doing fine, so don't worry about me," came a slightly high-pitched but calm voice. However, behind that calm, Max could sense a joy that couldn't be fully concealed. "Thank you very much. An oddball named 'Einstein' is always sending me magazines. I especially enjoyed that German cryptographic book, and for a whole week."

Max was about to reply, but he couldn't find the words.

"What's the matter? You call me out of the blue, and now you clam up? That's not like you."

"I have a favor to ask. It's just that it's a pretty big ask."

In a dimly lit room in a large house's basement in the New York City suburbs, the screens of several computers emitted pale light, and the keystrokes sounded like a techno-incantation. In front of those computers sat a pale boy with thick glasses who looked as tall and thin as a straw—or at least, that was the scene Max was picturing. The boy was over six feet tall, and weighed 140 pounds.

"I promised I'd do anything for you. You saved my life."

Max talked for about thirty minutes. The boy listened silently. People talking to him for the first time never knew whether he was listening or not, and Max had been no exception. He knew now, however, that the boy was absorbing every single word he uttered.

"Can you do it?"

"Lighten up, Doc. It's no big deal." His voice sounded much cheerier than the first words out of his mouth—just like old times. "I can do you that sort of favor any time you like. I would've never expected you to come to me with a request like that. I won't ask why; you seem stressed. Or, like, really stressed."

"You've gotten good at understanding people."

"Oh? Am I doing you another favor by not prying?"

"You are." Max heard him chuckle. "I'm counting on you, kid." He was about to end the call.

"Doc . . . I wouldn't bother if it were the president calling me with this request. But I'll do it for you. I won't ask why for now, but please tell me someday. I'm too curious."

"I'd love to, if I ever get the chance."

"Take however long you need to—I'll be waiting. If I have one virtue, it's patience. But you already know that. Besides, I know I won't be dying before you anyway." He chuckled again.

Max recalled what the boy's mother had told him three years prior: "You're the first person he's smiled at besides me. I wonder if you two have something in common." Then she'd hurriedly taken that remark back—this had been at the psychiatric ward of a university hospital in upstate New York.

Click. The sound of the phone hanging up on the other end. Max kept his phone to his ear for a while, listening for a voice he knew wouldn't be coming. There could be no cold feet now.

CHAPTER 29

Max woke up to a noise. He'd lain down on the sofa and fallen asleep. Katya was standing by the door. The floor and desk were covered with blueprints and photographs. Max got up and sat in a chair. Katya stepped over the blueprints.

"Your eyes are bloodshot."

"I'm leaving for Aztec Labs soon."

She looked surprised, and silently began to pick up the photographs and blueprints. Max looked outside. The vans were still in the same place.

"I'm going alone."

Katya stopped moving and looked up at him.

"It'll be a dangerous job, and it's got nothing to do with you."

Katya put the blueprints on the table and stood in front of Max.

"You have some nerve, Professor. You're the one who wrapped me up in all this. Ninety-five percent of it is your responsibility."

"What about the remaining 5 percent?"

"My curiosity." Katya stared at Max, her eyes blurry with tears. "I want to help you—and Aska, too."

Max looked at the blueprints on the table. "The place is like an exhibition hall for surveillance cameras and infrared sensors. No idea how many there are," he said, pointing at the red marks.

"Even if you're lucky enough to sneak past the walls into the grounds, you'll be spotted by the time you enter the building. The only thing going our way is there doesn't seem to be a minefield on top of everything else."

"We just have to pray that's the case."

"It doesn't seem feasible unless you take a small army in with you," she said, eyes glued to the blueprints.

"How did you figure out the layout of the rooms?" Katya pointed to text on the blueprint. Laboratory, P2, P3, P4 laboratory, changing room, dining room, restroom—that text wasn't there the night before.

"I thought about how I'd set it up. This is how I picture it given the locations of the rooms, the electrical system, and the plumbing."

"What's this thick pipe?"

"It's the main water pipe. It's three feet or so in diameter and is linked to the sea. A person could probably swim through it, but I haven't got that kind of courage. The rooms that have a bunch of pipes running through them are either experiment rooms or medical rooms."

"Look how many there are. That's ten or more large rooms. Water pipes, electrical wiring. I'm guessing they must also be conducting experiments here. Experiments on people."

"There's no doubt something's going on there."

"This must be the computer room. The electrical wiring says it all. The Roadrunner supercomputer is installed here. And that's where we'll find the information we're looking for."

"Our only objective is to get Aska back. We can leave the rest to Feldman."

Katya looked at him and shook her head.

They snuck out the back door and had Nancy drive them to San Francisco International. Max told Nancy to act as usual at the house.

She was confused, but agreed. From the way Max had been acting, to the van parked in front of the house, she knew that something was happening. As they had done before, Max and Katya flew to San Diego and rented a car to reach La Cruz. Using false names, they checked in at a motel that was closer to Aztec Labs than where they had stayed before. This time they were in the same room.

"Just sent Feldman an email. I told him we're going to try infiltrating Aztec Labs," he told Katya.

"Knowing him, he was against the idea," Katya said.

"I immediately got a call on my cell. He started screaming, but he quieted down when I said this phone is probably tapped."

"And that's not impossible."

"That's what he said." Max shrugged. "I think it's okay for now. He just urged us to reconsider. He was worked up to the end of the call."

"But he can't stop us anymore anyway." The laboratory blueprints were arranged on the table. They'd done a rehearsal of the infiltration twice before sundown. "We're overlooking something important. How do we get to the research building from the outer walls? The walls are ten feet tall, and they're electrified. And both have surveillance cameras."

"We already have that little problem solved."

"How?"

"You'll understand when we get there," Max said, eyes on the blueprints.

"Aska is somewhere in one of these rooms." Katya pointed to the three rooms marked in red. One was next to the medical office, another was in front of a large laboratory-like room, and the third was a small room inside the operating room. Logically, she would be near a place where medical checks could be done. "You should sleep. You probably haven't slept since last night."

"I slept on the plane."

"That was barely even a nap."

She was right, his body felt weighed down and sluggish, and his brain power was fading. Max lay down on the sofa. He ruminated on what they were about to do and soon dozed off.

It was ten o'clock when he was awakened by Katya. He'd only slept for about four hours, but he felt lighter. Coffee and pizza were on the table. After eleven, they left the motel. They parked in the parking lot of a small supermarket on the outskirts of town and walked the rest of the way. After about thirty minutes, Aztec Labs came into view. They crawled closer to the wire fence side, avoiding the surveillance cameras. This was where the guards had stopped them before. The laboratory building could be seen about a hundred yards beyond the barbed wire. In the intervening space, there was a lawn with a few trees.

"Which cameras were in the blueprints?" Max silently pointed to the outdoor lights standing at intervals. Some had surveillance cameras attached. There were no blind spots in the grass. He removed a large cutter from his backpack, for severing the barbed wire.

"The time limit is one minute and thirty seconds. I need to run behind that tree."

"It's not an unreasonable distance. You used to be a football player."

Max looked at his watch and held the cutter.

"But what about the electricity and the cameras? Do you have some magi—."

Before Katya could finish, the area was covered in darkness.

"What is this?" Katya said in the dark.

"Magic." He cut through the wire fence. Max pushed Katya into the lab and ran. Just as they'd discussed, they stood behind a tree in the center of the lawn with their backs against each other. The area turned bright once again as the outdoor lights turned back on. The private power generator had activated.

"A power outage? Or is God on our side?"

"I may not be a sorcerer myself, but I am friends with one."

"Is this any time to make jokes?"

"I once had a computer genius for a patient. He had terminal lymphoma. He came to me after all the hospitals in the East gave up on him. He was young, and his cancer was progressing quickly. I did everything in my power for him. After all, I couldn't let a boy with a 190 IQ die."

"A boy you treated in collaboration with your brother's doctor, Dr. Hamilton."

Max nodded. "The only treatment left was gene therapy. It was the first time a gene with anticancer functionality was injected directly into the bone marrow as a treatment method. I hadn't even tried it through animal testing yet. He offered a deal before the surgery. He promised me he'd do anything if I saved his life. And now he's the genie to my Aladdin." Max was looking at the clock with his arms outstretched.

"And you obtained a magic lamp."

"He asked me how many zeroes I wanted at the end of the figure in my bank account, and whether I'd enjoy reading the president's emails."

"I'd have taken him up on that first offer."

"I replied that they were both too heavy for me, so I got a rain check for the magic."

"So, you rubbed the lamp and got a power outage?"

"I remembered him saying he was familiar with the systems of electric power companies and telephone companies. He'd also offered to make my telephone and electricity free for the rest of my life. Power outages in California are practically a summer event at this point."

"From here we'll run into problems, though. Right now, we're stuck. We can't move."

"The power company's electricity is already on. That means their private generator should be off again."

"Then your next wish will be granted soon?" As soon as the words were out of her mouth, the area turned dark once more. The two ran as fast as they could. It took one minute and thirty seconds to switch to private power generation again, and they had to reach the third research building by then. The instant they crouched down in front of the door of the building, the lights came on. This was the only blind spot from the cameras. The door had a card slit and a PIN panel next to the handle. Everything was as shown in the blueprints.

"Can your genius genie also operate the door key?"

"I'm listening to how to do it." Max took his computer from his backpack and inserted the card connected to the cord into the slit. A string of numbers appeared on screen, and it kept shifting at dizzying speeds.

"Yet another gift from him, I take it."

"He gave me this on my birthday. I used to gripe about losing door cards, and he gave me this."

"Don't tell me you've been walking around with that thing this entire time?"

"For half a year he was in the hospital. Every time I met him, he asked how useful it was."

Eventually, the numbers began to fill in from the first digit. Looking at the clock, it was 1:08. Not even ten minutes had passed since the first power outage. Anxiety filled Max's heart. It was going too smoothly.

"How old is the computer whiz?" Katya interrupted Max's train of thought.

"He'll be 18 next month."

"Introduce me to him sometime."

"If you're willing to go to the New York Medical Youth Center."

The numbers on the screen were searching for the last two digits.

"He dug up the grave of his father, who died in a car accident, and set fire to his body."

"That's a crime that doesn't suit a genius."

"He was molested by his father when he was a kid. Sometimes he has seizures and hurts himself. When we first met, he had no nails on half of his fingers."

The numbers stopped in time with Katya's sigh. The door unlocked, and they entered. The entire building was lit, and the corridors were quiet. Their footsteps echoed off the linoleum floor. As they walked down the hallway, they heard a voice from a room.

"That's the laundry room over there in the corner. The door's unlocked." Once inside, they saw an overflowing laundry basket. "Find something that fits," Max said, rifling through the lab coats.

"I'm not too into wearing dirty clothes." Katya took a clean lab coat from the shelf and handed it to Max. They returned to the corridor and walked toward the laboratory.

Suddenly, Max stopped. "I feel like someone's watching me." He looked around. An uneasy feeling came over him, but there were no people in either direction—only sterile white surfaces.

"Must be in my head," Max said quietly, and he started walking again.

Around the corner, there was a corridor with one side made of glass. Labs were lined up behind the glass, and inside men in lab coats operated micromanipulators while looking at the attached screens, which displayed an egg. There was an inverted microscope next to each.

"A convenience store open 24 hours a day," Katya said, looking sideways at the laboratory.

"The room at the end was top secret." Max grabbed Katya's arm as she began to walk. "Dr. Otto Gerhard," he whispered as he saw through the glass a man in a lab coat.

"Who's that?"

"A doctor—and one of Dr. Mengele's right-hand men."

"Dr. Mengele? You mean the Angel of Death? The doctor you spoke of at the graveyard in Domba—who experimented on humans and killed them for sport?"

"He's the man in the middle," Max said, pointing with his eyes.

Gerhard stood in the center of the men in lab coats and was giving instructions. High nose bridge, thin lips. Max didn't know the color of the eyes behind those glasses, but there was no doubt about the skull with the protruding bones. His hairline had receded, but his skin tone was that of a man in his forties. Max's line of sight was fixed on the screen.

"They're pulling out the egg cells' nuclei. And those egg cells probably aren't a cow's or a sheep's."

"What are they trying to do?"

The tip of the pipette approached the egg on the display and a new nucleus was inserted. The door behind opened, and they heard voices. They saw the reflection of three men walking toward them. Max and Katya walked away.

"Around that corner, there should be a room leading to the computer room." Katya looked down and hid her face, pretending to be discussing and whispering. The two quickened their pace. There was a door around the corner. Max pulled the doorknob, but it was locked.

"There was no lock on this door in the blueprints," said Max.

"They added it later. The laboratory is past this door."

"How do we get in?"

"Any advice from your boy genius?"

"Insufficient explanation of the situation."

"Step aside." Katya pushed Max away and crouched in front of the door. Then she removed a tiny clip from her hair and inserted it into the keyhole.

"It's an ordinary cylinder lock," she said to herself. "I can do this." She concentrated on the keyhole, and the door opened with a clink.

"Another of my special skills. I told you I was good with my hands." She pushed Max into the room. "My second apartment had an auto-lock thing. It was faster to pick the lock than call the super." After a few seconds, they heard voices and footsteps passing in front of the door and moving away. A faint light and warm air surrounded them. "What's that?" she asked under her breath, facing ahead and into the room.

Max's eyes were also fixed forward. On the central platform

stood a cylindrical glass container about three feet tall and a foot and a half in diameter. It was filled with a brownish liquid, and a small animal resembling a mouse floated in the vat.

"It's a fetus!"

"It's three, no, two months old."

"Is that a specimen? No way . . ." She approached the cylinder, unable to believe her eyes. It was a four-inch fetus with pink skin. It hadn't opened its eyes yet. It bore a vestigial protrusion of a tail. It twitched, and Katya moved back.

"It's alive!"

"It's an artificial womb. The glass tube is the uterus, and the liquid inside is amniotic fluid."

The fetus slightly opened its mouth and swallowed the liquid. A tube extended from the fetus's abdomen to the top of the cylinder. The tube pumped nutrients and blood into the fetus in place of an umbilical cord.

"There's no time." Max grabbed Katya's arm and headed for the next room. The two stood there in a daze. The glass cylinders were lined up under the white lights. Spanning from one and a half to two and a half feet in diameter, they were reminiscent of a backlit objet d'art. They entered the room as if drawn by magnets. "They're about three to seven months old. Some are even developed enough to be placed in incubators."

"There has to be at least thirty."

"More than fifty, no doubt."

The two weaved between the glass containers. Some of the fetuses were about a foot tall, already had distinct fingers, and were sucking their thumbs.

"They're all female."

"Daughter 7, Daughter 8 . . . 14 . . . 15 . . . Mother 7, Mother 8 . . ." Max read the labels on the cylinders. "They're clones. They're human clones," he groaned.

"They're cloning Dona and Aska here."

"They 'grow' them and then extract their genes."

"Every one of these fetuses has the gene for life. They're going to take bone marrow fluid from the fetuses and use it for gene transplantation. They're trying to extend their lives using these children. And fetal telomerase is the most effective."

"If you take bone marrow fluid from fetuses, they'll surely die."

"That's why the villager said that the pregnant women were taken. When cloning technology wasn't established yet, the fetuses had to be removed from pregnant women."

"Unforgivable!" Katya gently traced the glass with her fingertips. Max pushed Katya to move on to the next room with him. Glass tubes and utensils were on a large table. It was the preparation room for cloning experiments. "The computer room should be at the end of the hall."

After making sure there was no one in the hall, they went out. "The computer room door is a card-type door." Max took out his computer and inserted the card into the slit. The door opened with a thud. There was no one inside. It was chilly, and the air-conditioning was purring.

"The Roadrunner. The current fastest supercomputer in the world." Katya stood in front of the supercomputer in the center of the room. The box-shaped computer hummed as it continued to calculate. "The research results should be stored somewhere." Katya sat down at one of the computer terminals along the wall and began typing.

"There we go. But we still need a password."

"Let's get out of here. Our objective is Aska."

"Hitler, Adolf, Eva, Braun, Third Reich . . . ," Katya said as she tried potential passwords, her fingers dancing over the keyboard.

Ten minutes passed. All the passwords Katya entered returned error messages.

"Give up. It's impossible."

"Just one more minute." Katya didn't look up from the keyboard.

"What's Hitler's birthday?"

"How should I know?"

"Let's try all the years from the late 1800s up to 1900. It's no use." She looked up at Max, nearly sobbing.

Max reached over her shoulder and typed GOD IS ETERNAL. It worked.

"Did you rub your magic lamp again?"

"The words that open all the doors. That's what Father Yunov said before he died. It's the perfect Nazi password. No one would ever guess it."

Katya started typing again.

"First, we're going to connect to the web and move all of this data to your university computer. The same thing we did at the Eoghan Institute."

Letters lined up on screen. Most of the text was in German.

"It's the genetic information of Dona and Aska. They are also analyzing the molecular structure of purified proteins. Their scientific prowess is a sight to behold."

"Past research data has also been stored here. I'm sure it's a treasure trove."

"That's a massive amount of data."

"There, just connected it to the university's computing center." Katya took her hands off the keyboard. "When I press Enter, everything will be moved from this computer to your college folders." Katya pressed the key with gusto. "In ten minutes, the treasure trove will be ours. If you analyze this data, you'll find the key to your cure. I'm sure of it."

"Let's hurry and find Aska."

"Five minutes left." Katya started up the computer next door and typed.

The screen shifted as blueprints appeared. They were the same as those they had seen in the architect's directory. The difference was that each room had a number. And the number contained a name.

"Two-thirds of your guesses as to the room layout were correct, but the problem is the other third," Katya said.

"'Experimental body storage.' What does that mean?" She moved the cursor to a number. The screen turned into an enlarged view of the blueprint.

"It's on the third floor. If we go out and turn right, there should be a warehouse. The door leads to the staircase. From there, we can go up to the third floor," Katya said, tracing the path.

They went out into the hallway and saw no one.

The corridor on the third floor was quiet. The lights were off, and the emergency lights provided the only illumination.

"Here," Katya said.

"What about the key?"

"It's open." Katya opened the door. Darkness spread before them. Max took a step forward while covering Katya.

"Stop!" echoed a voice.

A dazzling beam of light hit them head on. They covered their eyes.

"You're . . . !" Max shouted. He thought he saw a familiar face in the light. "What are you doing here?"

A blow to the head stopped him, and he toppled forward.

"Katya . . . ," he spoke, fading fast. His consciousness dimmed before he could check to see where she was.

● ● ●

VIII

THE GENE OF LIFE

CHAPTER 30

Where am I? What the hell happened?

His cheek was on a cold surface—vinyl floor tile. He tried to move, but a shooting pain seared his brain. He froze and waited for the pain to subside.

A light went on. The brightness was blinding, stabbing through his eyes into his brain. He squeezed his eyes shut. He opened them again and squinted, to find three men standing in front of the light. Each was a blurry shadow. Each was staring at him.

He turned his head, trying to figure out where he was. He saw a large room with plain concrete walls, lit by fluorescent bulbs in the ceiling. A steel desk and a few chairs were lined up along the wall. It looked like a basement or warehouse.

Where's Katya?

"It's a pleasure to meet you, Professor Maximillian Knight," said an arrogant voice; it was so shrill it bypassed his ears and shot directly into his skull.

Max took a deep breath, and the world came in sharper relief. He tried to move so he could look in the voice's direction, but his wrists throbbed with the attempt. His hands were cuffed behind his back. He braced himself against the pain and bent backward so he could look up. As his eyes adjusted, he could make out the men's outlines. The tall, slender, balding man in the center wore glasses. He was staring at Max. The men to either side of the tall man, though shorter, likely weighed around twice as much as he did.

The man in the center took a step forward.

"Dr. Otto Gerhard," Max said quietly.

"I'm honored you know my name." A smile warped his smooth, light-complexioned face, which reminded Max of a reptile.

Animated by nervous energy, Gerhard was rubbing his fingers in front of his chest. His fingers were long and thin, and they moved like a bunch of wriggling snakes. Gerhard took another step forward, and the men to either side of him followed. He stood before Max, grabbed a chair, and sat down. He leaned over to the large man on his right and whispered something to him. He removed Max's cuffs. Max put his hands on the floor to lift himself up; he didn't want to stay at this man's feet. His heart and soul were almost audibly screaming.

"If it isn't the shadowy scientist who lurked behind Mengele. They say you were even more talented than the Angel of Death himself." Max's voice was so hoarse it shocked him.

He tried to get to his feet by holding onto the legs of the desk, but he fell to his knees. His legs were not cooperating, and he knew that couldn't stem from a mere blow to the head. He looked up at Gerhard; the bastard was staring down at him with glee.

"Why, thank you," he said. "It's truly an honor, coming from the mouth of Professor Knight."

"I also hear you're a degenerate obsessed with human

experimentation. You're especially fascinated with the moment life vanishes, and you've taken hundreds and hundreds of lives, or so I've read. It was written that your sheer cruelty and coldheartedness surpassed the Angel of Death."

Max could see the muscles of Gerhard's face shift as his expression changed. Gerhard ordered the two large men beside him to wait outside the room. They looked unhappy about it, but did as they were told when Gerhard pointed at the door.

"At last, it's just the two of us. It irritates me to have to look at those useless nitwits' dull faces. More accurately, it's not so much 'irritation,' as it is the urge to kill."

Gerhard lifted Max to his feet by the armpits. Max held his breath against his strong body odor. He reeked of formalin, alcohol, and a host of other chemicals—smells that had soaked into Gerhard's body over many years. This was the smell of death.

Max held onto the desk to keep himself on his feet. He grimaced at the pain in his head. Gerhard enjoyed Max's suffering, and trailed his soft fingers along the back of Max's neck. Chills and goosebumps all over. He tried to brush them away, but he couldn't muster the strength. He must have been drugged.

"Where are Katya and Aska?"

"Let's not discuss such trifling matters. This is the momentous meeting of two magnificent scientific minds."

"I'm the type that can't concentrate when I've got something weighing on my mind."

"They're safe and sound. Are you happy?"

"Prove it."

"We are the greatest scientists in the world. We must trust each other." Gerhard took off his glasses and wiped the lenses with a handkerchief. "I read your papers on restriction enzymes and vectors. You made groundbreaking discoveries. The theory and implementation of gene therapy will change the way we think about life itself. Your paper on clones that appeared in *Nature* last year was also revolutionary. It facilitated my research immensely. Frankly, were it not for those papers, my research would be ten years behind."

"It leaves a very bitter taste in my mouth, knowing I lent a hand to a fiend like you. I could never go as far as you did—I could never do what you did to Gehlen, Yunov, and your own body."

"You were simply unlucky. I had the great fortune of gaining access to the genes of Domba. Besides, you were only allowed to experiment on animals, and reached the limit of what you could accomplish. You did amazing work, and you truly possess incredible talent. It's no wonder the world has dubbed you a genius."

"I'm not happy being praised by you."

"There is no greater honor. A genius knows genius when he sees it. Why are you still only a candidate for the Nobel Prize? The nobodies of the world cannot grasp the importance of your discoveries, which will forever alter humanity's notions of life and death. They're just a whirlwind of empty-headed imbeciles of no worth whatsoever."

"I've learned so much from those 'empty-headed imbeciles.' They raised me."

"And that is why you cannot be more than them. The 'decency' and 'ethics' they make so much of are hindrances to science. They're the clamorings of those who've reached the limits of their own ability, and are trying to hide their incompetence. If you change that frame of mind, you free yourself from the limits of the weak." Gerhard's expression was as ripe with self-regard and self-confidence as his words. "There's no substitute for human bodies when it comes to experiments. The human body is God's masterwork. I experimented on people from the very start. Human cells are far easier to handle than animals'. Has the potential of using human cells never occurred to you?"

"Can't say it has," Max said. But, the thought had crossed his mind, and more than once.

"Behold, Professor." Gerhard stood in front of Max and spun in place with his arms outstretched. He was light on his feet, and moved with the agility of a much younger man. Then he rolled up a sleeve and stuck his arm before Max's eyes. His skin was smooth and unwrinkled. "I am my own research subject, and these are the results. I am a work of art!"

"You're right; no one would ever believe you're over a hundred years old. You've got the body and the energy of a man in the prime of his life. But your soul is rotten. Don't you smell it? The stench of death. I know what that smell is. But you wouldn't understand in a million years."

"Don't let me down. I think you have the greatest intellect in the world. Apart from me, of course."

"Then you've got the wrong idea. Don't put me on the same level as your stupidity."

Gerhard shook his head and heaved a sigh. "I've made a tremendous discovery: eternal life."

"There's no such thing."

"You're looking at it."

"Eternity is a long time."

"I'll show you. I'll live to 200, then to 300! That is what my research is for!"

"It's not people that control people's lives. Nor can they."

"I am chosen by God. My existence is proof of that."

"Then God made a mistake."

"Are you calling God incompetent?"

"Even God makes mistakes. Though if you ask me, you're the Devil's chosen. In which case the Devil chose correctly. You yourself might be the Devil."

A deep laugh came from Gerhard's lips. "Me, the Devil? That suits me fine. The Devil is a being worthy of eternal life. I am he who surpasses all."

"Eternal life is a dream. To say nothing of everyone being able to live forever."

"It's enough for only the chosen to enjoy eternal life. They shall be the lords of this world, a handful of authorities wielding power over their disposable underlings. Is that not the ideal state of things? That way, only the superior strain survives."

"And who are the chosen? The rich? Those already in power? Who decides? Would they be the ones to decide they're the chosen, or would you be the ones to decide? Before long, the world would be nothing but the rich and powerful."

"Why don't you join us? Join the fold of the chosen who shall create the Fourth Reich. I would love to have you as my partner in science."

"No! I couldn't handle the honor of such a thing."

"Think about what it would be like if Newton, Galileo, Bach, or Michelangelo survived to modern times. Perhaps Galileo would have demystified yet more of the secrets of the universe. Bach would be composing even more music that stirs the hearts of all the world. And to this day, we are in awe of the sculptures of Michelangelo. Think how much more magnificent civilization would be if the geniuses of the past had eluded death," Gerhard spoke with enraptured eyes.

"But what about Nero, Hitler, Stalin, or Pol Pot eluding death? Has that thought escaped you? The world would've been reduced to the playground of monsters like them, and would've been ruined as a result."

"They would all have caved in to the allure of eternal life. They must have wanted to continue researching, composing, sculpting, and painting. And the only way to do that is to obtain immortality," he said, ignoring Max's answer. He looked up at the ceiling, and then cast a soulless glance Max's way. "You could see where every branch of science is headed. Wouldn't that be splendid? I was born during the age of coal, lived through the age of oil, and experienced the atomic age. I will one day be able to experience nuclear fusion as well. We will create miniature suns and hold them in the palms of our hands. I was there to witness humanity go from mechanical calculators to electronic calculators to computers. I'm currently living through the age of fakery, the internet age. I look forward to what comes next. But the greatest advance of them all was a human. What is a human being, Professor? Can you answer that?"

"I never thought you'd ask me that. To me, what makes a person a person will forever remain a mystery."

"Humanity—all life—is a cluster of proteins created by DNA, animated by electrical signals. When a life form dies, it rots and returns to the earth. Where does this 'soul' you speak of enter the picture?"

"Do clusters of proteins have wills? Do they feel love or hate, sorrow or joy? I am a human being. A person. And people love each other and give birth to the generations after them. That's part of what makes them people. Human beings are clusters of proteins with minds and souls!" he shouted, staring at Gerhard. Max hadn't known he had that speech in him. "You're trying to tack centuries onto your life, while life itself arose from chains of amino acids 3.6 billion years ago. Humanity as we know it exists thanks to the continuous evolution that started then. And humanity, too, will continue to evolve over time. Life exists alongside the flow of time. Do you mean to hit the stop button? Immortality is impossible."

"In a few months I'll be able to acquire a more advanced immortality. I will live forever." Gerhard's face was confident. He smiled, intoxicated by the glory of it.

Max sighed. This man was insane.

"Join me. Let's journey through this century, and the next. We'll shape a new world with our own hands." Gerhard stared at Max. There was a weird glint in his eyes. They were the eyes of a madman. "I looked you up. I know everything about you. Your IQ, your grades in school, your hobbies, your favorite foods, even your tastes in art and women. And I also know about your illness." Gerhard smiled triumphantly. Max looked away in spite of himself.

"You fear the passing of time. People can put up with change if it's gradual. Even if they can't, they can brace themselves mentally and force themselves to accept what they must. But people's hearts cannot deal with abrupt, radical change." Gerhard was staring at him intently. His eyes radiated with the cruelty of a snake playing with a mouse.

"Father Yunov chose death of his own free will," Max said, glaring back at him. "He found a peace greater than what life could offer him."

"All he did was return to nothingness. He was nothing more than a coward who wasted the life I so graciously granted him. Not a trace of his existence remains on this Earth. He was the plaything of a make-believe god, unable to see the truth!" he spat.

"There are fates worse than death. To him, there was greater happiness in death."

"You disappoint me."

"I wasn't trying to please you."

"If you won't serve me as my loyal partner, you can serve as my guinea pig. Your intelligence is precious and valuable, but so, too, is your body. I'd like to watch as you age, but I'm afraid I don't have the patience for that. So, I'm going to make you age faster. That much is possible for me now, too. I've taken one step closer to godhood."

"You've got that backward. You've taken a step closer to becoming the Devil himself. In fact, you already are that evil."

"To a man who's conquered death, neither God nor the Devil is anything more than a figment of mankind's imagination." Gerhard grinned. "Take him away!" he shouted at the door.

The door opened, and two large men came in. Max's hands were cuffed behind his back, and the two walked him out of the room. One had a gun. The other, who was in a lab coat, held a stick and a file that looked like a patient's chart. A skull tattoo was visible on his wrist, only partially concealed by the lab coat. He opened the door at the end of the hallway. There was a narrow passageway within the dim room, and doors lined both sides. There was an eight-square-inch iron grill in the door. Max could tell there were people there, but it was silent.

"The test subject is here," the man with the tattoo said.

"So, people are the guinea pigs here? You're going to have problems with animal rights groups about this."

"People come way cheaper than monkeys. This place is near the Mexican border, so there's no shortage. We can get as many fresh specimens as we like."

"You're kidnapping people from Central America that cross the border illegally?"

"No one cares if they disappear. No one even notices."

He rapped on one of the doors with his stick. There was no response from within.

Max was taken to a room at the end of the hall.

"Katya! Are you in he—"

A sharp pain exploded at the back of his neck, and he tumbled to the floor.

"Stop that!" Katya screamed, but Max couldn't tell from where. The stick was a stun gun.

"Shut up! He may be the great Professor, but that won't earn him, or you, any mercy." He removed Max's cuffs and shoved him into the room. Max's knees gave, and he ended up kneeling on the floor. The man rapped on the door with the stun gun and left. Max could hear the main door close with a thud.

The men's footsteps echoed in the hallway, eventually fading away.

"Katya, are you there?" Max shouted through the iron grill.

"I'm here!"

"Are you injured?"

"I'm okay. Are you?"

"I'm okay. I saw Gerhard."

"They were waiting for us. But why?"

She was right; they'd known about the mission in advance. *How?* The suspicions that dawned on him suddenly became clear. *But that can't be. There's just no way.* Max banged his head against the grill and shook off those thoughts.

"Who was with him?"

"Don't say another word. They're probably listening."

"Okay."

Silence. Max sat on the bed and looked around. The room was lit by what little light entered from the hallway through the grill. Max tried to think. The heavy lead in his body spread all over. He felt sluggish, still experiencing the effect of the drugs.

Suddenly, the light went out. In the complete darkness, all he could sense was the presence of people, silent but there. Max counted slowly. The light came back on after he reached two hundred.

He lay down. His mind refused to piece together the complex interlocking chain of events. His hands were still numb from the cuffs. Max closed his eyes, and his consciousness rapidly receded. Gerhard . . . the fetus in the glass cylinder . . . Feldman . . .

Joe, you . . .

CHAPTER 31

How much time had passed?

The main door creaked open, and the click of boots echoed off the walls. He could hear the locks of separate rooms unlocking, and people stepping into the hallway. Max sat up in bed. He grimaced at the pain in his joints, but the sluggishness was gone.

The footsteps stopped in front of the room. The door was unlocked, and rammed violently open. There stood two men. One man was thin and over six feet tall, and the other had on a lab coat. The man in the lab coat was the one who'd taken him here, the man with the tattoo.

Max had his hands cuffed behind his back once again, and he was dragged out of the cell. Standing beside the thin man, Katya looked at Max with frightened eyes.

"You're bleeding." Katya put a hand on Max's forehead.

"It's just a small cut."

The two men looked at the clock and spoke in low voices. A faint smile occasionally curled the thin one's lips; he was looking at Katya.

"What time is it?" Max asked the tattooed man.

"It's almost five."

"In the morning, or in the afternoon? I want to know the exact time."

"It's 4:54 a.m.," he sniggered.

The thin man pushed Max to make him walk out into the hallway. The men walked quickly as they rushed the two of them forward.

"Faster!" The tattooed man shoved Max's shoulders. Max staggered and lost his balance, but narrowly avoided falling down.

"Don't be so rough. He's wounded!" Katya said. She held Max up by the arm.

They stopped at the first room around the corner. The men exchanged glances and opened the door. The dreary room had a table at the center and a steel desk in the corner.

A savage blow hit the back of Max's neck. His body lurched, and his mind went blank. He collapsed to the floor.

"What are you doing!?" But Katya's voice was muffled, as if she were underwater.

Out of the corner of his eye, he saw the man with a black stun gun.

Katya opened her mouth to scream. The thin man was holding her in place from behind.

"Lower the voltage. It's more fun when she's conscious."

"Stop!" she said hoarsely.

The man with the stun gun placed it on the back of Katya's neck.

Max tried to scream stop, but couldn't. He was dragged by the handcuffs to the corner of the room. His body was too leaden to move.

"You're gonna get chopped to pieces anyway, so we're gonna show you a good time before that happens." The thin man taped Katya's mouth shut.

Everything flowed in slow motion. Katya's despairing face, the men's laughter . . . Max desperately kept himself from slipping into unconsciousness. Katya's white skin seared into the backs of his eyelids.

They held Katya on the table. The thin man turned his back on Max and tried to remove Katya's jeans. Max could hardly see the man with the tattoo. *Was he holding Katya's arms from the other side of the table?* The tattoo man's upper body was bare. Max looked around, still groggy. He saw a lab coat in the corner, beside it was Katya's jacket. The stun gun was sticking out of the pocket of the lab coat. When Max stretched out his arm, he was stopped by the pain in his left wrist. One of the handcuffs was fastened to a desk leg. The thin man took off his pants and threw them behind him.

Max desperately stretched his arm again. Just four inches away. He put all his strength into it. The desk moved and his fingertips touched plastic. The thin man, whose lower body was now exposed, turned around. His expression changed, and he moved away from Katya.

At that moment, darkness swallowed the room. Max stuck out the stun gun, and it came into contact with something soft. With a moan, a heavy body fell down on him.

"The power's out. What've California's power companies come to?" the tattooed man said.

Max pushed the thin man aside. He fumbled in the darkness for the man's pants; the key to his cuffs had to be in one of the pockets.

"Get it over with so I can have my turn with her."

His hand felt the fabric. Rummaging through the pockets, he found the key. He searched for the keyhole of his cuffs, but it was tricky in the dark.

"What're you doing? We've got no time. We need to take them to the lab before Dr. Gerhard shows up."

Then the lights came back on. Max and the tattooed man's eyes met. Astonishment dawned on his face.

When he saw his friend lying half-naked on the floor, he pounced. Max took a blow to the chin, and the stun gun slid to a corner of the room. Max kicked the man with all his might, and he flew across the room, his back smacking against the wall.

Where's the key? Max looked around but couldn't find it. It flew somewhere when he'd taken that hit.

The man with the tattoo groaned and got to his feet. Max froze. He was holding a handgun. He kicked Max in the stomach. Stomach acid flooded his throat.

The man raised his foot against Max once more, but he suddenly jerked upward. His eyes rolled back as his body spasmed, until, at last, he dropped to his knees and fell forward.

Katya was holding the stun gun. She was still in her underwear. Max looked away and unlocked his cuffs with the key he found under the table. He picked up her jacket, went to her side, and put it over her shoulders. He gently pulled the tape off her mouth.

"Don't say anything," she whispered. She was pale, shivering, with tears welling in her eyes.

After they were sure the two men were out cold, they taped their mouths shut and bound their hands. Katya finished dressing, then glared at the two as she pointed the gun at them. Max took it from her. Then the power went out again.

"Don't leave my side." Max gripped her hand. "Do you know where we are?"

"We're on the north side of the computer room. From the exit . . ." Katya's voice cracked as she started crying. Max hugged her tight to him. "I'm okay. But if the lights had gone out seconds later, I would have killed them." She started walking. "Were these power outages caused by the computer wiz, too?"

"Five a.m. It was extra time to spring us out. We should've been either rushing down the coastline in a motorboat, or toasting with some wine right about now."

"He saved me."

The lights came back on. They'd switched to a private generator.

"There should be a staircase around the corner," Katya said, as they dashed down the hallway.

They climbed the stairs to the floor above the basement.

"Do you still have any magic lamp wishes left?"

"He's an honest sorcerer."

"How many more times?"

"Until he hears from me, the power is set to go out twice in quick succession every thirty minutes for the next three hours. It was his suggestion. But somebody's bound to tip off the power plant at some point. The rest will be a battle of wits between him and the power plant engineers. I am sure he'll win."

"Is it possible that the laboratory is generating its own power the whole time?"

"It is possible, but you've seen the size of the place. Supplying power to the entire complex through private power generation is probably only for emergencies. And I bet that'd only last for a few hours at the most."

"I don't plan to be around by the time the next wish is granted."

Max grabbed Katya's arm and stopped. They could hear footsteps from beyond the corner ahead of them.

Max turned the nearest door handle, and it opened. A few seconds later, the footsteps of several people passed in front of the room.

"What . . . is . . . that?" Katya whispered.

Max turned to face her. Katya was staring across the room. Cold air enveloped them. Slowly they walked over to the opposite side of the room. Their field of view suddenly opened up, and they saw that they were in a 1,000-square-foot atrium. The hallways above curved around the portion of the atrium at the second-floor level. In the center of the room, four glass cylinders glowed in white light. Several large apparatuses were along the wall. The cylinders were huge, each around ten feet tall. Inside them were not fetuses, but the bodies of adults.

And those bodies were staring at them.

"They're alive . . ." Katya clenched Max's arm. It was true—they were inhaling and exhaling the fluid in which they floated.

"This . . . this is . . ." Max was at a loss for words. *This isn't the real world. Is this the world of death?*

A body without a head was inside one of the cylinders in the back. Next to it was a cylinder with a brain inside. The grayish lump was floating in fluid. In another cylinder was a head. There was a hole in the back of that head; its contents had been scooped out. Its face was . . .

"Gerhard . . ."

Katya buried her face in Max's back. She was shivering.

"They're clones of Gerhard." Max approached the cylinders. The two bodies were staring at them. They had thin hair, pointed noses and light blue eyes; there was no mistaking them. The headless body was also Gerhard.

"Gerhard cloned himself."

"But . . . what is all this? This is madness!"

"He even played around with his own body."

"But why? He wasn't making some friends for himself, was he?"

They stood there dumbfounded.

"Drop the guns!" shouted a shrill voice from above.

Max pointed his gun at the voice. Gerhard was standing in the corridor. Katya leaned even closer. He could feel her fear. Max held her in his arms and moved behind the glass tube. Ten guards were standing on either side of Gerhard, and they all held automatic rifles. A small figure moved beside Gerhard.

"Ich bitte dich, bitte verschone ihr Leben," the figure said in a high-pitched voice. "Please, please, help them!"

"Aska!" Katya called out.

"The girl likes you two. She's begging me not to kill you." Gerhard grabbed Aska's arm and dragged her away. Aska yelped.

"Don't hurt her!" Katya shouted.

"Throw away your guns and come."

"Your threats are empty. You can't kill her. No one else in the world has her genes."

"I have already generated her tribe's telomerase. And I'm culturing the embryonic stem cells as well. I no longer need her."

One of the guards wrapped an arm around Aska's neck and stuck a gun to her head. Katya started to run out from behind the cylinder, but Max grabbed her arm.

"You're lying," Max said. "You can't shoot her."

Gerhard raised his hands, signaling the guard. The guard's arms moved, and Aska shrieked.

"Don't let him trick you, Katya. He does need her. Aska's genes are even better than Dona's. Her cells can regenerate dozens of times faster than Dona's could."

"But he made a clone of Aska!"

"No, he just tried to. He hasn't succeeded yet. They can't make clones of Aska. Her DNA has far more genes than the average person. Those genes interact with each other and activate as she grows. Aska is an enigma. There's no way of knowing what will happen within her body in the future. The girl holds stupendous possibilities."

Katya's line of sight moved from Max to Aska. Aska was grimacing in pain.

"You are the genius scientist, Professor. I want to bring you to our side. So, you already worked it out, Professor Knight." Gerhard grinned. "Aska's genes are more advanced than those of her mother and her villagers. If her genes could be analyzed and integrated into my genes, I would obtain true immortality. But I've already taken a sample. I have no use for her anymore."

"I wouldn't be so sure. Aska will continue to evolve."

"No matter what happens, I will achieve eternal life."

"Can't be done. Try examining the third and ninth chromosomes.

They both contain genes related to telomerase and embryonic stem cells. Even Aska will die eventually."

"Her third chromosome is the same as Dona's. It's not unique to Aska."

"The question is the period her ninth chromosome will start activating. That will serve as the switch that turns on cell apoptosis. It's that cell death that leads to evolution. The signs of aging must be slowly materializing in your body, too."

Gerhard was speechless. His grin was gone, and for a moment, he looked afraid.

"Humanity is evolving. Evolution will go on forever, as long as humanity continues to exist. It's death that moves evolution forward. Evolution can only happen if we accept death and plant the seeds of the next generation." Max signaled for Katya to stand back. Behind them, a giant compressor was making a low hum. "Her cells are undergoing apoptosis. Death may come for her later, but as long as she's human, she can't evade it forever. Once a living thing becomes immortal, it stops evolving. And that's just impossible. Eternal life will never be anything but a fantasy. Besides, there's no point to immortality."

"You're wrong. I will make eternal life a reality! I'm just a step away. All that stands in the way are technical hiccups," Gerhard replied. He'd come back to his senses, and his evil smile returned.

Max looked at the huge cylinders. "Brain transplants?"

Gerhard's body reacted. He stiffened.

"You plan to transplant your brain into clones of you, so the body won't reject the transplant. The brain will replace the new cells with further-activated embryonic stem cells. In theory, it should be possible."

"Again you live up to your reputation, Professor Knight. I greatly admire your acumen. You are correct. With your assistance, I could realize that plan in the near future."

"You can count me out. All you're doing is toying with

human lives. You don't even regard your own clones as independent existences."

Gerhard faced a corner of the room. A man's silhouette was standing there, covered by darkness. Max and Katya stared in his direction until he stepped into the light.

"Joseph Feldman, is that you?" Katya asked.

The shadow didn't reply.

"He asked me for a transplant of this child's bone marrow fluid. In exchange for your necks. He's the one who informed me that you had snuck in."

"What do you mean? . . . Joe?"

Again, Feldman didn't answer.

"There's something that humans want, no matter how, and that is life. There is no substitute. Now put the gun down. Won't you reconsider?" Gerhard's voice echoed.

"Joe, say it isn't true," Max pleaded.

"You can't blame him. Everyone is afraid of death, especially old folks like him." Gerhard beckoned to Feldman. Feldman obeyed and took a few steps forward, emerging into the light.

"The prisoners of Auschwitz were meek and submissive. They accepted their destiny and resigned themselves to their deaths. If all Jews were as docile as they were, we could have taken a different approach."

Feldman's face stiffened. The handgun he was holding slowly moved up.

"You . . ."

The muzzle stopped at Max's chest.

"Joe, why are you doing this?"

"Even I don't know," Feldman said. He paused for a few seconds. "No, I do know. I stopped to think about the life I led. Suffering, sadness, hatred, anger . . . and nothing else. I want to start over. They promised to give me a new life. To give me eternal life." A faint smile appeared on Feldman's face. "And I'm tired. I've been tired since I was dragged to a concentration camp when I was 7. Sixty-six years. A long time, I think you'll agree. And through all that time, I thought only about erasing Nazis from this Earth. That was all there was to my life. Isn't that just too sad, too lonely a life?"

"You chose that life."

"What will pass through my mind when I die? Conversations with the love of my life? Time spent with my wife? Fishing with my children? Parties with friends? Dinner with family? I never experienced any of that."

"And it's not too late to do so."

A deep laugh came from Feldman's lips. "I'm 73 years old. Next month I'll turn 74. Look at this hand. The veins are showing, and there are blemishes all over. My eyesight is poor, and my joints ache in the morning. More than half of my teeth are false. My hair is white. These are the ravages of time. I'm sure you can picture what my hair used to look like. It was a beautiful brown. But by the time I left the camp when I was 10, it had turned the color it is now. I was silver-haired as a boy. From then on, hunting Nazis was all I could think about. Can that be called a full life? That is why I've decided to start anew."

"It's your fault for not letting go of your hatred. You chose that life for yourself."

"I had no other choice."

"Bullshit!" Max cried. "You did have a choice, Joe! Everything stemmed from the choices you made."

"The Nazis said they would return the lives they took. I've made up my mind. I will live a second life. And this time it will be my own life."

"So, you made a deal with the Devil."

The gun pointed at Max's chest moved a little. "Eternal life and wealth. You could live alongside Katya. Continuing your research is everything to you, I imagine. You can continue for decades, even centuries. It would be a whole new life. Why don't you join us? They will make it possible for us." Feldman sighed lightly and stared at Max.

"You have plenty of reasons to accept the offer."

"I'll decline, Joe. I want to live my own life, the one life I'm fated to live. If I'm lucky, I can forge a new destiny for myself."

"All you have to do is close your eyes a moment. You have talent. The world won't begrudge you an extended life, no matter how you choose to go about it."

"That's not the issue. There are many ways people choose to live on. And that includes the way they live their lives."

"The ends justify the means. There is value in living on. If you die, you simply cease to be."

"Stop this. This isn't like you. You saw Father Yunov. Living was more painful than death for him. I'm sure he's feeling relieved right now."

"Then you're just waiting for death. The symptoms of your condition have already begun, haven't they, Professor?"

"I'll cure myself my way. I won't sell my soul like you. That's how I'll live my life on my terms."

"Is that all you have to say?" Feldman heaved a sigh.

"Let's return to the real issue," Gerhard said. "Shoot him! It's your ticket to eternal life, Joseph Feldman!"

Feldman's hand trembled. Max knew Feldman was suppressing the shaking by sheer willpower.

"Stop! Don't kill him!" Aska shouted.

Beside the compressor, Katya looked tearfully at Aska.

"Do it!" Gerhard looked at Feldman and Max in turn.

"I'm begging you, Professor. Throw away the gun and listen to him. I don't want to shoot a friend."

"You can't shoot me." Max slowly lifted his gun.

A gunshot rang out. A crack formed on the surface of one of the huge glass cylinders.

"No!" Gerhard shrieked.

Max kept pulling the trigger. Soon the magazine was empty. Cracks in the glass cylinders expanded, fluid broke through and gushed out. Glass shattered and tinkled all over the floor. Fluid flooded the room. The bases of the other three glass cylinders swayed in the deluge, and slowly tilted to their sides. The guards stared down in disbelief.

Silence.

All eyes were focused on the man on the floor. His body shuddered a few times before he got to his feet. His dripping skin glistened like a thin pink membrane. Countless veins showed through.

The man slowly looked around the room. His eyes fell on Katya, and he reached for her.

Katya's shriek and the ring of the bullet were nearly simultaneous. Feldman stepped back with his gun still trained on the man. Blood poured from the holes in the man's forehead and chest. The man pressed down on his chest and looked at the blood in his hand; he fell to his knees and fell forward.

"My clones!" Gerhard's face grew pale, and dark blood vessels rose to the surface. In a matter of seconds, he had become unrecognizable.

The deluge smashed the cylinder containing the head and brain. Blood mixed with the fluid and colored the floor deep red. The brain quivered on the ground.

"Kill them! Kill them all!" Gerhard's face contorted with rage. He grabbed an automatic rifle from the hands of a guard and pointed it at Max.

"Stop!" Katya screamed as she leapt in front of Max.

A shot rang out.

Gerhard slowly turned to Feldman. He looked at him, mystified. Feldman lowered his gun. Gerhard staggered over to the railing. The gun dropped from his hand and clattered to the first floor. Gerhard tumbled over the railing. His skull cracked, releasing black fluid that spread across the atrium's floor.

"Why?" Max looked up at Feldman.

Aska shook off the guard's arms and bolted toward the staircase.

"Over here, Aska!" Katya shouted.

The lights went out again, and darkness engulfed them.

CHAPTER 32

The door swung open, and the lights switched on. The intensity of the light hurt Max's eyes.

Several men were standing in the light. Three of smaller stature were in the front, and Max couldn't tell how many were in back, but there were probably more than ten. Under the stairs, Katya and Aska were crouching and hugging each other.

"The man of the hour is finally here." Feldman got to his feet and stood by Max's side. Blood flowed down his right cheek from where a bullet had grazed him. "Benchell, I presume."

The three shadowy figures didn't answer. "Sorry, but we're going to put an end to this little game," said the small man in the center.

A gun was aimed at them from among the backlit silhouettes.

"Stop!" Feldman shouted at them.

"Gerhard's dead. If this man dies, eternal life will slip away forever. The only researcher of the gene of life that can replace Gerhard is Professor Knight."

The small man in the center looked to the small man to his left, who nodded slightly. "How about you help us, and we don't kill Aska or the woman."

"I told you already. I have no intention of lending a hand to evil."

The small man trained his gun at them again.

"Wait!"

Feldman thrust Max away and raised his gun at the exact same moment the small man's gun fired. Feldman shuddered and crumpled in a heap.

"Joe!" Max ran to Feldman and lifted him off his back. A red spot was spreading in the right shoulder of his suit.

"There's another gun in my right pocket," Feldman whispered, his eyes shut. "Shoot the short one on the right."

"But why?"

"Just trust me, Max."

Max gently stuck his hand in Feldman's pocket. It was there all right.

"I can't shoot a man."

"Save the world, Max," he wheezed, his eyes opening slightly.

"On your feet, Professor Knight!" yelled the small man in the center.

Max laid Feldman back down and stood up. He looked down at the old man, whose eyes were piercing him even through his heavy eyelids.

"One shot's all it takes." Feldman's lips were quivering.

Max aimed and fired. The small man on the right fell to his knees, bleeding from the left side of his chest.

The group gathered around the fallen man. Max lowered the gun, the shot still ringing in his ears.

"What happened?"

"The man on the right is Benchell."

"Come!" Feldman shouted to Katya. "Hurry!" He took the gun from Max and pointed it at the circuit breaker. He fired. Sparks flew from the breaker, and the lights went out. Now wrapped in darkness, they could hear the men shouting among themselves.

"Catch them! Kill them if you have to!"

The sound of footsteps mixed with shouting as the beams of their flashlights crossed and intersected. Some of the lights rushed down the stairs. Feldman fired off a few rounds in their direction. The lights vanished, and the sound of their footsteps ceased.

"Block the exits! Don't let them get away!" a voice shouted from the darkness.

A door at the end of the corridor opened. Light from the hallway lit the room.

Max put his arms under Feldman's and pulled him to a dark corner.

"There's a small box in my chest pocket," Feldman said, as he trained his gun on the corridor. "Hit the switch. It's a tracker. It can transmit radio waves to the outside even from inside this place."

Max took it out and flipped the switch.

"That was the end-operation signal. Now go to the roof. A rescue copter will be there in fifteen minutes. The copter will stay for five minutes before taking off."

Katya dragged Aska by the hand, and they rushed to where the other two were.

"Go! There's no time. I'll fend them of—"

But Feldman didn't get to finish before a guard stepped out from behind the demolished cylindrical base. Feldman pulled the trigger and drove hot lead into the guard's chest. The man collapsed in front of them. Feldman took his gun and his flashlight.

"Take the gun!" he shouted at Max, before firing blindly at the corridor. Max picked up the gun by Gerhard's corpse and slipped behind the damaged cylinder base.

The men were no longer in the hallway. The small man who'd been bleeding from the chest was gone, too.

"Hurry to the roof. They ran to call for backup."

Max rushed over to Feldman.

"They only got me in the shoulder. I can walk," he said, brushing Max's helping hand away and staggering to his feet. He left his gun since it was out of bullets, and took a gun from Max.

Katya gripped Aska by the arm as Max pushed them into an adjacent room. The lights were out there as well, since they shared the same circuit breaker.

"Do you know where the stairs leading to the roof are?" Max asked Katya.

"The third floor's central staircase goes up to the roof."

"How do we get to the third floor? We can't get into the hallway."

"There must be a fire escape. We should be able to get to it from the next room."

The four moved to the next room. The guards were still nowhere in sight. Feldman's flashlight lit the wall; there was a door with a plate that read EMERGENCY EXIT. It was locked. Feldman pointed his gun at the keyhole, but Katya pushed him away, picked the lock, and opened it. They rushed up the fire escape to the third floor. The whole floor seemed empty. The guards were rushing through the first and second floors. Sure enough, there was a staircase at the center of the hallway. Max, now at the head of the group, ran toward the stairs, and Aska and Katya followed.

When they got to the roof, Max squinted. The sunrise had dyed the area bright red. The sun-drenched waves were sparkling. As the sea winds blew against them, they heard the helicopter, which had already landed at the edge of the building. They also heard angry shouting from below. Several men appeared on the roof of the neighboring building.

"Hurry. They found the chopper—"

Gunshots. The men were firing at them. Max grabbed Katya and Aska and dove for cover behind the guardrail.

"Get low and run toward the chopper."

"Where is Joe?" Katya asked. They couldn't see Feldman from where they were.

"You two go first." Max returned to the third floor. The door to the room beside the fire escape opened, and there stood Feldman. "Hurry, Joe. The chopper's here!"

Feldman took his gun in both hands, pointed it inside the room, and fired. The shots echoed across the floor.

The magazine was already empty, but he kept pulling the trigger, a dazed look on his face. Max put a hand on his shoulder, but he was stiff as a rock. Inside the room, a man in a gown lay on the floor with his back facing them, riddled with bullet holes.

"What are you doing? Hurry!" He dragged the unmoving Feldman from the room. "We've got no time. They've seen the chopper."

By the staircase leading to the roof, Katya pulled Aska by the hand, and signaled for them to hurry.

"Go!"

"I can't just leave you here," Katya said.

Max grabbed Feldman's arm and ran while dragging him along. Feldman followed Max's lead, like a doll without its own will. They made it back to the roof. The chopper was hovering about twenty inches above the concrete. The gunfire had intensified, and the guards were shooting from the neighboring building's roof. Two men were firing back from the copter using automatic rifles, but they were outgunned. They saw one of the men whipped back. He'd been shot. The whir of the rotors grew louder. The chopper was lifting higher.

"Don't go! We're over here!" Katya shouted, but the rotors drowned her out. "It's gone." Katya hugged Aska.

Feldman watched the chopper as it flew off, his face empty of emotion. The men on the roof of the other building were pointing at them and shouting.

"Come on! We need to get out of here!" Max smacked Feldman on the cheek.

Feldman came to his senses. "Let's go back to the room." He grabbed Max's arm and went back down the stairs.

Katya was about to enter the room, but she held Aska tight and covered her eyes. A man was lying in a pool of blood. Feldman looked around.

"What are you looking for?" Max asked.

"There must be something that will help us escape. He'll have secured some sort of escape route for himself," he muttered half to himself as he looked at the wall.

"This is the research building's east side," Katya said. "There should be a three-foot-square space close to the wall that leads to the basement."

They gathered in a corner by a large closet. Feldman opened the closet door and pushed the clothes to either side. "It's an elevator!"

Just then, they heard people running and yelling.

"Hurry!"

"Where does it go?"

"Just get in. They're coming!" Feldman pushed Katya and Aska into the closet. Max followed them, and the second the elevator closed, they heard the door to the room open.

"Geht es Ihnen gut? Bitte antworte!" said a man's voice. "Are you okay, sir? Please answer!"

The elevator went down, and stopped underground. A concrete passageway, too cramped for two or more to stand side by side, stretched before them. Feldman picked up a flashlight from the elevator and started walking. The concrete looked cold to the touch. Five minutes later, they reached a staircase. When they lifted the hatch at its top, they found themselves inside a boathouse on a private beach.

The engine hummed. Feldman rested his arm on the motorboat's side as he looked at the laboratory. At Feldman's signal, Max turned off the motor.

A hush fell over the ocean. All they could hear was the gentle licks of the waves on the boat.

"We're going to let the current take us into the open sea," Feldman said. "Then we'll turn the motor on again. The laboratory must be in quite the uproar."

"Now you can tell us what the hell happened back there. Benchell, he . . ."

"Death always hangs over Nazis like a shadow. No, they themselves were death incarnate. That's why they were always afraid of their own repugnant death-shadows. They were trying to run from it. That explains why they wanted to obtain eternal life."

"What a pitiful existence," Max said. "So, how did you know Benchell was the guy on the right?"

"His purpose in life was to take lives. He delighted in dealing death, and in seeing the panic and anguish of those who died by his own hand. He never delegated the killing if he could help it. They say he even cut open people's chests and ripped out their still-beating hearts. And then he'd—" Feldman noticed Aska and Katya staring at him, and swallowed the rest.

Max wiped his hands on his pants. Shaken, he could still feel the gun in his hands.

"We hunted Benchell down five times in the past. During two of those encounters, we shot him to death. Another time, we killed him and made it look like a car accident."

"I don't understand, Joe." The word "clones" came to mind, but it wasn't possible. He was talking about the 1950s and the 1980s.

"Benchell was cautious. He hardly ever showed himself in the presence of others. When he had to appear in the open, he used decoys. He would search for men with similar physiques and facial features and perform plastic surgery on them. It was impossible to determine who was really Benchell by the face alone. More than sixty years have passed."

"So, you killed body doubles?"

Feldman paused. "More or less. But we only found out after the fact. Benchell sightings typically occurred years apart from each other, and intel that he was still alive never stopped coming in." Feldman paused again. "It was my last resort. I didn't know what Benchell looked like anymore. That's why I had to sneak into their midst."

"But sneaking into their midst wouldn't be enough to find out," Katya said as she stared at Max, waiting for him to back her up. Max didn't know how to reply.

Feldman nodded slowly. "He changed everything about himself. He altered his face with plastic surgery, replaced his fingerprints with skin grafts, and changed his eye color and vocal cords. He lost weight to change his frame, and even trained himself from being left-handed to right-handed. He transformed into a completely different person. In fact, I'm sure even he forgot what he 'truly' looked like. But there was one aspect he could never change."

"His heart? His soul?"

"That's right. He could reshape his body, but he could never change his cruel and cunning personality—that is to say, his soul."

"So, that's why you created that whole situation."

"Your first step was luring Benchell out however you could," Katya said. "Then you had to create a situation where he'd want to kill by his own hand. That's what the real Benchell would do, after all."

"You two acted too quickly. If you had waited longer, we would have been able to guide you from the inside. But I underestimated you; I didn't think you could do anything on your own."

"You mean like back at the Vatican?"

"I mean like the first raid on Aztec Labs."

"Don't tell me that was all part of your plan, too!" Katya's expression changed.

"It was because you two made a move of your own that we were able to completely trick the enemy. Gerhard and Benchell both believed in it—that I was on their side. And yet they didn't appear before me. It was thanks to your actions that I was able to remove that last shred of doubt."

"So, you got all the players to show up by reporting our infiltration."

Feldman nodded.

"I never want to go through that again."

"I won't make you go through that again."

"One more thing," Max said, staring at Feldman, "when did you start capitalizing on me? From the very beginning? From the time you found out about Aztec Labs? Or was Simon's bombing at Dörrenwald part of your plan, too?"

"We needed your—"

Max raised a hand. "Forget I asked. I don't want to be any more disappointed in my fellow man."

"We didn't start using you until recently. I learned who you two were during this mission. And I'm beginning to think people are not to be discarded."

From the shore, a deep rumbling noise, plus the sirens of police cars.

"They must have destroyed the lab in order to hide their secrets. We informed the police ten minutes after the copter took off. And we informed DC at the same time. The fire trucks and police cars from all over town must be flying over as we speak. That chief of police won't be able to hide, either. The attorney general will have called. However . . ." Feldman turned his eyes from the lab to Max. "I did wrong by you, Professor. There must have been a small library's worth of information a scientist would love to have—including information that might have provided a key to a cure for you."

"I have the best assistant I could ever ask for. And I've got a charming girl by my side, too."

Katya smiled and pulled Aska into a hug. Feldman looked on quizzically.

A red pillar of flame spurted from Lab Building Two's central section.

"It's over." Feldman's whisper blew away with the salty sea breeze.

Katya held Max's hands, and Max squeezed hers. The soft sound of the waves washed over them.

• • •

EPILOGUE

At a sprawling white sand beach tucked under a cliff, cheerful music was playing from the fast food restaurants along the road, mixed with the laughing voices of young men and women.

Sunrise Beach, San Francisco.

Max was leaning against the railing, and looking out to the sea. Feldman was next to him, lighting his cigar. Katya and Aska were buying ice cream across the street. Two weeks had passed since the events.

"What became of the Nazi war criminals at Aztec?"

"Three escaped, but they'll get caught. A headless snake is as good as dead. What's more . . ." Feldman looked at the ocean. "The lab is slated for closure. After the bombing of a P4-level laboratory complex, that's to be expected. We were lucky that a biohazard was avoided. And the Aztec Foundation will crash and burn along with their lab."

"Let me ask you something," Max said, staring at Feldman. "Did you really want to catch Benchell, Gerhard, and the rest more than you wanted to live forever?"

"Someone who didn't experience Auschwitz or any other concentration camp wouldn't understand." Feldman blinked repeatedly, as though he saw a mirage in the distance. "The line between life and death is thin, Professor. We humans are so fragile, our lives so fleeting."

"All the more reason to desire eternal life, no?"

"The present is beautiful because it must end. Those are your words, Professor. The present is all there is. I've realized that eternity has only ever been an illusion."

An elderly couple walked leisurely down the boardwalk, hand in hand. Feldman watched them as they went by. "One thing I regret is not having experienced that."

"It's not too late, you know," Max said, grinning.

"I'll do my best."

"I've got your back."

"I have one more regret," Feldman said, smiling awkwardly. "That I never got to raise a son like you."

"You're on your own there, bud. It's not like there's no chance of it happening." Max patted Feldman on the shoulder with a smile on his face. "That reminds me, back then, in that room . . ."

Max flashed back to the voice he'd heard by the door back then. *"Geht es Ihnen gut? Bitte antworte . . . Mein Führer!"* They called the man lying bloodied on the floor their Führer.

Feldman's forehead was sweating. His face contorted with pain, and he sucked in gulps of air. His grip on the railing tightened.

"Was that man a clone, or was he . . . ?" Feldman said. "Let's not talk about it. I don't want to think about it anymore." He drew a deep drag on his cigar, as if to distract himself. The pleasant aroma wafted Max's way. "What about her? Will she be all right?" Feldman asked, looking at Aska.

"Her village doesn't exist anymore. She lost Dona, Davi, the people of Domba, and everything. She could hardly speak two weeks ago. But now she's beginning to smile sometimes. Together with Katya, I plan to look after her for now. Then she can decide for herself what she wants to do."

"She can't live in an urban setting, can she? If I'm not wrong, her immune system isn't up to it. She'll be hundreds of times more susceptible to viruses and bacteria than the average person."

"She was too sheltered. A little dirt goes a long way toward building up a person's immunity. I just need to build up her immune system a little at a time. So far, she's adapted with surprising speed. Which might also be thanks to her genetics. She's got a potential life span that's centuries long."

"What about your illness?"

Katya and Aska came back. They handed Max and Feldman some ice cream. Feldman smiled and accepted the ice cream from Aska.

The phone in Max's pocket rang. He faced away from the group and took the call. The bright orange sail of a windsurfer was floating past. Max nodded along to what the voice on the other end was saying.

"I can visit you tomorrow."

"Thank you." Click.

Max faced the sea. The sparkling sun stung his eyes.

"Good news, I'm guessing," Katya said.

"That was Dr. Hamilton. It seems Alex's condition has improved, if only slightly."

After they returned from Aztec, Aska allowed Max to take some of her bone marrow and transplant it into Alex.

"You need to start the treatment, too."

"It's only just started."

"The future's bright."

Max turned to face her.

"Excuse me." Feldman bowed, and headed for the car, enjoying his ice cream on the way.

"He's going back to Israel," Katya said, watching Feldman walk away.

"He's a hunter. I'm sure he's got his next job lined up."

"And we ours."

When Max and Katya returned to Allon, the lab's computers were filled with Gerhard's research materials and the results. Telomeres, embryonic stem cells, clones . . . it was more than enough to revolutionize life science as they knew it.

"To think this was the legacy of the Nazis," Katya said. "These findings could win Nobel prizes for the next ten years."

"That's what you've always wanted."

"All I want is to continue my research alongside you." Katya looked at Max, then at Aska. "Aska wants to be a doctor. Looks like she really loves how you look in that lab coat," she added with a smile.

Aska smiled at them, bashfully.

"You'll be a great doctor," Max said. "Though you need to learn this country's language first. There's no rush. You've got more than enough time."

"How about Nancy?" Katya said, out of the blue. "For Joe, I mean. He's looking for a woman, right?"

"He's looking for someone to spend the rest of his days with."

"She might be a good match for him."

"Then who's going to look after me?"

"You're still scared?" Katya grabbed Max's hand.

"I told you, didn't I? I'm a wuss."

"There's nothing to be scared of. Holding down a home. Having kids."

Max didn't answer.

"You were chosen by God. I said it once, and I'll say it again."

Max gave her a curious look. Before, the word "God" had always made him uncomfortable, but now he accepted it.

"God knew you would overcome the trial he set before you." Katya leaned her head on Max's shoulder. Max inhaled her perfume.

Aska smiled as she watched them.

"Let's go," Katya said. "We need to fulfill our promise to your brother."

Max nodded, and together they walked off, Katya pulling him by the hand.

Kids in roller skates zoomed past them. Max suddenly stopped. He felt as though he'd heard a voice. That strange echo whispered in his soul and spread across his whole body. It sounded like both a voice from high above the heavens, and a voice arising from within himself.

"What's wrong?" Katya was looking at him like he was crazy.

Max didn't answer. He pulled Katya and Aska toward him.

To his right, the vast Pacific Ocean shone in the sunlight.

ACKNOWLEDGMENTS

History will remember 2020 and 2021.

As of March 2021, COVID-19 has infected around 120 million people and precipitated the deaths of around 2.6 million worldwide. And the battle is ongoing.

These years, marked as they are by both death and resilience, caused the preciousness of life to stand out in sharp relief the world over. Many of the world's cities and towns have had to undergo lockdowns, with people no longer able to live as freely as before. Meanwhile, healthcare professionals, researchers in various fields, and we in the general public continue to combat this time of hardship as we all carry out our respective roles. Given these circumstances, I think 2020 and 2021 have caused humanity to contemplate the totality of life—which is to say, both life and death—on a deeper level.

Publishing the English translation of *The Gene of Life* during such a time feels a bit like the hand of destiny at work. I wrote the novel in 2002, a year that gave rise to a fresh new sense of life's essence through discoveries in genetics and clone science. I'm truly grateful and truly delighted that, nearly twenty years later, we can publish the English-language translation.

I'd like to express my deep gratitude to the translator, Giuseppe di Martino, for providing an on-target translation, and to the editor, Janice Battiste, and proofing editor, Francis Lewis, for giving us a lot of suggestions; thanks in part to their efforts, the book turned out fantastic. I'm also deeply grateful to Akira Chiba, the head of Museyon, for affording me this opportunity, and I hope we continue to be of like minds. I thank Takaki Kondo for helping us with publicity. And I look forward to working further with film director Toshinari Yonishi, who made a heavy-hitting trailer for the book. Thank you all for your support.

The publication of *The Gene of Life* in English follows last year's publication of the English translation of my novel, *The Wall*. I thank everyone who was involved in making that happen.

Lastly, allow me to end on a positive note by repeating the following aphorism from *The Gene of Life*:

"Enjoy life, for it is both beautiful and short."

ABOUT THE AUTHOR

After working as a scientist for the Japan Atomic Energy Research Institute, **Ted Takashima** moved to California, where he studied at the University of California. He has published more than thirty books in the action/thriller/suspense/mystery genres in Japan. His novels include *Intruder*, which won the 1999 Suntory Mystery Award; *Pandemic* (2010), which foretold the global spread of COVID-19 in 2020; and *The Wall* (2020), a redemption story set against the backdrop of a refugee crisis at the Trump border wall with Mexico.

Thank you for reading *The Gene of Life*. I hope you enjoyed it! If you did . . .

• Help other people find this book by writing a review.
• Sign up for the Museyon newsletter, so you can find out about my next book. www.museyon.com

See you soon!
Ted Takashima